The
Thirty
Before
Thirty
List ☑

Tasneem Abdur-Rashid is a British Bengali writer, born and raised in London. A mother of two, Tasneem has worked across media, public relations and communications for over fifteen years, in the UK and the Middle East. She holds a BA and MA in Creative Writing, and she is the anonymous writer of the bestselling novel, *Desperate in Dubai* (2011). *Finding Mr Perfectly Fine* (2022) is her debut romcom, and her latest novel is *The Thirty Before Thirty List*. Tasneem is also the co-host of the award-winning podcast, *Not Another Mum Pod*, which empowers women who feel voiceless with a platform to share their stories. She won the coveted SHE Award for Arts and Culture (2023) for her commitment towards bringing under-represented voices to the fore.

You can find Tasneem on Instagram: @tasneemarashid

First published in the UK in 2024 by
ZAFFRE
An imprint of Zaffre Publishing Group
A Bonnier Books UK company
4th Floor, Victoria House, Bloomsbury Square, London, WC1B 4DA
Owned by Bonnier Books
Sveavägen 56, Stockholm, Sweden

A CIP catalogue record for this book is
available from the British Library.

Paperback ISBN: 978-1-83877-818-7

Also available as an ebook

1 3 5 7 9 10 8 6 4 2

Typeset by IDSUK (Data Connection) Ltd
Printed and bound in Great Britain by Clays Ltd, Elcograf S.p.A.

Zaffre is an imprint of Zaffre Publishing Group
A Bonnier Books UK company
www.bonnierbooks.co.uk

TASNEEM ABDUR-RASHID

The Thirty Before Thirty List

ZAFFRE

For my sisters: the ones I share my blood with and the ones I don't. I'm eternally grateful for you all ♥

Chapter One

I never ran for the Tube. It wasn't worth getting sweaty and flustered when another would come approximately two minutes later. That day, though – the day that completely changed the course of my life – I ran, trying not to curse my parents as I did. I had been late for work two days in a row that week and I couldn't turn it into a hat-trick. I had a new boss who didn't know I was pretty amazing at my job and that it wasn't a biggie if I was occasionally late, because I always got the job done. I was at the stage where I had to prove myself all over again, despite being there for two years and smashing all my performance reviews.

Showing up late for the third consecutive day would make me look like *that incompetent brown girl*. The one who only worked until she reached her true goal in life – to get married and have kids. I wasn't being paranoid. Nicola, an ex-colleague, actually said that to me when we met. Not in so many words, of course, but the sentiment was there, beneath the casual, 'Ah, you'll probably be off getting married and having kids soon, won't you?'

It wasn't even my fault I'd been late. Not really. I knew I was too old to blame my shortcomings on my parents, but it really *was* because of them. On Monday, as I was about to leave the house, Ma made me throw out the kitchen rubbish, recycling *and* food recycling. As I went to open the compost box, everything spilt out onto my feet and ruined my shoes completely. I had to clean up the sticky, soggy and stinky mess from the front path, wash my feet and hunt around for my only other pair of black ballet pumps before I could leave the house again.

On Tuesday, I was putting my jacket on when my dad started lecturing me about how I was getting old and how I needed to find a husband, how they didn't grow on trees and I needed to be proactive, blah blah blah. An argument ensued, I lost track of time and there you had it, I was late once again.

That day, it was completely my fault. I forgot to set my alarm, woke up late and had to leg it out of the house without a shower or doing my makeup. Flying onto the semi-full carriage, I threw myself into the nearest available seat, panting heavily and trying to catch my breath. The fact that running for the train winded me said a lot about my fitness. It was something I was planning to work on . . . one day. Today my only goal was getting to work on time.

'Hey, you dropped this,' a voice said quietly. Startled, I looked up at the man who'd had the audacity to speak to me. He was sitting across from me and he held out the newspaper I'd dropped in my haste. Who *did* that on the London Underground? You were supposed to avoid eye contact at ALL COSTS. Speaking to a stranger was borderline harassment.

'Thanks,' I replied warily as I grabbed the paper from TubeGuy while trying to avoid his gaze. He was obviously a weirdo. A free newspaper was hardly something I couldn't live without. There was a discarded one on the seat right next to me. What did he want? The last time a stranger started up a random conversation with me on public transport, he ended up trying to convert me to Mormonism.

Arranging my expression into its most authentic RBF, I hoped that my lack of enthusiasm would discourage any further contact. I didn't have time to make friends. I needed to spend the first ten minutes of the Piccadilly Line journey to

Hammersmith doing my makeup. I couldn't show up to work completely barefaced, not with a new boss watching me.

Obviously, I realise that men go to work without makeup all the time and no one thinks they look unprofessional and this is another manifestation of the patriarchy and all that. And it's true. But for me, makeup is a shield. A mask. A barrier. Without it, I feel exposed. I wish I was the sort of person who is comfortable in their own skin, but I'm not. In fact, I'm in a constant state of *dis*comfort.

Trying my best to ignore TubeGuy and everyone else around me, I placed the newspaper on my lap and planted my giant tote on top of it so I could fish out the products I'd thrown in that morning. Up until this low point in my life, I'd always thought applying makeup on public transport was a bit cringe. It wasn't that hard to schedule an extra ten minutes at home to save yourself the embarrassment of trying to fill in your eyebrows in front of everyone ... or so I thought. Ha. Served me right for being so judgy.

I hated drawing attention to myself, but I hated the thought of Sheila condemning me even more, so putting aside my fear of public ridicule, I began with a quick dab of concealer under my eyes and on a couple of blemishes, evened out my complexion with some pressed powder and managed to apply mascara without stabbing my eyeball.

As I worked on making myself presentable, I could feel TubeGuy watching me. Feeling like a zoo exhibit, I tried to block him and everyone else out as I hastily brushed on a bit of blusher to add some life to my sallow complexion and went straight to lip gloss next, because I couldn't risk lipliner and lipstick on a moving carriage. It was bad enough as it was, trying to put makeup on when I could only see a tiny part of my face in the compact mirror. The lighting wasn't great either, so there was every chance that I had made myself look like a geisha.

I glanced up then to find TubeGuy's eyes on me like he was watching a movie. Looking around the carriage, I found that there were two other people gawking at me as well: an older man who really should have had better things to do than witness my glow-up and a middle-aged woman with flawless makeup who looked like she was smirking at me. I bet she had never found herself in such an embarrassing situation. I bet she was the type who sent all of her outfits to the dry cleaners to get pressed because she was too busy being fabulous to bother with trivial chores. I was still waiting for fabulous to come to me; until then, I would have to make do with 'flabulous'.

If I had the guts, I would have said something like, 'Would you like to take a picture?' But I didn't. Instead, I sent all three of the nosy-Nancys bad vibes and tried to block them out.

Then came the hardest part, which I saved for the end: taming my unruly and uneven brows. My right eyebrow behaved and it was a nice, tidy shape in a few seconds. But just as I began work on the left, the train jerked so violently that a woman standing in the aisle knocked into me, causing my hand to swipe a long, black line across my face.

'Sorry,' she mumbled, not very apologetically. She wasn't even holding on to the handrail, of course she was going to bash into someone!

'It's OK,' I muttered back, my face burning. I couldn't bring myself to ignore her apology completely, especially not with at least three other people watching. I tried to rub the smear off, but I only managed to ruin the makeup underneath it as well. Now not only did I have a black smudge, but I also had a patchwork cheek too.

'You were doing such a good job until then,' TubeGuy said, loud enough for me to hear him over the noise of the carriage rattling through the tunnels. Ms Fabulous chuckled and

I glared at her before looking at him, snarky reply ready to go. But then he grinned cheekily at me, flashing a set of perfect pearly whites. My rebuff died on my lips. This man was bloody fit. Like, seriously hot. Actor hot. No, *model* hot. Clear, smooth complexion. The right amount of beard. Luscious, light brown hair. Greyish-green eyes. I tried not to let my jaw drop. *Maybe he wasn't a weirdo after all?*

'Thanks, I think,' I replied, trying to switch my face from astonishment to impassive, so that he wouldn't realise how in awe of him I was. 'Serves me right for not doing this nonsense at home.'

'To be fair, you didn't really need all that,' he said and I raised my good eyebrow, confused.

'What do you mean?'

He looked a bit sheepish then. 'I just meant that, erm, you looked fine without it.'

This time, my jaw did fall ajar. Was TubeGuy *flirting* with me? I was so out of the game – well, to be fair, I hadn't ever been *in* the game – that I didn't realise what he was trying to say and I went and embarrassed him completely unintentionally.

'Oh, thanks,' I said. But as soon as the words left my mouth, I realised that it could be that he wasn't complimenting me at all. He could have been insulting me. I began to backtrack, feeling like an idiot. 'I think? Or are you trying to tell me that my makeup application skills are crap?'

It was his turn to look uncomfortable. 'No! It was supposed to be a compliment. Not that my opinion matters, obviously. Or anyone's opinion, really. Especially a man's.' Heat flared in his cheeks and I found myself smiling. How had my life become so exciting so quickly? Just that morning, as I got ready for work and threw on my usual, uninspiring workwear of trousers, top and blazer, I wondered exactly how and when my life became so . . . mundane.

I was twenty-seven years old, for crying out loud. Hardly geriatric. Yet my routine screamed OLD PERSON at me. Worse than old person. Because, unlike actual old people, I didn't have a child or spouse to take care of. I didn't have my own house and mortgage to think about. I was acting like an old person without the shackles of marriage, offspring and commitment. How had that happened?

But that day, as I looked into TubeGuy's friendly eyes, desperately trying not to bite my nails from the nerves . . . suddenly, I didn't feel quite so old. Maybe this was my moment to do something interesting for a change, live a little and engage with him instead of burying my head in a newspaper.

Only now that he had gone and complimented me, I didn't know what to say in response. I wasn't cool or witty. I didn't have banter. I was the sort of person who faded into the background and I usually liked it that way. My days consisted of going to the same paralegal job I had for the past two years; my second job since graduating with a first-class degree in Law. My nights were made up of a combination of watching Netflix with Ma, reading or chilling with my family. And the most exciting thing I ever did at the weekend was meet up with my best mate Dina, or my cousins and go for a meal/ movie. Both, if we were feeling particularly ambitious.

There was a reason why I had never dated anyone. It wasn't because I was a devout Muslim or that my parents were too strict. They weren't. In fact, Ma was always telling me to go out more.

'When are you going to tell me that you've met someone?' she had asked me a few weeks before.

'When it happens, I guess,' I spluttered into my tea, my cheeks turning pink.

'Can you hurry up? Your thirties are just around the corner, you know!'

How could I not know when I was reminded every month, mostly by her only sister, my Aunt Lottie – short for Lotifah, not Charlotte.

The reason I was still single was because I had whatever it was that was *less* than having zero 'game'. I couldn't maintain eye contact for longer than a millisecond with any man I was remotely attracted to. The fact that this good-looking man was talking to me, despite getting a glimpse of my insecurities, was mind-boggling.

'So . . . how was your weekend?' TubeGuy asked, like it was the most normal question to ask a stranger on the Tube. I looked into his eyes, framed in the thickest, darkest lashes, feeling a stirring in the pit of my stomach.

'It was all right,' I croaked, my throat feeling unusually dry. *All right?* Was that the best I could come up with? Pulling out a three-day-old bottle of water from my Mary Poppins bag, I took a quick swig, trying to calm my nerves. If I left my answer at that, there was a chance he would give up trying to converse with me.

I heard Aunt Lottie's voice in my head, screeching at me to hurry up and find a husband. *'How will you ever get married if you can't talk to a man?'* Fair point. Taking a deep breath, I attempted to prolong the conversation.

'How was yours?' I managed to mumble.

'*So* good,' he said, his entire face alive with enthusiasm. 'Went to see the new Marvel movie on Friday night and then on Saturday we went to this interactive art installation thing at the Tate. It was so cool.'

TubeGuy started telling me all about the exhibition and I observed him as though I were watching a performance, completely enraptured, barely registering the actual words coming out of his lips. This whole experience was surreal, but I decided to enjoy it instead of questioning his motives. Maybe there were still decent people in the world who weren't after something. Not every strange male was a potential murderer/rapist/abuser/threat.

He moved his hands a lot when he spoke. His fingers were long and slender and his nails were neatly trimmed. He was fair-skinned, but I couldn't tell if he was English white or European white, not that it mattered. His accent was pure London though, like mine. A little rough around the edges and I liked it. He was wearing a black leather biker jacket over a plain white T-shirt and denim jeans that hugged his muscular legs. There was a slightly worn sports bag on his lap, with a leather notebook on top of it, so I guessed he was probably on his way to work. His hair was light brown, longish at the top, and he had the same colour facial hair, which was perfectly sculpted to make the most of his sharp jawline. His nose was a bit on the large side, with a bump on the bridge which I thought made him look strong and regal. He was beautiful and as he spoke, his face was animated, his grin easy.

'Sorry, I talk a lot,' he said when he finally came up for air as the train pulled into Caledonian Road Station. 'What did you get up to?'

This was my time to shine, to say something really witty so he would remember the girl on the train for something other than dodgy makeup skills. Unsurprisingly, nothing interesting came to mind.

'I also watched that movie,' I told him.

'Oh really?' He looked pleasantly surprised. 'Did you like it?'

'Loved it. But then, I'm a die-hard Marvel fan.'

'What? No way! So am I! Who's your favourite character?'

'Iron Man,' I replied, without skipping a beat. 'All day, every day.'

'Not Thor, with this golden mane and muscular physique?'

'Nope. Brains over brawn any day. They're both funny, but Tony's humour is clever. Thor's is more slapstick.'

'Tony, huh? You're on first-name terms with him then?'

'Hey, I cried in *Endgame*. Buckets. I think that earnt me the right to call him by his first name.'

The train began to slow down and as it crawled to a stop at King's Cross, TubeGuy grabbed his bag and notebook and stood up, along with half the carriage. I stared at him in disappointment. Just when I had finally started loosening up, he was going to get off.

I opened my mouth to say goodbye to him, but it turned out I didn't need to. He didn't get off the train, he changed seats to one right next to me.

'Now I'll be able to hear you properly,' he smiled, turning his body so he was facing me.

Having TubeGuy beside me was a completely different sensation from having him across from me. I couldn't see him as well, but my other senses came alive. I could smell him now, a mix of soap and sandalwood. I could feel his warmth where our bodies met on the armrest we shared. It was intoxicating.

I caught Ms Fabulous smiling wistfully at us, like she couldn't believe that she was watching a real-life romcom play out in front of her. I felt bad for cursing her earlier.

'So which camp are you?' I croaked, trying to steady my starved, beating heart. 'Black Widow or Captain Marvel?'

He waited a moment before he answered. I could tell that he was taking my question seriously, which I found crazily endearing. I hoped he would hurry up and answer. I still didn't know when he was getting off the train and I was suddenly desperate to know if he was more of a curves guy (aka Team Black Widow) or a power guy (Team Captain Marvel).

'Neither,' he said thoughtfully, his eyebrows knitted together in concentration. 'I like Gamora.'

'Huh? The green one?'

'Yes, the "green one",' he laughed. 'She's also determined, resourceful and forgiving. She had a tough upbringing, what with Thanos and all that, but despite that, she had a heart of gold.'

'Are those characteristics you look for in a . . . friend?' I found myself asking without thinking. Because if I had been thinking, I would have completely clammed up. This wasn't like me at all, to engage and almost *flirt* with a stranger on the Tube.

'I guess so, hadn't really thought about it,' he replied. 'Does that mean to get your attention, someone would have to be super smart, super funny AND super rich and successful?'

'Definitely,' I joked. 'Building a skyscraper and naming it after themselves is a bare minimum. So is flying.'

A homeless man got onto the train at Holborn. He looked young, in his thirties maybe and cold. It was September, my birthday month, and the weather had turned recently. It was at that point when it was warm in the sun, but cold in the shade; almost like being in-between two seasons, between daylight and nightfall. He must have been freezing at night.

As he approached us, his head down, his weathered fingers wrapped around a battered paper coffee cup, I took out my purse and grabbed the only cash I had on me – a ten-pound note. I stuffed it into the cup and offered the man a small smile. TubeGuy did the same, pulling out his wallet and putting a note into the cup.

'Thank you,' the man whispered, his watery blue eyes looking as exhausted as the rest of him. 'Both of you.'

'Our pleasure,' TubeGuy and I replied in unison.

The man moved on and waited by the doors. When he got off at Covent Garden, TubeGuy turned to look at me.

'That was nice of you,' he murmured.

I shrugged. 'Not really. It's going to be cold tonight. Giving a thirsty person water, or a cold person warmth, isn't being nice. It's normal. You did the same.'

'Yeah. But my friends usually tell me off for it.'

'Mine do too. What do your friends say?'

'Stuff about alcohol and drugs. But I don't know, I feel like you can't judge a stranger without knowing their situation.'

I nodded in agreement. 'One hundred per cent.'

'So, what do you do apart from being nice to random people on the train?' he asked as we left the station and plunged back into the tunnel.

'Oh, I have the most boring job in the world. I'm a paralegal. What about you?'

'I'm a personal trainer, but I'm training to be a physiotherapist as well,' he replied.

'That sounds a lot more interesting,' I smiled. That explained his physique then. 'Who's your craziest client?'

'It's this sixty-five-year-old who's completely addicted to exercise.' He began to tell me about his client and how he called in the middle of the night once asking if he could have a midnight training session. I only half listened because the train slowed down and as it did, I felt that twisting in my stomach again. I needed to know his name. I needed to know where he was getting off so I could mentally prepare myself. I needed to know how I could continue this conversation after we parted ways. I somehow needed to gather the strength and courage to ask for his Insta, or at least his Snap.

'Hey, what's your name?' I forced myself to ask as I geared up towards asking him for his contact details. 'I can't believe we've been talking all this time without knowing each other's names.'

'I know, right? This is the first time I've ever done anything like this,' he said. 'I'm Noah. Well, Nuh in Arabic but I guess most people find it hard to pronounce, so they call me Noah.'

Arabic? Did that mean he was *Muslim*, like me? And he had dropped it into the conversation so casually, like it was normal that a guy that looked like him could *actually be* someone like me. Of course, he could have been an Arab Christian and therefore not marriage material. But who cared? I needed some experience before I got married anyway.

It was beginning to feel like the stars were aligned; like there was a superior force – God? Fate? Destiny? – pushing us together. Of all the Tube carriages in all of London, whizzing around underneath the city, I got on the same one as this potential Muslim who loved Marvel movies, art exhibitions and looked like a model for beard oil? And forget all that – *he seemed interested in me as well.*

'Hi, Noah,' I said as the train slowed down once again, approaching Piccadilly Circus. 'I'm Maya.'

I offered him my hand to shake and he took it. His was warm and strong and I think I held onto it for longer than I should have.

He looked at me then. I mean, he had looked at me numerous times throughout the journey, but now he *really* looked at me, like he was seeing me properly for the first time. My heart began to pound and my skin prickled in anticipation as I waited for him to make the next move.

Piccadilly Circus. Noah opened his mouth and was about to say something when he suddenly jumped up.

'Shit, it's my stop,' he exclaimed, making a dash for the doors as they began to beep. 'I can't be late. New client. Call me!' I stared at him, glass now between us, partly shocked, partly horrified. How was I supposed to call him? We didn't exchange numbers. Was that it? Was it all over before it began?

Noah must have realised this too, because he was mouthing something frantically at me, gesturing with his hands, but I couldn't make out the words. Then the train began to move and he was gone.

Chapter Two

It wasn't meant to be, I told myself as the blasted train sped through another blasted tunnel, creating a greater distance between us. I tried to stop the disappointment in my gut from seeping into my chest. Stuff like this happened all the time. *Worse* things. Anyone who has seen *Before Sunrise* knows what it really means to lose the love of one's life after a chance encounter. This wasn't a fraction as romantic, or heartbreaking. We knew each other for all of twenty minutes. *It wasn't that deep.*

With a sigh, I leant back in my seat and tried to ignore the ache in my throat and the empty seat beside me. It probably still smelt like him and I resisted the urge to press my nose against the old, discoloured fabric, reminding myself that it housed a lot more than just Noah's scent.

Feeling cold and empty, I took out my earphones. I needed a distraction from all the 'what might have beens' racing through my mind. As I did, something caught my eye, discarded on the carriage floor next to a newspaper. I leant forward to take a closer look. It appeared to be a notebook.

Just as I was wondering if I should pick it up and check the contents, despite the potential germ-factor and breach of privacy, I suddenly realised it was Noah's. He had been holding it when he sat across from me. I remembered him gathering it up with his bag when he changed his seat to be closer to mine.

I reached out and picked up the notebook, cradling it in my fingers like it was made of ancient papyrus and might disintegrate into nothing if I wasn't careful. The cover was black leather and I traced my fingers across the embossed 'N. K.' on the front. I could tell that it was used often from the worn creases in the leather and spine. And I was dying to find out what was inside.

'You have to open it,' Lucy, my colleague and friend, declared after I got to the offices of Wiser, Hall, Steadman and Associates and offloaded the story onto her. 'How else will you find out who he is?'

The open-plan office was still quiet, as most people came in at nine and it was only a quarter to. Lucy and I were two of the firm's eight paralegals. Three of us sat on the same side of the room and the third was a Desi guy called Arjun, who always sauntered in after nine, slightly dishevelled from his previous night's antics. Our desks were arranged in a sort of circle, so we were facing each other, which was a blessing and curse. It was useful when we needed help – and like now, when Lucy and I had something really important to chat about – but Arjun was a total distraction. If he wasn't on the phone, he was gossiping about the partners and other solicitors. The only time I got any proper work done was when he went to make himself a cuppa, because he spent ages chatting to everyone in the office on the way to and from the little kitchenette at the back of the room.

'It's hardly going to have his full name, address and phone number on the first page,' I reasoned. 'This isn't the nineties.'

'There may be hints though,' Lucy mused. 'Snippets of information that will help us find him.'

'Us?' I laughed. 'What are we, Sherlock Holmes and Watson?'

'Is that really the only detective reference point we have? In this day and age? Two middle-aged men?'

'Nancy Drew?'

'Better. Or *The No. 1 Ladies' Detective Agency*.'

15

'Who's a detective?' Arjun asked, flinging his bag onto his desk and falling into his seat with a theatrical sigh. I looked over at him and I had to admit that despite his messy hair and dark circles, he still managed to look good in that slightly unkempt, geek-meets-model way, with his tailored suit and Italian leather shoes courtesy of the Bank of Mum and Dad. 'I'm bloody shattered. When is this week going to be over? I swear it feels like Friday.'

'It does,' I agreed. 'But Sheila already thinks I'm useless after rolling up late twice this week. Let's pick up this convo after lunch.'

'Coming after 9 a.m. doesn't make anyone "late",' Arjun argued. 'It's not the Victorian times. This isn't the workhouse.'

'Feels like one,' Lucy said darkly. 'I stayed until after eight every day last week.'

The main door swung open and Sheila, my new manager and one of the three partners, strutted into the office in a power suit and sky-high, red-soled stilettoes. Just looking at her walk in those deathtraps made my ankles ache. I wished I was the sort of woman who looked sexy and powerful, but the best I could do was pretty and cute, with my huge, round eyes and signature dimple on my right cheek. Ma loves telling everyone the story of how when I was born, she and Dad had a big fight immediately after her C-section because he wanted to name me Dimple. It's not unusual for Bengalis to give their daughters nicknames like Lucky, Baby, Beauty and so on, which everyone in their extended family uses. Their real names were often Arabic ones, but only for official purposes.

Ma, who had been born and raised in the UK and had no interest in honouring quirky Bengali traditions, burst into tears and refused. Still hormonal and in agony after her emergency surgery, she was hysterical and made such a ruckus that the midwife burst into the cubicle she was in and kicked my dad out for

16

upsetting her. My younger brother, Malik, still calls me Dimple to wind me up, which often earns him a whack with a pillow.

'Shh, they're coming this way,' Lucy hissed, staring intently at her computer screen. Arjun did the same and I quickly pulled open one of the case files I was working on.

'Morning,' Sheila greeted us stiffly as she clacked past. 'Maya, do you have everything for the meeting at eleven?'

'I do,' I confirmed, smiling warmly at her. 'The room's booked from 10.30. I'll set the tech up then.'

'Great.'

Once all the partners were safely in their glass offices, the three of us let out a collective sigh.

'Tea?' Arjun asked. I nodded and followed him to the kitchenette, where I proceeded to recount the morning's events as the kettle boiled.

'You have to read the notebook,' he said, throwing two extra-strong PG Tips into a big mug with some milk, cardamom and a cinnamon stick before heating it in the microwave. 'I don't do "white man's tea",' was his usual response whenever anyone questioned his method.

'I feel bad,' I replied, my resolve getting weaker with every passing moment. 'What if there are really personal things in there?'

'Like what?' he scoffed as we waited for the kettle to boil, as part of the second step of his pseudo-masala chai. Ma made it at home all the time, but she did it over a stove and it took ages. There was no stove in the kitchenette of Wiser, Hall, Steadman and Associates. I watched as he took the teabags out of the now-beige milk, infused with spices and put the bags into individual mugs. Pouring the hot milk into the two mugs, he added boiling water and let it all brew for a while, before reheating both mugs in the microwave. Two heaped teaspoons of sugar completed the process and, honestly, it was *so* good. I personally couldn't be bothered to make it like this myself in the office, or even at home. Yorkshire Tea with a dash of cold milk was perfectly adequate. But Arjun's milky, spicy number was pretty epic for a microwaved job.

'Personal stuff. You know, family dramas, a broken heart . . .?'

'Maya, this is a grown-arse adult man we're talking about, not a teenage girl. It'll probably be meeting notes or something equally banal.'

I hadn't thought of that. 'But it's a proper leather-bound book, embossed with his initials. It looks too important to be work stuff.'

'If you don't look inside, you'll never know.'

For the rest of the day, while I prepared meeting rooms and AV equipment, wrote up minutes and completed mindless admin tasks, my mind kept drifting to the notebook that was slowly burning a hole through my desk.

Arjun was right. It could contain something as ordinary as work notes. I had known Noah for less than half an hour, but I could tell he wasn't the type to pour his heart out onto a piece of paper.

At 4.56 on the dot, Arjun grabbed his jacket and bag and left the office before anyone could stop him and ask him to do something that would take him over the 5.00 p.m. threshold.

'What are you doing tonight?' Lucy asked, like she always did, as if the answer was going to be anything other than, 'Not much, just going to chill with my family.'

'Are you seriously not going to peek inside?' she continued, slipping on her jacket and stuffing her phone and charger into her bag.

'I don't know,' I admitted. 'I really want to.'

Lucy put her bag back down. 'Er, well you're not doing it without me. Let's do it.'

'What, right here? In front of everyone?'

I looked around the sparse office. It was past five now and only a handful of people remained on the other side of the room, where the family law lot sat. They took their jobs a lot more seriously than those of us in commercial and employment and never left before six.

'No one will know, it'll look like we're working. Let's do this.' Lucy sat down and wheeled her chair closer to mine. Inhaling nervously, I pulled the notebook over to us. The leather felt softer than the first time I held it and I waited a moment, because once I did this, there was no undoing it. Then, muttering 'Bismillah' – in the name of God – I opened it to the first page.

It was blank.

'What the hell?' I looked over at Lucy in a panic. 'Is that it? Have I been stressing over this bloody thing all day for no reason? Now I'll never know who he is! He's gone, forever!'

'Calm down, turn to another page,' Lucy said soothingly and I could tell from the tremble in her lip that she was desperately trying to stop herself from laughing. I turned the page and let out a breath.

There, on the top, in scrawling blue ink, was written '*30 BEFORE 30*'. And below it:

1. APPLY FOR PHYSIO COURSE

- UEL (open day: 24 Nov)
- KCL (open day: 11 Nov)
- SGUL (open day: 1 Dec)
- LSBU (open day: 14 Dec)

Find out application deadline.
Fees?

Lucy and I stared at the information.

'He wants to be a physiotherapist?' Lucy murmured, her eyes bright. 'This is good stuff, Maya! Now you know something personal about him.'

'Well, he said he was already training to be one, I think,' I replied, still staring at the page and at the way he formed his letters. The ink didn't look like a standard biro either, possibly a fountain pen. He was serious about becoming a physiotherapist then, it wasn't a line he told women on the train. What other information did this book hold? I was itching – *no, desperate* – to know more.

'He told you about his future plans between Turnpike Lane and Piccadilly Circus?'

I shrugged. 'It was a deep convo, Luce. We really connected.' I omitted the fact that most of it was about the Marvel universe.

'Let's see what else is there,' Lucy said, grabbing the book from me and this time, I complied with no fuss. Ethics were secondary when it came to finding love, after all.

'There's one on each page, see!'

I snatched the book off her and sure enough, there were more. But each item on the list was on a new page:

2. READ ULYSSES ✓

Challenging but epic read – glad I got there in the end.

And then . . .

3. PARTICIPATE IN A TRIATHLON

Choose between:

- Dorney – Windsor, 21 May

- Dorney Lake – Eton College, 31 July
- All Nations Supersprint – 7 May

'I wonder what this is,' I mused out loud as I flicked through the rest of the book, my eyes landing on some of the headers: *10 – Complete the Whole 30 programme; 15 – Go skydiving; 22 – Pay off credit card*.

'Omigod, I think I know,' Lucy exclaimed. 'He's made a list of thirty things he wants to do before he turns thirty years old!'

I turned to Lucy and then back to the book. *12 – Trek Snowdon*. Who could be bothered to do stuff like that?

'A fitness freak who's also planning to do a triathlon,' Lucy laughed. 'If this list is anything to go by, he is *not* the man for you, Maya.'

'Why not?' I snapped. 'I'm very active, thank you very much, in case that's what you're implying.'

'I'm not "implying" anything, babe. I'm saying it how it is. Your idea of being "active" is hitting Oxford Street once a season.'

She was right. I was the most inactive person I knew.

'What do I do with all this then?' I asked, deflated. The last thing I expected was for this notebook to prove to me all the ways that Noah was wrong for me.

'Forget about it and move on. And if you ever happen to run into him on the Underground, get his number so you can return it.'

'That's it?'

'What other options are there? You're hardly going to tick off his list for him! Can you imagine going skydiving?'

We both laughed weakly and I shuddered at the thought of jumping out of a plane *for fun*, not because the tail had caught fire and it was the only way to safety.

With a sigh, I stuffed the book into my bag and put on my coat. 'Come on, let's go. Netflix waits for no one.'

'Actually, the whole point of it is that it waits for *everyone*.'

'You're so bloody pedantic.'

'Duh. I'm not the best paralegal at this firm for nothing, you know.'

Chapter Three

The rest of the week plodded by. The mundanity of my routine didn't give me comfort though. Something had shifted on Wednesday and I felt restless. My mind kept wandering to Noah and his notebook and the list he'd painstakingly curated. I wanted to know what else was on it, but I stopped myself from looking because it felt too intrusive. Aside from the quick glance with Lucy, it lay untouched on my desk at home, surrounded by my own books, stationery, makeup and other things that I had no place for anywhere else in my bedroom.

Home was a three-bedroom terraced house on a side road off Turnpike Lane in north London. It wasn't the most glamorous of locations – far from it, with all the litter, knife crime and growing number of discount shops. But the station was a five-minute walk away, all the halal grocery shops and takeaways were even closer and you could get to nicer areas pretty quickly. I wondered if Noah lived in one of those nicer areas. He was already on the train when I got on, so he must live somewhere between Wood Green and Cockfosters.

On Friday night I met up with my bestie Dina, who I'd been friends with since Year 7. The only Muslims in the class, we instantly connected over our abstinence from pork and intense love for James Blunt. We had been glued together ever since and even went to the same sixth form and university, although she studied Biomedical Sciences and I went for Law. After we graduated, we were forced into spending time apart since we were on different career paths on opposite sides of London. And then she got married to her university love, Mohammed, had a baby and our weekly meet-ups became more of a monthly thing, depending on her childcare situation.

'Guess what?' Dina said the moment we sat down in our favourite local steakhouse with an adjacent shisha lounge. Not that we ever did shisha. The one time we tried, I got so dizzy that I thought I was going to throw up. Dina actually *did* throw up. She didn't make it to the loos in time before her dinner expelled itself from her smoke-ridden body. Nowadays, we just ate good food, caught up on the week's/month's gossip and then split an indulgent dessert. Our idea of excitement was having an After Eight at half-past seven.

'What?' I asked obligingly. Dina was always starting conversations with 'Guess what?' The answer could range from 'I tried this new place for lunch' to 'My cat is dying of cancer'. I knew this from experience.

'I'm pregnant.' She looked at me eagerly, her green eyes dancing and her loosely wrapped hijab billowing around her face as she bounced up and down in her seat.

'OMG, CONGRATULATIONS!' I squealed, grabbing her hands and squeezing them tight. 'I can't believe it! Sami is going to have a sibling! How are you feeling? How many months are you? How is Mohammed? Is he crazy happy?'

'Slow down,' Dina laughed, squeezing my hands back, her cheeks pink. She proceeded to tell me that she had had the twelve-week scan a couple of weeks before and continued explaining every change in her body in minute detail. I listened to it all, nodded and smiled in all the right places as I tried to keep up with all the medical terminology.

Our starters arrived – crispy calamari and chicken lolli-pops, like always – and she dug right in, the massive smile on her face revealing her newly installed braces. Yes, she missed the boat at fifteen, but evidently, that boat was able to come back twelve years later.

As Dina carried on chatting away about the baby, Sami and Mohammed, the restlessness inside me began to grow. She said they were going to go for a 3D scan the next day. That was when we were supposed to go shopping for autumn clothes. It was starting to get a bit chilly and I was still wearing all my spring and summer clothes. I didn't bother mentioning it. She had obviously forgotten in her excitement and saying anything would be pathetic under the weight of such amazing news.

After we had analysed the scan pictures to death, trying to figure out the sex of the baby, I filled Dina in on my own life.

'Are you telling me you've only flicked through the book and haven't read all thirty of his plans?' she demanded, her eyes wide with bewilderment.

'How can I? This is personal stuff, Dina. I can't just read all the intimate plans he has.'

'Doing a course and reading a book is *not* intimate! You need to read the rest of it! And even better – you should actually *do* the things on his list!'

'What's the point?' I scoffed, taking a bite of the calamari.

'There'll be clues to help you find him! Not just to see him again, but to return his notebook. Look, you already know about the three triathlons he's looking into. All you have to do is show up.'

'Who says I want to find him? He's so different from me. He's a fitness freak and I don't think he's Muslim. But you're right, I should try and give the book back to him.'

'Didn't you say he mentioned Arabic?'

'Yeah, but he's probably an Arab Christian.'

Dina rolled her eyes. 'Right, cos there are *sooo* many of those around in our ends. What if he *is* Muslim and what if you need someone different to encourage you to experience new things? Maybe the whole point of you finding this list was for you to do the things on them.'

'I don't need to experience new things! I'm happy the way I am!' I started getting defensive, my voice level rising as I stabbed at the steak on my plate.

'You're happy spending your days in a boring job, your evenings watching TV with your mum and your weekends eating out with me?'

'Yes, I am! Because that's real life, Dina. You do the same thing! Your routine is always the same.'

'That's because I have no choice! I'm a mum and a wife. But I'm sick of nothing interesting ever happening. I'm sick of the same old playgroup with the same old mums who look at me like I don't belong with their bougie buggies and designer handbags. I'm sick of barely leaving the house without a baby. And when I do get some me time, all I do is go to the same old restaurant with the same old . . .' Her voice trailed off as she realised what she was about to say. My cheeks turned crimson with humiliation and I stared down at the meat I had been massacring on my plate.

Dina's voice softened. 'Sorry, Maya. I didn't mean it like that. Of course I love you and you're my favourite person to spend time with. I'm just feeling a bit out of sorts. I'm happy I'm pregnant, I really am . . . but I'm also in a constant state of exhaustion and instead of things easing up with Sami starting nursery at three, I'm going to be doing it all over again. And I'm jealous of you! You can do whatever you want with your time but instead, you do the same crap over and over again! You take your life for granted.'

Later that evening, I lay in bed with my stomach grumbling because I'd lost my appetite after Dina's careless remarks. It was still early, well before midnight anyway, but I didn't feel like watching whatever Bollywood movie Ma and Baba had on downstairs.

I wondered if what Dina said was right. Maybe the whole point of my Tube encounter wasn't about Noah, but about the list. My life *was* boring. I never did anything out of my comfort zone. There's a fine line between comfort and complacency and I had the feeling that I had slipped into the latter. I couldn't remember the last time I did anything remotely out of the ordinary.

And while I was wasting my life away, my best friend was moving onto another stage of her life. She was married and I wasn't. She was a mum, I wasn't. And once the new baby came along, she would have even less time to do the same boring things with me. She was constantly evolving. Maybe it was time I did the same.

Climbing out of my double bed, I turned on my lamp and rummaged around on my desk until I found The Notebook. I traced my fingers over the soft leather and the embossed initials before opening it.

The idea began to form as my eyes rested on Noah's easy scrawl, imagining how he felt as he compiled his list. Did he google 'cool things to do before you hit 30'? He didn't seem the type. I bet it all came naturally to him.

I probably should have made my own bucket list, but then it would have been full of things I already liked and wouldn't have pushed me to try so many things that were out of my comfort zone. Also, if I were being completely honest with myself, there was a little part of me that hoped that I might run into him at some point as well. I decided I had to do all the things on his list in the same order he had written them, so I could grow at the same pace as him. I could only assume that there was some sort of thought process behind the chronology.

A tingly sensation began to brew in my belly, something I hadn't felt in years. The more I thought about this project, the more excited I became. Yes, doing everything on the list would be difficult, maybe embarrassing as well. But it was going to be fun! It was going to get me out of the house, trying things I would never have thought of. Then, as if that wasn't enough, I decided to add another layer to the adventure: I wouldn't peek ahead at the items. I would do them as and when I got to them. Each new item would be fresh and exciting.

Closing the book, I turned my lamp off and got back into my soft, warm bed and snuggled under the heavy duvet. The next day would be the beginning of a brand new me.

Chapter Four

The following morning, the excitement I had fallen asleep with had faded into a dull ache in my chest. My phone calendar alerted me that I was supposedly going on a 'Shopping trip with Dina' at 10 a.m. I doubted she realised.

It may have been just a missed date – insignificant in the grand scheme of things – but as soon as the baby came, she would have zero time for me. And I knew that I was being incredibly selfish, but I was scared. I was being left behind so fast that if I didn't do something to catch up, then soon Dina would be out of sight forever.

'Morning, Ma,' I grumbled as I dragged myself downstairs and found my mum in our narrow, galley kitchen making breakfast for her and my dad. She was still in her cotton nightgown and her hair was pulled into a messy bun.

'Have you made me breakfast too?' I asked hopefully.

'I didn't think you'd be up so early, sorry,' she replied. 'But I can whip up something now if you'd like?' I watched her deftly remove the sunny-side-up eggs from the pan and onto a pre-warmed plate with two slices of toasted sourdough, mashed avocado and some grilled cherry tomatoes, all the while keeping an eye on the Deshi tea that was simmering on the stove.

'It's OK, I'll have cereal.' I grabbed the box of Coco Pops that I had hidden behind the rice tin. In this house, if I don't hide my stash, my younger brother Malik will eat it all. I've lost count of the number of times I've reached for my cereal, or anything really, like the bread, or milk, to find it's gone. The worst part is, he leaves the empty boxes and cartons where they are, so I don't realise it's finished until it's too late.

'Aren't you meeting Dina today?' Ma asked as she washed the dishes, moving with speed and accuracy despite the early hour. Everything Ma does, she does quickly. She never dawdles or lingers. She's always been on the go, from as far back as I can remember.

My parents aren't well-off. They do all right but Ma always has to work; we need the extra income. She is a Special Educational Needs teacher at our local primary school, which is a pretty tiring job. When we were younger, her days were always a whirlwind of school runs, work, batch cooking, cleaning, mending, activities, extended family responsibilities. I don't think I ever saw her sitting around and relaxing when I was growing up.

'I was supposed to,' I replied. 'But she's got family stuff going on. She's having another baby.'

'A baby? Mashallah! That's wonderful news!' Ma put down the tea caddy. 'How many weeks is she? How is she feeling?'

I shrugged, trying to keep the misery from showing on my face. 'She's fourteen weeks and she's OK, Alhamdulillah.'

'Wow.' Ma fell silent as she steeped the teabags in hot water, making the drinks the usual English way. I knew she was wondering when I would take a leaf out of Dina's book. Not by getting knocked up obviously, but by progressing in life. Every so often she'd tell me off about how I was getting older and I needed to find a husband and did I need her to set me up the Bengali way? I probably did, to be honest, but I couldn't bring myself to ask her to. Most of my Muslim and Asian friends had parents who were so traditional that finding their own spouse wasn't an option. They'd shave their heads for a mother like mine; young, sort of cool, with the perfect East/West balance. And most importantly, who actively encouraged her daughter to find her own marriage partner.

'I'm going to take this to the other room,' I muttered, putting my bowl and tea onto a tray and then carrying it over to our living room. Baba was there, watching Bangla TV as usual, and he nodded to me as I sat down on the other end of the cream leather sofa with my tray on my lap.

'Kita khobor?' he asked. What *was* new? Dina had a foetus; I had a notebook and met a boy on the Tube. I couldn't tell him any of those things. My mum might have wanted me to date, but my dad certainly didn't. I knew this, without him ever explicitly saying it, through the random comments and observations I'd heard over the years: *Girls from good families don't talk to boys; Look how Polly's daughter married an English boy, tawbah tawbah; Chi chi chi, it must have been a love marriage, God forbid.*

I opened my mouth to reply with something trivial about work when Ma called out, 'Hoonrayni, the cha is done, breakfast is ready,' and I was saved by the yell. Baba got up from his place and straightened out his lungi before strolling to the dining room like a boss man. Despite being 'modern', Ma was also traditional in many ways. She still made breakfast for my dad nearly every day and she also never called him by his name. Not in front of anyone, anyway. Like many Bengali women from previous generations, she called him variations of 'listen' or 'are you listening?' If she was speaking about him, then he was 'Maya's dad'. I was used to it now, of course, but as a child I thought 'Hoonrayni' was Baba's real name.

I turned on the TV and mindlessly flicked through the channels as I ate my cereal. Was this it? Was this how my life was going to be for the next ten years, until someone was desperate enough to marry me? Was I going to be living with my parents in my thirties, eating the same cereal from my child-hood Peter Rabbit bowl and watching them potter around and live their lives while letting mine dehydrate?

'Why do you look so miserable?' Malik poked his head round the door and raised an eyebrow at my fluffy onesie with the bunny ears on the hood. He was dressed for the day in a bomber jacket over a hoodie, expensive-looking jeans and one of his many pairs of exclusive trainers that littered the porch. Malik got onto a graduate scheme at a top firm as soon as he finished uni with a first in business and he now had a really good job that paid ridiculously well. So well, in fact, that he recently brought an architect round to draw up plans for a kitchen and loft extension to the house that he was planning on paying for himself.

'It's Saturday, Affa. Shouldn't you be going out, doing something fun?' Despite how generous he is to our parents, calling me 'Affa' – the respectful title for an older sister in Sylheti – is about the only respect my brother shows me. He spends most of his time taking the mick, bossing me around or lecturing me. He's two years younger than me, but the way he carries on, you'd think he was a decade older.

'I'm not in the mood to go out,' I shrugged, turning my attention back to the TV. I didn't bother telling him that I did have plans, but my best friend of sixteen years was too busy popping out babies to bother with little things like shopping.

Malik sighed. 'All right. Well, if you change your mind, a bunch of us are going out this evening. Why don't you join us?'

I stared at my brother like he had grown a third eye during our conversation. He *never* invited me out with his crew. To be fair, if I was a tall, good-looking, immacu-lately coiffured twenty-five-year-old Bengali boy, I wouldn't want my unfashionable and boring older sister cramping my style either.

'What?' he said, a little defensively. 'I always ask you out, but you never come!'

He didn't. But I didn't want to start a fight so early in the morning. 'I'll think about it,' I replied eventually. 'Where are you off to now?'

'Breakfast, shopping, you know, the usual.'

'With that girl you're hiding from me?'

'No!' Malik glared at me, nodding towards the partially open sliding doors that joined the living room to the dining room, where our parents sat eating their breakfast. He clearly didn't want them to know that he was dating someone. He probably didn't want me to know either, but it was obvious from the way his face lit up when she called and how his voice became all soft and mushy when he answered.

'All right, calm down,' I said. 'What's the big secret, anyway? Has she got a droopy eye? Is she an older woman? Is she divorced with three kids?'

Malik rolled his eyes. 'Your imagination is insane. You're in the wrong line of work, Dimple.'

'Well, something must be the matter, otherwise you would have told me about her,' I shrugged. 'Come and chill for a bit and fill me in.'

'Can't. I don't want to be late. Bye!'

My brother left the room and, once again, I was alone with the TV for company. The fragrance of his expensive aftershave lingered in the air and my pitiful bowl of Coco Pops was getting soggier and more unappealing by the second. I could hear the faint sound of Ma's laughter through the door. Everyone, it seemed, had things to do with people they loved. Everyone except me.

My phone beeped and I took it out of my onesie pocket to find a message from Lucy:

LUCY WORK: Have you read the rest of the notebook???

I smiled and tapped a response:

MAYA: No . . .

LUCY WORK: Why the . . .?

MAYA: Huh?

LUCY WORK: The . . . The ellipsis. It implies you're about to do something with the notebook.

MAYA: Something like what?

LUCY WORK: Like read the rest? Burn it? Make a TikTok out of it so it goes viral and you find him again?

MAYA: I applaud your creativity but I have other plans.

LUCY WORK: Like?

MAYA: I've decided to do the stuff on the list.

LUCY WORK: What???!! You're going to do a TRIATHLON?

MAYA: Fine, not everything. But the things I can't do, I'm going to replace with something more doable.

LUCY WORK: Woah. You've given this a lot of thought.

MAYA: I have. Everyone's right. I'm boring and predictable and I need to experience more things.

LUCY WORK: Go, Maya! Here to help if you need it x.

Later that evening, I opened the notebook and re-read the first thing on Noah's list: *Apply for physio course*. I had no interest in becoming a physiotherapist, but I could do with learning something new. I hadn't studied since my degree. I'd always wanted to do a master's degree, but I started working soon after uni and the idea fell to the wayside along with other fanciful notions I'd entertained when I was younger, like going blonde and travelling.

Opening my laptop, I started to browse courses and as I checked out various London university websites, the idea of studying again became more and more appealing. When I originally started my degree, the plan was to go on to do an LLM, a master's in Law, then do my Solicitors Qualification Examination (SQE), smash out training contract and then become a solicitor. But the thrill of earning my own money took over and now, six years later, all that had changed was that I was now a senior paralegal instead of a junior one. I did less photocopying and admin, but that was it. If Noah could go to uni at what appeared to be twenty-nine years of age, then surely, I could at twenty-seven?

I filtered my searches to show part-time courses in London. I'd carry on living at home of course, so I didn't have to waste money on rent. Like my parents would let me move out, even if I wanted to. The only time people like me moved out was either with a groom or in a coffin! I was surprised to find there was a scholarship specifically for British Muslims. I clicked on it out of curiosity but as I read through the eligibility criteria, I realised that I ticked most of the requirements. What seemed like a fanciful idea an hour before was beginning to feel achievable.

Before I could change my mind, I opened Word and began to write a personal statement explaining why I deserved the scholarship. At first, I found it difficult. I'm not great at bragging about myself, but soon my fingers flew across the keyboard as I listed out my achievements, my motivation, my experience. In minutes I had written two pages. It would do for now. I would go back and edit it the next day, when it had had some time to rest and I'd had time to think over anything else I wanted to add.

I got back into bed, still wearing the same onesie I had been in all day, and called Dina to find out how her 3D scan went, but it rang through to voicemail. I tried not to let the fact that I hadn't heard from her all day bother me.

With a sigh, I wrote out a message to her asking her how she was and then switched off my lamp and squeezed my eyes closed.

I lay there for ages, willing sleep to come and take me away from my thoughts. But my mind was in overdrive, mulling over the statement I had written, thinking of new things to add, wondering what else was on the list and if Noah was stressing out over losing his notebook.

Taking out my phone, I googled 'Noah' and 'north London'. Vague, I know, but it wasn't like I had much else to go by. I couldn't exactly search 'Cute possibly Middle Eastern guy called Noah who might live in north London somewhere on the Piccadilly Line and lost a notebook'.

Noah's London estate agent. Nope.

Noah Homeware. No.

Noah's Ark children's hospice. Definitely not.

This wasn't going to work. I typed 'Noah personal trainer London' and this time, there were loads of hits. I went through them one by one but none of them appeared to be him. What sort of personal trainer didn't have social media, or a website, to bring in new clients?

Anyway, it didn't matter. My journey with the list wasn't about finding Noah. It was about trying new things. And if I *happened* to come across Noah while doing so . . . well, that would be the frosting on the donut, wouldn't it?

Chapter Five

I spent most of Sunday holed up in my bedroom fine-tuning my university and scholarship applications. Ma popped her head in around noon, expecting to find me asleep. She could barely contain her shock when she saw me dressed and typing away furiously on my laptop.

'What's happening?' she asked, peering over my shoulder.

'I'm applying to do an LLM,' I told her nervously, turning to face her. Ma had really pushed me to do this when I first graduated and I obviously hadn't listened. I braced myself for the, 'Didn't I tell you all those years ago?'

'What? Where has this come from all of a sudden?' Ma sat down on the bed; her forehead wrinkled in concern.

'I feel like my life is stagnant,' I admitted. 'It's not really going anywhere. It doesn't look like I'll be getting married any time soon, so I might as well invest in my career if I'm going to be alone forever.'

'Is this all because Dina is having another baby?'

'No!' I said defensively. Ma raised an eyebrow and I looked down, slightly embarrassed to have this conversation. 'Well, not entirely. But it did make me think. I'm twenty-seven and I've never been on a date, let alone had a child. Who knows when or if I'll ever meet someone worthy enough to marry? I need to create a future that I'll be content with if I end up alone.'

'And what if going back to university makes it harder for you to settle down? Where will you find the time to meet someone? You know I'm happy to put the word out, if that's what you want—'

'I could meet someone there!' I interrupted hastily, before she decided to put her matchmaking headscarf on. 'But that's not the point. The point is to go out in the world and make something of my life, instead of waiting around for life to happen to me.'

Ma sighed and stood up. 'I think you should go back to university if it's something you want to do, but not because you're bored. It's going to be tough doing it while working. No more loafing around in bed watching TV all night and sleeping in until late at the weekend, going out on Friday nights. You'll be too busy.'

She left my room, taking with her my laundry basket and some of the wind in my sails. I was so excited about this, but now I felt deflated, despite her reaction being reasonable. Everyone was going to question my motives for going back to studying at this age instead of putting all my time and energy into securing a husband. I needed to find a way to deal with them instead of letting it get to me. I wondered what Noah was going to tell everyone about going back to studying now, at nearly thirty. I bet no one would question *his* motives. He would be seen as driven, motivated, striving for success. No one would ask him if it would hinder his chances of settling down. In fact, it would make him a more attractive marriage candidate.

My phone rang as I was reading through my applications. Glancing at the caller ID, I saw Dina's smiling face looking out at me. We had taken that picture together a few years ago in Hyde Park, the day she got the worst sunburn of her life. It was one of those scorching, humid days when the whole of London seemed to be out in the park, pink and white flesh glistening and burning under the heat as they lay there baking on the grass like rotisserie chickens. My toffee-coloured skin did all right in heat, but poor Dina's marshmallow complexion didn't fare as well. She was sore for days afterwards and refused to go out without a sunshade and medical-grade factor 100 sunscreen for the rest of the summer.

'Hey, Dina,' I said with forced cheeriness. I didn't want her to realise how disoriented I'd felt since she shared her news with me. If our lives were a racetrack, she was more than halfway through the race, jumping effortlessly over all the hurdles, whereas I was still casually strolling along the plain tarmac, tripping over every rock and stone.

'Hey, Maya,' Dina sang out. There was nothing forced about her good mood. I could feel it radiating through the phone. 'I have *so* much to tell you! Are you free tonight?'

Of course I was free. I was always bloody free, wasn't I? The childish, petty part of me wanted to pretend I had plans of epic proportions. But the more rational, mature part of me knew that playing games would only deepen the crack in our friendship.

'Yeah, I am. Do you want to come over? Have dinner with us?'

'I need to have dinner at home, Mohammed's been moaning about how he hasn't seen me much lately. Like it's my fault he's been on-call all week. But I can come round after Sami's gone to bed, like nine-ish?'

'See you in a bit.'

'Later!'

'What's this about going back to university?' Baba walked into the dining room as I set the table for five; the fifth being Nani, my maternal grandmother. From the kitchen came the aroma of garlic, chillies and gochujang and my stomach growled in response. Dina was missing out; Ma's cooking is seriously the best. Better than anything I have ever eaten in a restaurant. Her hands are like magic, turning everything she touches into a thing of beauty. And she doesn't only cook Bengali curries either, although those were amazing as well, given that she learnt from both my grandmothers. Nani loves east-Asian food, so that night's dinner was tom yum soup, vegetable spring rolls, pad thai, dynamite shrimp and Korean fried chicken. Heaven.

'I want to do a master's in Law,' I replied, avoiding his gaze as I set out cutlery and chopsticks on the placemats.

'Education is never wasted,' he mused. 'Although it would have been better if you did it straight after your degree. How are you going to pay for it?'

Nearly all my dad's concerns began or ended with, 'How are you going to pay for it?' I didn't – couldn't – blame him. He's a first-generation Bengali Brit who came to the UK at twenty-three years old, got beaten up almost daily for being a 'smelly Paki' and had to work hard to make it to where he is today. Which isn't anything spectacular – he works for the social services department at Tower Hamlets council – but it's not like he had anything handed to him on a silver platter. He worked in a restaurant for pennies every spare moment, throughout school and college, so he could save up to go to uni without getting in debt. Even now, he does GCSE maths tutoring two evenings a week because he's not only used to grafting, but he's also petrified that a rainy day will come and he won't have the back-up funds for it. I'm pretty sure he has saved up enough to see us through a tsunami.

'I'm going to apply for a scholarship,' I told him. 'I'm only going to do it if I get the funding for it. And I'll do it part-time, so I can work at the same time.'

'Hmm,' Baba said non-committally. I knew that 'hmm'. It was the prelude to the real issue on his mind. I went into the

41

kitchen to bring the bowls of food to the table, bracing myself for the next line of questioning, when the doorbell rang, saving me from the inquisition.

'NANI!' I cried out as I opened the door to find my little grandmother on the other side in her usual beige trench and a white headscarf pinned neatly under her chin. My uncle waved from his car that was parked on the kerb and I guided Nani into the house and helped her with her coat. As always, she was in a simple saree underneath. She always wore various shades of white, beige, cream or, if feeling particularly rebellious, blossom pink or light grey. In our culture, widows are supposed to wear white and Nani tried to adhere to that custom as closely as possible.

'Yallah, amar Maya ni?' Nani always greeted me like this and it made me smile each time. Of course it was me. Who else was it?

'Bala asoin ni, Nani?' I asked her how she was, as I hung her coat up and took her through to the dining room. 'Ma Chinese khani randi soin afnar lagi.' This wasn't entirely true. Ma had cooked a combination of Chinese, Thai and Korean food for Nani, but going into that much detail would have required me to explain the nuances and my basic Sylheti was inadequate for that sort of technical conversation.

'Don't you think it's time we started finding suitors for you?' Baba continued when Nani was deposited at the table next to him and as I carefully set down the bowls of steaming hot soup. Malik, as always, sat expectantly, not bothering to offer any help. 'I mean, by all means, study if you want, but you need to progress in other areas of your life as well.'

'Yeah, Maya,' Malik chose that moment to participate, grinning evilly at me. 'You need to progress in other areas of your life. Our lineage is at risk of dying out.'

'Pretty sure lineage continues via the male heir, not the female heir,' I retorted. 'What, or shall I say, *whom* are you progressing with right now?'

Malik glared at me and I stuck my tongue out at him like a five-year-old. 'Don't start things you don't want to finish, little bro.'

'Kita mati rai?' Nani asked what we were talking about and Baba gave her the lowdown as I scurried away back to the kitchen to bring the rest of the food out.

'Eh-reh,' Ma called out to Baba from the kitchen, where she was putting the final garnishes on the noodles. 'We've spoken about this. Maya will find someone when she's ready.'

'And why has no one spoken to me about it?' Nani demanded, in Sylheti of course, because despite living in England for nearly fifty years, she still pretended she couldn't speak a word of the language. 'I'm only the head of the family, that's all.'

'We didn't really speak about it,' Baba replied, glaring at Ma. 'You spoke and I listened, but now that she's about to embark on a two-year course, things have changed. Are we going to wait another two years before we start looking? These things take time and the moment she's on the other side of thirty . . .'

Baba let the implication dangle in the air like a dead fly stuck to a web.

'Look,' I interrupted, before my parents got into an argument over me and my lacklustre love life, 'I'm open to meeting people, OK? You do what you have to do and I'll do what I have to do.'

'What?' Ma stared at me from the doorway as I sat down in my usual seat. 'Are you saying we can put the word out? Look at biodatas?'

'If you want to look at dodgy marriage CVs that basically say everything about nothing, that's up to you. Just don't expect me to meet anyone who is shorter than me, without a decent job, or outside the M25.'

'Deal!' Ma beamed at us as she placed the bowl of sweet, spicy and tangy noodles in front of us with a flourish. 'Let's eat.'

Throughout dinner, all my parents and grandmother spoke about was how they were going to find me a husband. They talked about creating a 'biodata' for me, a Bengali version of a marriage CV that detailed everything any prospective partner's parents would want to know about me: my age, height, occupation, education and family background, complete with a carefully styled photo that showed me in the best possible 'light'. And that wasn't just a phrase; they literally meant that they needed a picture where I didn't look too dark-skinned. Nani was adamant that we get it done before she left for her annual trip to Bangladesh in a few days, so she could vet the contents.

As I listened to them go on and on about which uncle to speak to, which aunty to visit, whose wedding to attend to show me off, I felt my skin prickle with unease. *This is normal*, I told myself, over and over again. *Everyone does it. The fact that you HAVEN'T been doing this for the past four years is what's weird.*

I didn't enjoy a single bite of my food and even Malik kept darting worried glances in my direction. As soon as my parents finished eating, I leapt up from the table and cleared away quickly, so I would be free before Dina arrived. The knock on the door came as I was drying the last dish and I ran to open it before Ma could.

'Come upstairs!' I said, closing the front door firmly behind her and all but dragging her up the stairs to my room.

Being older than Malik, I was lucky enough to get the second double bedroom in our little house, while he was stuck with the box room which could barely accommodate his ego, let alone all his swag. I felt bad for him; he earnt so much money and could be living it up in a bachelor pad in Canary Wharf. Instead, he chose to do the 'proper' Bengali thing and stay at home with our parents.

Dina took off her coat before collapsing on top of my double bed and nestling back against my stack of colourful pillows and cushions. I gave her a quick once-over, trying to gauge whether her pregnancy had changed her appearance. She unwrapped her hijab and her brown hair tumbled out, a mess of curls around her face. As always, her freckled face was makeup-free. She was wearing a beige hoodie over ripped jeans that she had patched up herself from the inside, so as not to show any skin. I let out a breath. She looked exactly the same.

'Well?' I asked. 'How was your scan? Tell me everything!'

Dina closed her eyes for a moment, a small smile dancing on her lips. 'Maya, it was so beautiful. I was feeling really nervous about having another baby, especially when I'm just about coping with Sami, but seeing the baby in 3D has changed everything. I'm ready.'

'Well? Is it a girl or a boy?' I asked in excitement. 'Is Sami getting a brother or a sister?'

'Is it OK if we keep it a surprise? I feel so nervous about everything.' Dina looked imploringly at me and I tried to swallow back the disappointment. She had told me it was a boy when she was pregnant with Sami. What was different now?

I didn't ask. Instead, I told her that she was going to be an amazing mum to both children. As Dina continued talking about the baby and Sami and her in-laws and husband,

I felt my heart grow tighter and tighter in my chest. I really was happy for her and there wasn't an iota of jealousy in me.

I just wished my life was moving forward too.

Chapter Six

'So? Have you read any more of the notebook?' Lucy asked the second I got into the office on Monday, before I had the chance to take off my jacket or put my bag down.

'No, but I've started doing the stuff on the list,' I replied, settling into my seat and turning my computer on.

'Already? That was quick!'

'Only the first one. His first point is to do a physiotherapy course, which is obviously irrelevant to my life, but it got me thinking about what I could do to further my own career – or my knowledge at least.'

'Interesting,' Lucy mused. 'I like where this is going. So what did you decide?'

As I scrolled through my emails and made a note of all the things Sheila wanted me to get on with that day, I told Lucy about the scholarship and master's degree I wanted to do. Arjun rolled in at some point and – unlike Lucy, who was completely supportive of my plan – he thought I had lost the plot.

'You want to go back to uni? Now? At this age? All for some guy you don't know?'

'It's not *for* a guy, it's for me. I've been inspired by him, that's all,' I corrected him, a tad sharply.

'Hmm, if you say so,' he said, sounding dubious. 'Anyone want a microwaved masala chai?'

When I got home that evening, the first thing I did was read over my scholarship and university applications. I had emailed them to Dina the night before for her thoughts, but she hadn't responded and the more I delayed it, the greater the chance of me changing my mind. I knew I could carry on editing a word here or there forever, but I needed to take ownership of what I'd done and then go for it and let fate, aka God, decide what would come of it. If the tingly sensation in my gut was anything to go by, then I had made the right choice. With a 'Bismillah' I hit send and then went downstairs to see if Ma needed any help.

'I sent my application,' I told her as she took the dish of steaming hot macaroni out from the oven, the cheese beautiful and golden with the sauce still bubbling underneath.

'That was fast,' she replied, setting the food down onto a heatproof mat at the table. 'You really want to do this?'

'Yup. I do.'

'OK, well, Insha'allah khair. Whatever is in Allah's plan will happen. Can you call your brother and dad to come down and eat?'

'Sure. BABA! MALIK! COME DOWN AND EAT!' I yelled.

Rolling her eyes, she muttered, 'I could have done that my flippin' self.'

My dad and brother came thundering down the stairs and soon we were all tucking into another one of Ma's delicious dinners, as Baba filled us in on his day at work. I've been listening to stories about his colleagues since I was little and was totally invested in Gifty's paranoia, Sandra's marital dramas and Bernadette's OCD tendencies.

'I spoke to Mitu this morning,' Baba suddenly told Ma, referring to his younger brother who lived in east London. 'He's already got someone he thinks would be a good match for Maya.'

I froze, my Buffalo chicken wing halfway towards my mouth, which became locked in a gaping position. I looked over at Malik, who was grinning like he had heard the funniest joke in the world. Ma shot me a nervous look and quickly rearranged her expression to look reassuring.

'Oh?' she said. 'Do we have a biodata for him?'

'Not yet,' Baba replied, ploughing through his dinner like he wasn't talking about something as life-changing as marrying me off to some dude I didn't know. 'Insha'allah he'll send it through tonight.'

'We'd better make one for Maya,' Ma mused, talking about me as if I wasn't sitting right there. 'Let's do that after dinner.'

'Make what?' I demanded when I finally got use of my mouth back. I knew I had agreed for them to start looking but still, this all seemed a bit quick for my liking. I had only just submitted my course application!

'Your biodata,' Ma said calmly.

Malik began to chuckle. 'Better start prepping for an interview, sis.'

'I don't know why you're laughing,' Ma frowned at him. 'While we're at it, we might as well make one for you.'

'What?' he spluttered. 'I'm not getting married!'

'Ever?' Ma and Baba both turned to glare at him and I breathed a sigh of relief that the spotlight was off me for now.

'Not right now! I'm only twenty-five.'

'So? You have a good job, plenty of money,' Ma reasoned. 'Unless your heart is elsewhere, of course. Is there something I need to know about?'

'Yes, Malik,' I narrowed my eyes at my brother who was beginning to look as though he wished he hadn't opened his big mouth. 'Has the viscount got his beady eyes on an unsuitable viscountess? There are rumours milling around in the ton, according to Lady Whistledown.'

'What the hell are you on about?' he asked, confused, as Ma and I began to laugh.

'Nothing,' I giggled, finally picking my fork up again. Maybe all this marriage malarkey wouldn't be entirely awful if my brother was forced into participating as well.

After dinner, instead of joining my parents in watching the latest cooking competition show they were addicted to, I headed back up to my room. Now that I had checked off task one on the list – applying for a course – I was ready to tackle what was next.

Sitting down at my little desk – the same one I had during my undergrad, where I spent hours and hours poring over massive Law textbooks and past papers – I carefully took out the leatherbound book from my tote and opened it. I had started to carry the book around with me – in case I ever saw Noah again and had to return it, of course. Not because I had started to form an unhealthy attachment to it or anything. I turned to the second page:

2. READ ULYSSES ✓

Challenging but epic read – glad I got there in the end.

His handwriting wasn't the neatest, but I noticed there was an artistic flair to the way he crossed his Ts and curled his Ys. I wondered if that meant that he was creative and my heart lifted at the thought. I was neither sporty nor arty, but I liked that there seemed to be so many layers to him.

Reading a classic would be a doddle, I decided as I closed the notebook. Noah had already done it and he was the active, Marvel-watching type. I had done English Lit for A-levels, so it would be easier for me. The fact that he had persevered demonstrated that he was a hard worker and didn't give up easily, making him all the more attractive in my eyes.

It had been a while since I had finished a book, I was ashamed to admit. As a teenager, I would devour them and throughout university I always made sure to have a bestseller in my bag. These days I ended up listening to podcasts on my way into the office. Sometimes. Mostly it was music.

The next day, instead of going to Pret, grabbing a sandwich and coming back to the office to eat it during my lunch hour, I found the nearest bookshop to our office in Hammersmith so I could buy *Ulysses* for myself. I couldn't remember the last time I went to a bookshop, or the library and the familiar scent of books took me straight back to my childhood, when Baba would take me to our local library in Wood Green and spend the afternoon reading newspapers while I browsed the books. When and why did I let life become so dull? Why had I stopped enjoying simple pleasures like reading a good book? Was it laziness or an inability to see beyond my Groundhog Day routine?

Well, whatever it was, that streak was *over*. My life was now unpredictable and I had no idea where the next task would take me.

Browsing through the latest paperback releases, I picked up a romcom that looked like fun and last year's Booker Prize winner before I ambled over to the classics and found *Ulysses*. It was MASSIVE. I knew it was big but I hadn't expected it to be quite so huge. Did I have to read the whole thing?

Chapter Seven

After struggling through hundreds of pages of bloody *Ulysses* I was definitely immersed. Immersed in a stream of consciousness that was supposed to be revolutionary but made me go cross-eyed. And the worst part was, I still had *a thousand pages* to go.

Bloody Noah and his bloody list! Why couldn't he have chosen something like 'read a Russian novel' instead? I could have managed a bit of Dostoyevsky or Tolstoy. But this . . . this was *torture*.

'You can't give up,' Lucy admonished me at work the following week, as I sat during lunch with the brick of a book opened up in front of me. I could have sworn that my biceps were more toned after holding it so much. Even the muscles in my palms ached from trying to hold it open for hours at a time.

'But I gave it a go,' I moaned, rubbing my eyes. 'I've read five hundred pages, Luce!'

'More than a third. Imagine how accomplished you'll feel when it's done!'

'It's going to take ages. I should be getting on with other stuff on the list.'

'Why don't you? You can carry on reading while you complete other tasks.'

'Fine,' I huffed. I couldn't remember what came next in the list so I took out the notebook and flicked through the pages. 'Let's have a look, Stalin.'

'If you're going to compare me to a dictator, at least choose a more fashionable one,' Lucy retorted.

'Like whom?'

'Sheila. Sheila's a fashionable dictator,' Arjun whispered, throwing himself onto the free chair in our little chill-out corner. 'She's had a word with me about my timings. Apparently, I'm always coming in late and leaving early.' He stared at us, waiting for our outraged denial.

'Ummm,' Lucy began. 'Well . . .'

'Oh, piss off,' he grumbled, pulling a sandwich out of a paper bag and taking a delicate bite. 'This place has become a bloody matriarchy and I'm sick of it!'

3. PARTICIPATE IN A TRIATHLON

Choose between:

- Dorney – Windsor, 21 May
- Dorney Lake – Eton College, 31 July
- All Nations Supersprint – 7 May

'Oh, it's that triathlon thing we saw the other day.' I groaned. 'I can't do it. Don't try to make me.'

'Can you swim?'

'Just about. And there's no way I can become good enough to be able to take part so soon. Unless you want me to drown? In which case, go ahead and sign me up, murderer.'

'Fine, calm down,' she rolled her eyes. 'No need to be so dramatic. Let me think . . .' Lucy tapped on her chin thoughtfully.

'I think—' Arjun began and we both turned to glare at him.

Arjun gave us the finger before stomping back to his desk, while Lucy continued to *hmmm* out loud while she pondered.

'I know!' she said finally. 'You obviously can't do a triathlon and I'm not sure if you should try and find Noah at one either. It's a bit stalkerish.'

'Agreed.' I felt relieved. 'So that's it? We move on to the next item?'

'That's *not* it, Maya. The list is about experiences and doing different things, changing the course of your life. So you need to adapt it to something you *can* do.'

'Which is?'

'Running! You're going to start running. It's one-third of a triathlon. You're going to train for Race for Life.'

'What? Isn't that 10K? There's no way I'll be able to do that! I can't even run for the bus!'

'I think there's an option to do 5K. Look into it. You're a paralegal, I'm sure you can figure it out. Anyway, Sheila's coming and our lunch hour is up. I don't want to be the next Arjun.'

Later that evening, I took Lucy's suggestion on board and researched Race for Life. The race wasn't for a few months and there was a 5K option that was more achievable than 10K, so I quickly signed up me and Lucy, giving us each a £500 target to raise. I also discovered an app created by the NHS called Couch to 5K that would help me train without having to waste money and join a gym. As well as getting fit and getting out of the house, I could also raise money for a good cause. It was pretty much win-win all round.

The downside of this plan was, of course, the fact that I would have to exercise. Movement and I weren't the best of friends. We were barely acquaintances and were more like enemies. I was the girl who ran for the bus, tripped over her own shoelaces and ended up falling into dog poo. True story.

But maybe this would change things. I was doing something *good*. God wouldn't punish me for that by landing me in shit – both the real and proverbial kind. In fact, He might reward me for my good deed. Hopefully in the shape of a tall, brown-haired man named N-O-A-H.

As I screenshot the confirmation of our participation and sent it to Lucy, I considered how, in a couple of weeks, my sixteen-year-long friendship with Dina had changed. I should have been doing this list malarkey with her, my best friend, not my work colleague. She hadn't replied to my last few texts or emails, or returned my calls. I picked up my phone to write out a text to her and then stopped. The words were stuck on the tips of my fingers as well as in my throat and for the first time in all these years, I didn't know what to say to her.

I revealed my training plans to my family as we sat down for dinner a short while later, omitting the inspiration behind my newfound desire to jog through the tired streets of Wood Green.

'You? Run?' Malik started laughing so hard that he almost choked on his mango lassi. It was Pakistani food that day: spicy and creamy butter chicken with homemade naan and a sweet and tangy chickpea chaat on the side. Baba picked up some fresh shingaras from Ambala – the pyramid-shaped ones with the flaky pastry stuffed with spiced potatoes and peas. Along with the mango lassis that I made when I was helping Ma earlier, it was a bit of a feast for a Thursday.

'You could do with joining me,' I replied smoothly as he reached for his umpteenth naan. 'Since we're bride hunting for you and all that.'

'I'll be hunting you in a minute if you carry on like that!'

'I think it's a great idea,' Ma interrupted before the bickering became a full-blown row. 'We could *all* do with getting fitter. When are you going to start, jaan?'

'Five thirty a.m. tomorrow, so I have enough time to get back, shower and get ready for work.'

'Five thirty?' Ma looked queasy. 'I think I'll join you when you go at a more decent hour.'

Baba grunted and reached for more butter chicken. I didn't think he was up for it either.

I spent most of the evening ploughing through *Ulysses* instead of chilling with my usual Netflix shows and although it was tedious, sometimes sending me to sleep, I still felt a massive sense of accomplishment when I hit the 700-page mark.

I didn't feel quite as enthusiastic about my upcoming run when my alarm went off the following morning. My eyes heavy with sleep, I snoozed it a couple of times and eventually managed to drag myself out of bed the third time.

'Bloody Noah and his bloody list,' I muttered to myself, not for the first time, as I staggered to the bathroom down the hall and splashed cold water on my face. 'Bloody Lucy and her bloody ideas.'

Somehow managing to stuff my lethargic legs into my tatty leggings with a hole in the knee and pulling a faded hoodie over a crumpled T-shirt, I stumbled down the stairs and almost tripped over a figure sitting on the bottom step.

'What the hell?' I croaked, grabbing hold of the banister to prevent the fall. 'Malik? Is that you?'

'Who else is it going to be?' Malik grumbled, standing up and stretching. 'I could do with improving my fitness so I thought I'd join you on your runs.'

'Wow, OK. At least now I don't have to worry about getting mugged, stabbed or raped while I run around in the dark,' I replied, trying to see the positive side of my brother – my endless teaser and tormentor – witnessing my attempts at moving my legs fast enough to constitute 'running'. This was London after all and the semi-grimy side. Anything was possible.

We ventured outside the house, closing the front door gently behind us so as not to disturb our parents. The sun had yet to rise and the sky was still dark. Our street was completely still, but it was quiet most of the time anyway. Malik began to do stretches and gestured for me to copy him, so I half-heartedly followed suit, trying to ignore the fact that he could comfortably reach his toes whereas my fingers could barely pass my knees.

'So, I was planning to do Couch to 5K,' I admitted to Malik when he was finished showing off his elastic-band moves.

'Wow, you really are a total beginner, aren't you?' he teased. 'I'm going to jog and listen to music. Shall we take a brisk walk to Ducketts Common and then we can do our own thing there?'

'Sounds like a plan.' Pulling my hoodie tighter around my body, I followed Malik as he all but ran to the common. I don't know how someone with such short legs (he's only five-seven, which is on the tall side for a Bengali guy, but short for the UK average) could walk so fast. I'm short myself, at five-four and almost broke into a jog trying to keep up with him.

'Slow down,' I panted as we approached the common. 'What's wrong with strolling leisurely?'

'I thought you wanted a proper workout?'

'I don't! I want to learn how to run so I can participate in Race for Life!'

That stopped Malik in his tracks. He turned to gawk at me. 'Since when have you been interested in races or charity? First, a master's, then marriage and now this? You need to tell me what's going on and don't feed me some *Eat Pray Love* BS, all right?'

With a sigh of resignation, I told Malik about Noah and the list, ignoring his chuckles and eye rolls.

'It all makes sense now,' he laughed. 'I've been telling you to live a little for years and you've never listened. And then some good-looking guy comes along and suddenly you're adventurous?'

'Hey, it's not because of him! I was inspired by his list, that's all.'

Malik shrugged. 'Whatever the reason, I'm glad you're trying new things.'

As Malik jogged away, leaving my novice self far behind, I turned on the Couch to 5K app and listened to the narrator's soothing voice coax me into a fast walk and then a slow jog for thirty seconds. At first, it wasn't too bad. I completed the half-minute jog easily enough. OK, everything wobbled and I should have tied my hair back, but if this was what running was all about, it was relatively easy. The sun began to rise soon after I started running so I stopped and watched the sky turn from coal to flames. It was magnificent and I couldn't help but smile, despite my parched throat and throbbing bones. Maybe this waking up at dawn business wasn't as bad as I thought it was going to be.

It got harder the second time though and as my boobs leapt around in my completely inappropriate balconette bra and my heels pounded against the concrete pavement in my flimsy Converse, I realised that I was totally ill-equipped for this. By the third time I started running, my knees were aching and I was certain that my right boob hit my chin at one point. If I was going to do this, I needed to invest in some proper running gear. By this stage, Malik had lapped me at least four times and then told me he was going to head home. As desperate as I was to give up and join him, I waved him goodbye and ploughed on.

Despite the discomfort and aches, I felt a steely sort of calm take over me, even when it began to rain. Out here, at this hour, there was no Noah, no list, no Sheila, no impending marriage. Just me, the breeze, the raindrops and the adrenaline urging me to go on. By the time I started hobbling back home with blistered feet, I was shattered but exhilarated.

'Wow, you did it!' Ma exclaimed in surprise when I stumbled through the front door like a wet, bedraggled cat. 'I didn't think you would.'

'I'm so tired,' I gasped as I filled a glass with cold water from the tap and gulped it down. 'But I'm glad I did it.'

'Well done, jaan,' Ma gave me a little hug. 'Go and have a shower and get ready for work, I'll make you some breakfast.'

Malik had already left the house, thank God, so there was no one to fight over bathroom time with. I showered away all the sweat and grime and managed to change into one of my many outdated shirt and trouser combos reserved for work before heading downstairs. My legs were throbbing in exhaustion and they wobbled with every step I took. I found Ma waiting for me at the dining table, a plate of masala omelette and paratha at my usual place setting, as well as a cup of tea and a glass of juice. For the record, my mum never made me breakfast on a weekday. In fact, she rarely made me one on the weekend. For starters, she was too busy, always rushing out to the school she worked at before I came downstairs. And even if she wasn't, I'm old enough to sort myself out. Having said that, different rules seemed to apply to my brother, who always managed to wangle a breakfast out of our poor Ma.

'What's going on?' I asked warily, sitting down at the table and eyeing the plate of food like it might have been laced with arsenic.

'Does something have to be going on for me to make my favourite daughter some breakfast?'

'Why aren't you at work?' I tentatively tore off a piece of the buttery paratha and tried it with the spicy eggs. It tasted normal. Divine, in fact. My stomach rumbled in agreement and I pushed aside my reservations as I shovelled the rest of it into my mouth.

'I've got an appointment this morning. I'll go to school after. I thought I'd use the opportunity to have a quick chat.'

Ah ha. Here it was. The big reveal and reason behind the special treatment I was receiving.

And then it hit me.

Ma had an appointment.

She had cancer.

I knew it. I could feel it in my bones, as real as my heartbeat and the blood pounding in my ears.

That's why she had taken the morning off; she had an oncology appointment. That's why God had pushed me into signing up for Race for Life. She'd been looking a bit tired lately, but being the self-absorbed, horrid daughter that I was, I carried on with my life like I was the only thing that mattered. Water filled my eyes as the magnitude of what was unfolding began to take hold of me.

'What stage is it?' I choked out as the tears spilt over.

Ma looked at me, startled. 'Why are you crying?'

'Tell me what stage, Ma! I need to know how much time we have left.'

My mum rolled her eyes, her stoicism shocking me into silence. How could she be so calm? It must have been caught early for her to react like that. But then, Ma hardly ever cried. When my grandfather passed away, she went silent and withdrew into herself and if she cried, it was in private because I never saw her tears. I sat there, gulping and hiccupping as snot mixed with tears dripped down my face, while she watched me like I was a complete crazy person.

'Calm down, Maya,' she said, trying to be patient. 'There's no need to be so dramatic. It's still at the early stages.'

I took a deep breath to steady myself, before reaching for some kitchen towel and blowing into it. It was just like my mum to play it down. 'OK, that's good news,' I rasped. 'What type is it? What's the course of action?'

'Why are you calling him "it"? That's a bit rude. Like I said, it's early days, so the next step would be to arrange a meeting, I suppose.'

'What sort of meeting? Like treatment, you mean?'

Ma frowned at me. 'You're not making much sense, Maya. Why would you need treatment?'

'I know *I* don't need treatment; I'm talking about *you!*' I exclaimed, throwing my hands up in exasperation. Why did my mum always have to be so evasive? Why couldn't she answer my questions, instead of talking in riddles?

'Me? Maya, I don't understand what you're saying. Why would I need treatment?'

'Because you have cancer?'

Ma looked startled then. 'Cancer? What on earth are you talking about? I don't have cancer!'

'You just said you did. You said it's at the early stages!'

'Honestly, Maya, sometimes I wonder if all this is because you used to fall out of the bed all the time as a child. I don't know where you got cancer from. I wanted to talk about the boy, the one your chacha suggested for you.'

'What about him?' If I was confused before, by then I was feeling utterly bewildered. How had we gone from my mum being diagnosed with cancer to a potential marriage prospect?

'We sent them your biodata and they want to arrange a meeting. That's all. No one has cancer, Alhamdulillah. *Jesus.*'

That was a first. Allah and Jesus both used to convey exasperation.

'Your dad and I have spoken about it and we think it's better to invite them over to our house for nasta, so we get to meet the family and see if they're compatible with us. Maya? Are you listening to me?'

I was listening, but I knew I was making my stupid face. The one where my eyes went vacant and my jaw slackened. It was either that or my pissed-off face and considering the fact that I felt like I had got my mum back from death's door, I couldn't bring myself to look angry. But seriously. *They wanted me to meet a random guy at my house?* My safe space?

I grunted something and Ma continued. 'Great. They're coming next weekend, so don't make any plans with Dina.'

'Next weekend?' I managed to choke once I got the use of my larynx back. 'Why so soon?'

'Why not? It's better not to delay these things. If we dilly-dally, he might get snatched up by someone else.'

'He's hardly the last samosa at iftar,' I muttered under my breath. Or at least, I thought I had, but Ma's radar ears managed to pick it up.

'Maya! You agreed that we could start looking for you if you went back to university! Shall we not bother then? Because if you're going to give me a hard time every step of the way . . .'

Ma left the threat hanging in the air like an ash cloud and I scowled, too scared to protest more. I didn't want her to rescind her support of me going back to studying either.

'I'm not,' I grumbled once the silence became too much to bear. 'It's come as a surprise, that's all. I didn't think things would move so quickly. I haven't even seen my own biodata!'

'I'll email it to you. And that's how these things work,' Ma said, her tone gentler. 'Anyway. They haven't told us if they prefer Saturday or Sunday, but keep both days free regardless.

We need to sort the house out before they come and I need your help to do it. As it's nasta and not a proper meal, we'll have to make a lot of snacks.'

Ma rattled on about new curtains and deep cleaning and I tuned out. All I could think was that a man was coming to view me, like I was an object; a house he was considering buying. And I had no say in the matter.

Later that afternoon, while I was at work, an email from Ma came through with the subject YOUR BIODATA in capital letters.

Dropping everything I was working on, I hurriedly opened it up and scanned the boring parts quicky – my name, age, address, education, family background – until I got to the 'about me' section: *I am a family-oriented, God-conscious woman who prays five times a day and dresses modestly, despite not observing hijab. I enjoy spending time with my family, cooking and learning. I am looking for a partner with similar goals and interests.*

I blanched.

That was it.

I read and re-read the offensive paragraph, my anger increasing each time. Modestly dressed? God-conscious? There was no mention of the fact that I was going back to education either, probably because it would make it look like I wasn't ready to get married. My mum also knew perfectly well that I was as good at cooking as I was running! And why did she mention hijab, wasn't it obvious from the pictures?

Oh, God. The pictures! I opened the other attachment in the email to find a photo of me from three years ago at a family wedding. It had been brightened so much that not only did my pink shalwar kameez now look white, but my brown complexion was also more pine than walnut. In a nutshell, neither the picture nor the description were anything like the real me.

Was the real me, with my dark brown skin and inability to cook, really such an unattractive prospect that they had to completely dismantle me and rebuild me like Lego before creating this atrocious CV?

I already knew the answer to that.

Chapter Eight

MAYA: Hey, call me when you're free! Feels like we haven't spoken in forever!

I typed out a message to Dina the following week when I was in the throes of scrubbing all the doors in the house in preparation for the weekend's 'dekha dekhi' meeting, where the potential in-laws would find out that my skin tone was five shades darker than the picture they had seen.

The groom's family had postponed the meeting, much to my relief, and the date had been set to teatime on Sunday. Ma had gone crazy with the house prep – as if they were going to decide if they liked me or not based on the angle of the sofa.

I was desperate to talk to Dina about everything but she was always too busy to talk: it was her father-in-law's sixtieth, Sami was ill, she was out with her husband, she had guests round. And in those few weeks, my life had completely changed. I had the LLM and scholarship on the horizon, I had Noah's list pushing me to do all these new things, I had the dekha dekhi coming up. I had read over half of *Ulysses*, for God's sake. That in itself was probably my greatest achievement in life. I had taken up running and was working up to being able to run 5K without stopping. I had signed up for Race for Life.

Over the weekend, I had also already completed numbers four and five on the list. Number four was watching *2001: A Space Odyssey*, which was actually pretty amazing. Number five was going to a jazz concert. I knew nothing about jazz, or any music beyond the UK Top 40 if I was being honest. I hadn't even been to a concert before, so I had no idea what to expect. I would have preferred my first live-music experience to be something recognisable, but the list said otherwise and that was the whole point of the process.

Lucy took the lead in organising the night out. She booked us tickets at The Jazz Cafe in Camden last Saturday, which I imagined to be a cosy basement cafe with mood lighting and leather armchairs. But then I googled it and I found everything from hip hop to R&B gigs and I texted Lucy in a panic:

MAYA: Lucy! I looked up Jazz Cafe but it looks like a club with strobe lights and everything?

Lucy, whose phone was permanently glued to her right hand (thank, God), texted back instantly:

LUCY WORK: Relax Maya. That's only on Friday nights. We're going to an authentic jazz night on Saturday, don't worry.

Lucy was right, I didn't have to worry. We arrived early and as soon as we passed security and entered the venue, my mind was put at ease. On the stage was a band I had obviously never heard of. There was a saxophonist wearing dark glasses, a pianist, two trumpet players and a singer who both sang and performed spoken word, so I guessed it was more of a modern interpretation of jazz. Lucy had booked us a table overlooking the main floor and I was relieved not to have to stand among the throng of unknown people and be able to enjoy the music – it was enchanting and a completely different experience to hearing music on the radio. On the radio, music seemed to reach my ears, but live, it went beyond, until I wasn't only listening to it, I was feeling it.

Back in my little house in north London, my phone pinged with a response from Dina and my heart strained against my chest. What if she had outgrown me and my stagnant progression through life? What if she no longer wanted or needed me as a friend?

DINA: Sorry been so busy!!! Can come over tonight if you're free?

MAYA: Sure. But you might have to watch me scrub the skirting boards.

DINA: What?

MAYA: I'll explain when you get here.

DINA: Be right there!

Putting my phone down, I decided to carry on scrubbing because Dina's 'Be right there' could be anything from appearing in ten minutes to rolling up after a couple of hours.

I was relieved that she had responded. We had never gone without talking to each other for this long before. Her absence had felt like a missing limb. There was so much I wanted to tell her about my life and hear about hers. But more than anything, I wanted to feel that our bond was stronger than the distance that was growing between us.

Once I was done with the skirting boards, I moved on to the windowsills and then the kitchen cabinets. I listened to my Cleaning Yo Crib playlist on Spotify as I worked, trying not to think too much about the fact that all this cleaning was a prelude to what married life was going to be like.

Damn. Married life. I was meeting a man for *marriage purposes* and all I knew about him was that he was a couple of years older than me, my uncle's friend's son and he worked in finance. Unfortunately there was no picture attached to his biodata which made me even more hesitant to meet him, but according to my chachi, my uncle's wife, he was 'very cute'. And this, they believed, was enough for me to go on before meeting him in the flesh. The thought made me nauseous, but a deal was a deal. I had agreed to it and I had to see it through. And if I was truly being honest with myself, this wasn't solely to placate my parents. Somewhere, deep down, a part of me was interested in meeting a partner and settling down. Maybe I could hash the whole thing out with Dina. Lucy was great and all, but she didn't get my context and my culture the way my childhood friend did.

Two hours later, the house was almost done but Dina still hadn't arrived. I grabbed my phone to call her to find a message she had sent half an hour before:

DINA: I'm so sorry Maya, I fell asleep when I was putting Sami to sleep! I'm so exhausted. Rain check? Maybe at the weekend?

Something inside me clenched painfully.

Ignoring the prickle behind my eyes, I texted back a simple 'OK, no problem' even though I wasn't available at the weekend and carried on scrubbing and scrubbing, until my hands were red and raw and there wasn't a fingerprint or smudge in sight.

The next day, I was more than ready to tackle number six on the list: attend an art class. After a quick Google search,

I found an adult art class that had a session with availability straight after work. Lucy wasn't free, and although I was reluctant to go on my own, I forced myself to book a place before I could change my mind.

Ma was annoyed that I wasn't coming home straight after work. She wanted me to help her iron all the curtains before Sunday after she had taken them down and washed them. Like anyone was going to be looking at the curtains! I wondered if male suitors had to go through this nonsense? Probably not, even though where they lived was more important, given that there was a big chance of the bride moving in with his family after the wedding. London house prices were so ridiculously high that most of the new brides I knew moved in with their in-laws while they saved up enough money for a house or flat deposit.

I was nervous as I walked up to the Victorian building near Old Street, flanked on either side by newer towers of glass and chrome. But that was London all over, wasn't it? Old juxtaposed with new, the present nestled against the past. I hoped I didn't stand out as an uncreative imposter who was only there because of a list written by a stranger.

Pushing open the heavy, wooden door, I entered a square foyer with a staircase in the centre. The old, panelled walls were dark and gloomy and the floorboards creaked as I took a nervous step forward and peered through the open door on my left.

'Hello! Welcome!' A petite, pretty woman with dark skin and coal-coloured curly hair called out as she hurried towards me.

'Hi,' I replied shyly, extending my hand, which she grabbed and pumped up and down vigorously. 'My name's Maya. I signed up for an adult art class?'

'Yes! Of course. Hello, Maya, welcome, welcome! My name is Nandini. Do come in and get comfortable. May I offer you a drink?'

'Thanks, water would be great.' I followed Nandini through the doorway and into a dimly lit room, with candles and lamps casting interesting shadows and flickers on the wall. There were chairs set up in a half circle, with easels in front of them and Nandini gestured for me to take a seat. Not wanting to take centre stage, I chose a seat nearer the edge of the semi-circle and put my bag down before shrugging my coat off and draping it on the back of my seat. Nandini returned with a glass of water and she kindly took my coat from me before rushing off to the door to welcome someone else.

The seat next to me was empty, but the one after that was occupied by a small, milky-complexioned woman with bright red hair, rummaging through her handbag. She didn't look over at me so after a few seconds of trying to make eye contact, I gave up. The pair next to her had come together and were chatting quietly and at the other end was a group of three. Maybe coming here without a friend wasn't such a good idea after all. It would have been nice to have someone to talk to.

Getting up, I decided to go to the toilet before the session officially began, which would kill a few minutes and save me from having to sit there alone before the model arrived. In the bathroom, I stood in front of my reflection for a few minutes, killing time. I didn't have a *bad* face. In fact, as faces went, it was pretty decent, varying in degrees of attraction depending on where in the world I was. In Bangladesh, I would have been considered pretty if it wasn't for my dark skin. I had the typical big eyes, straight nose and small lips combination they loved out there. But my shade of brown was borderline offensive in Desh and my hair wasn't straight enough, so I was far from being a beauty. Over here, I was more average. Small lips weren't in fashion, nor were small boobs and flat bums. But Noah was interested in me. I think. As the days passed, my memory of him and our encounter on the Underground had faded, like a painting left out in the sun. Maybe I had got the whole thing wrong and all he wanted was someone to chat to, to liven up an otherwise boring journey to work.

But he had gestured for me to call him when he got off the carriage, right? Or did I imagine that? Maybe he was only being kind. If he really wanted to keep in touch, he would have asked to exchange numbers, not accidentally left behind an obscure notebook that contained zero information on how to reach him. Why was I bothering with his stupid list?

With a sigh, I washed my hands and went back to the studio. My head down, I skulked over to my seat, telling myself that I was there to try something new, experience something different. It wasn't about finding Noah; it was about finding myself.

Sitting back down in my seat, I looked up to see that the model had arrived and so had another man, taking up the seat right next to me. He was brown and was also on his own. Our eyes met and I could tell that he was as surprised to see me as I was him. It wasn't every day you ran into brown boys at art classes.

I looked away and focused on the model instead. He was a tall, blond, white guy and he was wearing a robe. Thinking nothing of it, I listened to Nandini start the class and tell us to pay attention to shadows and light, to try and see beyond what our eyes could see, whatever that meant. She talked about creating feelings and conveying emotions, about depth and symmetry. Then, she walked away and began playing soothing, classical music and the model stood up and let his robe fall to the floor. And he was completely and utterly butt naked.

My jaw dropped and I quickly averted my gaze as I felt heat creep up my cheeks. I discreetly darted my eyes around the room at the other 'artists' – they all looked completely at ease as they analysed the naked man before them and began to draw. Everyone except the brown guy. He looked as mortified as I did and once again, our eyes met. He smiled wryly at me but I didn't smile back. I couldn't! I didn't want anyone to think I was there on purpose.

Feeling queasy, I tried to think of what I could say to get out of this situation. It wasn't that I was a prude or I had an issue with the naked form. I didn't want to look at a man's wiggly bits for no reason! It wasn't exactly attractive, was it? Let's be real. It was gross.

'Strange for you to be here,' the brown guy said, startling me. Yes, it was, but it wasn't his business, was it?

'Why? Because I'm a brown woman?' I snapped, narrowing my eyes.

'Because you're a Muslim woman,' he corrected, nodding at the keffiyeh wrapped around my neck.

'And I guess you're a judgemental Muslim man,' I retorted. 'How original!' Ten minutes before, I was desperate for someone to talk to me and now I was regretting it. If I had known that God was going to be answering prayers at that moment, I would have asked for something more meaningful, like Sheila being replaced by a manager who appreciated me.

The redhead began to draw with long, sweeping strokes. Eyeing her technique, I tried to copy her.

'Now who's judging?' Mr Judgy quipped, picking up the conversation as though two minutes hadn't passed and the matter hadn't already been concluded.

'Do you mind? I'm trying to focus here,' I replied stiffly as I continued to scrawl randomly across the sheet.

'Doesn't look like you're focusing,' he said, assessing my 'work' dubiously. 'It looks like a toddler's scribbles.'

'Speaking of *focusing*, why don't you *focus* on your *own* work?' With gritted teeth, I pointedly turned my back away from him and continued to draw without looking at the naked man under the spotlights in front of me.

'I wonder what compelled a visibly Muslim woman like yourself to attend a class like this,' he mused as if I had never spoken. 'And don't tell me it's because you're an artist. You're obviously not.'

'How am I visibly Muslim?' I gaped at the man, flabbergasted by his audacity. Was he for real? 'This scarf is around my neck, not my head! And even if it were, what's it to you? Instead of trying to analyse me, a random woman who you will never see again, why don't you look inside and ask yourself why a *Muslim man like yourself* felt compelled to attend this class?'

'I'm supporting my friend,' he admitted, looking abashed now as he began to draw what looked like a stick man on his paper.

'Your friend is the model?' I scoffed, my reflexes causing me to turn away and end up being treated to the model's naked glory. I quickly looked down, anger bubbling closer to the surface. 'So it's fine for your friend to be naked, but not fine for me to be here? How does that make any sense? And anyway, I came here by accident if you must know.'

'Now *that's* what doesn't make sense. I find it stupefying that you "accidentally" came to a life-drawing class.'

'Did you just call me stupid?'

'No! I said "stupefied".'

'What? Who talks like that? This isn't *Harry Potter*.'

'What's *Harry Potter* got to do with anything?'

'Stupefy? You know, the spell that . . .' And just like that, I suddenly felt exhausted. Why was I arguing with a complete stranger? I bet Noah would have got the Potter reference.

Bloody Noah and his blasted list. The predicament I was currently in was largely to do with him. 'Oh, forget it.'

Nandini was walking around the room like Mary Berry on *Bake Off*, commenting on brush strokes and shading and shadows and both Mr Judgy and I stared at our respective disastrous drawings in dismay as she drew closer.

I needed to get out of here before I made a bigger fool of myself, but I didn't want to come across as rude or incapable. And then I had a brainwave.

Picking up my phone, I put it to my ear and said 'Hello?' as though I was answering a call. 'Oh no, what happened? Is she hurt? Oh gosh, yes, I'll be there. I'll meet you at the hospital.' I put the phone away and started gathering up my belongings.

'Is everything OK, dear?' Nandini asked, hurrying over to me.

'I'm afraid there's been an emergency,' I replied, trying to sound panicked as I went over to the coat rack where Nandini had hung up my coat. 'I have to leave, I'm so sorry.'

'Oh, I'm sorry, dear. What happened?'

What did happen? I hadn't expected her to actually ask me. 'My . . . g-gran,' I stammered, as I tried to remember what I had said during my fake phone call. 'She had a fall.'

My gran, as far as I knew, was absolutely fine and in good health. She was probably at that very moment watching a Bollywood movie on Star Plus. Did they have Star Plus in Desh? I had no idea; I hadn't been since I was seven years old. *Astaghfirullah, forgive me, Allah*, I beseeched God in my head. *Please don't let anything happen to Nani!*

'Oh my goodness! I hope she's all right,' Nandini exclaimed. 'Is she here in London?'

Why was she asking me all these questions? It was an emergency! I had to leave! And yes, my grandmother did live in London, not too far from me in fact, but I didn't want to admit it. She was on holiday in Bangladesh right now, but that was beside the point. I wanted the story to be about someone else, it felt less ominous that way, less like I was jinxing her.

'No . . .' I replied, wracking my brains. 'She's . . . back home. As in . . .' My eyes fell to the keffiyeh I had wrapped about my neck, a gift from Dina from when last visited. 'Palestine.'

'Oh, poor thing. How is access to medical care over there? Is she in the West Bank?'

I tried to recall where Dina's family was from, but couldn't for the life of me remember. My eyes landed on the giant crucifix above the window. 'Erm, she's in Bethlehem,' I guessed solemnly, picking up my bag and flinging it over my shoulder.

'Terrible what's happening,' the redhead chose that moment to pipe up and acknowledge my existence. 'What's the situation on the ground like?'

'Yes, would love to hear your thoughts on that,' Mr Judgy joined in, his eyebrow raised mockingly at me. 'I wouldn't have pegged you as Palestinian.'

I looked in his eyes and I could instantly tell that he knew I was lying about my grandmother – and possibly about Palestine as well and I immediately regretted the lie. To be honest, he had really nice eyes. The same shape and colour as almonds. In fact, he would have been attractive if he wasn't so annoying.

But forget that. I needed to get the hell out of that room and fast, before I was asked any more questions I didn't know the answer to. 'I'm half Palestinian,' I lied. 'And erm, the situation is awful,' I replied vaguely. 'I'm so sorry but I really have to leave. Bye!'

With that, I legged it out of the room, down the hall and back into the cold night. It was only when I was safely on the Tube that I remembered that during my phone call, I said that I would 'meet them at the hospital'. How I was planning to go to a hospital in Palestine in one night, God knows. Dina hadn't been in years because of how dangerous it was.

Shoulders sagging, I took out Noah's notebook and under his review of item number six – 'Fantastic night – Ally is bants' – whatever that meant – I wrote 'Never again'.

Chapter Nine

Sunday – aka doomsday – had arrived; the day a stranger was going to come to my house with his parents and siblings and based on a brief chat, decide whether or not he could see a future with me. I got to do the same back, only the stakes were higher for me of course. They always were for women.

Since my potential father-in-law was friends with my dad's brother, also attending the meeting were my chacha, chachi and their twins, Pretty and Pinky. If Nani had been in London, she would have been there too. But maybe it was a good thing she wasn't. She would have stressed everyone out more.

I didn't know much about my suitor, only the basics that my uncle had told my dad. His name was Zakariya, he was twenty-nine and five feet, ten inches tall, grew up in Camden, had an older sister who was married and a younger sister who wasn't, worked in finance and came from somewhere in Sylhet that was acceptable for my grandmother's elitist mindset. Ma thought that he sounded perfect on paper. We were supposed to meet and talk to see if we were compatible off paper as well.

I googled him, of course, but all I found was a LinkedIn profile that had no picture – I didn't want to click on it because then he would know that I had viewed it – and an Instagram account that was private, so I couldn't see any of his posts.

It was three in the afternoon and they would arrive at any moment. The house was gleaming, without a speck of dust in sight. Ma and Chachi were in the kitchen frying samosas and handesh so they would be piping hot and fresh when they arrived and all I had to do was wait in my room with my cousins until I was summoned.

Ma had wanted me to make something for the guests so that she could tell them that I had made it with my own fair hands. Everyone knew that I wasn't the best cook. In fact, it was a running family joke that started when I was twelve and attempted to boil eggs without any water. I'd tried baking a cake the day before and I swear I followed the instructions to a T, but somehow, I still ended up burning the top. It was also really flat and the inside was so dry that when I managed to extract it from the tin, it made a noise when it clunked onto the plate.

In the end, I decided to order a cake from a local home baker and pretend I had made it myself. Ma wasn't impressed with the idea – she said something about deception being the root of most failed marriages – but agreed when she saw the state of the frisbee-like cake I had cooked to a crisp. The house still smelt a bit burnt, despite airing it out for twenty-four hours and burning scented candles, incense and the strong bakhoor Malik had got from Dubai last year.

'You look really nice,' my cousin Pretty said to me as we chatted in my bedroom. Her identical twin sister, Pinky, nodded in agreement. Ma made me wear a teal-coloured silk kurta and get a mani-pedi done, since my bare feet would be on display. I usually appreciated the fact that wearing shoes indoors was considered bad form (aka dirty) in my culture, but at moments like these, I wished we did. I debated buying a new pair of heels that hadn't been worn outside, but then the potential in-laws wouldn't know that they were new and would question my hygiene and lack of respect.

'It's nerve-wracking, isn't it?' Pretty mused, adjusting her cotton shalwar kameez as she got comfortable on my bed. The twins were two years younger than me but had already gone through this process a few times. I could tell from the simplicity of their outfits and minimal makeup that they had been instructed by their mum to tone it down and let me shine. They usually loved glamming up. I wasn't sure whether to appreciate the gesture or feel offended by it.

'God, I hate this part,' Pinky agreed. 'All that waiting always has my stomach in knots.'

'It's not as bad as the moment you have to walk into the living room and they all stare at you like you're a circus act,' Pretty countered.

I looked at one and then the other, as they went back and forth in this manner, my palms beginning to sweat. I wasn't that nervous before, but now I was. Walking into the room was going to be awful.

'The worst part is when you have to pour the tea,' Pinky said. 'Remember that time when I spilt some of it because my hands were shaking so much?'

'Ah, that was bad,' Pretty nodded along. 'The mum was horrified. Imagine a wife who can't pour a cup of tea without soiling the carpet.'

'Girls! You're not helping!' I interrupted, feeling sick. 'Is this supposed to give me confidence?'

'Just being realistic, babe,' Pretty giggled. 'We've seen it all already, at our ripe old age of twenty-five.'

I wondered how it worked when you were a twin. Did you both look at the biodata and then toss a coin as to who got to meet him? And if there was no chemistry, did you pass him on to your sister? I asked them this and they both laughed in unison.

'It doesn't work like that,' Pinky chuckled. 'Pretty and I are so different that suitors who tick my boxes don't necessarily tick hers, do they, Pree?'

'Yeah. Pink wants someone religious who prays five times a day and has a beard and I'm not bothered,' Pretty replied. 'So all the biodatas that are looking for someone in hijab go to her. It works out quite well.'

'Imagine if they knew that my hair is pink under my hijab,' Pinky giggled and we all laughed at that. My uncle and aunt threw a fit when she first dyed her hair.

'I still don't know how you had the courage to do it,' I said in between laughs.

'They shouldn't have named me Pinky!' she shrugged and Pretty leant over and gave her sister a hug. I couldn't remember the last time Malik and I hugged. Growing up, I would have traded him for a sister in a heartbeat; someone I could confide in about everything, share clothes and makeup with, someone who understood what it was like to be a female in our culture and society, someone who wasn't revered as the first and only son. Someone who didn't (unintentionally, perhaps) make me feel like a failure for being the inferior sibling in every way.

'So what do you know about this "Zakariya"?' I asked. 'His dad is friends with Chacha, right?'

'Yeah, they're friends but we've never met him. Uncle sometimes comes over with Aunty but he's never come round,' Pretty explained.

'We've met his younger sister Hasina though,' Pinky added. 'She's nice and chill. They're like us, not your typical family with crazy high expectations of a daughter-in-law.'

I wondered how they could tell that from meeting his mum and dad. You could never really know what someone was like unless you lived with them. I had heard so many horror stories of women who thought they were marrying into reasonable families, only to be treated like a slave once they moved in.

There was a knock on the door and Malik poked his head around. He was wearing one of his many tailored shirts and designer jeans, looking effortless yet expensive – a look I hadn't attempted replicating because I knew I wouldn't be able to.

'Dimple, they're here,' he announced. 'Come and peek out of Ma's window!'

The three of us jumped up and followed my brother out of my room and into our parents' bedroom next door, which faced the street. Peering from behind the net curtains, we watched as a bunch of people began climbing out of a white Mercedes. There was an older man, obviously the father, in a grey suit and blue shirt. The mother, I assumed, was the one in the burgundy saree and coiffured hair. There were two younger women, both pretty, one in hijab and one without. From my position behind the curtain, I couldn't tell which one was Zakariya's older sister and which one was younger. They both wore shalwar kameez. One was carrying a bouquet of flowers and the other was carrying a huge Ambala box full of mishti.

And then Zakariya himself climbed out from the driver's seat. I tried to get a good look at him as he straightened his charcoal-coloured suit, but his head was bowed down. He looked like he had a good body and a full head of hair, but that was all I could make out.

As they turned to face the house, we quickly ducked away from the window so we wouldn't be caught spying.

'He looks all right!' Pretty whispered loudly, in case they could hear us through the double glazing.

'This is so exciting!' Pinky chimed in.

I didn't feel excited. I felt sick. When I agreed to this whole 'looking for a husband' thing, it was to get my parents off my case. It was something theoretical, intangible, like a puff of smoke so far in the distance that when I reached it, it would be gone.

But the smoke had turned into fire and it was right outside my door.

The doorbell rang and the four of us looked at each other in a panic.

'I've got to go back downstairs,' Malik said. 'Chill, sis, it's going to be fine.'

'We'd better go down too and find out what's expected,' Pretty said, following Malik out the door. Pinky trailed behind and, my knees weak, I collapsed onto my mum's bed as I listened to the muffled voices in the downstairs hall.

This isn't a big deal, I told myself. I had done harder things in the past month, like nearly drawing a naked man and almost reading the whole of *Ulysses*. This was nothing compared to that. So why were my nerves holding me hostage like this?

I have never been a confident person. My whole life I had heard comments about how it was such a shame that my mum has fair skin, but I had inherited my dad's darker complexion. How it was unfortunate that Malik, a boy who didn't need good looks to progress in life, is lighter than me. He is more successful and accomplished as well. I am lesser in every way.

And now, this random guy I didn't know, along with his whole family, was going to judge me and my parents and our little house and our modest means. And my dark skin. And they were going to turn me down, I knew they were.

My phone buzzed with a message from Pretty:

PRETTY: Come down, they're in the living room. Your mum's in there chatting to them and she told us to get the tea etc ready!

Chapter Ten

I padded quietly down the carpeted stairs and paused outside the closed door that led to the joined sitting and dining rooms. Straining my ears, I tried to eavesdrop but could only make out a few words, so I went into the kitchen where the twins were standing in front of the cooker looking confused.

'What's happening?' I whispered, closing the door behind me.

'Chachi told us to make masala tea and re-heat all the savoury nasta,' Pretty explained, looking confused. 'She said all of us have to bring it into the room.' Noting my pained expression, she shrugged apologetically. 'At least you won't be on your own.'

No, I wouldn't, but the thought didn't bring me comfort. Yes, the twins had dressed down, but they were still pretty. *Really* pretty. At five-six, they were both a couple of inches taller than me and they were slim with curves in all the right places. But more importantly, they were fairer than I was. They would all be comparing me to them. What if they preferred one of my cousins over me?

You don't want *to get married right now*, I reminded myself as I filled a large saucepan with water and the loose tea leaves my parents had bought from a relative's tea estate in Sylhet, adding cardamom pods, a bay leaf and cinnamon sticks and letting it simmer before adding the Carnation Milk. *This is you keeping your end of the deal. Who cares if they reject you?*

I might not have been a good cook, but I could make a banging cup of masala chai – or cha/sa as we said in Bengali/ Sylheti – and I was good at organising things. As the tea gently brewed (the secret to a good cha is allowing the spices to slowly infuse without rushing the process), I got to work re-heating the handmade handesh and samosas. Although Ma and Chachai had been frying them earlier, some of it had become a little cold and given how important the guests were, needed to be served piping hot. Ma's flaky pastry samosas were delicious, as were her sweet handesh with jaggery – or 'gur' as we called the dark, sticky sugar – and her spicy spinach and potato pakoras were the bomb. My chachi had made the savoury yellow ones, called noonor gora or noonor bora depending on where in Sylhet you were from.

As I moved around the kitchen organising the snacks and bumping into my cousins, who kept getting in the way, I felt some of my nerves ease through focusing on the task at hand. For a minute, I forgot that I was about to be paraded in front of a bunch of strangers like a debutante. I was too busy making sure I didn't burn the pastries while re-heating them in the oven.

'Here, start putting everything on these platters and we'll take it all through to the dining room,' I told the twins, taking out the baking tray and carefully placing it on a heat mat. As I turned around to check on the tea, I heard a crash. Whipping around, I saw the entire foil tray of pakoras and samosas on the floor.

'Omigod!' I gasped, staring at the pile of now-ruined snacks. My mum was going to kill me.

'I'm so sorry!' Pretty cried, her eyes round. 'I went to lift the tray up and it was so hot that I dropped it!'

'Of course it's hot, it's just come out of the oven!' I whimpered, surveying the mess on the floor. 'What are we going to do? We've lost half of our food!'

'Five-second rule! Five-second rule!' Pinky interrupted, pushing me out of the way. She grabbed the hot pakoras and haphazardly started throwing them back onto the tray, wincing from the heat.

'What are you doing? We can't serve them that! It's been on the floor!'

My cousin ignored me and soon had everything back on the tray. Her fingertips sore and scalded, she ran the cold-water tap and stuck them under the flowing water.

'We can,' she said. 'No one will know! Unless you want us to lay the table with all the samosas and pakoras missing, jeopardise your chance of finding the one and deal with Chachi's wrath?'

'Not really,' I said weakly. She was right, we had no choice. Allah was probably punishing me for buying that cake and planning to lie that I had baked and decorated it myself.

'Whatever happens in the kitchen, stays in the kitchen,' I said solemnly and the twins nodded.

I glanced over at the tea to find that it had boiled right to the top and was about to spill over. Quickly turning the heat off, I began to feel panicky. Why was everything going wrong? And just when I thought all the potential kitchen disasters had been averted, I smelt something smoky coming from the oven.

'Oh no! The noonor goras!' I cried, flinging the oven door open to be hit by a plume of smoke and heat, which instantly caused the smoke alarm to start ringing. I grabbed the oven gloves and yanked the tray out, but it was too late. The once-beautiful yellow discs, made from rice flour, turmeric, onions and ginger, weren't golden anymore. They looked like the coal used to heat shisha pipes.

'Someone turn off the smoke alarm!' I coughed, mortified. God knew what our guests were thinking. I didn't have to wait too long to find out, because Ma came bursting into the kitchen, pushing past Pretty, who was frantically waving a dishcloth at the smoke alarm, trying to get it to stop its insistent shrill.

'What's going on in . . .' her voice trailed off as she surveyed the blackened noonor goras. 'Oh, for God's sake, Maya! I leave you in charge of something as simple as reheating and plating up some food and you manage to cremate it all!'

Well, we had cremated *some* of it, the rest we infected with bacteria and whatever else was stuck on the floor tiles. And it was done with the help of a certain pair of identical twins who had apparently lost their voices and were happy to let me take all the blame.

'Sorry,' I said glumly. 'What shall we do?'

'Bin the lot of it! And then help me take the rest in. Pinky and Pretty, grab the samosas and pakoras, Maya take the tray with the tea set. Pretty, come back for the cake once you've said Salaam.'

'The tea's still on the hob.'

'Put it in the teapot then! Shobta khowa lageh ni? Do I have to spell everything out?'

'OK, OK!' I snapped, my pulse quickening. Everything was happening so fast. Pretty and Pinky had left the kitchen bearing trays of contaminated savouries, Ma had walked out with the sweet handesh and mishti and I was left with the worst tray of all: the tea. With trembling hands, I strained the piping hot tea through a sieve and into the pot, wiping away any splashes and carefully began carrying it down the narrow passage, hoping no one would realise that the rattling of the cups and saucers was due to my nerves.

Ma was waiting for me by the door, her scowl gone and, in its place, a warm, loving smile that was clearly meant for my potential future in-laws, not me. If I wasn't so petrified, I would have laughed at her BAFTA-worthy acting skills.

'Don't grin, keep your head down, don't talk loudly and don't spill any tea,' she whispered so fast that I only just caught her words. Before I had the chance to gather my thoughts, she ushered me into the room, following close behind.

Grin? Ma would be lucky if I didn't burst into tears. Palms sweating and legs trembling, I walked into the living area with my head lowered. The talking stopped the moment I entered and my heart hammered away so hard that I was afraid the guests would hear it from across the room, like the beating of drums. Pinky and Pretty were hovering near the dining table, so I went over to them and carefully placed the tray of tea down with everything else, careful not to make too much noise.

Some of the women had congregated on the dining room side of our lounge, on the chairs arranged around the table. I could see them from the corner of my eye, a blur of bright colours. Even if I couldn't see them, I would have been able to smell them. The pungent mix of perfumes was making me feel nauseous. The men must therefore be at the other end of the room, but there was no way I would look at them.

I could feel countless beady eyes on me, analysing every part of me; watching my trembling hands as I moved the teapot to the table, measuring both the thickness of my hair and the thickness of my waist. I didn't look up. I was too afraid of accidentally catching someone's eye. I kept my gaze firmly on my newly manicured toes, wishing I had worn socks, regardless of how ridiculous they would look with my outfit.

From Ma's briefing last night, I knew that now was the time to go and join them all, but my feet felt like they were glued to the carpet and I couldn't move. I wasn't sure where I was supposed to sit either – at the table with all the women or in the living room with the men? Ma gave me a little poke but still, I was frozen. How embarrassing would it be if I sat with the men and then got told to go and sit with the women?

'Here, sit down,' Ma said eventually. She gestured towards a seat that was in between the two sections of the room. I forced my leaden feet to the chair, flinching when it creaked.

'This is my daughter, Maya,' Ma said in Sylheti and I murmured 'Assalaamu Alaikum', my gaze firmly on my feet. I heard a few 'Wa Alaikum Salaams' but I still couldn't bring myself to look up. I had managed to figure out quite a bit by looking down though. I worked out that the potential groom, Zakariya, was sitting at the far end of the room, on the two-seater sofa with his dad, judging by their trouser legs and socks. I knew it wasn't Baba because he didn't sit like that and wouldn't be wearing socks either. I guessed that the older man was the one in plain navy socks and his son's had multi-coloured stripes. Although it could easily have been the other way round.

If my dad was on the single armchair, I guessed that my chacha was sitting with chachi on the three-seater sofa, with my potential mother-in-law next to her. I could tell by the hem of her burgundy-coloured saree.

Zakariya's sisters were around the dining table, along with my cousins and Ma, but I still wasn't sure which sister was older and which was younger. I guessed that the one closest to me was the younger one, judging by her trousers, which were dangerously short at calf length. It was from that direction that someone asked, 'So, Maya, what do you do?'

I wasn't expecting to have to speak or look up so soon. I swallowed nervously, but my throat was so dry that everything in my mouth felt like it was stuck together. I took a moment to compose myself, plastered a smile on my face and then forced myself to look up, but only at the women and not at the guy across from me. I was dying to know what he looked like, but I didn't want him to think I was checking him out.

As I explained what it was that I did, I looked over at my potential future mother-in-law. She was attractive for her age.

She didn't wear a hijab like my mum. Instead, her hair was expertly coloured without the slightest hint of grey and was done in a professional-looking updo. She was on the pale side, with slanted hazel eyes and full lips. I wondered if Zakariya looked like her and although I could have looked in his direction, I didn't. I could see him from the corner of my eye, of course, but not clearly enough to discern his features or anything. He seemed tall though and slim, but that's about all I could make out.

It took a few minutes for me to overcome my initial fear as the mum and I made some small talk. The dad didn't say anything, nor did the potential groom, so minutes passed and I still had no reason to look over at them. By that point, I desperately wanted to, but I had built up the idea of looking at him to be something so big and embarrassing that the more seconds that passed, the harder it became.

After a while, Mum nodded at me, indicating that it was time for me to pour the tea and dish out the snacks, so I got up and walked back to the dining table with wobbly legs. I didn't know how much sugar to put in each cup, which meant that I would have to bring the tray over to the coffee table and bend down as I did it, right in full view of everyone. I decided there and then that I was never going to meet anyone like this ever again. Next time – IF there was a next time – I would meet them in a coffee shop, or restaurant, or even my local library. Anywhere but in my own home. This was making me feel like I was being pimped out by my parents.

I got on with the task at hand and I offered the ladies tea first, which was the wrong way around, but I wanted to delay coming face-to-face with the guy as long as possible. There is no such thing as 'ladies first' in my culture. In fact, sometimes when we had a lot of guests, my mum didn't sit or eat at all, she was too busy serving everyone else. And regardless of whether she ate or not, the men always ate first. They got the food when it was piping hot, fresh off the stove. It was only after they had finished eating and we had cleared up that we got to sit down. By that point, the table usually had crumbs or stains decorating it, as well as half-filled bowls of lukewarm curry and thrice-heated kebabs, reminding us that others had already eaten there.

When I got to Zakariya, it was impossible for me to ignore him any longer, so I looked at my feet and mumbled, 'Do you take sugar?', my hands trembling again. When he replied, 'One, thanks,' I finally looked up at him. When I saw who it was, I inhaled sharply and almost dropped the hot tea all over his lap. It was *him!* The obnoxious man from the art class!

As recognition dawned on him, the corners of his mouth tilted upwards in a little smirk. I obviously couldn't say anything so I carried on with the tea malarkey, feeling annoyed and disappointed in equal measure. There was a moment when I let myself wonder if this meeting would go well . . . and now, it was over before it had begun.

Dejected, I went back to my seat and slumped down in my chair, not caring that my body language was negative. Everyone else continued to slurp their teas, Ma putting on her best hostess-with-the-mostess face, Baba making smart and intellectual comments about Bangladeshi politics and Malik putting on a great show of being charming and polite. It was like something straight out of *The Stepford Wives*.

I could feel Zakariya looking at me and I ignored his gaze for a while before finally meeting it. We locked eyes and I decided not to look away this time. Instead, I glared at him and he stared back at me unabashedly. The seconds passed and I started to feel silly, but I was too stubborn to break the impasse we had reached . . . until he winked at me! The nerve! I quickly averted my eyes, hoping no one else had noticed and thankfully, the continued sound of voices indicated that no one was paying any attention to us.

Ma got up and started handing out the samosas and pakoras and I shifted my gaze back to Zakariya, who I found was already looking at me. This time, I narrowed my eyes at him and gave him my fiercest glower. He raised a dirty samosa to his lips and took a massive bite. Stifling a laugh, I subtly covered my mouth to hide my grin, feeling a thousand times better than I did ten minutes earlier. He might have thought he had the upper hand, but the reality was, he was eating a pastry that had fallen on the floor. If that wasn't empowering, I didn't know what was.

Chapter Eleven

When our guests finally finished eating, Pretty, Pinky and I started loading the trays with the empty cups and crockery to clear up. I couldn't wait to get out of the living room and into the safety of the kitchen so I could tell the girls who Zakariya was. To my annoyance, his older sister, Halima, got up to help us, which meant I couldn't offload. Then, to make matters worse, his mother, younger sister Hasina and Ma decided to follow us into the kitchen too, getting in the way as we attempted to tidy up without dropping anything (again).

'Which of today's delicious treats did you make?' his mother asked, placing her hand on my arm and peering into my face, as if she was trying to figure out what I looked like without makeup. I tried not to extract my arm from her grip as I replied in a monotone that I baked the cake and shaped all the samosas. She looked pleased with my lacklustre response and Pretty suppressed a snigger as she put the leftovers into old butter, ice cream and one-litre yoghurt tubs. (I've lost count of the number of times I've opened what I thought was Anchor Butter to find homemade ginger and garlic paste instead. The worst is excitedly grabbing a tub of chocolate ice cream, dessert spoon poised, only to discover a soul-crushingly disappointing frozen mutton curry inside.)

'You like cooking then?' his mother continued, as if it was the most important thing to know about me. Before I could reply, Ma jumped in with, 'Oh, Maya is a bit of a whizz in

92

the kitchen, you know! She's always whipping up these fancy meals that put me to shame!'

By fancy, she must have meant mushy pasta with Dolmio sauce. I rolled my eyes at Pretty, which didn't go unnoticed by Hasina, who seemed to pick up on everything. She looked at me as if she were trying to figure me out and I wished her luck with that, because even *I* didn't know who I was half the time.

I was desperate to tell the twins about my meeting with Zakariya earlier in the week, but it was impossible with his sisters in hearing distance. And just as they left the room and I was about to combust, Malik came in to tell me that Zakariya wanted to talk to me alone.

'I don't want to!' I hissed, begging my brother with every part of me. 'I'm not feeling it, M. Please don't make me!'

Ma stopped midway between putting the teacups away and both she and my brother stared at me like I was crazy.

'Have you lost the plot?' Malik whispered back. 'He's a decent guy and he's good-looking! Get over yourself and meet him. I'm going to bring him up to your room.'

'Maya, please, don't ruin things,' Ma implored, grabbing my hands. 'They're a good family. Proposals like this won't come every day!'

'I can't believe you want him to come to my room! It's my safe space.'

'Stop being so dramatic, what is this "safe space" nonsense? Keep the door open so it's not bejjoti. I don't want your reputation tarnished.'

Ma all but shoved me out of the room and I glared at my brother's back for a moment before legging it upstairs. The last thing I wanted was to be standing there like an idiot when Zakariya came into the hallway and having to lead him to my room myself.

Panting, I flopped onto my bed and then leapt back up, smoothed out the sheets and chose the desk chair instead. Sitting on my bed would have been too provocative. I didn't want this 'Zakariya' to get the wrong idea about the situation and think I was interested in him. The saddest part was, I might have been if I hadn't known that he was a judgemental know-it-all who talked too much about things that weren't his concern.

Before I could spend any more time gathering my thoughts, there was a tap on the door and Malik walked in, followed closely by Zakariya, who was towering over him.

'Affa, this is Zakariya,' Malik said. He gestured to Zakariya to take a seat on my bed and I bristled as he did. To be fair, it was either my bed or the floor, but still, it felt horribly intrusive. I should have stayed on my bed and let him take the chair. I expected Malik to join him and make small talk but then my snake of a brother turned around, walked out of my room and closed the door behind him.

Staring at the door that my mum had specifically told us to leave open, I wondered if I should get up and open it again. Before I could, Zakariya spoke.

'Fancy meeting you again,' he began with a knowing smile, leaning forward. 'How is your ailing grandmother?'

So that was how he was going to play it. I opened my mouth to respond and before I could think it through, I squinted at him and said, 'I'm sorry? Have we met before?'

My response threw him and he shifted in his seat, not quite as confident as he was a moment before. 'At that drawing class in the city? You had to leave early because your grandmother was taken ill in . . . Palestine?' As the words came out of his mouth, I could see in his expression that he was doubting himself. He had seen my biodata for God's sake. He would have known if I had a Palestinian grandmother.

I put on my best sheepish look and shrugged helplessly. 'Palestinian grandmother? I'm as Bengali as they come. Sorry, you must have me confused with someone else.'

A silence followed as he struggled with what to say next, since his plan to embarrass me and put me on the spot was obviously failing. I did nothing to ease the awkwardness. He deserved to feel uncomfortable after the discomfort he had caused me during that class.

Clearly at a loss for how to respond, Zakariya instead got up from where he was perched on the edge of my bed and began nosing around my room. I watched him wordlessly as he took in the plain beige walls, matching carpet and similarly coloured duvet.

'You like . . . beige, don't you?'

'It's not beige,' I said defensively, wracking my brains for a colour that didn't have such a bland reputation. 'For your information, it's . . . stone. And I like things to be simple and unfussy.'

'You're hardly "simple" and "unfussy",' he mused, going over to my bookcase and flicking through the titles. He raised an eyebrow at *Ulysses* perched on the end of the shelf like a bookend and then I thought I heard a snicker upon his discovery of the handful of spicy TikTok sensations that I should have donated to a charity shop before the Big Marriage Meeting. But how was I to know that my parents – the same people who warned me about *looking* at boys – would allow a full-grown male into my bedroom, unchaperoned?

If his prying into my taste in books wasn't excruciating enough, he then moved on to my photographs. There was the one of Pinky, Pretty and me in Cornwall the summer after GCSEs that Ma had taken. One of Malik and me in Bangladesh when we were kids, wearing vest tops and shorts and drinking fresh coconut water straight from the fruit. There was one of my mum and dad on their wedding day and then a really embarrassing one: me, on my own, dressed up to the nines in a full-length gown at Dina's wedding. He spent the longest looking at that one. I felt the heat rise to my cheeks as I stomped over to him.

'Do you mind?' I snapped, snatching the frame out of his hands. 'This is private stuff, you know.' I put the frame back on the shelf facing the other way so the photo wasn't visible and made a mental note to replace it with something less personal, like our next-door neighbour's cat.

'Well, it is on display, not hidden away in an album,' he reasoned, going over to the chair I had vacated and sitting down, crossing his outstretched ankles and making himself comfortable.

'I wasn't expecting you to start digging through my room,' I retorted. 'If I had known you would be this nosy, I would have put everything away.'

'I'm glad you didn't. A person's boudoir speaks volumes about their personality.' He leant back in the chair, eyeing me with an interested expression on his face, and I resisted the urge to push him over. His confidence was bordering on arrogance and while a part of me found it endearing, the bigger, more sensible part, found it annoying.

'Oh, really? And what does my "boudoir" say about mine?'

'You're studious. You love your family. You're smart.' He nodded to *Ulysses* then and I held back a snort. 'You prefer staying at home to going out. You're soft beneath that prickly exterior. A bit shy and introverted, despite the image you're trying to portray.'

I forced my jaw not to drop open, shocked by his brazenness. Soft beneath that prickly exterior? How dare he! Like I was some sort of ripe jackfruit. He probably expected me to swoon at his charm, but I rolled my eyes instead. What a load of codswallop. So what if what he said was spot on? Anyone could have figured that out.

'But what I'm really curious to know –' he continued, staring at me with a half-smile on his face '– is why you're pretending that we haven't already met?'

'Because I wish we hadn't!' I blurted out, unable to contain myself anymore. 'You didn't exactly leave a good impression!'

'What did I do?' he asked, looking genuinely confused, which irritated me further.

'Forget about it. It doesn't matter.' I sighed and looked down at the floor.

It had been such a long week. I had put my blood, sweat and tears into preparing for this visit. I let my parents create a marriage CV. I cleaned every inch of the house. I bought a new outfit. I gave it my best shot and what happened? The guy turned out to be a judgemental git that I had already met before. How was that for bad luck? I was exhausted. Physically, mentally and everything in between.

'It obviously does matter because whatever it is, it's impacting the way you're behaving towards me today. You're not going to give this a chance, are you?'

'Of course not. And who cares? You might think you know me after poking around my room for five minutes, but you don't. So why don't we call it a day and stop wasting everyone's time?'

'Are you serious? Just like that? I don't know what I did that was so terrible.'

'Like I said before, it doesn't matter. Forget it.'

'You know what? Fine. Let's forget it. We're obviously incompatible. But can you tell me what I did?'

'You really want to know?' I finally looked at Zakariya again and I was surprised by the intensity of his expression. It felt as though he truly did want to understand why I disliked him so much. I had no idea why he cared, but maybe he was one of those guys who couldn't deal with rejection.

'Yes!'

I took a second to gather my wits, before letting him have it. 'You made a comment about being surprised that a "visibly Muslim girl like me" was at the class. Do you know what it's like, being a brown Muslim woman in London? I get judged everywhere I go, from white people to our own people. I can't win either way! You judged me without knowing me, or why I was at the class, even though you were there yourself to support your naked friend!'

By the time I got all this out of my system, I could feel my cheeks burning and I was waving my hands around like a lunatic. He looked surprised and then incredulous as he digested my revelation.

'Well, it was a valid observation,' Zakariya said after a beat, his voice a lot calmer than mine. I tried to take my own volume down a notch, reminding myself that our families were downstairs.

'Seriously?' I hissed from between clenched teeth, crossing my arms like a child and then uncrossing them when I realised it probably made me look immature. 'It was judging a woman, without knowing her, because of the colour of her skin!'

'OK. Fine. If you insist. So that's it then? No point in talking further?' His voice still quiet, he stood up and stepped closer to me. Uncomfortably so. I inhaled deeply and his expensive, manly scent went straight to my brain and made me feel lightheaded. Why did he have to be so bloody good-looking? This would be so much easier if he wasn't. I tried to take a step backwards, but my bed was right behind me and if I moved back any further, I would fall onto it. And Lord knew what sort of invitation that would have been.

I contemplated his question and I hesitated for a second before saying no. I looked away from him because suddenly, staring into his eyes made me feel funny. There was something about the way he was looking at me, the intensity of his stare, which was making my legs turn to jelly. Swallowing nervously, I lifted my eyes again to meet his. 'There's no point.'

'Right. I'll go back downstairs then.'

With one last long, hard look, he turned around and walked out of the room, closing the door firmly behind him. And as soon as he did, I didn't feel triumphant like I thought I would. I felt horribly deflated. And alone.

Chapter Twelve

It had been a fortnight since the disastrous dekha dekhi meeting and the atmosphere in my house had become so tense that I had started avoiding going home straight after work. Instead, I was going running, occasionally with Malik, meeting Lucy and trying (and usually failing) to see Dina.

Ma and Baba couldn't understand why I didn't want to progress things with Zakariya. Apparently 'there was no vibe' and 'his older sister is hard work' weren't good enough reasons to say no. Whenever they got the chance, they would try to persuade me to meet him again, listing all the ways he made sense for me.

'He ticks all the boxes!' Ma insisted the day after the meeting, as I got in from work and was taking off my coat. 'Not only is he good on paper, but he's also tall and good-looking. You can't figure a person out from one little meeting. You need to see him again!'

'Ma, please let it go,' I said, trying to squeeze past her and upstairs to my safe space. 'We didn't connect at all. We've got nothing in common.'

'Do you think your dad and I had anything in common when we met?' she argued. 'And we've been married for nearly thirty years!'

'I need to go and change. I don't want my clothes to smell of curry!' This tactic didn't work though, because as soon as I came down to set the table, it started up again. Then again through dinner. And again while clearing up. It was unbearable.

What was I supposed to tell my parents? That I had met Zakariya before at a nude drawing class? And that I didn't like his holier-than-thou attitude? And that I was too busy getting through Noah's list to waste time and energy on a man I wasn't interested in? And speaking of Noah . . . what if I did run into him again? I didn't want to be committed to someone I had settled for when Noah was still out there, somewhere.

I desperately wanted to talk it all through with Dina, but I hadn't heard from her since the day she blew me off. Lucy was great . . . as great as someone who wasn't Muslim, or at the very least, South Asian could be. She didn't get the whole family pressure thing, about upholding traditions, fulfilling societal expectations. She – and most of my social-media feeds – were all about self-love, self-care, setting boundaries, putting yourself first, living your truth, prioritising your mental health.

HA. As if it was that simple. I tried saying this to my parents and not only was I scoffed at, but I was also told that 'living your truth' was a selfish person's way of saying 'do what you want with no consequences'. 'Putting yourself first' was another way of saying 'to hell with everyone else'. And as for 'setting boundaries' . . . they laughed at that one. Well, Baba did. Ma rolled her eyes and said that if we wanted to live like shada manush, then how about she started with charging me rent and board?

Malik was also on at me about rejecting Zakariya. It was during one of our morning runs and after some probing about why I had rejected a perfectly decent 'catch', that I finally spilt out the sordid truth.

'Is that it?' Malik stopped jogging so abruptly that I knocked into him and the two of us almost toppled onto the tarmac. 'You're offended because of *that*?'

'Malik, you don't get it,' I replied tersely. Because he really didn't. 'You're an Asian boy, the only son, a good-looking, fair-skinned success, with clout akin to royalty. You don't know what it's like being me, the stick I get for merely existing. The way Zakariya made me feel that day at the art class . . . It just wasn't good, OK?'

'Look, Dimple,' Malik replied, his voice gentler this time. 'Take it from me, as a red-blooded bloke. He spoke to you because he was interested in you. But he obviously didn't know what to say. He probably wanted it to sound like banter but it came out wrong. Don't shut this whole thing down so hastily.'

One Friday morning during work, Dina finally texted me:

> DINA: It's been too long and I know it's my fault. Please come round for dinner tonight, I miss you x.

Ordinarily, I would have leapt at the opportunity to enjoy Dina's amazing cooking skills and company, but something inside me felt reluctant. It *had* been too long. So long, in fact, that I no longer knew what to say to her and how to act around her.

'Go,' Lucy said encouragingly when the entire morning had passed and I still hadn't responded. It was lunchtime and we had popped outside so I could get some fresh-ish air and Lucy could vape. 'You guys have been friends for far too long. She's made a move and reached out to you. Ignoring her is dishonouring your friendship.'

Deep down, I knew that Lucy was right. Pushing aside my fears, I texted back and then ignored the queasiness I felt the rest of the day.

It was freezing when I left the office for Dina's house and I wrapped my coat and scarf tighter around me as I walked to the station and then proceeded to take them off the moment I went underground because it was so warm. I swear, it's the drastic changes in temperature that make me snotty all winter.

As always, as soon as I got on the carriage, I did a quick look around to see if Noah was there. He wasn't, of course. He never was. The chance of him getting on the train at the exact same time and in the exact same carriage as me was about the same odds as me winning the lottery. And I didn't even play it, because gambling is haram in Islam. But still, I lived in hope.

'Maya! Omigod, I've missed you so much,' Dina exclaimed as she threw open her front door. 'How is it that we only live a few Tube stops away from each other, but I never get to see you?'

Err, because you decided I was too boring for you and you're too busy with your own fulfilled life?

I didn't say this. Of course I didn't.

'Err, because you're too busy being super-mum and superwoman, that's why,' I replied a little stiffly, giving her a half-hearted hug back. I moved to pull away, but she drew me in closer and squeezed tighter.

'I'm sorry for being AWOL lately. I really am,' she said when she eventually pulled away and I felt my anger and disappointment begin to thaw.

'I've missed you too,' I said quietly. There was a pause for a moment and then Dina smiled and switched the pace before it became too maudlin or uncomfortable. She had always been good at doing that.

'Come in,' she said, pulling me into the house and closing the front door firmly behind me. 'I was just getting Sami ready for bed.'

Dina continued to chatter as I took my boots, coat, scarf and cardigan off, hanging it all on the end of the banister before following her upstairs.

'Maya! Where have you been?' Mohammed greeted me, coming out of the living room in a white shirt and PJ bottoms.

'Salaams, Mo, it's been a minute. What are you wearing?'

'Don't ask,' he laughed. 'I started changing and then forgot. I've been on call for a week, my brain is wrecked.'

'Sami! Look who's here!' Dina called out and a second later a mini-Dina, complete with wild, curly brown hair and green eyes, came bounding out of one of the three bedrooms. Two-year-old Sami babbled something to me, in what language I had no idea, but Dina seemed to understand everything he said.

'Hi, Sami,' I said, scooping him into my arms and giving his chubby body a squeeze. 'Look, I have a present for you.' Putting him down and reaching into my tote, I pulled out the picture book I had bought for him on my way to the station. 'And this is for you, Deens.' I handed Dina a big box of Hotel Chocolat truffles.

'My fave! Thank you. Mind putting him to bed?'

'Sure. Will he let me? It's been a while.'

'He'll let anyone with a book. Thanks, hun. Switch on his night light when you're done, please and close the door otherwise he'll keep coming out of his room.'

Sami took me by the hand and led me to his colourful bedroom, stuffed with more books and toys than I had ever seen belonging to one child. Climbing onto his bed, he pointed to his book and I took that as an invitation to read it to him. Sitting next to him on the PAW Patrol bed covers, I opened the book and began to read it in my best actress voice, choosing different voices for the various characters. Sami didn't say a word but giggled and snuggled closer to me. He was so soft and warm and when the book was finished and I tried to put it away, he pointed at it again. And again. After the fifth read, he yawned and with a smile, I kissed the top of his head, which smelt like soap and berries and tucked him into bed before switching on his night light and turning the main light off.

Closing the bedroom door quietly behind me, I headed back downstairs. I could smell something delicious bubbling away on the stove and over the noise of the extractor fan and the TV playing in the lounge, I could hear Dina and Mohammed's laughter. I walked into the tiny kitchen to find the two of them squabbling about what herbs to add to the stew they were in the middle of cooking and I took a moment to observe the scene in front of me. Dina was smiling, Mohammed was rolling his eyes and there were jars of spices, discarded onion peel, little toy cars and plastic beakers all over the counter. The fridge was covered in magnets, photographs and Sami's 'art', but instead of seeing mess and chaos, I saw love. I saw comfort. I saw a family.

Maybe this was the whole point of marriage? To create a family; a club that only you belonged to, with its own schedules, own jokes, own values and goals. Maybe I had been short-sighted for not considering marriage to be an option until now? I kept thinking I had more time – there was no rush – but look at Dina. She met Mohammed at uni and she knew within a month of meeting him that she would marry him. It wasn't as simple as that, though. He was doing medicine and didn't want to get married until after he had qualified. She waited for years, growing weary and doubtful of his intentions. She thought he was keeping her hanging and that the reason he wouldn't put a ring on it was because his mum wasn't happy for him to marry outside of his culture. She was wrong on every count. He told his family as soon as he finished his final exam and they immediately came over with a formal proposal for Dina. His mum instantly fell in love with her – it's hard not to – and now look at them. Happily married for four years, careers, a property and offspring that was about to double.

'Tell me what's going on with you,' Dina asked over a gorgeous dinner of a tender lamb and aubergine stew, buttery vermicelli rice and a sweet and tangy fattoush salad topped with crispy flatbread.

'I don't know where to start,' I sighed, enjoying another mouthful of the stew, the lamb falling apart in my mouth.

'The beginning?' Mohammed suggested. 'I can't deal with stories that start in the middle.'

'Same,' Dina agreed.

Sighing, I took a sip of laban – a salty and refreshing yoghurt drink – and started from the beginning like I was asked.

'This is all so romantic,' Dina gushed as though hearing the story for the first time.

'Romantic? It's creepy. Ignoring people on the Tube is an unwritten rule,' Mohammed replied, unimpressed. 'I'm not sure I like the sound of this player.'

When I moved on to tell them about the list, Dina almost leapt out of her chair in excitement.

'I LOVE that! What an amazing idea. And the best part is, you might run into him again!'

Mohammed scoffed at this. 'It's cool you're trying new things, but please don't do it for the sake of a stranger playboy. It has to be for you.'

'It is for me,' I reassured him. 'It's getting me out of the house and trying things I never dreamed of. Can you believe I read the whole of *Ulysses*? It was over a thousand pages long!'

'And you've taken up running,' Dina said wistfully. 'I've always wanted to be able to run.'

'Why don't you then?' Mohammed added, unhelpfully. 'What's stopping you?'

Dina turned to glare at her husband. 'What's stopping me? Oh, I don't know. Maybe it's because I have a full-time job, a toddler, a household to manage, a husband who works long hours and no family close enough to help me? Not to mention the fact that I'm *pregnant*. Are those good enough reasons for you?' Dina's voice got louder and more high-pitched, her usually pale complexion turning pinker as she continued. 'Oh and let's not forget that my body is already wrecked after carrying a ten-pound baby, an emergency C-section and then breastfeeding for two years. And I haven't had a good night's sleep in years!'

Mohammed fell silent and I looked between them, feeling a little panicked. Maybe everything wasn't as perfect as it seemed. I reached over and clasped Dina's hand.

'I honestly don't know how you do it,' I said to her, as her eyes filled with tears. 'But I'm here for you, Dina. We're only three stops away on the Tube. If you ever need someone to watch Sami, call me! Or come round to mine and we'll go for a run together while my parents watch him. They'd be happy to. Or I'll come and look after him while you sleep!'

The tears Dina was struggling to hold in spilt over then, silently and I got up and gave her a hug. Mohammed, I noticed, hadn't said a word.

After dinner, I cleared the table and washed the dishes while Dina dried and put them away. Mohammed had a night shift at the hospital and I was glad to have some one-on-one time with her.

'Are you OK?' I asked her as I washed the last dish and Dina put the kettle on.

'Sort of,' she said quietly. 'No one ever really tells you how hard it is, you know? I'm lucky, I've married one of the good ones and he does as much as he can to pull his weight. But his hours are crazy and it's not his fault he's not around a lot. I feel so alone. Like my parents abandoned me.'

Dina's parents had moved to Australia to live with her brother shortly after Sami was born. I couldn't imagine having a child with no one around to help me. A wave of guilt hit me. I should have been there for her more, instead of selfishly focusing on my own life and resenting her for not having enough time for me. I was a terrible friend.

'You're not alone, you have me,' I told her. 'Now you go and sit down, let me make the tea.'

I was at Dina's house so late that in the end, I decided to stay over and she made me a makeshift bed in Sami's room. We spoke about it all: motherhood, marriage, family. I told her about Zakariya, my career plans, everything.

'My parents think I need to give Zakariya another chance and so does Malik. Apparently, one meeting isn't enough to tell that I don't want a future with him.'

'I agree,' she said simply. My jaw dropped open so wide that you could have fitted a golf ball in it.

'What? Why? You heard what he said at the class!'

'I know,' she shrugged. 'But people say silly things sometimes when they're nervous. He probably wanted to chat you up and it all went wrong. I mean, the first time I met Mohammed, I thought he was a right loser.'

'What did he say to you?'

'He asked me if my green eyes were real or if I was wearing contact lenses like a fake!'

'Woah. Stupid thing to say but he was what, eighteen? Nineteen?'

'Nineteen,' she smiled fondly at the memory, the way only someone truly in love could. 'But imagine if I judged him based on that one encounter. I wouldn't be here right now.'

'Hey, you were crying a minute ago,' I teased.

'I know,' she smiled ruefully back at me. 'Life can be bloody hard. But anything that's worth it is difficult, habibti.'

Chapter Thirteen

'You can't give up already,' Lucy said during the first lunch we'd had together in a while. Things always started getting busier in November, as the end of the year approached. We had so many contracts to check and cross-reference that we ended up eating lunch at our desks.

'I'm not giving up, I just took a break,' I replied, taking a bite out of my sandwich. It had been a while since I had attempted to check off another item from Noah's list. After the disastrous naked man event and with the distraction of the dekha dekhi thing, I didn't have the courage – or the inclination – to see what was up next.

'Come on,' she persisted. 'Let's have a look before Sheila gets back.'

From the steely glint in her eye, I knew that she wasn't going to stop harping on about it, so I retrieved the notebook from my bag and handed it over to her. I watched as she flicked through the pages, hoping it wasn't anything dangerous like 'join a cult'.

'Ah, this is easy and cute,' she exclaimed. 'And totally achievable.'

'Cute? Please don't tell me I have to adopt a stray cat. My mum would kill me. She has a phobia of litter trays.'

'Nope, guess again,' she teased, closing the notebook. I snatched it from her and looked inside:

7. VISIT LONDON'S 10 MAIN MUSEUMS ✓

British, Natural History, Science, V&A, Greenwich, Imperial War, Museum of London, London Transport, Design, Bank of England.

Fave – Natural History and the T-rex. Least fave – BoE. Boring.

'Oh,' I said, almost surprised at how easy it was. 'This is easy. And fun. And I've only visited half of those, mostly in primary school.'

'Time to visit them again and inject yourself with some culture. I wouldn't mind coming with you to some of them. We could make a day of it.'

'Let's do it! When are you free?'

'Not for a couple of weeks,' Lucy murmured as she browsed her calendar. 'OK, here we go. Weekend after next?'

'Sure. I can't believe I'm only on number seven. I thought I had done a lot more.'

'Well, you started in mid-September, right? It's not too bad but you'd better get a move on. You could be missing opportunities to bump into Noah.'

'That isn't why I'm doing all this! I'm doing it because—'

'Because you're broadening your horizon, blah blah blah, BS,' Lucy teased. I chucked my pencil rubber at her, narrowly avoiding hitting the side of her head.

'Hey, I see some workplace malpractice going on,' Arjun called out, sauntering into the office and casually sitting on the edge of my desk as though he didn't have the same workload as I did.

'And you'll probably witness some more if you don't meet your deadlines,' I reminded him darkly.

'Thanks for the reminder, Debbie Downer,' Arjun slid off the desk and threw himself into his chair. 'Can't get five minutes' peace around here without you lot breathing down my neck.'

If I thought that navigating Sheila and Arjun at work was difficult, it was like a spa retreat compared to what was happening at home.

It had been a month since the dekha dekhi and Ma had finally accepted that it was time to give up on the idea of me riding off into the sunset with Zakariya, Malik was spending less and less time at home – probably off with his mysterious girlfriend – and Baba was still in denial about both his kids; totally buying Malik's lies about working late and also believing that I was feigning indifference towards Zakariya. He thought I was being coy and needed a bit more time to come around.

In a few weeks, my usually functional and reliably boring family had turned into a dysfunctional hot mess.

'Baba, I'm not joking. I'm not interested in meeting Zakariya again. Please, can we move on from this now?' I implored after he pounced at me mere moments after I got in from work that evening.

'In my day, our parents would tell us who to marry and we agreed, no questions asked,' Baba muttered, his face darkening. 'We respected our elders and trusted their judgement. And now? You children think you know everything.'

'I don't think I know everything. But I do know that I don't want to marry him!' I argued, my voice rising with agitation. This wasn't the first, second or even third time that week we had had a similar conversation. All I wanted to do was sit and watch a bit of TV after dinner, but no such luck. I was getting carpal tunnel watching Netflix on my phone during all the evenings I had been avoiding them. I stood up. I would have rather been fitted with a hand brace than have to listen to my parents' nagging. 'I agreed to meet suitors and you agreed not to force me into anything. But you're not keeping your end of the bargain!'

'Fine, fine, sorry for trying to help you find a smart, educated, wealthy, handsome, respectable husband!' Ma interrupted, poking her head around the living-room door. 'We're such evil parents, boo hoo.'

I stared at my mum. She used to be the voice of reason in this house, but lately, it felt like my parents had been replaced by parodies of themselves. And all because I said no to the first proper proposal I had ever had? What would happen if I said no to a second, or a third?

'Girls these days,' I heard Baba mutter. 'Maya needs to realise how lucky she is to have such a dola proposal. It would have evened out the genes.'

With those parting, stinging words, he shuffled out of the living room, straightening his lungi as he did. I watched his retreating back, stifling the urge to run out of the front door and never come back. He seriously thought I was lucky because Zakariya was fair-skinned? How and why was that a *thing*? The threat of tears stung the back of my eyes and I blinked them away furiously, telling myself not to let his comments get to me.

It wasn't over though. I heard my dad stop and then his footsteps drew closer again before he stuck his head around the door. 'If you don't want this man, fine. But you can phone him yourself and tell him. Your chacha is too embarrassed to show his face to his friend and so am I.'

'What? Baba!' I exclaimed, jumping up from the sofa. 'The whole point of an arranged-marriage meeting is that the PARENTS arrange things! *You* have to call him, or chacha. Not me!'

'The whole point of an arranged-marriage meeting is to get married,' Baba replied stonily. 'I'll send you his number.'

Back in the safety of my bedroom, I took out my phone and stared at the contact card my dad had sent me: *Jakaria,*

Possible Damand. I couldn't help smiling at the way my dad, like a typical Bengali, had changed the Z into a J. But then I saw the bit about him being a possible son-in-law and my stomach clenched with guilt. They were really excited about this guy and all the possibilities that they thought were within their grasp. And I had ruined it for them. I had squashed their excitement like I had stamped on a balloon, all because I had run into him at a nude art class. Was it my fault for being unable to let it go? Was it the list's fault for taking me to that class? Was it Zakariya's fault for saying inappropriate things to me? The rational part of me knew that it was no one's fault, but the part of me that needed to compartmentalise things into boxes was struggling to make sense of it all.

Baba was expecting me to call Zakariya, but there was no way I would do that. It wasn't 1987. We had things like text messages and emails we could hide behind instead. Yes, it was the coward's way out, but I decided I didn't owe him anything. It's not like we were courting:

MAYA: Salaams Zakariya, I hope you're well. I know you know this already, but my dad is insisting that I let you know personally that I don't think we're a right fit for each other and therefore shouldn't progress things. All the best with your search insha'allah. Take care.

Before I could overthink my message and rewrite it a thousand times, I hit send. I wasn't surprised that he didn't reply, but even so, I kept checking to see if he would.

On the third Saturday in November, I woke up ridiculously early, went for a run and then showered and got ready to start my museum crawl with Lucy. We were hoping to see as many of them as physically possible, which defeated the purpose somewhat. When Noah compiled the list, he probably envisioned himself slowly making his way through the various exhibitions, soaking up all the culture and history, feeding his soul. I was planning to speed through them quickly so I could tick it off the list and move on to the next task, whatever it was.

It was going to be cold outside so I put on a thick knee-length jumper with jeans and my big sleeping-bag coat. Adding a scarf around my neck, a woolly hat and leather gloves, I went downstairs to rummage around in the cupboard under the stairs until I found my favourite boots with a thick heel, perfect for long walks. I could hear my mum rustling around in the kitchen but for the first time ever, I didn't bother to let her know I was going out. I couldn't deal with getting told off for the millionth time about rejecting Zakariya.

Outside the air was icy and sharp and I was grateful for all my layers until I got to the Tube. Peeling off my gloves, scarf and hat and stuffing them into my bag, I looked around the carriage for a sign of Noah and when I didn't spot him, I took out the romance novel I had bought the day I went to the bookshop. It had taken me a while to heal from the trauma of reading *Ulysses* and I was only just ready to read a book again.

'Maya! Hi!' Lucy called out when I emerged from the Underground twenty minutes later at Holborn Station. Unlike me, who looked like a sleeping-bag advert, Lucy looked effortlessly chic like she always did. Her glossy golden hair was loose over her shoulders and she was in a tan wool coat and cream-coloured beret. A Burberry scarf hung loosely around her neck and her knee-high brown suede boots over leather leggings made her already long legs appear even longer.

'Lucy, you look incredible,' I said, giving her a quick hug. 'Shall we ditch the museums and go shopping instead? You need to be my stylist.'

Laughing, Lucy linked her arm through mine and gently tugged me in the direction of the British Museum. 'Another day, babe. Today is about culture and all that.'

By lunchtime, we had seen most of the British Museum and the London Transport Museum, which was a short walk away in Covent Garden, and we were having a really good time. The Transport Museum surprised me with how fun and interactive it was. I took a selfie of Lucy and me with a 1962 double-decker behind us and sent it to Dina, with the caption 'You need to bring Sami here!' He would love playing on all those red buses. All this and more was on my doorstep and yet I barely bothered to see it. Noah's list was opening my eyes to so much more than trying new things; it was about perspective and making the most of what life had to offer.

'We should hit Kensington next and do Science, Natural History, the V&A and the London Design Museum,' Lucy said when we stopped for a quick sandwich in the piazza. It was far too cold to be eating outside, but I was on such a high from all the fun I was having that I didn't care that my fingertips were frozen and my nose had turned Rudolph red.

'How can we possibly do all that in, what, six hours? Well, do it properly. I want to enjoy it and savour it,' I replied, surprising myself with my reaction. 'Shall we pick two of them?'

'OK, let's save the Design one for another day and do the V&A, Science and Natural History seeing as they're right next to each other,' Lucy grinned. 'The V&A is my favourite. I love looking at all the clothes.'

Later that night, after showering, praying Salaatul Isha, the night prayer, and collapsing into bed, I checked my phone again to see if Zakariya had responded. There was nothing.

Chapter Fourteen

The next morning, I crept into Malik's room and nudged him, trying to wake him up. It was 7 a.m. and I had agreed to meet Lucy outside Hampstead Heath to complete number eight on the list: SWIM IN HAMPSTEAD HEATH POND! But now that I was on the verge of catching pneumonia, I couldn't bring myself to take public transport. I had woken up shivering in bed because every winter, my dad refused to turn on the heating until icicles formed on my eyelashes. I also needed moral support – something or someone to make sure I would see this through and wouldn't get off at a different stop and go shopping instead.

'Hmmm?' Malik grumbled after I resorted to tickling his nose to wake him up. His eyes slowly opened and he blinked them rapidly as he stared at me in confusion. 'What the hell, Affa? What do you want? It's still dark outside!'

'I need a lift,' I whispered. 'Shh, don't wake Ma and Baba up. I don't feel like seeing them.'

'Are you still avoiding them? It's been like, two weeks,' he closed his eyes again. I pulled the covers off him.

'Malik! Please!'

'Leave me alone, man. I'm tired! Get your own car!'

'I can't drive.'

'Learn then!'

We went back and forth for a few minutes and I almost felt bad for dragging my brother out of his warm, cosy bed so early at the weekend. But I rarely asked him for anything, so after a couple of seconds, the guilt was replaced by the sort of entitlement only the eldest child could have.

'Fine!' he growled after I opened the curtains and, feeling accomplished, I left him to get dressed while I made him coffee in a travel mug. Five minutes later, Malik appeared wearing a black tracksuit with the hood pulled up over his head and I followed him outside the house to where his BMW was parked on the street behind my dad's.

'Where to?' he said, taking the mug from me as he turned on the engine and pulled away from the kerb. 'And more importantly, why?'

'Hampstead Heath,' I told him, looking up the nearest gate to the ladies' pond on Google Maps. 'I'm going to swim in the pond there.'

'What? Are you serious?' Malik stopped the car, right there in the middle of the road and turned to stare at me as though I had told him I was pregnant.

'Deadly,' I shrugged nonchalantly, pretending that I didn't feel nauseous at the prospect. I was hoping that if I feigned confidence, I would eventually feel it.

'I'm getting worried about you,' he said as he began driving down our road again and onto Turnpike Lane. 'What's all this about? First going back to uni and then meeting biodata guys, going running and now this? I know you're old, but you're not old enough for a mid-life crisis. It can't be all about that list you found.'

'Relax, I'm just enjoying trying new things,' I replied. 'And the biodata thing wasn't because I want to get married. Ma and Baba said that if I want to do my LLM, then I have to be open to marriage.'

'And you had to try out this "new thing" in the depths of winter? You couldn't wait for the summer when there was less chance of you getting hypothermia?'

'No, I want to do it all chronologically, as it appears in the notebook.'

Malik shook his head at this, like he really couldn't understand or comprehend my reasoning. I didn't expect him to. It was my journey and only someone who had been living the same life as me, in the same skin as me, would understand it.

'I quite liked that guy, the one you turned down,' he said after a couple of minutes of driving in silence, as we drove past Hornsey and my old secondary school and towards Crouch End.

'Why?' I replied, still staring out the window.

'We had a good chat. He was decent and respectful.'

'Hmm,' I said non-committally. Decent and respectful? More like judgy with double standards. Who knew what my brother's decency and respectability yardstick was anyway? This was the boy who was so busy with his secret girlfriend that he barely spent any time at home. Although, to be fair, he was always there when my parents or I needed him. Nobody else would bother to drive me to Hampstead at the crack of dawn at the weekend. He also still lived at home when he could have easily moved out. He was renovating our family house with money he could have been spending on a deposit for a flat. He was actually very responsible, more so than a lot of boys his age. I couldn't imagine Arjun from the office doing for his family half of what my brother did for us.

Maybe Malik did know a thing or two about decency and respect after all.

As the car weaved through the narrow, tree-lined roads leading up to Hampstead, I wondered for the hundredth time if I was wrong to dismiss Zakariya. My parents, Dina and my brother all thought I should have given him a chance. That was a lot of people whose opinions I usually trusted who thought I was wrong.

The car pulled to a stop outside the heath and I climbed out wearily, cheering up only slightly when I saw Lucy waiting for me outside the gate. Malik sped away almost before I could close the door properly and Lucy faltered for a second and then came hurrying towards me.

'Maya,' she called out. 'I've been calling you and texting you!'

'Hey, what's up?' I replied, giving her a quick hug and bursting into laughter at seeing her dressed in a fluffy onesie with a furry coat on top and black Hunter wellington boots. 'I need to take a picture of your look.'

'Look, I read all about winter swimming and you need to make yourself warm as soon as you come out. I even brought tea and banana bread! But that's not the point.'

'What's wrong?'

'The pond's closed! It's closed for the winter and won't open until February. I tried to go there and the gate was locked and everything.'

'There's a gate?'

'Yes and a lifeguard. You have to buy a ticket. I can't believe we're both paralegals and we didn't research any of this.'

I tried to hide the enormous sense of relief I felt at not having to jump into an ice-cold pond in December and tutted sadly instead.

'What a shame,' I said, barely able to contain my grin.

'Oh, piss off,' Lucy laughed, shoving me. 'This isn't over. We're coming back here in February when it opens up again.'

'Fine, we will. But what do we do until then?'

'Let's have a look at the list and see what's next. We'll move on to that and come back to this one later.'

'Can't I go for a regular swim?'

'No! You can't!'

'All right, all right. Let's go for a walk at least, since we're here.'

Hampstead Heath was beautiful in the winter – a sharper, more melancholy sort of beauty than in the summer. Branches were barren, the grass was dead and muddy, but still I felt energised being in the cold and inhaling the fresh, crisp air.

'Let's stop here,' Lucy said after a while. 'I could do with a cuppa.'

Stopping at a bench, we sat down and she pulled out her Thermos and two paper cups. Handing one to me, she proceeded to take out a little foil parcel. Unwrapping it, I found a thick slice of moist banana bread, the scent of butter and vanilla tingling my nose.

'This is amazing,' I told her, scoffing down the entire piece in two bites. 'You should become a professional baker.'

'Since my research skills are so crap?' Lucy chuckled, taking a dainty bite out of her own slice.

'Well, that and the fact that this is the best banana bread I've ever eaten.'

Lucy sighed. 'To be honest, I've been questioning my future a lot lately. Your list and the fact that you've applied to do your LLM has made me think about what's next for me. And I've realised that there isn't anything next. Is this it? Is my life going to be like this forever?'

'Of course not,' I tried to reassure her as I took a sip of tea. It was weak and definitely not Yorkshire Tea, but I wasn't about to complain. Unlike Ma, who has been known to send me back to the kitchen to make her a new cup of tea if it was too weak, too strong or too tepid. 'We're only twenty-seven. We've got loads of time to figure out what we want to do with the rest of our lives.'

'Have we, though? I feel like I was twenty-one and graduating just the other day. I blinked and became twenty-seven. I need to hurry up and make up my mind.'

'Well, if you weren't the best paralegal at our firm, what would you be?'

'I don't know. Maybe a stylist?'

'I can definitely see you as a stylist,' I said and then looked at her fluffy legs sticking out from beneath her massive coat. 'Well, maybe not right this moment.'

'Oi, I'm pouring my heart out here.'

'Sorry,' I shrugged unapologetically, taking another sip of tea. 'What about starting a fashion thing on the side to see how it goes? You could start up an Instagram or TikTok account? Your style is amazing, Luce, it could really take off.'

'Do you think?' Lucy looked at me, her blue eyes huge and round. I could practically smell her fear. 'I don't know if I could handle putting myself out there for people to scrutinise. I don't have the confidence for it.'

Now it was my turn to stare at her. How was someone who was usually confident so unsure of herself? It made no sense to me. When I looked at Lucy, I saw a woman who was smart, sassy, beautiful and kind. I told her this and though her cheeks and nose were already pink from the cold, she turned redder.

'Enough about me, let's see what's next on the list. I'm assuming you brought the notebook with you?'

'I always have it with me,' I admitted sheepishly.

'I know! Let's have a look.'

Lucy opened the book and her entire face lit up. 'You're not going to believe this,' she grinned. 'This is going to be bloody amazing.'

'What is it?' Lucy thought my jumping into a bowl of ice was going to be 'amazing'. Her definition of the word was clearly warped.

I leant over and looked at Noah's artsy scrawl and began to smile.

'Looks like you've got your first client, Luce. Shall we say next weekend?'

Chapter Fifteen

'Morning, Ma,' I sang out as I ran down the rickety stairs to the ground floor the next morning.

'Why are you so cheery this morning?' my mum asked suspiciously and rightly so, since I had been avoiding her ever since the whole dekha dekhi palaver. She was in the kitchen, loading a plate with chilli omelette, spicy baked beans and toast. Freshly brewed masala tea simmered in a pan and I watched as she poured it through a sieve and into her favourite mug – one I had decorated for her when I was in primary school. Everyone but Ma woke up late on a Sunday. Whenever I asked her why she didn't sleep in for once, she said it was a waste of time.

'I'm feeling positive,' I shrugged, taking a swig of tea from her mug like I'd been doing since I was a child. It was strong, spicy and sweet. 'Can I finish what's in the pan?'

'OK, pour yourself a bit. I was saving it for Malik. Where are you off to today?'

'Shopping with my work friend, Lucy. I think I need a new look. I've been wearing the same old stuff for years and I don't think it's doing me any favours.'

'It's not,' a voice agreed from the doorway. Malik, who never usually rose before midday on a Sunday, chose that moment to saunter into the kitchen. 'Ma, I'm going out in a bit. Can I have some breakfast, please?'

I scowled at Malik as my mum handed her plate of food and the tea that I was hoping to drink to him. He grinned at me and went over to the dining room to sit down, while Ma began making another breakfast for herself. Entitled little shit. But as much as I wanted to blame him for his laziness, I knew it was largely my mum's fault for spoiling him – her precious only son, first of his name, heir to the iron throne.

'What's your problem with my style?' I demanded, entering the dining room with my bowl of Coco Pops. But even as I said it, I wished I hadn't. I knew I needed an image overhaul – and thanks to number nine on Noah's list – See a Stylist – I was about to get one – but hearing it from someone else wasn't going to make me feel any better.

'Listen, Dimple, are we calling this look you've been sporting for the past few years' "style"?' he replied, waving a finger at said 'look'. I was wearing a plain grey jumper, faded jeans and slightly tatty boots. It might not have been the most fashionable outfit but it wasn't *that* bad and I was going to be traipsing around London all day. I needed to be practical.

'Don't call me Dimple. And it might not be your style, but it's mine,' I replied sullenly, wishing I had never followed him to the dining room.

'You obviously know your "look" is boring, otherwise why are you overhauling it, *Dimple*?'

He'd got me there.

'Get lost,' I said childishly and he grinned as I wolfed down my breakfast and then stomped back to the kitchen to wash my empty bowl.

'Leave it with me,' Ma sighed. 'Ignore your brother. Go on, go shopping, have fun. It's good to see you going out and enjoying yourself more these days.'

Coming to Oxford Circus without Dina felt strange. Shopping was our thing and meeting Lucy instead almost felt like I was cheating on her.

Red double-decker buses rumbled by, black taxis and rickshaws blaring Arabic music zoomed past me; hundreds, maybe thousands of tourists ambled along, knocking into me because I was so lost in my own head that I barely registered them. Even my left arm missed Dina, the one that was always hooked into her right arm. She was the louder, the more assertive of the two of us, and I tended to follow her around. Not like a shadow exactly, I wasn't that much of a non-entity. More like a younger sister. I didn't know how I would choose new clothes without her guidance.

My shoulders slumped and my feet dragging, I forced myself into Selfridge's, where I was meeting Lucy. I knew it was expensive, but I didn't have the nerve or energy to traipse around a hundred different high-street shops. I guess the one good thing that had come out of years of working without much of a social life or fashion sense was that I had enough money to splash.

'Maya! Hi, babe!' Lucy came rushing up to me like a golden blur; beautiful, tanned skin, blonde hair cascading down her back in big curls, a beige coat over a cream jumper, cream trousers and tan suede boots. A brown Louis Vuitton tote was casually slung over her shoulder, completing her look. She looked like she had stepped off the set of *Made in Chelsea*, not Made in Edmonton.

'Hey, hun, ready to transform me?'

'I've been ready and waiting for over two years,' she laughed and I smiled weakly in return. 'You've got so much potential, but you hide beneath all these drab, baggy clothes.'

'OK, say it like it is, Luce.'

'The important thing is that we're here now,' she continued, ignoring the pained expression on my face. 'You won't regret this.'

Lucy headed off towards the escalators and I followed her, trying to inject some enthusiasm into my stride. She was doing me a favour by giving up her relaxing Sunday to revamp my look. I didn't want her to think I was ungrateful; I was just put out that everyone around me basically thought I'd looked like crap all these years and no one had bothered telling me before now.

'Not everything here is crazy expensive,' Lucy explained as we went up a level to women's fashion. 'There are nicer high-street brands here as well. Let's start there. We need to get you some classic staples that you can mix and match with more interesting pieces to create a stylish look. We have to work fast though. I've also booked you an appointment with a hairstylist.'

I'd tuned out by then and let Lucy lead the way. I let her pull things off rails, seemingly at random, before shoving me into the dressing room to try it all on. She made me try on things I'd never dared to wear before – jumper dresses, blazers, silky tops, jumpsuits, tailored trousers that fit properly – as well as boots, shoes and casual things like jeans, hoodies and fashionable trainers. We got a new coat and jacket and before I knew it, she had dragged me to a different floor where there was a salon.

'What are we doing here?' I asked, slightly panicked. The most I ever did to my untamed black hair was get a trim.

'You're getting a haircut. Didn't you hear me say so earlier?'

'But I don't have an appointment.'

'You do. I made one for you after Hampstead Heath. Are you not listening to anything I'm saying? You've also got a makeup session booked downstairs.'

Part horrified, part excited, I followed her into the salon and slumped into the seat, tuning out Lucy and the stylist as they lifted up bits of my hair and discussed what to do with it.

'Wait!' Lucy cried out, just as Hannah, the hairstylist, was about to cover my clothes with a nylon apron. 'Let me take a before pic. You're going to feature on my brand-new socials.'

My face heating up with the thought of having my sub-standard self out there for people to openly gawk at, I stood and let Lucy take pictures and videos of me. She had supported me through my entire life overhaul, the least I could do was help her launch her own styling brand.

'Right, I'll be back in a bit,' Lucy said as I sat back down. 'There's still a lot of work to be done. See you in an hour or two!'

I watched my friend leave and followed Hannah to the sinks, where she gently washed my hair, massaging my scalp so wonderfully that I almost fell asleep. So this was what self-care felt like? Why hadn't I bothered to pamper myself all these years? Thanks to living with my parents, I had enough disposable income, but spending money on myself so I could feel good had always felt like a waste. Maybe it was because my parents never did it. My dad is a first-generation immigrant, who came here to study and make a better life for himself and his family back in Bangladesh. Most of his extra income got sent straight back to his paternal village, where he supports his siblings and their children, from paying for their education to helping out with their medical expenses, marriages and emergencies. My dad and his only brother in the UK pay for it all.

Because of this, we've never really had much to spare. Ma has had to work hard throughout her marriage. She paid for all of our expenses when we were younger, as well as supporting my Nani with her extras. 'Me time' and 'self-care' were ideas for the privileged, not for people like my parents.

But maybe it was time for me to break the cycle and make a change.

I decided not to look in the mirror after my hair was cut, dyed and styled and wait for my makeup to be complete so I could look at it together, like a proper makeover moment.

After we left the salon, Lucy led me back downstairs to the huge beauty section with its various counters holding all sorts of lotions and potions guaranteed to make me look and feel spectacular. My dad would have had a heart attack if he knew what I had spent on what he would see as glorified Nivea.

During the makeup session, the artist talked to me about my features and complexion and the products and colours that would suit me the most. I listened attentively to all her advice, tips and techniques. Who knew you were supposed to put concealer on after foundation? I thought it was the other way round. Who knew that I could cover my pigmentation with a bright orange liquid called corrector? No wonder my makeup never looked flawless.

Lucy hovered around 'creating content' – I dreaded to think what was going to end up on her new accounts later.

An hour or so later, my makeup session was over and my bank balance was another few hundred pounds lighter as I had decided to buy everything the makeup artist had suggested. I was still in my old clothes, so Lucy insisted I follow her to the dressing room and change into one of my new outfits before I looked at myself, to get the full impact of my transformation.

'How am I supposed to change with my eyes closed?' I grumbled as she ushered me into a cubicle.

'I'm going to block the mirror,' she said, handing me a new pair of wide-leg trousers and a cropped jumper.

'What, you're coming in with me?'

'Yes! I won't look at your naked body, if that's what you're worried about. Although it's not like it's anything I've never seen before.'

I doubted my hairy, discoloured and stretch-marked body was anything like Lucy's perfect one. She was white and blonde. Her body hairs were invisible and if she had any stretch marks, the silvery lines would be barely visible on her pale skin. She wouldn't have darker underarms or knees. Her acne scars wouldn't leave black marks all over her back.

Apparently, my body was 'normal', but it wasn't on mainstream TV or in magazines, not even the South-Asian ones. Everywhere I looked, I saw smooth perfection and anything different was an abnormality.

True to her word, Lucy looked away so I quickly yanked off my old clothes and pulled on the ensemble she'd given me. When I was dressed, she fixed the hair I'd messed up by pulling the jumper over my head and then moved aside to let me finally take a look at the new me.

My jaw fell open as I stared at my reflection, barely able to recognise myself. The girl – no, *woman* – staring back *looked* like me, but so much more put together. I looked like someone who knew her worth and took care of herself, mind and body. My eyes prickling, I stepped closer and touched my new hair: chestnut, wavy, glossy, with no split ends and high- and low-lights that were so well-blended that they looked like they were given by God, not Hannah from the salon.

My new makeup was subtle and accentuated what I already had. My eyes looked more soulful and my lips were dark red, a colour I would never have dared to try myself. People – aunts, cousins, so-called well-wishers – had always told me that red was for fair-skinned women. I'd thought my complexion was too dark for bold colours. As for my skin, for the first time in my life I thought my shade of brown was beautiful. I had never worn a foundation that suited me perfectly. My shade was hard to match; brown but with a red undertone instead of a yellow one. I had spent most of my adulthood searching for a foundation that didn't turn me grey or yellow. The one

I was wearing was a mix of two shades and while part of me was pissed off that in this day and age people with my tone still struggled with makeup, I was also relieved that a solution actually existed.

I didn't look like an entirely different person, just a smoother, brighter, glossier one. My outfit – simple tailored black trousers, a cream jumper, black boots and a camel-coloured coat – didn't merely do the job of clothing my body, it did so much more. It told a story; one of happiness, success and confidence. The tailoring and cut were perfect, hugging my curves, elongating my legs, narrowing my waist. I was like Maya, V .2.0.

'I can't believe this is me,' I whispered, barely able to get the words out. 'Why have I never done this before?'

'Because you never had me helping you before,' Lucy laughed, glowing with pride. She looked like a mum whose daughter had won a beauty pageant. 'Come on, I think we need to go out and test your new look. But first, let's add this . . .' She took off the gold-plated bracelet she was wearing on her own wrist and clipped it onto mine.

'Lucy, what are you doing? I can't accept this!'

'You can. It finishes your look. You've gone for under-stated chic glamour and this is perfect. And it's also a thank you from me.'

'Thank you for what? You're the one who gave up your whole Sunday to transform me!'

'And you trusted me to do it. For the first time in a long while, I feel like I have a purpose in life, you know? Something that goes beyond the nine-to-five grind. I'm going to be a stylist and you believed in me.'

Tears springing to my eyes, I reached over and hugged Lucy and she hugged me back harder. I realised then that I wasn't the only one who was lost. We all were, in a way.

Some more than others, but we all had a certain amount of emptiness inside us, voids of time we were trying to fill. And although we succeeded in filling them, there was a difference between existing and *living*. Maybe finally we could both do the latter.

Chapter Sixteen

After our emotional moment in the Selfridge's changing room, I let Lucy persuade me to go to a fancy Japanese restaurant with her, so we could 'test out my new look' – her words. I didn't know what she meant by that. I was hardly a show-room car going for a test drive.

We stepped back onto Oxford Street, laden with so many bags that it was a struggle to keep track of them all. It was dark and the twinkling Christmas lights that decorated the street and all the shop windows created a magical atmos-phere that I've loved since I was a child. There's nothing quite like Christmas in London: the lights, the songs playing in all the shops, the spiced drinks. My family and I don't celebrate it though, unless you count the family roast dinner on Christmas Day and the baked salmon the day after because it's heavily discounted in Morrisons.

'Here we are,' Lucy said, pushing open the heavy glass door to the restaurant, which was just around the corner from Selfridge's. I followed her into the dimly lit room, where the waiter hurried to relieve us of our bright yellow bags before ushering us to a table at the back.

I slipped off my brand-new coat and brown leather hand-bag – a mid-range one because I wasn't ready to part with three grand for the sake of a fancy logo the way Lucy wanted me to – before carefully hanging my coat on the back of my chair and placing my bag on my lap. I hoped I wasn't going to ruin them seconds after I'd bought them. I had been known to spill soya sauce on my clothes before, with my chopstick-handling skills being borderline inadequate.

As I took my seat opposite Lucy, who had already begun to pore over the menu, I felt the uncomfortable sensation of someone looking at me. Turning around, I found Zakariya staring at me in disbelief. Our eyes connected and I instantly looked away, embarrassed. Why did he have to be in this restaurant, of all places? I hadn't heard from him at all since I sent the rejection text and now, he was right there, ready to make my dinner experience as awkward as all of our previous interactions.

'Don't look now, but remember that guy I had to meet for marriage a few weeks ago? He's here, in the restaurant,' I murmured to Lucy, who automatically turned to look.

'Lucy! I told you not to look now!'

'Sorry.' She didn't look particularly sorry. 'The Asian guy in the suit?'

'Yes! And don't you dare look at him again. He'll know we're talking about him!'

'Maya, I need to check him out properly! I didn't get a good look the first time!'

'You can't!'

'Just quickly!' Lucy, completely ignoring my pleas, looked over at Zakariya's table again. 'Ooh, he's a bit of a fittie, isn't he? You sure you don't want to give him another chance?'

The rest of the meal was torture. While I should have been enjoying my new hair and the way it elegantly swished around my face, I couldn't. I kept wanting to look over at Zakariya to see if he really was looking at me the way I thought he was. This was the second time I had run into him and the third time we had 'met'. Why did God keep planting him in my face like this?

'It's called coincidence, not divine intervention,' Lucy said with a giggle when I posed the same question to her. I felt my stomach tighten at her response. Not because she didn't believe in God. A person's faith, or lack of, had no bearing on how I felt about them. But it was at that exact moment that I missed Dina. She would have thought it was fate – or qadr – that we kept bumping into each other.

Lucy and I parted ways after dinner. Somehow, while she was wandering around the department store creating content, she had met a man and now had a drinks date, despite dating someone else 'casually'. I wasn't surprised. Lucy collected dates – or 'sneaky links' as she called them – like I collected Clubcard points. I was in awe of her talent and ability to put herself out there, time and time again.

It did, however, mean that I was now lumbered with all my bags. As I struggled to carry them while I took my phone out to book a ride home, Zakariya came out onto the pavement. I was hoping to avoid him altogether. The fact that he hadn't come over to say hello meant that he also wanted to steer clear of me. Whatever the reason, I planned to disappear to avoid any awkward conversation.

'Hey, salaams, Maya,' he said casually, watching me as I dropped a bag in my haste to book an Uber and get away from him. 'How are you? You look really different.'

'Wa alaikum salaam,' I mumbled back, my face heating up almost immediately. Why did he mention the way I looked? Was it a good 'different' or bad 'different'? Flustered, I ignored the comment and reluctantly answered his question, 'Good, thanks. You?'

'All right, considering. Do you need any help with those bags? What did you do, buy up the whole of Selfridge's?'

'No, it's OK,' I replied casually, grateful that the phone in my hand meant that I didn't have to look at him. 'I'm trying to book an Uber and the next one is available in . . . *thirty-two minutes*? What the hell?'

'It's hard to get them in central London these days,' he said and I couldn't tell from his tone if he was taking the mick or being serious. 'My car's around the corner if you would like a lift home.'

His offer came at the same time as I felt a drop of rain on my newly styled hair. I stared at my fifteen yellow paper bags in dismay and thought about all the beautiful new things they contained, not to mention my expensive hair and makeup. Was it worth ruining my epic makeover for the sake of my pride and dignity?

'I would love a lift, thank you,' I managed to croak as graciously as possible.

Within seconds, he had scooped up most of my bags and I trailed behind him with the rest, trying to match his long strides with my much shorter ones.

'Thanks,' I said, as Zakariya held the door of his fancy Mercedes open and I climbed inside, seconds before it really began to pour down with rain. He took the last few bags off me and stuffed them into the back of the car. When he finally got in, he was drenched. His hair lay lank and limp across his forehead and his eyelashes, which were abnormally and unfairly long, had drops of rain clinging to them.

'Here,' I said, pulling out a pack of tissues and handing him a couple. He took them gratefully and wiped his face, before switching the engine and the heating on.

'What's your postcode?' he asked, turning to me. I got the sudden, overwhelming desire to brush away a lock of wet hair that had fallen across his forehead. With a gulp, I told him and hastily averted my gaze as he typed it into his phone and then pulled away from the kerb.

We began to drive through London in silence. The radio was on, but so quietly that I could barely discern what song was playing. The rain was louder, beating down heavily on the windscreen, the wipers thrashing away but unable to keep up. Zakariya didn't seem to mind the rain or the silence. I glanced at him a couple of times. He had a nice profile, more so because of his beard and his straight nose. I thought back to Noah's nose. I remembered it being imperfectly lovely, but I couldn't remember why. He was fading from my memory faster than I thought he would. Painfully fast. Would I ever see him again, or was that morning on the Tube all the time I was destined to get with him?

'That's the third time you've looked at me.' Zakariya's low voice broke the silence and once again, heat rushed to my cheeks. Why did he always go out of his way to embarrass me?

'I'm trying to figure out why you're being so nice to me,' I replied stiffly, turning to look out the window. Not that I could see much in the dark and rain. London was a blur of lights and buildings.

'Why wouldn't I be?'

'We didn't exactly part ways on a positive note,' I replied frankly. Whatever game he was playing, I wasn't about to be a part of it. 'And you didn't reply to my text message either.'

'The one where you dumped me?'

'There was nothing to dump. It's not like we were dating!'

'Dating? Interesting term. Not very Islamic.'

'What am I supposed to call it, then?'

'Seeing each other? Courting? Talking? Getting to know one another?'

'Whatever you want to call it, Islamic or otherwise, we weren't doing any of that. Therefore, it was hardly a break-up text.'

'Have you sent a break-up text before?' His sudden change of tone surprised me. I raised an eyebrow and looked at him again. His gaze was straight ahead at the road, but he was smirking.

'Too many to count,' I lied, folding my arms across my chest. He looked at me quizzically, unable to determine whether I was winding him up or being serious.

We continued sparring as he drove up to Marylebone but somehow, by the time we got to Camden, we'd started having a normal conversation. By Holloway, we were talking about work and I ended up telling him about my list (omitting the whole 'Noah' part of it) and how I wanted to go back to further education. To my surprise, he seemed to understand where I was coming from and agreed that I should do whatever I needed to do to feel content. He told me about an Arabic class he was taking, because a job opportunity had come up for him to work in Dubai for a year. Like me, he was also feeling like life had become stagnant and he needed to shake things up.

'You know you don't need Arabic to work in the Gulf,' I told him. 'They speak English everywhere.'

'I know,' he replied with a shrug. 'But I don't want to be one of those expats who don't evolve or learn anything about their host country's culture. I want to make the most of it.'

I found it strange that he was planning to move abroad in the middle of trying to get married. If this was his intention, why had he put me through all the drama of meeting him? Forget the fact that my mum made me scrub every inch of the house until my hands almost bled, forget the fact that I was paraded around in front of him like a concubine, what was worse was how my parents had behaved with me since. I was the family pariah because I exercised my God-given right to say no.

Before I could persuade myself not to pry, I blurted the question out.

'Why did you meet me if you're planning to move abroad?'

We were passing Finsbury Park now, so we didn't have a lot of time before we arrived at Turnpike Lane, maybe ten minutes or so. If I didn't ask now, I would never find out.

'My parents aren't happy that I'm moving abroad,' he said, looking as pained as I felt. 'They're scared I'm going to meet the daughter of a Russian oligarch out there and their dreams of having a Bengali bahu would be dashed forever.'

'Wow. So they made you agree to meet prospective partners if you wanted their blessing? Hoped you would meet someone and take a wife with you?'

'Basically, yes. How did you know?'

I couldn't help but laugh at the irony of it all. I knew it wasn't as hilarious as I was making it out to be, but once the giggles started, they wouldn't stop. Zakariya continued driving but kept glancing at me in bewilderment as I snorted until tears filled my eyes. The look on his face only made me laugh harder.

'OK then,' he said when I finally stopped, minutes before we reached my house. 'I don't know if I *want* to know what has you in hysterics right now.'

'Our lives are a lot more similar than you would think,' I managed to say in between hiccups. 'My parents cut a similar deal with me when I told them I wanted to go back to uni.'

Zakariya laughed and shook his head. 'What a pair we are, agreeing to marriage so we can do what we want to do in life.'

'Pretty tragic really,' I replied. 'I'm glad I'm not the only one dealing with this.'

Zakariya pulled into my street and double parked outside my house. The rain had stopped a while before, but I felt the urge to stay in the car for longer. He was so easy to talk to, almost like a different person from the one who came to the marriage meeting. But obviously I couldn't. He had made it clear that he wasn't interested in marrying me or anyone. He was keeping his parents happy. Mistaking his good manners for anything more would be foolish and naive.

'Thank you so much for the ride,' I said, as he put the hazard lights on and began climbing out of the car. I stared at the door in surprise, wondering why he was getting out. Surely, he didn't think it would be appropriate to come inside the house and chat with my parents? This wasn't an American teen movie. My dad wouldn't pretend to be overprotective and tell us that we could hang out in my room if the door was open. My parents would *kill* me if they knew I was risking my reputation by accepting a lift from not just any man, but one who knew people in my extended family. I got the impression that they would be less concerned if there was a smaller chance of the grapevine finding out about my shenanigans.

I didn't have to worry though, because all Zakariya did was come over to the passenger side and open the door for me, before getting all my bags out of the boot and backseat and handing them to me carefully, so I didn't drop any of my precious new wardrobe into a puddle.

'I forgot to say that your new hair looks really nice,' he said as I thanked him again and began to walk towards the house. I turned back to gape at him, but he was already climbing back into the car.

Unable to stop the smile spreading across my face, I trudged up the path and let myself into the house. As soon as I got to my room, I dropped all my bags to the floor and collapsed onto the bed. What had happened? Were we friends now? Would I ever see him again? Was I reading into it too much? Probably. He seemed to be the sort of person who said whatever was on his mind, offensive or otherwise. Whatever it was, I hadn't felt this good in a long time. And the best part was, most of it was nothing to do with Zakariya, but everything to do with the amazing day I'd had with Lucy.

Chapter Seventeen

Christmas was quiet, more so than usual. Malik went away with his 'friends', but I was certain he was with a woman – one I was still waiting for him to tell me about.

I decided to spend Christmas with Dina. Lucy was away on holiday and so were the twins. Mohammed was working through most of the holidays so I went to Dina's on Christmas Eve for a sleepover and the following day I helped her make an epic meal of Palestinian-style slow-roasted lamb shoulder on a bed of buttery cracked wheat, with stuffed aubergines and cabbage leaves on the side. We made a halal, Middle Eastern version of pigs in blankets as well – beef sausages and medjool dates marinated in honey and spices and wrapped with Turkey bacon, which Dina jokingly re-named 'cows in dupattas'. This had us cracking up over how funny we thought we were, so much so that Dina was afraid that her waters were going to break four months early. When I say that I 'helped', really all I did was provide banter and childcare services while she did the bulk of the cooking.

We carried on talking throughout lunch and then, when Dina went to put Sami down for a nap, I cleared everything up and put the homemade kunafeh in the oven for dessert. I nearly burnt it of course, as I completely forgot about it while I was busy scrubbing the pans and baking trays. Luckily, Dina came down in time to save it. I watched as she poured rose syrup over the top of the shredded kataifi and inhaled the beautiful fragrance of sweet cheese, buttery pastry, nuts and rose water. No wonder Mohammed was obsessed with her. The girl had mad cooking skills.

'You think that's the secret to a happy marriage?' Dina laughed as I told her my theory, while she brewed Arabic-style tea. 'What's for dinner is the last thing on his mind. He's more interested in "dessert", if you catch my drift.'

I didn't immediately, but when the realisation hit, I burst into laughter. 'Ew, shut up, it's like picturing my parents together,' I complained.

'Speaking of marriage,' Dina said as she carried an ornate silver tea tray over to the coffee table in the living room and I followed her with two massive portions of kunafeh with vanilla ice cream. 'What's happening with you? Have your parents made you meet anyone else?'

'No,' I replied, settling into her comfy sofa and putting my plate on my lap. 'My mum thinks I have a secret boyfriend.'

'Poor aunty,' she said, taking a bite of the dessert. 'I bet she wishes you had someone.'

'I think she does,' I admitted. 'Oh my God, this kunafeh is amazing. It's so much better than the restaurant ones.'

'Thanks, habibti. Now, tell me more about Zakariya,' Dina brushed off the compliment. 'Is he a potential then? Your post-makeover encounter sounded romantic.'

'Not really,' I admitted. 'He told me he's not interested in getting married. He only agreed to meet me to placate his parents and he's planning to move to Dubai next year. His parents were giving him a hard time about it, hence meeting me.'

'Wow. I bet he's unsure now that you're in the picture.'

'I'm not in the "picture". It was one car ride and besides, I rejected him remember?'

'Oh yeah. That complicates things a bit.'

'A LOT, you mean.'

'I wish it didn't. He sounds like a good guy, this Zakariya.'

I contemplated Dina's words. She had always been sensible and was a good judge of character. I was also known to be sensible, although admittedly my people radar was a little off. But was a car ride all it took to make Zakariya seem decent in her opinion? What about the way he behaved in the art class?

'He probably wanted to start a conversation with you and said the first thing that came into his head,' Dina replied when I reminded her of that fact. 'It was a crap thing to say, but I don't know if he should be charged and tried based on one dodgy remark. If he reaches out to you again, which he might not since you rejected him, you should get to know him properly and make a more informed decision about his character.'

'Well, he's moving to Dubai and I'm going back to uni, so we're on different paths. It's not meant to be.'

When I got back home early the next morning, the first thing I did after greeting my parents – who were so engrossed in the Bollywood movie they were watching that they barely acknowledged me – was check out the next item on Noah's list:

10. COMPLETE THE WHOLE 30 PROGRAMME ✓

Smashed it like I knew I would and feel amazing! Need to make this a yearly thing.

What in God's name was the 'Whole 30' programme? It could be anything, from devil-worshipping to learning how to code. I was probably going to have to get creative with how I would adapt it to suit me.

I typed it into Google and immediately realised that it was a healthy-eating programme, which sounded a lot like a diet to me. Apparently, it wasn't, as weight loss wasn't the goal and people didn't count calories or carbs like with other diets. If I did this – which was a huge IF at that point – I wouldn't be able to eat dairy, wheat, grains, legumes or pulses, processed meats, sugar and some fruit. What sort of diet didn't let you eat fruit?

'It's only for thirty days,' Lucy voice-noted me when I sent her a text to complain. I could hear a lot of noise in the background and I immediately felt bad for disturbing her on holiday. 'Think of it like a detox.'

'Trust a bloody personal trainer to add some sort of crazy diet to his list,' I moaned in my reply. 'Why do I have to? Why can't I tailor it to my needs?'

'You need to tailor things that make no sense at all, like participating in a triathlon or doing a physio course. This does make sense. Everyone could benefit from an internal cleanse every now and then.'

I wasn't sure how and when Lucy became the authority on the way I interpreted the list, but I let her because it was easier with her support.

'Everyone . . . including you?' I asked hopefully.

Lucy sighed audibly through the voice-note. 'Fine. Including me. I've wanted to try this for a while anyway. No time like the New Year to try a diet.'

'You know you can't drink alcohol on this plan,' I told her. 'Too much sugar.'

The next message came a few minutes later, starting with another long sigh. 'Two New Year's resolutions in one then. Let's start on January first. It'll give us a few days to enjoy ourselves.'

'And give you New Year's Eve to go wild.'

'Exactly.'

After I finished bothering Lucy, I decided to check what was next on the list. The Whole 30 was called that because you did it for thirty days, not because you had to eliminate thirty foods like I initially assumed. It didn't make sense to stall the rest of the list for a whole month, especially if it was something I could do in tandem.

Taking the notebook out for the second time that day, I flicked through the pages that were getting more and more tired and worn from all my constant touching and analysing and checked out number eleven on the list:

11. TAKE ARABIC CLASSES ✓

Marhaba, Habibi!! Getting there, but got a long way to go!

I stared at the words in surprise. I had assumed that Noah was Arab, but how could he be if he was planning on taking classes? Having said that, my parents made me take Bengali lessons when I was younger. Maybe Noah's parents barely spoke Arabic at home and he wanted to brush up on it. Or maybe he was planning on moving abroad like Zakariya. My heart dipped a little bit at the thought. If Zakariya left the country, I would never see him again.

Unless we took the same class, I slowly realised. I could ask Zakariya. It would give me the perfect excuse to text him again, without looking like I was trying it on.

Unlike other items on the list, Noah didn't provide options for where to take the classes. For all I knew, he was doing them online. In fact, he probably was. Everyone did things online these days. I didn't want to though. I wouldn't focus half as much as if I did it in person. Plus, doing it offline meant I could meet more people and get out more.

Nerves tingling in my belly, I took out my phone and painstakingly crafted the perfect text after two failed attempts:

ME: Salaams Zakariya, hope you're well. Remember the list I told you about? Taking Arabic classes is on it. Any suggestions on where I can go to take them? TIA!

Hitting send, I leant back in my chair and waited. After checking my phone three times in one minute, I distracted myself by creating a meal plan and shopping list for my Whole 30 month, which was a lot harder than I originally thought it would be. I couldn't eat cereal, granola or yoghurt for breakfast. I wouldn't be able to buy something quickly whenever I needed to. I'd have to plan my meals properly otherwise I would fail. It looked like eggs were going to become my best friend.

It took me a while to create a meal plan that I would sort of enjoy – there were a lot of salads, soups, eggs and baked proteins on it, but I could live with it for a month. Potatoes were allowed, which meant that I could have jacket potatoes from the greasy spoon cafe next to my office if I needed to. Not with beans or cheese, though. Or butter. Tuna mayo it was going to have to be. If I could take up running, surely, I could cut back on some of my favourite food groups. No problem. Hang on, was mayonnaise dairy?

My phone buzzed and I grabbed it so quickly that I knocked over a stack of papers on my desk. But I didn't care because Zakariya had replied:

ZAKARIYA: Salaams Maya, I'm well thanks, how are you? Here's the link to the place I go. I go on Thursday nights, 6:30–8:00PM but I'm on level two now. Good luck!

I read the message again and then re-read another two times. It wasn't the mind-blowing reply I was hoping for. It was friendly enough, but apart from 'how are you?', which was a cursory response to my enquiring after his wellbeing, there weren't any questions; nothing to help me prolong the conversation. What could I reply to create an entire text chain? Nothing without appearing desperate.

Deflated, I replied with 'thanks so much!' and then put my phone away. He wasn't going to respond to that, so there was no point in staring at it all day. I emailed the college where he took his lessons, enquiring about dates, times, costs and availability, and then headed downstairs in my running shoes, hoodie and leggings.

The old me spent Boxing Day going sales shopping, indulging in a roasted salmon lunch and then watching Christmas movies while stuffing my face with halal mince pies (the alcohol-free ones – Malik bought a whole box with brandy in them a couple of weeks before that I had to give away to Lucy). This year was different. Lucy told me not to waste money in the sales buying things I didn't need or want because they were cheaper than usual, so I gave that a miss and went for a run instead. I was up to running three kilometres in one go now and thanks to all the stretches I did afterwards, I could nearly touch my toes. After my run, I showered and helped my mum cook for a change.

'Who are you and what have you done with my daughter?' Ma gasped in faux horror when I joined her in the kitchen, my sleeves rolled up, ready to be useful.

'Haha,' I replied. 'What shall I do?'

'Here, peel the potatoes.'

'Is that all?'

'Everyone has to start somewhere. Unless you want to descale the fish?'

'Potatoes are fine!' I said, hastily grabbing the peeler and getting down to it.

We worked in comfortable silence for a while, before Ma put a Christmas playlist on her phone and we sang along to all the classics together. Every so often she would show me what she was doing: de-scaling and filleting the fish, crushing garlic and squeezing lemons to make a fusion marinade with olive oil, dill, paprika, chilli flakes and coriander. The way Ma cooks is methodical but creative. She likes everything to be tidy and clean, but at the same time, she doesn't weigh or measure. Her ability to create great flavours is innate.

'Why the sudden interest in cooking?' she asked once the food was in the oven and I began clearing up the bits of peel that hadn't found their way to the food recycling bin yet.

I shrugged. 'I'm working on myself a lot. I guess it feels right to learn how to fend for myself as well.'

'Hmm,' she said non-committally. 'It's not because we're looking for a husband for you then? Or perhaps there's already a man in your life?'

'No way!' I spluttered. 'I have no desire to be the perfect, traditional wife, thank you very much. I'm learning how to cook for *me*, not for some man I don't know. And whoever I marry can pitch in with all the housework, thank you. It's not my job to be a cook and cleaner because I'm a woman. Islam says so.'

'All right, all right,' Ma laughed. 'Calm down, it was just a question!'

'Don't you get annoyed that Baba hardly does anything round here?' I said as I brushed the floor. 'You work full-time *and* you do everything around the house. It hardly seems fair to me.'

'Says the girl who also lives here and *also* hardly does anything round the house.'

'Ouch! That's not true! I might not cook but I do most of the cleaning.'

'Well, it would have been a great help if you did. It would ease my load considerably.'

'You know I'm a rubbish cook. Do you want me to waste perfectly good ingredients just so you can support traditional gender roles? I don't see you asking Malik to cook.'

'Touché,' Ma laughed. 'Useless, the pair of you.'

'Well, this useless person soon won't be eating much anyway. On New Year's Day, I'm going to start a programme called the Whole 30.'

'But you're not thirty yet.'

'No, it's thirty because you do it for thirty days.'

'Why? You don't need to lose weight and you're doing all that running. You need to eat well or you'll waste away.'

'It's like a detox, Ma. It's something I want to try. So don't include me in any meals for January, I'm going to make my own food.'

'You're going to make it yourself?'

'I am. So maybe after the month is up, I will be able to help you more with the cooking.'

'That's my girl,' Ma smiled, giving my shoulders a squeeze.

'. . . If you get Malik to do it too,' I added and dashed out of the kitchen before she could say anything else.

Chapter Eighteen

The Arabic language college replied to me the following day and as fate – or divine will – would have it, they had availability in their beginner's evening class on a Thursday, which was at the same time as Zakariya's level two class. They also had slots on Monday and Wednesday, but no one needed to know that. I replied to their email to let them know that I would be joining them the Thursday after New Year's Day with the fees in cash and sat back with a huge grin on my face. In a couple of days, I had organised and prepped for two items on the list and I felt massively accomplished because of it.

It had been almost four months since I embarked on this list-completing journey and I had already achieved so much. I had applied to go back to studying; I could run a decent distance without collapsing or having a heart attack; I had a beautiful wardrobe and had learnt how to apply my makeup properly; I had read bloody *Ulysses*. And now I was about to learn Arabic, the language of the Holy Qur'an and do a detox. As numbers ten and eleven would both take a while to complete, I excitedly moved on to number twelve, eager to find out what it was. I nearly choked on my tea when I read: *Trek Snowdon*.

Trek Snowdon? The only trek I knew anything about was *Star Trek* and even then, my knowledge was sketchy. I had never trekked for anything in my life, not unless you counted walking up Muswell Hill. How was I going to climb a mountain? Then I reminded myself that I hadn't been able to run before and yet there I was, running through the backstreets of Haringey three times a week, often in the dark, often holding my keys between my fingers should I need to use them as a weapon against a predator. Trekking a little mountain in Wales would be a doddle compared to that. Hopefully someone – i.e. Lucy – would agree to do it with me.

I had a vague recollection of reading this entry before, when I first flicked through the notebook. I wracked my brains for what else I had seen that day, but it all happened so fast that I couldn't remember. I decided not to check or try to recall what I had seen anymore and keep true to my plan of only reading the next items when it was time to do them.

Carefully putting the book back into my work tote bag, I went downstairs to wait for Malik to come home. He was due to arrive any moment and Ma, with a tiny bit of help from me, had cooked his favourite Bengali meal: creamy chicken korma, fragrant pulao rice and juicy lamb kebabs. I was in charge of shaping the kebabs and peeling the garlic. While that might sound easy, trust me when I say it wasn't. Ma made me peel TEN BULBS. Then she showed me how to blend and store them with a bit of salt and oil so we could use the paste for future curries. Despite scrubbing my hands and showering, the pungent smell of fresh garlic still lingered on my fingers.

What smelt infinitely better was the deliciously creamy korma. It had been teasing me all day, reminding me of Eid morning, for which the elaborate meal was usually reserved. I couldn't wait to dive in and make the most of the time I had before the Whole 30 programme started. With three days left to go until the New Year, I had to make every bite count.

The front door flew open as I began walking down the stairs and Ma rushed to greet Malik like he had been gone for ten years as opposed to ten days. He looked well: tanned and a little bit rounder in the face. It suited him and I went over for a hug once Ma was done gushing over how much she missed him and why hadn't he texted her more often. My parents barely looked at me when I returned from my sleepover at Dina's house. Trust me, only other South Asian girls know what it's like to be the eldest daughter with no other sisters and a princely younger brother. I had it better than some – and I supposed others had it better than me – but there was no denying that in our culture, sons are often revered. Daughters are loved, but that little bit less. You got used to it, *I* had got used to it. But if I ever got married and had both a son and daughter, I swore to make sure that the love and chores were distributed equally.

'Wow, who is this person and what have you done to my sister?' Malik exclaimed, appraising my new khaki co-ord; a vast improvement from my usual stained, woolly onesie.

'Ma used the same expression when I offered to help with the cooking the other day,' I responded dryly. 'So your lines are the same as our almost fifty-year-old mother.'

Malik grinned, kicking off his shoes and leaving them haphazardly in the hallway. 'Last week I would have said something about you looking like a fifty-year-old mother, but I guess I can't do that anymore. How the hell did you pull this out of the bag?'

'It's amazing what cash to splash and an entire day spent in Selfridge's can do,' I said, following him into the dining room, where I had laid the table earlier. 'How was your trip? And more importantly, how was the company?' I gave him a giant wink as I said this and he glared at me.

'It was epic,' he said. 'Thai food is so good and so cheap and I got a Thai massage every single day for less than a tenner.'

'Sounds like bliss,' I said wistfully. I had barely travelled. My parents weren't big on holidays. Baba visited Bangladesh every few years, once he had saved up enough. He spent thousands whenever he went because he gave a lot of money to his vulnerable relatives there and then there were presents for everyone he visited. The huge cost meant that he couldn't go often and he certainly couldn't take us all every time he went. I had only visited twice as a child myself and I could barely remember either trip. As for other holidays, I tried when I was at uni and the answer was a firm no. Girls shouldn't travel abroad alone. According to them, it was too unsafe and I couldn't remember what the other reasons were because I was so livid at the double standards; Malik had just returned from a boys' trip to Spain at the time. I hadn't bothered to try again. Fighting for what I wanted to do wasn't in me back then.

What if Noah had travel plans on his list? If he did, this time there was no way I would let my parents stop me. And if it wasn't on the list, I was going to do it anyway.

After our super indulgent dinner, Ma and I cleaned up while Baba and Malik relaxed in the living room; Baba chewing on crunchy betelnut wrapped in bright green paan leaves, his biggest weakness. I could hear the low murmurs of their voices and when I came in with mugs of tea and a plate of mishti, they fell silent.

'What's going on? Kita oiseh?' I asked suspiciously, eyeing them both.

'Kichu nai,' Baba said. At the same time Malik said, 'Baba's got another biodata for you.'

'I'm not interested,' I said immediately, before another word could be spoken on the topic. 'Not after what happened last time.'

'What happened last time?' Ma asked, entering the room and sitting down with her own mug.

'I'm not interested, Ma,' I repeated, this time my voice taking on a slightly pathetic, desperate tone. 'I trusted you last time when you told me that I had autonomy over whom I wished

I pursue, but it was all a facade. The minute I said no, you both turned on me and gave me hell! I'm not going through it again.'

'"Whom",' Malik mocked, chuckling over my choice of words. '"Facade", "autonomy" . . . I like that one.'

'Shut up, Malik!' I scowled at my brother. It was all right for him. He could do whatever he wanted without everyone getting their lungis and dupattas in a twist.

'Look, Maya,' Ma said calmly, using the same voice she reserved for difficult children at school. 'We were shocked last time, which was all. Zakariya was perfect in every single way, we didn't understand why you were rejecting him.'

For the hundredth time, Ma and Baba began reeling off the list of all the reasons why Zakariya was so great. He was educated. Successful. Handsome. Tall. From a good family. He had his own property (ignoring the fact that he didn't live in it and still lived with his parents). He was nice. Polite. Respectful. Fosha – aka 'light-skinned'.

'Oh, here we go,' I muttered. 'Maya is too dark, her complexion is too dirty to find anyone decent, she should be grateful.'

'I'm not trying to be evil, Maya, I'm saying it how it is,' Ma continued, ignoring the fact that I was putting on a rude, mimicking voice. 'You know what things are like in our culture. You get judged on the colour of your skin. The darker you are, the harder it is to find a good proposal. That's the way things are, there's no point in burying our heads in the sand.'

'Ma, you can't be serious,' Malik piped up, this time looking genuinely affronted. 'Plenty of my Bengali and Pakistani friends are with girls darker than them. Who cares?'

'Love marriages, that's why,' Baba scoffed. 'But it's the parents of the grooms who see the biodata first and if they're not happy with any part of it, the groom won't get a look in.'

I listened to them go back and forth, my insides churning with nausea, anger, sadness.

'Are you going to give me a bottle of Fair and Lovely again, Baba?' I finally said, trying to contain the emotions stewing inside of me. 'You know that cancer-causing concoction full of chemicals that you gave me when I was sixteen?'

Shortly after I sat my GCSEs, Baba came back from Bangladesh and along with the customary cotton shalwar kameez from Aarong, there was a bottle of the skin-lightening cream that my aunts had sent for me.

I was mortified.

I had grown up hearing comments about my offensive skin tone, how it was such a shame that Malik had inherited the fairer gene, how it was a great pity that I looked more like my dad than my mum, how it was so strange that Pretty and Pinky were whiter than me, though their mum was darker than mine.

'I'm sure I didn't,' Baba protested half-heartedly. 'And anyway, if I did, I was only trying to help you.'

'You didn't use that crap, did you?' Malik demanded, looking at me like he was disappointed.

'I did,' I shrugged nonchalantly. 'I used it for two years and it dried my skin so much that it began to crack. I guess that's how they made you fairer, by dehydrating your skin.'

'I can't believe you did that,' Malik muttered. 'You're crazy. Why would you?'

'Of course you can't believe it,' I snapped back. 'How would you know what it's like to be me, Prince Ali, Fabulous He?'

'What the hell are you on about?'

'*Aladdin*? Oh, forget it. All of you can forget it.'

With that, I got up and left the living room, leaving behind my tea that had now turned cold and held no appeal.

'I can't believe you made me do this stupid diet with you,' Lucy growled at me on our first day back at the office after the holidays. Admittedly, she didn't look as great as she usually did, more tired and less glowing, even though she had just got back from holiday. The same went for me, but that was my default setting anyway.

'I'm pretty sure you said something about wanting to try this "programme" for a while?' I replied airily, gently placing my new work bag on the desk. 'And speaking of supporting me and my journey . . .'

'NO, Maya! I am NOT doing another one of your crazy activities! This list is *your* thing, *not* mine. Yes, I'll support you where I can but if I don't want to do it, I'm not going to, OK?'

Gosh. Hangry Lucy was so different from sweet, funny, full of bread, cheese and pasta Lucy. I guess I would have to ask Dina if she fancied trekking Snowdon with me. And there was always Malik if I really got desperate.

'I like that you're wearing the outfits we chose,' Lucy said after lunch, nodding at the beige high-waisted trousers I was wearing with a fluffy white jumper and the bracelet she gave me. My hair wasn't looking as amazing as when I had first left the salon, but it was still lovely and far better than any style I had worn before. It was the first time she had said something non-work related all morning and I wondered if there was something else on her mind, other than the lack of food.

'*You* chose, you mean,' I corrected her. 'I would never have been able to buy this stuff on my own.'

She smiled and looked away, turning back to her computer screen. I opened my mouth to ask her if she was OK and if there was anything bothering her, but she got up then, probably to go to the loo. The question dissolved on my lips.

It was freezing when I left work that evening and I wished I had worn my giant padded jacket. My beautiful new camel coat made me look good, but did a rubbish job of protecting me against the harsh January cold, even with the blanket scarf wrapped around my neck and my new calf-skin gloves on my hands. But as I was seeing Zakariya later, sacrificing style for comfort wasn't an option.

The college where the Arabic lessons took place was in a backstreet in Whitechapel, a short walk from East London Mosque. It had been years since I had been to the area. We visited a lot when we were younger because Chacha and Chachi used to live in one of those gigantic brown brick council estates somewhere in Aldgate. Malik and I loved it. Growing up, there weren't many Bengalis near where we lived and visiting my aunt and uncle almost felt like going to Bangladesh. Their estate was mostly full of Bengalis with a few newly arrived Somalis and Jews who had been there since the Second World War. Children were allowed to play freely in the estate, a novelty for us since Ma never let us play in the streets at home. There were battered playgrounds with broken swings where we would play 'It' and 'Forty-forty' with brown girls in brightly coloured dresses paired with old jeans and sandals, their thick black hair slick with oil. Clothes hung out to dry outside every flat, from the balconies and windows, offering a much-needed splash of colour against the dull brick and iron bars protecting the lower floors from intruders. Lungis, sarees, dresses and shirts flew gently in the breeze and there was always a distinct scent of curry in the air.

My brother and I usually spent a week at Christmas and two weeks over the summer with Pretty and Pinky, running riot in the estate with all the other kids, feeling more like us than we ever did in north London. I loved it all.

Whitechapel had had a major facelift since the days of our childhood and I wondered how much longer the Bengalis and other communities would be able to continue to afford living and working there. Brick Lane, once known as Curry Mile, was almost entirely lost to London's bougie hipsters and it was only a matter of time before Bangla Town was completely gentrified and handed over to those earning big bucks in the nearby City.

It was dark as I walked past the synagogue and then the mosque and turned into a narrow side street with terraced Victorian townhouses on either side. The 'college' turned out to be in the basement of one of the townhouses and I carefully trod down the steel steps, taking comfort in the fact that Zakariya was going to be there and therefore it couldn't be too dodgy. I was getting serious Jack the Ripper vibes as I retreated further underground.

I needn't have worried though. The interior of the building was nothing like the gloomy exterior. It was bright and modern and there was a little reception area as soon as I entered. The receptionist, a pretty, petite girl in a light-blue hijab, led me to the room where the beginner's class took place. I was relatively early, so it was empty bar the teacher, who was still setting up. Ustadha Salma was a stout woman with a tightly wrapped white headscarf and a stripy abaya.

'Marhaba! Ahlan wa sahlan!' she called out to me enthusiastically in a thick, Arabic accent. I returned the greeting shyly and introduced myself as she gave me a form to fill in and I handed over the payment for the month. The desks were set up in pairs facing the whiteboard and soon the room was full of students and chatter. A girl called Nadira sat next to me. She was gorgeous, with a flawless golden complexion and silky honey-coloured hair. She said salaam and we small-talked quietly until the class began.

The hour and a half flew and by the end of it, I'd not only learnt my Arabic numbers up to ten, the days of the week and some other basic nouns, but I had made a new friend. Nadira had to rush off but we agreed to go for dinner after class the following week.

Pulling on all my winter paraphernalia and grabbing my bag, I trudged up the stairs, my heels clanging against the steel and my mind so full that I had completely forgotten why I had chosen the Thursday class in the first place. Until I heard him call out my name.

'Maya?'

I turned to find Zakariya at the corner with a couple of other guys, who walked away as I approached him.

'Hey, Assalaamu Alaikum,' I said, shivering. 'You, OK?'

'Wa Alaikum Salaam. Alhamdulillah, kaifa halik anti?' His classical Arabic, the dialect we were learning in class, was really cute and I smiled.

'Alhamdulillah, bi khair,' I replied slowly, trying my best to pronounce the words correctly.

'You joined then?'

'I did. Thank you for the recommendation, it was brilliant. I love the teacher, she's patient and thorough. Made a new friend as well.'

'Great. You getting the Tube?'

'Yeah, what about you? Not driving today?'

'Why, were you expecting a lift?' he joked, stuffing his cold hands into the pockets of his navy wool coat.

'I don't expect, I hope,' I joked back.

'Well, the most you're going to get today is a cup of chai while we walk to the station. Which way are you going?'

'Hammersmith and City to King's Cross, then the Piccadilly Line. You?'

'Same to King's Cross and then the Northern.'

We fell into step and easy conversation as we walked down to the busy main road and towards Whitechapel Station. Halfway down, he stopped at a stall and bought us two cups of masala tea and I accepted one gratefully. As we were about to carry on walking, he looked at me a little nervously.

'Are you hungry?' he said, almost as if he was expecting me to say no or tell him off.

'I am,' I admitted as I took a sip of my tea. 'My stomach growled through the entire lesson. It was so embarrassing.'

'Me too and it just so happens, that restaurant over there has the best Bangladeshi food in London. It's basic, nothing fancy, but the food is amazing.'

'Say no more,' I replied, my mouth already watering. 'Let's finish our tea and grab some dinner.' It was only after we entered the restaurant that I remembered that I was on the Whole 30 and couldn't eat rice, and I shouldn't have had the milky tea either. Not to mention the fact that I was wearing an expensive white fluffy jumper that I could easily spill curry on, ruining it forever. Oil and turmeric stains were a mission to get out. *And* my beautiful new coat and scarf would smell of curry when we left.

But we were already inside and Zakariya was about to sit down. If I said any of what I was thinking, he would regard me as some sort of high-maintenance coconut. So I swallowed my reservations and sat down across from him, delicately placing my coat, scarf and bag on the chair next to me.

Zakariya was quiet and contemplative as we waited for the waiter to arrive. He was in his work clothes; a suit and shirt and I wondered what we looked like together. Did we look like a couple or did we look like friends? We probably looked like siblings.

'What are you getting?' I asked him as we read over the menu and I tried to determine what was the most Whole 30 compliant. The restaurant served 'bhorta', a Bangladeshi speciality where the vegetables or fish are smoked and then mashed up and mixed with onions, coriander, chillies, mustard oil and spices. It's delicious but not without rice. For the fiftieth time in three days, I questioned my decision to do the Whole Stupid 30.

'Everything,' he replied. 'I want the buffet but I'll order some fresh paratha as well.'

We got our plates and headed over to the buffet station, where I gently lifted out some lamb and chicken, careful not to add any extra sauce to my plate, only whatever was already clinging to the meat. There was so much oil that it had floated to the top of the curry and created a shiny layer, like an oil spill in the ocean.

I returned to our table, where Zakariya's plate was piled high with pulao rice and four different curries swimming in oil. He looked at my choices in horror.

'What have you done to your plate? Where's the rice?'

'Erm, I'm not eating rice this month,' I said miserably.

'Why not? Don't tell me you're one of those nutters who doesn't eat carbohydrates?'

'I do usually, but remember that list I told you about? Doing this programme called the Whole 30 is part of it.'

'You don't look very happy about it,' he observed solemnly as he began to dig in with vigour with his hands. I picked up my cutlery. I had to do everything that was in my power not to ruin my beautiful new outfit.

'I'm not,' I admitted. 'But I wasn't happy reading over a thousand pages of *Ulysses* and I still did it. If I only do the things on the list that are easy, then what's the point?'

'True,' he agreed. 'And you found this list on the Tube, you said?'

'Yes. Well, it was in a notebook. But the notebook was left behind on the Tube.'

'I don't know if that's the coolest or craziest thing ever. To find a random list and then start doing the things on it, no matter how difficult or challenging they are . . . You're something else, Maya.'

I caught his eye; he was gazing at me almost in bewilderment. I shrugged.

'It's changed my life,' I said. 'The more things I do, the more I experience and the more I grow and get out of my shell. It's pretty liberating.'

'Hang on,' Zakariya said suddenly, 'is that why you attended the art class? Was it on the list?'

Surprised (but also not surprised) that once again he had opened up a contentious topic, I wondered if I should use the opportunity to tell him off again. But as I looked at his earnest face, I couldn't bring myself to say something that would alter the mood, so I nodded.

'Yep. Well, the list actually said I had to attend an art class and I booked that one without thinking. I had no idea what I was in for.'

'So you really were there by mistake? I'm sorry for my idiotic comments. I often say the wrong thing at the wrong time.'

'It's OK,' I shrugged amicably. 'It happens to all of us.'

The night flew by and we talked about work, the Arabic lessons, his move to Dubai and all the other things I had done, and was planning to do, on my list. When I told him about trekking Mount Snowdon, he looked at me in surprise.

'The charity I volunteer for is doing a sponsored Snowdon trek next month, I think,' he said. 'I wasn't going to go, but if you want to do it, I'll join you.'

He volunteered for a charity? Why was I so hasty in rejecting him? It made complete sense at the time. He was judgy at the art class and arrogant at the dekha dekhi. How was I supposed to know that he was, in fact, an endearing, Arabic-learning, charity-volunteering, mountain-trekking knight in shining armour who rescued annoying girls stuck in the rain? Yes, he was serious and he didn't laugh much, but who cared? If I wanted to laugh all the time, I would have looked for a comedian.

I'd had so many arguments with my parents about not giving him another chance and it was beginning to look like they were right. Now it was too late. He was no longer interested in me; his pride had been bruised and he was moving to another country. The most I could hope for was to be his friend.

Zakariya polished off three full plates of food and dessert, while I watched him miserably, wishing I could do the same. He also insisted on footing the bill, his justification being that there was no point in me paying for my share since I ate so little. I let him. It was the first time I'd had dinner with a man that wasn't some guy I was doing a project with at uni and it felt nice to have someone look out for me.

Afterwards, we walked down to the station together and caught the same train to King's Cross, the conversation still flowing like a river. There weren't any pauses, comfortable or otherwise.

On the train, we sat across from each other and I couldn't help but compare him to the last man I had conversed with on the train. Zakariya – or Zak as he preferred his friends to call him (I was a friend now? Wow!) – was the opposite of Noah. He was as dark as Noah was fair, his build leaner and narrower, his style muted and subtle. He was also shorter, with shiny black hair. Noah's was more of a medium brown and looked coarser than Zak's.

In the looks department, Noah was a head turner, but Zak was also attractive. Not in the obvious, 'look at how hot I am' kind of way, more in a slightly geeky, well-mannered sort of way, if that made any sense. I wasn't sure whose look I preferred, but based on personality and the fact that I had spent much more time with him, Zak had definitely taken over the role of Leading Man in my life.

King's Cross Station came far too quickly. We both got off, with Zak hanging back so I could alight first. His manners were impeccable and I wondered if his dad was like that with his mum. His dad hadn't looked chivalrous. He looked like any other uncle who didn't have a beard and chewed too much paan.

'This is where we part,' I said brightly a few minutes later. I felt an odd, tugging sensation deep in my ribcage. 'Thanks for dinner and the Arabic school recommendation.'

'It was my pleasure,' he replied, giving me an easy smile in return. 'See you next week, Insha'allah.'

'See you.'

I turned and began to walk in the direction of the Piccadilly Line and it took all my willpower not to look back to see if he was watching me.

Chapter Nineteen

The next couple of weeks raced by. Work was extra busy, as it always was after Christmas and New Year's when clients suddenly woke up to the fact that they hadn't done anything in the past month and were behind on their deals and contracts. Between work, Arabic classes, Arabic homework and running, there was very little time for much else.

Zak and I hadn't hung out after class again. The week after my first lesson, I saw him briefly as we were entering the building and then Nadira and I went for dinner after class. The two weeks after that, I didn't see him at all. I had lost count of the number of times I picked up my phone to text him to see if he was OK, but I always stopped myself. Desperate wasn't a good look on anyone, least of all me.

Lucy and I were also on day twenty-two of the Whole 30. We had become used to the restrictions and our complexions and hair were beginning to look brighter and more lustrous. We had also got to a point where we stopped accidentally adding dairy to our tea and feeling hangry all the time. I had, anyway. Lucy still looked weary and was less patient than usual. I had asked her more than once if she was OK, but she claimed it was because she missed sugar and alcohol. I couldn't force her to tell me what was on her mind, so I decided to let her come to me whenever she was ready.

'Maya, check this out,' she said one day, entering the little kitchenette where we often ate lunch together. I was in the middle of devouring my baked salmon and avocado salad and put my fork down to take her phone from her.

'You did it!' I cried, taking in her brand-new Instagram page. The first post was a stylish black and gold logo with the name StyledByLucy in simple lettering. 'It looks amazing! So classy and elegant. Congratulations, Luce!'

My grin faded when I opened the next post. On the screen was a before and after picture of me and it was simply horrifying.

I stared at the screen, at the girl on the left. Me. Did I really use to look that bad? I couldn't have done. But the photographic evidence was right there, in my hand, my shortcomings highlighted by the 'after' picture on the right. Dry, frizzy black bush on the left. Sleek chestnut waves on the right. Blotchy, discoloured complexion on the left. Smooth, glowing brown on the right. Unruly, uneven eyebrows versus perfectly manicured beauties. Drab, ill-fitting, functional jumper and jeans combo beside a tailored, flattering, stylish trousers and top ensemble. The left me – the old me – oozed misery and insecurities. The one on the right radiated confidence and happiness.

Neither were me. *Both were me*, depending on the day and circumstance. But the picture didn't paint a 3D, layered, nuanced story of me. Maybe the caption did, I thought in desperation. Maybe the caption conveyed that I wasn't a miserable ogre before the makeover and while I loved my new look, it didn't completely change my life as the photo implied. My eyes anxiously scanned the words, my heart pounding:

Hey everyone, let me introduce you to my lovely client, Maya, who came to me for some simple style advice and ended up going for an entire image makeover! Maya was a beautiful woman hiding beneath boring, dull clothes that did nothing for her figure. She had thick hair that was in desperate need of some TLC and needed a little guidance on what makeup worked best for her and what clothes would suit her fuller figure. Six hours was all it took to transform Maya's life. And here's a secret – she went home with a mysterious man later that evening! I saw her climb into his Mercedes myself. DM me if you want to be #StyledByLucy #fashionblogger #style #london #selfridges #MACCosmetics #fashion #OOTD #imageconsultant #makeover #beforeandafter #makeup #trends #glowup #glow #hotgirlwinter

What. The. Hell.

'Lucy!' I squeaked, my face turning pale. As pale as it could get, that is. 'You need to edit this! You can't put the bit about me going off with Zak. My mum will kill me!'

'Oh, Maya, don't worry about stuff like that. I've hardly got any followers. Is your mum on Instagram?'

'Well, no, but what if—'

Lucy laughed and casually put her arm around me. 'Trust me, babe, no one you know will see this. You know how the algorithm works. Now let me show you the TikTok I made.'

I didn't know anything about algorithms. And I doubted she did, but I didn't protest further. I didn't want to upset her or seem ungrateful after everything she had done – and was still doing – for me. I let her show me the video she made of the transformation. It was really good, with upbeat music and smooth transitions. If I wasn't looking at myself waddling through Selfridge's and sitting on the salon chair with a hundred pieces of foil sticking out my head like Medusa, I would have liked the video. It *was* me, though. It was my very personal, very private life that was now online for everyone to mock.

'Can you at least un-tag me?' I implored once I could speak again.

'Oh, OK, sure,' Lucy said, her voice losing some of its enthusiasm.

'Lucy, you've honestly done an amazing job and I'm so grateful to you and proud of you at the same time,' I said when I realised that if I didn't explain myself, our friendship could easily go down the plughole. 'It's embarrassing for me, seeing myself looking so frightful. It's really unforgiving and I'm not used to putting myself out there like that. That doesn't mean I'm not excited for you, I am. It's my own insecurities.'

'Oh, babe, I'm so sorry you feel like this. You were beautiful before, Maya, you just needed a bit of help figuring out how to make the most of what you had.'

'If you say so,' I shrugged. I couldn't see an ounce of beauty in the 'before' Maya. And the more I looked at it, the more stupid I felt. There was no way Noah was remotely interested in me that day on the Tube. How could he have been?

'I do, but I'm going to delete the posts. I don't want to upset you or stress you out.'

'No way!' I interjected. 'You can't. This is your business.'

'*You're* my business,' Lucy shrugged. 'It's fine. Maybe one day I'll find someone else who can help me. But I suppose I could post pictures of my own outfits and stuff.'

'No!' I insisted again, firmer this time. 'I said I would do it and I meant it. I needed a moment to get over the initial shock and shame. I'll be fine in a bit.'

'Are you sure?' Lucy looked at me doubtfully. 'Honestly, Maya—'

'I'm sure,' I said resolutely. 'Please. It's fine.'

That evening, when I got home and prayed, I asked Allah not to let anyone I knew see the picture or video of my transformation. If Network Aunty thought I was gallivanting around London with a random man in a Merc, then my reputation would be shot to pieces. I had managed to get through my teenage and university years with it intact and I had zero desire to ruin it now.

I got into bed earlier than usual that night and as I was about to switch off my bedside lamp, my phone pinged with an incoming notification – a new follow request. I was about to ignore it and go to sleep, but then I decided to check it out. *ZakHussain16* had requested to follow me! What the actual hell? How did he find my account? There were numerous Maya Rahmans online – how did he find the right one? It took me a millisecond to decide whether to accept his request. In that fraction of time, I weighed out the pros (I could stalk his own accounts, we could become better friends, I would learn more about him) and the cons (he could stalk my account, he would learn more about me). There were thirty-three per cent more pros. Maths didn't lie, I had to accept based on hard facts.

Accepting his request, I followed him back and waited anxiously for him to accept. About an hour later, I was into the semi-private Insta world of Zakariya Hussain and then spent the next hour going through all his content. I didn't have a huge amount of experience with the accounts of Muslim, Bengali men. In fact, my entire frame of reference was based on Malik's social media, which was full of the usual: hanging out with the boys, food, holidays, snapshots of the City. You wouldn't be able to tell he had a girlfriend from his social media. Or that he had a sister. It was a carefully curated archive of the Malik he wanted outsiders to think he was.

Zakariya's was different. It seemed less intentional than my brother's, a mishmash of quotes, books, food, travels, Islamic stuff. His sisters featured prominently – weddings, Eids, family outings – and I wondered why my brother never included me in his, even though there was a picture of him on mine. Was he ashamed of me? Did I not fit the image of himself he was trying to portray? A suave, finance man with money to blow, living his best life, etc., etc.?

I wondered what Zak would think of my page. It was sparse, with no pictures of me. I never felt like my photos were good enough to be immortalised online. Instead, there were lots of scenes of London and the odd food post. It was pretty boring, actually. Now that he followed me though, I would have to think of interesting things to share. It felt like pressure.

Before I put my phone away and went to sleep, I did yet another Google search for Noah. I did it every week or so, in case something new popped up. It hadn't. He was fading faster than I had anticipated. The arrival of Zakariya had shifted my focus away from the stranger on the train, who I felt I knew intimately because of his list. A part of me felt guilty for thinking of Zak when I had been carrying a piece of Noah around with me for over four months. That piece of him had become a part of me. We were forever intertwined because of the experiences we had shared.

Maybe that was all it was ever destined to be. Maybe Allah put him in my path so I could find the notebook. Maybe it wasn't about Noah himself.

I contemplated DM'ing Zak, asking him how he found me, but I didn't. If he wanted to talk to me, he knew what to do. Putting my phone on silent, I switched off my lamp and snuggled under my heavy duvet. It was still freezing and my dad was being tight about when we could turn the heating on. He had it on a timer to come on for an hour at Fajr time, just before dawn and an hour in the evening. Whenever we complained, he reminded us that he was the one paying the bills. I wondered if he would ever stop acting like he was still poor; the boy who had come to the UK at twenty-three with nothing but twenty pounds in his pockets and the naive belief that his Queen's country and its people would welcome him, as a member of the Commonwealth. He was born after India became independent, but British values, the language and the belief in monarchy remained in the region for a long time afterwards. Baba never realised that he would be seen as a dirty pest when he got here; the lowest of the low.

And so we wore socks at night in the winter and we let my dad do whatever he needed to feel safe.

Chapter Twenty

'To our last day of the Whole Dirty 30,' Lucy said, raising her glass of water as a toast.

'To our last day of this hellish lifestyle,' I replied, tipping my glass towards her. 'May we never again have to give up life's simple pleasures for the sake of our health.'

'Amen. Or for the sake of a man.'

'Ameen.'

Clinking our glasses, we sat back and ate our last Whole 30 lunch; tuna salad for me, steamed fish and vegetables for Lucy.

'How's StyledByLucy getting on?' I asked Lucy as we began to eat.

'Good. Really good,' she replied. 'I'm on 513 followers on Instagram and 194 on TikTok. I know that doesn't sound like much but it's only been three weeks, so I'm doing all right. The posts on you have had the most engagement though, much more than my outfit of the day or styling tips ones. I need to find someone else who wants to be transformed.'

I tried not to visibly blanch when she mentioned the posts of me. I was happy for her, I really was and the whole reason I agreed to let her help me was because I wanted to support her passion. It was tough, though. When the post first went live, I checked back after a couple of days and some of the comments were awful. People who didn't know me, who hid behind the comfort of their usernames, were tearing me to pieces. There weren't many, to be fair. Most of the comments were generic:

'Wow, she looks amazing!' or lazy heart and fire emojis. There were three in particular that stood out, which Lucy deleted – but not before I had seen them. One was something about how I looked crap before *and* after. Another commented on my discolouration and the last called me a fake and a catfish, adding something about my man getting the shock of his life when I wiped my makeup off.

Those three comments were enough to negate all the positive ones. They plagued me for days. I kept looking at myself in the mirror, wondering if I was that ugly, that disgusting, that complete strangers felt the need to insult me in public.

I didn't tell anyone how I was feeling, though. I rarely did. Maybe I needed to add something else to my list about learning to talk about my feelings more, instead of believing them to be invalid or unimportant.

'What are you going to eat tomorrow?' I asked Lucy, pushing the negative thoughts out of my mind. 'I'm going to have eggs and paratha for breakfast with a big mug of sweet masala tea. And I'm going to finally enjoy rice and curry for dinner.'

'I'm desperate for toast,' Lucy replied, with a dreamy look on her face. 'Toast with lashings of butter. And I'm going to go for drinks and get shit-faced in the evening.'

'It's a Wednesday. How will you deal with work on Thursday?'

'I'll figure it out.'

After lunch, we both went back to our desks and I began the mundane work of combing through some new contracts for any errors or irregularities. Halfway through my stack of papers, I checked my phone to see a new email from the organisation that I had applied to for sponsorship for my master's. My heart stopped and my hands instantly turned clammy. The subject didn't reveal whether I had got it or not, with its vague 'Application Outcome'.

I looked around the office to see if Sheila was around before I opened the email, my chest tight with anxiety, straining against my ribcage and pushing against my throat.

'OH MY GOD! I GOT IT!' I shrieked, jumping up from my seat in a fashion that was very unlike my usual calm and quiet demeanour.

'Got what?' Arjun and Lucy asked in unison.

'I got the scholarship! They're going to pay for my LLM!' Tears filled my eyes as Lucy rushed over and threw her arms around me. Arjun joined us and soon the three of us were jumping around the office like loonies, still holding on to each other.

'What's all this?' Sheila's steely voice cut through our laughter; we stopped jumping and instantly fell silent. Lucy and Arjun slunk back to their desks while Sheila glowered at me. She was smiling, but she wasn't. Her big white teeth were showing, but her eyes were annoyed. *Oh, Sheila, what big teeth you have! All the better to eat you with, my dear.*

'Sorry for the noise,' I gulped, edging towards my seat before I suffered the same fate as Red Riding Hood. 'I had some good news, that's all.'

'Oh? What's that then? Are you getting married?'

What? My eyes darted over to Lucy and Arjun, their expressions of confusion no doubt mimicking my own.

'Er, n-no,' I stammered. 'I applied for a scholarship and found out that I got it,' I said as I backed away and slowly sat down in my seat.

'A scholarship? For what?'

'I want to do an LLM,' I replied, my throat dry.

'Oh? You know you don't need a master's to be a paralegal, Maya,' she said icily, before abruptly turning around and slithering back to her office.

Exhaling deeply, I ignored the looks of horror mixed with pity on my colleagues' faces, Sheila's words already replaying over and over in my mind. There were no congratulations, only the not-so-subtle reminder to stay in my lane and the assumption that as a brown woman the only possible accomplishment I would want to celebrate was getting married.

The worst part was, Sheila was brown herself. What did that mean? How could she be racist towards me when we shared the same colour? Surely not. But then there were a subset of MPs, evil brown MPs, I call them, who capitalised on their brownness to make decisions that then destroyed brown people. Sheila was definitely giving me evil MP vibes.

The hope and joy I had felt moments earlier had dampened to a vague sense of relief. For the rest of the afternoon, I kept quiet and silent, just the way I used to be.

'Guess what,' I announced when I got home that evening. My mood had improved considerably by the journey home, partly because I got a seat all the way to Turnpike Lane for a change, but mostly because I had decided to text Zakariya with my scholarship news. His reply came instantly and I spent the rest of the afternoon texting him discreetly instead of working. It was my passive-aggressive way of giving Sheila the finger.

'What's up, Dimple?' Malik drawled, sauntering down the stairs.

'Oh, wow, fancy finding you home before midnight for a change,' I replied sarcastically, taking off my scarf and coat and draping them across the banister. 'Trouble in paradise?'

'Everything's fine, thank you for asking,' he scowled at me, shooting a glance at the open living room door where the sounds of Bangla TV could be heard.

'Guess what, Baba!' I entered the living room where my dad was watching the news in Bangladesh.

'Kita oiseh?' Baba replied distractedly, his gaze fixed on the screen.

'I got the scholarship to do my master's! Law school, here I come.'

'Congratulations, Affa, I knew you'd get it!' Malik exclaimed, thumping me on the back. 'Well done!'

'Good news,' Baba's reply was lacklustre. He wasn't the most enthusiastic of people. As someone who grew up sharing a room with five brothers and used to study by candlelight on the hallway floor because it was the only space available, he isn't often impressed with success that hasn't come with odds-defying hard graft. 'How much will that save you?'

'Over twenty grand,' I told him with a flourish. He perked up at that.

'Fantastic! Fantastic news!' he said, showing delayed enthusiasm. 'Fantastic, what a relief.'

Rolling my eyes, I went to find Ma, hoping for a better response.

'Oh my goodness, Maya! Congratulations!' she exclaimed, tears instantly filling her eyes. 'Give me a hug. Well done!' Now *that* was a response. 'I wish you had told me earlier; I would have made something more special for dinner.'

'What did you make? Tonight's my last night on the Whole 30, I was going to have grilled chicken and salad for dinner.'

'Well, come home straight after work tomorrow and I'll make you something special. Is there anything you fancy?'

'Anything with carbs, dairy and sugar, please. Preferably all three at the same time.'

'Deal, my darling. I'm so proud of you!'

Now all I had to do was get offered a university place and my plan to become a solicitor in approximately five years would be underway.

Later that night, once I'd had my final Whole 30 meal and gone to bed excited at the prospect of having paratha the next day for breakfast, a text from Zakariya came through. I smiled when his name popped up on my home screen, my stomach instantly fluttering with anticipation.

Although we had been messaging each other all afternoon, this felt different. It was dark and I was snuggled up under my duvet in my fluffy onesie with matching socks. Hardly the most romantic of outfits, but it wasn't like our conversations constituted romance. They were friendly, sure, but no one would be able to misconstrue our communication as anything but platonic.

But still. It was dark. I was in bed, about to fall asleep. It was just the two of us; no Lucy looking worriedly over at me after my run-in with Sheila, no Arjun huffing and puffing across from me. No threat of Sheila suddenly bursting into the room – and bursting my bubble with it:

ZAKARIYA: Hey you awake?

I waited a few minutes before I replied, as was the norm when trying to appear aloof and mysterious, I assumed. Not that I had a norm, exactly. I had never been one to enjoy late-night texting sessions with random boys. There was never anyone I liked enough to bother wasting my time on. The only guy I had really fancied during my university days was a Japanese international student called Kaito, who never looked at me. All I did was look at him though. I used to dress up for the lectures I knew he would be at. Once I had to do a presentation on the case for a co-habitation law reform and I spent days choosing the perfect outfit. Looking back, I now realised that my 'cute' outfit wasn't cute at all (a floral dress over skinny jeans and cardigan) and the thick black kohl that rimmed my eyes was more Marilyn Manson than Cleopatra. He caught my eye once during my whole presentation, as I stumbled and mumbled my way through my argument about how the UK needed to loosen its hold on the traditional institution of marriage. I know now that it didn't mean anything. I mean, I was at the front of the class talking, he was bound to look at me at some point. At the time though, it meant *everything*. I spent hours analysing the look he gave me, droning on and on about it to Dina, replaying that moment over and over on a loop. The more I thought about it, the bigger the incident became and I was convinced that it wasn't a 'look', it was a message.

So I did what anyone would. Rather than slide into his Instagram DMs, I *threw* myself into them with something ridiculous like, 'Hey! How are you? Fancy finding you here!'

I waited days for him to reply, agonising over what he would say, certain that it would bloom into a romance. I imagined him saying things like, 'Wow! I've been looking for you online for ages!' Or, if I was really lucky, 'Maya Rahman, I've been waiting for this moment all year.'

His reply came all right. A friendly but completely humiliating, 'Hey do we know each other?'

I was mortified. The boy I had spent the good part of a semester dreaming about, whom I was convinced beyond doubt was into me too, didn't even know who I was.

That was the first and last time I approached anyone. Since then, any time I caught the eye of an attractive male, I told myself it was an accident:

MAYA: Hey. I am indeed. What's up?

Zak's reply came immediately. He clearly didn't feel the need to wait a few minutes first – the thought of him sitting there waiting for my reply made my cheeks heat up:

ZAKARIYA: I've got some news for you, Ms Scholarship Winner

MAYA: You do? Will it beat being Ms Scholarship Winner?

ZAKARIYA: You can be the judge of that.

MAYA: Well????

ZAKARIYA: I asked my team leader at the charity I volunteer for if you could join us on the Snowdon trek without having to fundraise, since there isn't much time. They never let people do the fun part without the fundraising part.

MAYA: Oh wow, thanks for trying. What did they say?

ZAK: So soon you'll be Ms Snowdon Climber as well as Ms Scholarship Winner! 🏃

MAYA: Yay! Thanks so much, can't wait!!! 💪 ☺

Gulp. I *could* wait. I had been starving myself for the past month, how was I supposed to climb a mountain so soon? All my energy had been burnt for fuel. I was too weak! I couldn't admit that to Zak, not after he went out of his way to help me. Besides, the trek was on my sacred list, so I had to do it no matter how tired or scared I was.

Chapter Twenty-One

'I can't believe you're making me do this again,' Malik mumbled a couple of weeks later as we drove through quiet London streets in the dark, well before sunrise. We were supposed to be at the coach stop by six in the morning and in Snowdonia National Park by 10.00 a.m. The trek was around six hours there and back so we would be back in London by ten that night. It was going to be a long, tiring day, but instead of dreading it, I felt excited. So far, except for *Ulysses* and the life-drawing class, I hadn't regretted a single item on Noah's list. Everything had contributed to bettering my life somehow, whether it was a fun experience, a day out or a makeover; my life was better because of it.

'As far as I remember, this is the first time I've attempted to trek Snowdon,' I replied blithely, like I didn't know what he was talking about.

'Let's hope you do trek it, instead of realising it's closed when you get there,' he said, shooting me a dirty look.

'I appreciate you taking me and not expecting me to get a cab with a potential rapist at five-thirty in the morning.'

'The Brother of the Year award goes to me.'

'It would, if you were a brother who confided in me,' I said, giving him a sideways glance. 'When are you going to tell me about this girlfriend of yours? When you're standing at the altar?'

'Altar? What are we, born-again Christians?'

'You know what I mean.'

There was silence as Malik continued to weave through random side roads as he made his way south of the river, which was like crossing county lines for us north Londoners. I expected him to fob me off with another snarky comment and was surprised when he began to talk seriously.

'I don't see much point in advertising things unless it gets serious,' he said eventually, staring straight at the road ahead.

'Well, it must be a little bit serious at least. You guys went on holiday together.' I tried to keep my voice light and non-accusatory. Malik's and my interpretation of being good Muslims were different. We both prayed, fasted and paid our yearly Zakat to charity. But whereas I didn't believe in getting super physical before marriage, Malik thought it wasn't a big deal. To me, intimacy was sacred and should be enjoyed within the sanctity of marriage. It wasn't something my parents had preached openly to me. Can you imagine my dad breaking the birds and the bees down for me? It was something unsaid, that you just knew to be the case. Whether you listened to your religion or culture was another story. Malik clearly didn't and since he was finally opening up to me, I wasn't going to ruin it by preaching to him.

'Yeah, but a holiday is different from a lifetime together,' he replied. 'I don't know if she's the one I want to spend the rest of my life with.'

'Tell me about her then,' I suggested, trying not to pry too much. I was bursting to know more about this girl who had my brother confused, but if I came across as too pushy then I knew Malik would withdraw. 'I know you think I have no life experience, but maybe I can help you figure things out.'

Malik looked at me sceptically. I knew he thought I was naive because I had never dated, but that didn't mean I was completely clueless when it came to life.

'She's white.'

Oh.

I immediately understood why it was such a big secret. Interracial marriages are a lot more common now than they were when I was growing up, but there are still only two people in our entire extended family married to white people and that was done with a lot of drama, tears and threats of being cast out. The biggest issue was that of religion. If the partner converted, then the more traditional family members were a little placated at least. If they didn't, certain uncles and aunties were renowned for boycotting weddings and making a big fuss about the scandal.

'How old is she?'

'A couple of years older than me,' he admitted.

Shit. And there went another one. I had no idea how he was going to persuade my parents if things came to that. I tried to be positive, but I knew my parents and my grandmother. This wasn't going to go down well. 'How long have you been together?'

'About a year, on and off.'

'A year!' My brother had been going out with a girl for an entire year and I was only finding out about it now? Why hadn't he told me?

My facial expression must have given my feelings away because he nudged me gently. 'Telling you would have been too much pressure. I needed to figure things out without you making digs at me or expecting me to propose.'

'OK,' I said, taking a deep breath and trying not to feel too hurt by his lack of trust. It wasn't as though I had told him about Zakariya. It would be hypocritical of me to get offended when I was hiding things myself. 'Tell me what makes you unsure. Is it the cultural differences? Because you know it can still be done if you really want to. It'll require a bit more effort and convincing, that's all.'

Malik thought for a moment, his brows furrowed as he expertly navigated the London streets that were becoming busier as the sun rose higher.

'There's the obvious,' he began. 'She's white. She's not Muslim.'

'OK,' I said slowly when he stopped talking. 'What is she? Christian? Atheist?'

'She's agnostic, which I guess is better than being an atheist.'

'Much better,' I agreed. 'The fact that she isn't sure might mean that she's open to exploring the concept of faith and religion.'

'I guess so,' he said quietly, still thinking.

'What else?' I probed gently. 'What's she like?'

'She's kind and funny. She respects me and I respect her.'

'So what's the problem? Why aren't you sure about her yet? It's been a year, Malik. If this was an arranged marriage, you probably would have been married six months ago!'

'I don't know,' he shrugged. 'She's really into her career. She has a full-time job but she has side hustles as well. I like that she's driven but I'm worried she won't want a family.'

'Is this speculation or have you spoken to her about it?'

'I can't! If I do, she'll think I want to marry her and that's too much pressure.'

Once again, I bit my tongue and tried to hear him out.

'I'm worried about raising a family with her, Dimple. She could convert to Islam, but she might not be a practising Muslim, you know?'

'You're hardly the pillar of piety yourself,' I couldn't stop myself from retorting. What the hell was my brother on about? Was he really one of those men who held themselves to one set of rules and had another for the women in their lives? The thought infuriated me and I turned to glower at him, my decision to remain non-judgemental flying out of the window.

183

'This is messed-up, Malik,' I said. 'Sorry if you don't want to hear it, or you regret telling me, but I'm your older sister. If I don't hold you to account or tell you what's what, then I'm failing you.'

I proceeded to tell him off for his hypocrisy and double standards for the next five minutes. She was good enough to mess around with for over a year, but not marry? My blood was boiling.

'If you're not interested in a future with her, she has the right to know so she doesn't waste her time on you. But the fact that you've let it get this far and judged her for things you do yourself, is messed-up!'

We had arrived by this point and Malik had parked behind the private coach, the hazard lights on as he waited for me to finish telling him off.

'Are you done?'

'For now!' I glared at him and got out of the car. 'Do the right thing, you bloody fool. She doesn't deserve this!'

As I yanked my fleece undercoat and raincoat out of the backseat, together with my backpack and water bottle, I gave him one last death stare before I got out, still shaking my head in disappointment as he drove away.

There was a queue of people outside the coach, chattering away while warming their hands on travel mugs, and I approached them nervously. I eyed the mugs of tea and coffee with envy. I was too scared to drink a thing that morning in case it made me need the toilet during the journey. Scanning the crowd for Zakariya, I quickly spotted him talking to a really pretty, tall brown girl with shiny jet-black hair tied into a high ponytail. She was dressed like me, but with her height she looked so much better. She laughed at something he said and I felt a twist inside my gut. What was I doing here? This was Zak's space, not mine. A place where he laughed with women who looked like they belonged on the cover of one of those Asian bridal magazines. I wouldn't fit in.

As I debated turning around and skulking away, Zak spotted me. Smiling warmly, he beckoned to me and I had no choice but to contain my nerves and walk over to them.

'Maya! Assalaamu Alaikum! You made it.'

'Wa Alaikum Salaam,' I replied, offering him a stiff smile that was more grimace. Of course I had bloody made it! We had texted last night to confirm all the details. Why was he acting like he wasn't sure if I would come? Was this for the benefit of his lady friend, who was looking curiously at me?

'Salaams, I'm Zara,' she said, offering her hand to me and smiling a perfectly straight, white smile. I made a mental note then and there to visit the dentist and get my teeth whitened. They weren't bad, but they didn't dazzle like hers did. I was suddenly desperate for dazzling teeth. 'Zak is rubbish at introducing people. If I waited for him, we would complete the entire trek and I still wouldn't know who you were!'

'Salaams, Zara, I'm Maya. It's nice to meet you,' I lied, taking her delicate, manicured hand in my unkempt paw. She was speaking about him as if they were a couple and all the excitement I had felt at the day I was going to spend with Zakariya was replaced with nausea. Why had he invited me on a date with him and his . . . whoever this 'Zara' was.

Zara.

Zara and Zakariya.

Her name was an anagram of his. Well, partially. It sounded like a couple name, much better than Zakariya and Maya. Our couple name would be something hideous, like Makariya.

Zara began to chat animatedly about how she had got into fitness a few years ago and how she had wanted to do this trek for ages. She only recently started volunteering for Islamic Relief, blah blah blah. I tuned her out. All I could see was Zakariya's reaction to her endless chatter. His eyes were bright as he absorbed her energy. The more she talked, the more deflated I became. I knew I would never be able to match that sort of vibe. If she was the disco ball in the centre of the room, I was less than the shadows dancing on the wall. I was the wall itself.

'Hey, sorry I'm late, everyone.'

I was about to throw myself in front of the oncoming traffic when a deep voice came from behind me and I turned around to see the HOTTEST guy I'd ever seen. Literally. He was even hotter than Noah. I remembered Noah as polished and groomed; this man looked like he had rolled out of bed and straight onto the Tube, and still looked bloody amazing. He had chestnut-coloured messy hair and a beard that wasn't sculpted like a royal park; more organic and natural, but still somehow neat and groomed. His eyes were almost hazel and he was so tall that he towered over us all. I forced my bottom jaw to stay connected to my top one as I soaked in his beauty.

'Sorry, aşkim, don't kill me,' he said to Zara, throwing his arm around her. She elbowed him playfully and leant into his embrace. I looked at Zak to gauge his reaction, but he seemed genuinely happy to see this man. Could I have been wrong about the chemistry between him and Zara?

'Salaams, Adam,' Zakariya said, smiling. 'This is my friend, Maya. Maya, Adam. See, Zara? I am capable of introducing people.'

'Once doesn't make you capable,' Zara retorted. 'Babe, did you get me a coffee?'

'I did, indeed. Skinny latte, extra hot.'

'I've trained you well, haven't I, Turkish?'

'You have indeed. I aim to serve.'

Ordinarily, I would have found all this cutesy behaviour a bit sickly, but instead I was relieved. Zara was with Adam not

Zakariya! My spirits lifting, I raised my eyebrows at Zakariya and he shrugged. 'They had their nikah recently, so they're still in that loved-up honeymoon phase.'

'What's up with calling him Turkish?' I asked quietly so they didn't overhear. They were now talking to others in the crowd and I felt myself relax a little. The fact that they were Islamically married explained why they were comfortable with PDA in front of everyone, although I couldn't imagine myself being tactile in public. I found it difficult to be myself in large groups, especially when I didn't know anyone. My anxiety was beginning to kick in and I asked myself why I agreed to come on this stupid trek with a bunch of strangers. I should have done it on my own.

'He's Turkish,' Zakariya shrugged, like it was normal to call someone by their ethnicity instead of their name.

'You'd better not start calling me "Bengali",' I said, half serious, half trying to be witty.

'Why would I? You're not my fiancée. You're some random who's following me around,' he retorted. *Ouch! Was that supposed to be a joke?* There was something in his tone that suggested that it was a dig at me, disguised as banter.

'Oh, really? More like you're some random who followed me to an art class and then showed up at my house, trying to marry me,' I snapped, smarting at the implication that I wasn't good enough to earn a nickname.

An uncomfortable silence followed and we both stood there, not knowing what to say next. We had *hours* left to spend together. If it was going to continue like this, there was a good chance of me jumping off the edge of the mountain.

Chapter Twenty-Two

The team leader came out of the coach and introduced himself as Musa. He was a short, broad man in his mid-forties, I guessed, with a big greying beard and a bit of a belly. He also had the strongest cockney accent I had ever heard on an Asian man and I suppressed a smile as he handed out forms for us to fill in, explained what the schedule was and checked our names off a register. When the formalities were complete, we all shuffled on to the coach, around thirty of us in total. Everyone seemed to know each other apart from me and, once again, I regretted my decision to do this without a proper friend by my side.

I climbed up the steps and waited behind Adam and Zara, wondering where I was supposed to sit now that things were awkward with Zakariya. He solved my dilemma by asking me if I preferred the aisle seat or window. Grateful, I told him I preferred the aisle – I didn't want to be squashed between him and a wall. I didn't tell him the reason, of course. He agreed genially and sat down. I sat next to him, hoping we had moved on from the earlier catty remarks.

Zakariya, I soon discovered, either had thick skin or didn't hold grudges. Given the fact that he had been there for me multiple times despite my rejecting him as a potential husband, I guessed it was probably the latter.

Taking our coats off and stowing our bags, we settled into our seats and within seconds, Zak was fast asleep. So much for wondering what we were going to talk about for the entire journey. It looked like I wouldn't need the conversation starters I had devised in my head and later wrote out in Noah's notebook.

With a sigh, I took out my AirPods and looked over at him, sleeping away with his head against the window. He looked really cute with his eyes closed; his long, unfairly thick eyelashes resting across the crest of his cheeks. I was acutely aware of the (lack of) distance between us and though we were both in fleece hoodies, I could feel the heat emanating from his body. He smelt good too; spicy and warm, like Arabian oud and cinnamon. I swallowed nervously and looked away. Maybe sitting next to him wasn't such a great idea after all.

'Maya, do you fancy a snack?' Zara asked and I turned to her. She was in the aisle seat across from me. Adam, next to her, had fallen asleep as well; his head rested on her shoulder and he was snoring gently with his mouth slightly ajar. I caught Zara's eye and she smiled good-naturedly.

'That boy is always either eating or sleeping,' she said, pretending to be annoyed. But I could tell that she wasn't. 'Too bad he's going to miss out on these bad boys.' She held a plastic Tupperware out to me, containing still-warm samosas.

'Thanks, I'd love one. I didn't get a chance to have breakfast this morning.' I took a delicate triangle from the container and bit into it. It was delicious, despite being lukewarm instead of piping hot. It had the right amount of chillies and spices in the mince, which was moist and juicy. I savoured every last morsel.

'Yum, these are amazing,' I told Zara. 'Did you make them?'

'Yeah, right,' she laughed. 'Don't take the mick, but my gran made them. She makes loads every month, freezes them and then fries them whenever she fancies.'

'Are you telling me your grandmother fancied eating samosas at five in the morning?'

'Haha, no. But she's a darling and wanted to pack me some food. Here, have another.' She handed the box over to me again and I gratefully accepted.

As we bonded over our shared love of samosas and began talking more freely with each other, I learnt that Zara wasn't Pakistani like I originally assumed, but Bengali like me. Her height had thrown me. Bengalis are notorious for being petite, including the men. If the shared motherland between us wasn't bonding enough, I then found out she was a north Londoner as well, so we spent a good while longer trying to figure out if we had any mutual friends or family.

'How did you meet your husband?' I asked her once we had eaten her samosas and the spicy omelette paratha wraps she had also brought with her.

'We used to work together,' she explained. 'And I guess he sort of grew on me.'

'How were your parents about you marrying someone who isn't Bengali? If you don't mind me asking.'

'They're fine,' she said with a shrug. 'Him being Turkish was never the issue.'

The way she said this sounded like there were other issues and I wondered what they were, but I didn't know her well enough to ask.

'What was a problem initially was that he didn't practise Islam,' she continued as she finished off her coffee, more honestly than I would have expected from a virtual stranger. 'I wanted to be with someone who was more conscious and on the same page as me. But he's grown a lot and not for me. His aunt died and it changed his perspective and lifestyle. He's come a long way and I think the timing is finally right between us.'

As Zara put away all the empty containers and wrappers into a plastic bag, I leant back in my seat and glanced at

Zakariya again, wondering what God had planned for us. Zara's story sounded complicated, despite her simplifying it for me. It looked like mine was going to be complicated too.

The journey to Wales was long. I listened to a podcast for a bit, then an audiobook before my AirPods needed charging – and so did my phone if I wanted the battery to last throughout the trek. At some point, I must have fallen asleep because I woke up with my head on Zakariya's shoulder and my right arm casually draped across him. Mortified did not adequately convey the horror that tore through me when I realised what I was doing.

'Oh my Lord!' I squeaked, yanking my body away from him so quickly that I almost toppled off my seat. My half-open bag went flying and out spilled the contents, which among other, less embarrassing items, included a tampon. Half toppling, half climbing out of my seat, I squatted unattractively in the aisle and hurriedly stuffed the incriminating items back into my bag. The coach driver chose that moment to brake hard and I fell backwards. Hard.

'It's OK, you're OK,' Zakariya murmured, taking my hand and helping me back into my seat, where I moved as far away from him as possible. My hand burned from his touch and I sat on it to make the electricity die down.

'I'm so sorry, why didn't you wake me up?' I looked around the coach to see if anyone had spotted my fall, but Zara and Adam had thankfully slept through the commotion.

'I couldn't bring myself to,' he said unapologetically. 'You looked so peaceful; I didn't want to ruin it. Plus, you look nice when you're not frowning or scowling.'

I didn't know what to say to that.

'Anyway, check out the view. We're almost there.' Zak changed the subject and I was relieved. I had suffered from enough humiliation for one day.

I looked beyond him to the view outside the window. All around us were various shades of green pierced with rock and stone; jutting up high and dipping low as the coach made its way through the park to Llanberis, where we would be starting our trek.

'It's so beautiful,' I said. 'I can't wait to climb it.'

'Same.'

Amidst all the God-given greenery, my falling asleep on him and then falling off my seat slowly faded away into insignificance.

The walk began after we'd all been to the toilet, done our midday prayers and some stretches. As the charity was a Muslim one and most of the volunteers were Muslim, we all prayed together in congregation, with Musa leading the salah. As soon as we finished the last step – greeting the angels on our shoulders – I jumped up, raring to go. There was something about fresh, unpolluted, crisp air that I found energising. According to Musa, the path we were taking was the longest, but the easiest. It was going to be around nine miles there and back and a climb of almost a thousand feet. I couldn't wait.

We were told by Musa to stick together, which we sort of did. Some of the fitter members of the group ploughed ahead, the less energetic lagged behind. Zak, Zara, Adam and I were in the middle for a while, but after an hour, they had moved ahead and then it was Zak and me, walking in comfortable silence, stopping every so often to absorb the scenery. The path was mostly gravelly with occasional steps, but although I slipped and tripped once or twice, I didn't feel scared of rolling down the mountain. Zak made sure to walk close enough to me for me to grab him whenever I lost my balance.

By the time we reached the summit, I was hot, sweaty and tired, but totally buzzing from the high of being so . . . high. The view from the top was magnificent and I inhaled it all in;

the clouds swirling around us, the rocks piercing the sky, the various hues of green blending into an artistic masterpiece. I pulled out my water bottle for a much-needed drink and it immediately slipped out of my hand. Before I could grab it, it casually rolled down the mountain.

With a sigh, I collapsed onto the ground and focused on my breathing as I waited for my heart rate to settle, hoping no one had noticed.

'What do you think?' Zakariya asked, sitting down carefully beside me, his legs outstretched in front of him. 'Beautiful, isn't it?' I drew mine close to my chest and smiled at him.

'It's . . . I don't know how to describe it. I feel so in awe, but at peace at the same time. Everything else feels so small right now. Me, my list, my life. We're all tiny specks in this infinite universe.'

'I know what you mean,' he replied, staring out at the view. 'Sometimes life feels really confusing, or difficult. It's easy to become consumed. That's what I love about nature. It sort of helps me recalibrate.'

I wondered what he meant by life being difficult or confusing and a tiny part of me wondered if it had anything to do with me.

'What sort of confusing things?' I asked, keeping my voice light and my gaze firmly on the rolling green hills before me. From my peripheral vision, I saw him turn to look at me for a moment longer than necessary.

'All sorts,' he said, his tone indicating that he wasn't prepared to reveal anything further. 'Anyway, it's nearly time to pray. You getting up?'

'Sure.' Disappointed that this was the end of the conversation, I got up and followed him back to the rest of the group, who were forming the lines for the late-afternoon prayer, Asr.

Zakariya offered to recite the call to prayer, which he did in the most beautiful, melodic voice. Time stood still, his voice like nectar to my ears, and when I was able to tear my eyes from him, I noticed quite a few other girls watching him, mesmerised.

Performing our salah at the top of the summit was something else. Every time my forehead touched the ground, I felt a wave of peace engulf me. Up here, I felt closer to God than I had ever done. When it was over, I slowly took off the scarf I had placed around my head like a makeshift hijab and wrapped it back round my neck, but as I walked towards Zakariya, I was beaten to it by two giggly uni students who flanked him on either side. Stopping dead in my tracks before I embarrassed myself by approaching him, I tried to ignore the pang of disappointment and jealousy that had a firm grip on my heart and turned away.

'What's up with you two then?' Zara asked me as we began the slow descent down to sea level.

'Huh? What do you mean?'

'You and Zak. Don't pretend there's nothing going on! I saw you cuddled up with him on the coach.' Grinning, Zara gave me an indiscreet wink and I stopped myself from pushing her over the cliff.

'We weren't cuddling! It was an accident,' I protested weakly, knowing full well that it was futile.

'If you say so,' Zara said sceptically, linking her arm through mine as we continued our steady descent downwards and I tried my best to watch my footing on the rocky path instead of watching Zak disappear further out of sight with his fan club.

Chapter Twenty-Three

The coach journey back felt strange, more tense than the ride there, but that could have been because we were both awake the whole time. We were acting normally – I shared my sandwiches and cake with him, he shared his wrap and crisps with me; we chatted about the trek, browsed our phones, talked about books we were reading and podcasts we were listening to (he was a massive fan of self-help and productivity books and pods) – all the while being careful not to accidentally brush each other's arms or get too close. He also revealed that he was more of a DC guy than a Marvel guy – which was a red flag in my eyes. DC Comics were so much darker than Marvel, which made me wonder if he was more complicated than he let on.

Malik was waiting for me when I arrived in Victoria at around ten in the evening, so I bid Zak a hasty farewell, relying on the blanket of darkness to hide his features from my unsuspecting brother. The two giggling girls hung around, obviously hoping to get onto the Tube with their crush. The thought annoyed me, but there wasn't much I could do about it. Hugging Zara goodbye and waving to Adam and Zak, I jumped into Malik's Beemer and didn't look back.

The next few weeks were a blur of completing other items on the list:

13. WATCH CITIZEN KANE ✓

Greatest movie of all time!!!!

'Ma,' I called as I stomped down the stairs in my PJs, 'do you want to watch a movie?'

'Ooh, the new Shah Rukh Khan one?' Ma poked her head out of her bedroom excitedly. 'I've been saving that for after Ramadan.'

'Uh, not exactly,' I replied vaguely. 'It's a classic. It's supposed to be the GOAT.'

'The goat?' Ma looked baffled as she followed me downstairs and began rummaging through the snack cupboard for microwave popcorn. 'A film about a goat?'

'No . . . G.O.A.T. Greatest of All Time?'

'Sure, why not?' Ma obliged amicably as popping noises began to sound from the microwave, instantly transporting me to my childhood. We never used to go out much as a family – there wasn't much time or money to spare – but one thing Ma always did was put on a film on a Friday night and we would sit together in our little living room after dinner, the coffee table laden with Morrisons' own-brand snacks, watching the latest Bollywood blockbuster.

As the film began in black and white, with ominous music creating tension, I kept glancing at Ma to see if she was enjoying it.

Two hours and a very confused mother later, I could safely say that she hadn't. And neither had I, to be honest. I wasn't a film buff or critic to appreciate the lighting and cinematography enough for it to outweigh the subtlety of the story.

'Well,' she sighed when the sled was tossed into the fireplace and the end credits appeared, 'that was . . . interesting. Maybe next time we can watch something more . . . colourful?'

'What's next on the list?' Dina asked one evening. Mohammed was working nights, so she'd asked me if I wanted to come over and stay for a couple of days. I happily agreed; cuddles with Sami were long overdue. As soon as I got in, I persuaded Dina to take some time out for herself while I watched him and she gratefully accepted. While she went for a pregnancy massage and then came home to sort out her hospital bag, I fed Sami his dinner, bathed him and got him ready for bed. I did all this without flooding the house or getting his dinner all over the kitchen floor. It felt good to be helpful. Maybe I wasn't entirely useless at all things domestic.

'I haven't checked yet,' I said as I finished off the lamb and barley soup Dina had made. We had it with crusty bread and it was gorgeous, like I knew it would be and perfect for the chilly night. 'Let's have a look.'

Retrieving the notebook from my bag, I opened it to the page I had bookmarked and turned it over to see what number fourteen had in store.

'Oh for God's sake,' I muttered, my stomach instantly churning. 'I have to eat escargot.'

'Oh no,' Dina covered her mouth in horror. 'Are they halal?'

'I don't know, but I'm not going to research it. Ignorance is bliss and all that.'

Dina made a face at me and I shrugged. I didn't see why they wouldn't be. They were practically the same as prawns. You couldn't slaughter them with a prayer, like you did with chickens and sheep.

'Do you have to do everything on the list?' Dina asked as we took our bowls to the kitchen and cleared up. 'It's not sacred, Maya. You can miss things if you want.'

'I can't,' I replied, panicking at the thought. 'The whole point is to do everything on it. Otherwise, it's meaningless. It won't have the same effect.'

'But you're not doing everything. You're not doing a triathlon.'

'I know, but I'm doing something that's in the realm of possibility. Like I didn't sign up for a physio course either, I'm doing what's relevant to me.'

'And eating snails that are possibly haram is relevant to you how?'

She had a point there.

'Look, all I'm saying is, this list is great and all and it's wonderful how it's getting you to try new things and become a more confident person, but it's not your purpose in life. We're Muslim. Our purpose is to be the best people we can be, under the guidance of God. Why don't you change it to eating something equally as gross as snails, like lamb balls or lamb brains or something?'

I made a face and she grinned triumphantly. 'See? The thought sickens you, right? Do that instead, if you insist on doing it at all.'

'Fine,' I grumbled. 'But you're doing it with me.'

'Deal. I'll cook them, the Palestinian way.'

The next day, true to her word, I came back to Dina's from work to find that she had indeed cooked something she called nkhe'et and baid ghanam for our dinner, which we would apparently eat with hot Arabic bread, salad and wedges of lemon.

The thought made my stomach turn, but I consoled myself with the fact that it wasn't snails and it was halal. And since the entire Levant region enjoyed these delicacies, how bad could it be?

'I can't do this,' I squeaked when we sat down to eat at the dining table, eyeing the bowl of beige lamb brains, patterned and squiggly. A shiver ran down the length of my spine and all the hairs on my body – and I had a LOT of hair on my body – stood on end. The testicles didn't look as bad, they were fried in ghee and could have been any part of the body. I ate liver and heart when my mum cooked it, the Bengali way, heavy with spices. But this . . . there were no spices in sight. The brains looked just like . . . brains.

I swallowed down the bile that rose up my oesophagus and took a sip of water. 'You go first,' I told Dina, my voice strangled. 'How are you not feeling sick right now? You're the pregnant one!'

'I like it,' Dina laughed. Grabbing one of the flatbreads, she tore off a piece and scooped up some of the brains, squeezing lemon juice over them and then popping them into her mouth. 'Mmm, so good,' she murmured. 'Not as good as Mama's, but almost.' I blanched.

'When is your mum getting here?' I asked, delaying the inevitable.

'Next week, Insha'allah,' she replied, taking another bite. 'Don't change the topic and hurry up and try some,' she added.

Inhaling as deeply as possible, I recited a prayer, whispered 'Bismillah', and did the same as Dina. *Mind over matter! Mind over matter!* I chanted to myself over and over, as I chewed and swallowed it, gulping water to wash it down.

'Well? What do you think?'

'It's not my thing,' I admitted. The texture was horrible; pasty and mushy. If it wasn't for the bread giving me something to chew, it would have all come right back up.

'Have a piece of baid ghanam next,' Dina instructed. She did the same thing with the bread and lemon and I followed suit. This wasn't too bad. At least it was chewy and had flavour. It was like heart, but more tender.

And then I remembered that it was lamb testicles and once again, I fought the urge to retch.

'OK, I'm done. Sorry, Dina, I can't bring myself to eat anymore.'

Dina laughed and helped herself to a plateful. 'It's OK, I didn't think you would. Go check the microwave, there's something else there for you to have for dinner.'

'What? You serious?'

'I wasn't going to let you starve, was I?'

In the microwave, I found a plate of chicken pesto pasta and I had never felt so relieved to find something so ordinary and inoffensive.

'Thank you so much,' I almost wept in relief when I returned to the dining room, avoiding the lamb's bits that were at the centre of the table.

'Now you can tick off that ridiculous item on that crazy list of yours.'

When I got home that evening, still feeling a bit queasy whenever I thought of the grey mush I had allowed into my mouth, I decided to distract myself by online-stalking Zak. It had become a bit of a habit for me.

Staring at his Instagram page, I wondered for the thousandth time why he hadn't been in touch properly since Snowdon, aside from the occasional meme. Had I done or said something on that trip that had made him write me off, even as a friend? Or maybe I was looking into it too deeply and he was merely busy. He hadn't posted anything on his page since then either. Analysing the feed that I had already memorised was proving to be utterly futile.

When I finally came to terms with the fact that stalking Zak wasn't going to make him magically contact me, I decided to reach out to him myself. Before I lost the nerve, I quickly typed out the first interesting thing I thought of. I hit send and it was only after the message was released into the ether, once it was too late to backtrack, that I thought to proofread.

And when I glanced over what I had written . . . SHIT. I stared at the two little blue ticks that meant it could no longer be unsent:

MAYA: Did another item on the list and had to eat lamb balls.

I had written BALLS instead of BRAINS. For God's sake!

I was contemplating throwing my phone behind my headboard so I wouldn't be able to look at it again until I somehow managed to retrieve it when I saw that he was typing a reply.

My breath trapped in my lungs, I waited.

Zakariya is typing . . .

Then the typing stopped and there was no response.

When Ramadan came along, I decided to take a break from the list and thinking about Zakariya and connect with God instead.

I spent the four weeks being as Islamic as I possibly could: waking up for dawn prayers, attending the nightly Tarawih prayers at Wightman Road Mosque, abstaining not only from eating and drinking, but lying, swearing, backbiting and gossiping. Arabic classes were paused during the Holy Month as they clashed with iftar time and I barely heard from Zakariya the whole time, apart from one of those generic 'Ramadan Kareem' WhatsApps I got on the first day.

Despite there being no classes, I still practised my Arabic whenever I could. I watched TikToks and listened to audio classes. I wanted Ustadha Salma to be proud of me when we returned.

Ramadan wasn't all fasting, praying and reading the Qur'an, though. We also saw more relatives than we had seen the entire year. My aunts, uncles and other friends and relatives hosted elaborate iftar parties and we returned the favour. It all became a bit too much because every Bengali cooked the same thing for iftar. By the end of the month, I wanted to hurl the plates of pakoras and samosas across the room. But that wasn't the reason why I refused to attend the last few iftar parties. I was sick of everyone asking me why I was still single.

'I can't take it anymore,' I complained to the twins. It was an hour after we had finished eating and the three of us collapsed onto Pinky's bed after the mammoth clean-up session which, as usual, the men didn't bother participating in.

'Me neither,' Pretty moaned. 'I can't stand the sight of pulao and Deshi roast chicken, anymore. All I want for iftar is something plain and simple, like a chicken and mushroom pie or a roast dinner.'

'I would kill for a roast dinner,' Pinky agreed, unwrapping her hijab and pulling her fuchsia hair out of its bun. 'But stop talking about food! I feel so sick, I've eaten way too much.'

'That's not the only thing I can't take,' I groaned, rubbing my swollen belly. 'I can't take people asking me about when I'm going to get married. It's driving me insane!'

'To be fair, you've always been a sandwich short of a picnic, Maya,' Pretty giggled.

'Why are all our idioms so anglicised?' Pinky mused. 'When have any of us ever taken a sandwich to a picnic?'

'If you mention the word "samosa" or "pakora", I will literally kill you,' Pretty threatened.

'Guys! Stay on topic,' I implored. 'How do you cope with all the comments about your marital status?'

Pretty looked uncomfortable. 'We don't get it as much as you,' she admitted reluctantly. 'You being on the shelf longer than us and all that.'

'In fact, when you're around, it eases the pressure on us,' Pinky added.

'Thanks a bunch,' I said, half-heartedly throwing a cushion at Pretty.

'We aim to please,' both twins said in unison, proceeding to cackle at how funny they thought they were. With a sigh, I picked up my now-lukewarm cup of tea and vowed to stay at home and pray for the rest of Ramadan.

The first weekend after Eid-ul-Fitr, Lucy and I arranged to try doing the pond swim again. Well, to be more accurate, Lucy arranged it and virtually bullied me into agreeing. I could hardly say no after she had booked tickets in advance and when it was my list and my life-changing journey she was trying to help me with.

'You sure you're OK with doing this?' I asked her, as we stood shivering in our full-length swimming gear by the edge of the pond, staring at the green water in apprehension. It was bigger than I expected, so Lucy and I decided to swim just one lap and had left our towels on the other side of the pond. Spring had arrived, but despite what the deceptive, cornflower-blue sky and daffodils suggested, it was still cold when it was windy. I was petrified of jumping into the ice-cold water that awaited below, more so than when I had had to eat lambs' testicles and brains. This was going to be, by far, the hardest challenge yet.

'Of course,' Lucy replied. 'I was going to do it before, wasn't I?'

'Yeah, but that was before you had a go at me for making you do stuff on the list with me,' I replied.

'Oh, yeah. Sorry about that.'

'What was going on with you, Luce? There's no way that was just hanger.'

'Nah, it wasn't.'

I waited for her to tell me more despite it being an inappropriate time and setting for such a deep conversation. Eventually, she sighed. 'Some stuff has been going on with a guy I'm seeing on and off,' she replied. 'I don't really want to go into it, but I'm sorry for taking it out on you.'

'It's OK,' I replied, reaching over and giving her arm a squeeze. 'I'm sorry for making you do this stuff with me. It's not your list or your commitment; it was wrong of me to drag you along on this journey.'

'Hey,' Lucy interrupted. 'No one can make me do anything, OK? I've been doing this with you because I want to support you. If there's something I really don't want to do, I'll tell you.'

'Promise?'

'Promise. Now shall we do this or not?'

'Count of three?'

Turning to face the water, we counted down, still holding hands. On 'three', I took a deep breath, squeezed my eyes shut and jumped in.

The feeling was like nothing I had experienced before. The cold didn't engulf me – it beat the crap out of me. It was like being electrocuted. Every inch of my skin was shocked senseless.

Gasping as I came up for air, I found Lucy, who looked equally as stunned as I did. A moment later, adrenaline kicked in and once we became acclimatised to the water, I felt more alive than I had done in a long time.

'Shall we d-do the l-lap?' Lucy managed to say, her mouth frozen. I nodded, because talking would be too difficult and swam after her, my limbs slicing through the water like a knife through butter. Lucy was clearly a more competent swimmer than me in terms of form, but while my style was basic and I looked like a dog paddling in a pond, I was quite strong and had a lot of stamina, thanks to all the running I had been doing for the past seven months. Halfway through the never-ending swim, I almost began to feel warm, as every part of my body united with the rest, working in unison to move through the water.

We swam silently and I focused my mind on the task rather than letting it cloud up with worrying thoughts like it usually did. *Would I ever see Noah again? Did Zakariya hate me? Why was he ignoring me? Was he really going to move to Dubai? Why hadn't I received a university offer yet? What if I failed the course? What if I lost my job because I was too busy studying?* I pushed it all aside and swam until there was nothing there but the water and me.

'OK, I'm done,' Lucy panted when we finally reached the other side, reminding me that it was the water, me AND her. I nodded, too exhausted to speak. I had somehow pushed my muscles through the burn and felt like I was going to collapse – and possibly drown.

Dragging myself out of the pond, I welcomed the towels that were waiting for us and dried off as fast as I could, my entire body shaking uncontrollably from the cold, as I part shuffled, part ran towards the changing rooms before I turned into an ice cube. I don't know how I peeled my wetsuit off with my numb fingers. It felt like it took forever, but I finally managed to shower and change into the woolly onesie I had brought to wear. The cold shower was nothing compared to swimming in the pond.

When I got back to Lucy, she was sitting on a bench drinking tea from a Thermos and eating banana cake. I joined her and took out my own flask, taking a long swig before gratefully accepting a piece of cake. We sat there in silence, the hot tea warming us up from the inside and gently defrosting us. The tip of Lucy's nose was bright red and her usually shiny, blonde locks were a frizzy mess, sticking out of her head like a lion's mane. Mine was no doubt worse, but I didn't care. I had just swum outdoors for the first time like a complete BOSS. If I could do that *and* eat questionable parts of an animal without throwing up, I could do *anything*.

Lucy grinned at me as though reading my thoughts and I smiled back. We didn't need to talk; we both knew exactly how the other was feeling. And it was pretty bloody amazing.

Chapter Twenty-Four

Despite the invigorating weekend I'd had, when Monday came along, I awoke with a sense of dread – a feeling that was becoming all too familiar. Prior to Sheila joining the firm as partner, I didn't *love* my job, but I didn't hate it either. But now, every morning I would awake to knots of anxiety in the pit of my stomach, wondering if I should call in sick.

With a yawn, I checked the notifications on my phone, the breath dying on my lips the instant I saw that I had an email from one of the universities I had applied to. Bracing myself for rejection – because anything other than soul-crushing disappointment was too alien to comprehend – I opened it, my eyes scanning the text for 'rejection'.

It wasn't a rejection.

It was an acceptance.

I stared at the words on the screen, my eyes filling with tears. I was going back to university to do my LLM, it was being paid for in full and my life was finally going somewhere beyond thirty items on a list made by a man I didn't know.

Energised, I pushed the covers off my body, got out of the warmth of my bed and rushed to the shower. If I hurried, I would still make it in time.

I was struck by an overwhelming sense of déjà vu when I half-walked, half-ran to the Tube station and threw myself onto the Piccadilly Line train that was already at the platform, just as the warning beeps began to ring, indicating the imminent closing of the doors. You don't want to be partially inside the carriage when those doors close, trust me. I've been there and it's pretty painful, not to mention embarrassing.

As I rummaged around in my makeup bag, I thought back to the morning I met Noah and how my life had changed for the better since. I knew it wasn't because of him per se, it was because of the list and my own perseverance and determination, but he did deserve a little credit. If I hadn't met him that day, I would still be the same Maya I was more than seven months ago; a shadow, going through the motions of life without actually living.

Carefully brushing on some powder and blusher, I looked around the carriage, half expecting to see him. I didn't, of course. As always, the train was packed with commuters who wanted nothing more than to avoid eye contact with me and everyone else. I wished God would throw Noah in my path again, instead of constantly planting Zakariya on it. I knew that I didn't really know Noah, but I felt like I did. We had connected instantly during our short conversation and I felt as though I had got to know him more because of the list. I knew that he was driven and ambitious, adventurous and open-minded. I knew that he had goals and dreams and he was determined to achieve them. I knew that he appreciated literature, films, art and history. He was the full package as far as I could tell: good looks, great charisma, intelligence. What wasn't there to like about him?

Then there was Zakariya, who had all but told me he wasn't interested in me and had only met me to keep his parents quiet. Zakariya, who judged me the moment we met and made me – a girl he didn't know – feel guilty for being at an art class I had accidentally attended. Zakariya, who showed up at my house and made me more uncomfortable. And then proceeded to help me out: driving me home, recommending the Arabic class, buying me dinner, taking me to Snowdon. Ignoring me for weeks after. Preferring DC to Marvel.

The sad reality was that neither man was into me, I realised as I sat on the train. If Noah had been, he would have asked for my number before he ran off the train that day. If Zakariya was, he had plenty of opportunity to give me an inkling. The fact was, I was wasting my time, energy and brain space thinking about them. Right now, I could have been listening to a podcast or reading a book, or working harder at evening out my eyebrows. I could have been engaging in a riveting conversation with the man across the carriage with the unkempt beard, vacant look in his eyes and a vague scent of beer wafting from his direction. OK, maybe not. But my point was, I was wasting my time. It needed to stop. Neither deserved my attention and thoughts, *especially not Zakariya*. I needed to focus on myself, my career, my education and my list.

Emerging at Hammersmith, I took out my phone to tap through the gates and for the second time that day, I received news that both winded me and filled me with joy at the same time. It was from Mohammed: Dina was finally in labour, two weeks after her due date!

Without wasting another moment, I sent HR an email, turned back around and headed to the hospital, texting Mohammed that I was on my way.

'Maya, salaam'alaykom!' Dina's mum, Aunty Noura, greeted me when I finally made it to North Middlesex over an hour later.

'Salaam, Aunty,' I replied, giving her a brief hug, relieved that she had arrived in time for the birth of her second grandchild, but also worried. Her and Dina's relationship had always been strained and I hoped and prayed that her presence proved to be helpful, not stressful.

'My poor daughter has been in there for hours and no one's telling me what's going on,' she said loudly for the benefit of the labour ward receptionist. 'I'm so worried. Ya Allah, protect my daughter! Ya Rab, deliver this baby safely! My Lord, listen to my prayers!'

I gulped. I had forgotten what Aunty Noura was like. But then I heard the most deafening, wretched wail coming from one of the closed doors. It sounded like Dina. Stricken, I turned to stare at Aunty Noura, who also began to moan.

'Ya Allah! Ya Rab! My poor baby! Have mercy, Ya Arhamar Raahimeen!'

As Dina's mum proceeded to call all her relatives and speak to them in loud, fast Arabic above the sounds of the screaming and moaning from the labour rooms, I snuck over to one of the midwives.

'Is everything OK with my friend?' I asked her quietly. 'Dina Al Farawi? Are there any updates?'

'Nothing to worry about,' the midwife reassured me. 'She's doing great, there are no complications. It just took a while for her to dilate to the full ten centimetres, that's why she's been in there a while.'

'But all the screaming . . . it's really worrying,' I managed to say, feeling faint as another long, primal moan pierced my ears.

'All very normal. Your friend is incredibly brave, she didn't want an epidural and is surviving on gas and air only. Don't worry and be strong, OK?'

'Shu? What did she say?' Aunty Noura all but yelled at me as I approached her and I repeated what the midwife had told me.

'Huh!' she scoffed, folding her arms across her ample bosom. 'These midwives have no clue. Babies should be delivered by *doctors*. Australia is much better than this God-awful country with its God-awful NHS!'

'Don't they have midwives in Australia, Aunty?' I asked innocently.

'Oh, be quiet, child, I can't hear myself think!'

Three hours later, baby Sama entered the world at nine pounds and two ounces. She was beautiful like her mummy, with a head full of dark curls and the chubbiest, rosiest cheeks. Dina looked exhausted, but happy. She had to have a bunch of stitches after the delivery and I couldn't fathom how she was managing to smile after all that.

'Dina, you're bloody amazing,' I whispered as I stroked her damp, sweaty hair while the baby lay naked on her chest.

'I'm not,' she replied, barely able to speak. 'It's the baby who's amazing. Isn't she beautiful?'

After some cuddles and a cup of tea, I took my leave so she could rest and enjoy this time with her family. As I turned to go, I caught Dina staring in awe at her baby, like she was the most precious thing in the world, and a lump formed in my throat. I didn't know why; I was truly thrilled for her. I guess I just hoped that one day, I would experience the same.

Later that night, after texting back and forth with Dina and making sure she was OK and didn't need anything, I took out the notebook and flicked through the now worn pages and found number fifteen:

15. GO SKYDIVING ✓

AMAZING! BEST THING EVER!

It wasn't the best thing ever. Holding a newborn baby that had grown inside of you was truly amazing, not jumping out of a stupid plane.

But I didn't have a baby. Or even someone to make a baby with. And if there was one thing in this world that petrified me more than snakes, tarantulas and walking through Edmonton at night, it was the mere idea of throwing myself out of an aeroplane. Life in London was dangerous enough as it was. Every time I left my house, I was at risk of getting stabbed, raped or at the very least, mugged. I didn't need to participate in thrill-seeking activities for a buzz.

But I had to do it. This was number fifteen, exactly half-way through the list. I had come so far. My comfort zone had been shed so long ago that I no longer knew where it was. I had grown with every task I had completed and I didn't regret a single one, not even *Ulysses*. I HAD to do it, whether anyone wanted to do it with me or not.

But maybe there *was* someone – well, two people – who were crazy enough to join me:

MAYA: Who wants to go skydiving with me?

I posted into the group chat I shared with my twin cousins. Pinky's response came instantly:

PINKY: Hell yes, I'm there. When and where?

Pretty's took a while longer and when it came, I felt a massive grin spread across my face:

PRETTY: Only if it's in Dubai.

Three weeks later, I was on a plane with the twins, on our way to an extra-long weekend in Dubai. I would have liked to have gone for longer, but Sheila wouldn't let me take more than three days off because of the 'short notice'. No one else had booked leave and Lucy was fine with me handing over my urgent tasks to her, but she still refused on 'principle'. God, I hated her more and more each day.

Persuading Sheila to give me the time off was almost as hard as persuading my parents to let me go. I didn't understand why they were so strict about me going abroad. Everyone I knew travelled! Although to be fair, Dina used to lie to her parents and pretend she was going on work trips all the time. She was quite possibly the only teacher who had travelled to thirteen countries in two years for 'work events'.

It was my chacha and chachi – the twins' parents – who stepped in and had a word with Ma and Baba. I overheard Chachi saying things like, 'Restricting kids too much will only lead to resentment and rebellion'. Ha. I was hardly a rebel, but if I had to act the part to get to see the world, I would.

In that time, between visiting Dina and her newborn, running and work, I had done two more items on the list. Number sixteen was 'Take Mum to a West End musical – *Mamma Mia? Grease? Back to the Future? Wicked?*' Underneath, as always, he had written his own little comment on how it went. This time, it was: '*Wicked* was simply wicked!' It was cute that he wanted to treat his mum to a show and I was more than happy to do the same for mine. Since she had persuaded my dad to let me travel, I was also feeling particularly benevolent towards her.

Ma wanted to see *Grease*, her all-time favourite non-Bollywood movie. If there was one celeb she loved more than Princess Diana, it was Olivia Newton-John and so we made a night of it with a fancy Indian meal on Shaftesbury Avenue afterwards. Our throats were sore from singing along to all the songs at the top of our off-key voices, but it was worth it. I hadn't seen Ma let go like that in a long time and I decided to do things with her more often.

On that note, I forced her to enjoy number seventeen with me, which was watching *The Lord of the Rings* trilogy. I was ashamed to admit that I hadn't seen any of the movies. I always pretended to know what people were on about whenever they mentioned hobbits or the Shire. Once, when Arjun had come back from the Peak District, he said something about it feeling like 'the Shire' and I had responded, 'Which shire is Peak District in then? Is it Yorkshire?' In my world, anything beyond the M25 was the stuff of legends and fairy tales.

Ma quite enjoyed the first movie, although almost jumping out of her skin at some parts. By the time we got to the second though, she was fast asleep and snoring on the couch. When it was time to watch the final film, she politely declined.

'Maybe next time we can watch the latest Karan Johar instead?'

'If you had to compile a list of thirty things to do before you turn thirty, what would you put on it?' I posed the question to the twins once we were safely in the sky and the cabin crew were going around with drinks. The three of us had adjacent seats on the left side of the plane, with me on the aisle and Pinky in the middle.

'There's so much I want to do,' Pinky mused. 'I want to travel more. I'd love to write something, like a novel or a collection of short stories. Maybe learn a new skill like knitting or sewing.'

'Sewing would be cool,' I said. 'I'd love to be able to make my own clothes. Not that I have an eye for fashion. And I'm clumsy with my hands.'

'You'd probably poke your own eye out with a needle,' Pinky agreed. 'Remember that time you cut your finger with scissors when your mum used to make us do craft sessions in the holidays?'

214

Pretty laughed at that. 'Your hands would become a pin cushion. You'd bleed all over the fabric.'

'All right, all right,' I interrupted. Maybe not sewing then. 'What about you, Pretty? What would you do?' I peered around Pinky to look at Pretty, who was staring out of the window. At what, I didn't know, as it was nighttime and we were too high up to see anything but darkness out there. I waited for her to say something crazy, like bungee jumping or going to Coachella.

'I'm hoping I'm married before I turn thirty,' she admitted quietly, still looking out of the window.

'Woah, that's deep,' I said, downing my apple juice in three gulps. 'I don't think I could put a timeline on something like that. It'll happen when it happens.'

'*If* it happens,' Pinky agreed. 'It's not destined for everyone, you know. And who needs a man anyway?'

'Thanks for giving me hope,' Pretty muttered. 'I knew you wouldn't understand. What's so wrong about wanting to get married? You want to get married too! If you didn't, you wouldn't be attending all these dekha dekhis!'

'I don't mind getting married, but it's not a goal! It's a "nice to have". That's different,' Pinky rationalised calmly.

'How is it different?'

The sisters began to bicker and I tuned them out and put on my headset instead. We had six hours of this flight left and four days together. I didn't want to ruin it by arguing or getting too deep, so I left them to it and settled down with a film instead.

Our skydive was booked for Sunday, our last day. This was intentional in case we became so traumatised by the experience that we weren't able to enjoy the rest of the trip. Given that none of us were rich, we were in a hotel apartment that was clean, modern and spacious, but not overly glam or luxurious like most of the city.

On Friday we went to the Sheikh Zayed Mosque in Abu Dhabi for Jumuah prayers, which was a magical experience. Pretty and I had to wear hijabs and abayas and I enjoyed it more than I thought I would. Maybe it was because we were in the mosque, or because we were in a Muslim country, but I felt good wearing it and blending in with the other women who wore it. I felt like I was a part of a global family and community. A woman I didn't know walked past me and gave her Salaam to me, which never happened to me as I wasn't a visible Muslim most of the time. That moment of solidarity reminded me that I was part of something bigger than myself and my family.

The mosque was huge and looked like something out of *1001 Arabian Nights*, with its brilliant white domes and pillars made from marble. After the congregational salah was over, I sat in the women's prayer hall for some time while my cousins explored and took pictures. It was so peaceful and serene. Pressing my head to the floor in prostration, I prayed for God to grant me peace in this life and the next and guide me towards what was best for me, whatever or whoever it was. I also prayed for the courage to get through the skydive on Sunday without getting hurt or humiliated. I was trying my best to block it from my mind, because whenever I thought about it, I could feel acid churning in my stomach. It wasn't the jump itself that made me want to go back to London, it was how my body was going to react to the shock of it. What if I threw up in the sky and bits of my vomit landed on everyone else? What if I weed myself and it soaked through my jumpsuit and onto the instructor? Or worse . . . what if my bowels decided to release themselves mid-jump? There was a plethora of things that could go wrong, anatomically, each one leaving me completely disgraced forever.

Ya Allah, I beg you, please have mercy on me and let me find the courage to jump and please get me through it with my dignity intact, I beseeched, my forehead pressed so firmly on the ground that I could feel it getting carpet burn. *I promise I'll be a better Muslim if you do! I'll help Ma more around the house and I'll pray more regularly and I'll do ten extra fasts and I'll give a hundred pounds to a charity for . . .* My mind went blank. There were so many valid and important causes. Palestine. Syria. Sudan. The Congo. Droughts. Floods. Famine. Clean water. Healthcare. Refugees . . .

. . . *Orphans,* I decided. Looking after orphan children was considered one of the most noble charitable acts. The Prophet Muhammad, peace be on him, was an orphan and looking after orphan children was mentioned a lot in the Holy Qur'an.

We went back to Dubai after visiting the mosque and then spent the evening on a desert safari, which was a lot of fun. After a thrilling (and sometimes scary) bout of dune bashing followed by camel riding and sand boarding, we were taken to a camp where we enjoyed a barbecue dinner, had our henna done and chilled with a pipe of shisha for the twins. Later that night, there was a belly-dancing show. We all clapped along to the music, maybe a bit too enthusiastically because suddenly the vigorous dancer was standing right next to me, flinging her red hair this way and that, bumping my shoulders with her hips and using her body to tell me that I should join her.

No flipping way. My face scarlet, I shook my head vehemently. She took this as a sign that I was interested and proceeded to grab my hand and hoist me to my feet, wiggling her ample bosom in my face and grinning almost maniacally. I began to feel sorry for her at this point. Her job wasn't easy – trying to coax unwilling participants into dancing with her was probably the least of her problems. She probably had to fend off the ones who were a bit too willing, all the while acting like she was having the time of her life when all she wanted to do was curl up in bed with a good romcom and a tube of Pringles. She probably hated being ogled day in, day out, forced into jiggling her belly while onlookers analysed every inch of her flesh.

The story I had conjured felt so realistically woeful that I decided to give in to make her happy. Plastering a fake, toothy smile on my face, I wiggled my hips back at her and shook my hair out in what I hoped was the same sexy way she did. Her expression changed as I joined in and copied her moves to the rhythmic drumming. It was quite fun, letting go like that. I had never danced in front of anyone before. I was always the girl at the mehndi party who clapped along quietly in the corner, trying not to draw too much unwanted attention to herself. Forget being a wallflower, I was more like wall-paper. Completely unnoticeable.

But no one here knew me, besides the twins, who were hooting and cheering me along. I was on the other side of the world. There were no aunties insulting my complexion. No grannies asking me why no one wanted to marry me. No uncles comparing Malik's successful career to mine. It was just me and the music, dancing in the middle of the Dubai desert under a diamond-studded sky.

Chapter Twenty-Five

On Sunday morning, the three of us sat waiting in the cool, air-conditioned marble lobby of our apartment block, waiting for the taxi that was going to take us to the Skydive of Doom. Browsing through my camera roll, I looked for the best pictures from the previous couple of days to post to Instagram. We'd had a chilled Saturday, starting off with a morning at an exclusive ladies-only beach, followed by spa treatments and then shopping and shisha. As I scrolled, I could hear familiar music playing from Pretty's phone and the two of them cackling away.

'I can't believe you posted it!' Pinky chastised her sister while Pretty continued to chuckle.

'I had to; it was gold!'

'What are you guys laughing about?' I asked suspiciously, still trying to place the music. I knew it from somewhere, but I couldn't remember where.

'Check Pretty's Snapchat,' Pinky managed between giggles. I obliged and absentmindedly went through the pictures and videos she had been posting, albeit never in real-time like you were supposed to on Snapchat. There was Pretty and I at the beach – only our heads, of course. The best thing about going to a ladies-only beach was being able to wear whatever we wanted without having to worry about modesty. For Pinky this was particularly special, as she was able to feel the sea breeze on her pink hair. I tapped through the rest: sea views, our meal, Pretty seductively blowing a plume of smoke from the shisha pipe. There were pictures from Friday as well: the majestic mosque, a video of the three of us squealing and screaming as the 4x4 flew over burnt orange sand dunes, Pretty getting her henna done.

I tapped again to change to the next video. I heard the music first – the pulsating, expert drumming from the desert camp – and then the blurry video slowly came into focus. And there I was, in all my sweaty-faced, wild-haired glory, dancing with the belly dancer. Calling it 'dancing' was being extremely generous. The blood drained from my face as I watched myself wiggle and shake out of time to the music, my forehead creased in concentration, my arms flailing like a drowning octopus, my boobs bouncing along with the rest of me and my hair swinging around my head like a jinn's. It was like watching a car crash.

That night, I had found myself truly letting go for the first time in my *life*. I felt powerful, sexy almost. I thought I looked like Shakira.

I looked nothing like Shakira. I didn't even look like her aunt twice removed. I looked like the ghost of Shakira's sunburnt doppelgänger, who had died and now haunted the desert.

Swallowing away the lump that had formed in my throat, I turned to Pretty, who had the decency to look guilty. 'I can't believe you posted this,' I managed to say, my throat so tight that getting the words out was an ordeal. 'How could you?'

'It was just for laughs,' Pretty replied lamely. 'It's not that deep. I can delete it if you want. Hardly anyone has seen it anyway.'

'Thanks,' I said flatly, looking away. Not that deep? That girl didn't post pictures of herself on Snapchat until she had edited them to perfection, but it was fine to post a video of me looking like a maniac?

'Ahmad's here,' Pinky announced, jumping up.

'Who the hell is Ahmad?' Pretty asked, clearly grateful for the change of subject and pace.

'The taxi driver. Come on, let's go. We have an aeroplane to jump out of.'

I didn't have time to process the awful video because the next traumatic event was already looming. Not for the first time, I cursed Noah and his blasted list as I sat waiting on the plane, strapped to my instructor.

We had spent the past few hours being trained and briefed on the procedure. I barely listened to a word they said, I was so furious about the video. This trip was supposed to be epic. It was the first time I had gone on holiday with the girls and I was going above and beyond what was required from me to complete the list. I was beginning to make my own list, forge my own path. And now it was tainted.

Pinky sat next to me and Pretty was across from us. Both had their eyes squeezed closed and their fists scrunched up so tight that their knuckles had turned white from the pressure. Above the sound of the plane, I thought I could hear Pinky muttering prayers. Feeling faint from nerves, I closed my eyes and did the same, reciting every dua that came to mind. Ayatul kursi for protection, the travelling dua, the one the Prophet Yunus – or Jonah, as he was known in the Bible – recited when he was stuck in the belly of the whale. When I ran out of the relevant ones, I prayed whatever came to mind: the sleeping dua, eating dua, the prayer for rainfall. Everything and anything to calm myself down.

The speed with which life was racing by was insane. One minute I was in London, excited about finally getting my place at uni and holding Dina's baby . . . and the next I was on a bloody plane, strapped onto a burly South African man called François, about to fall to my death.

One by one, the others in our group leapt out of the plane. Then it was Pretty, followed by Pinky and before I knew it, it was my turn. I stood frozen, unable to move closer to the opening.

'I can't do this!' I shouted above the noise of the plane, as François all but dragged me to the opening where we were going to fall from 13,000 feet. My legs began to shake so violently that if he hadn't been strapped to me, I would have collapsed.

'You can, Maya! I'll be with you every second, don't worry!' François shouted back, a massive grin on his face. 'You won't regret this, trust me. No one ever does. But if you don't do it, you *will* regret it.'

The opening was right in front of us now. The wind was fierce, whipping violently around us. I squeezed my eyes closed, my heart lodged in my mouth, pounding louder than the wind. Lenny, the cameraman, gave me a thumbs up and promptly jumped out of the plane. I stifled a scream. *Ya Allah please do not let me die today! Please don't injure me! Please let the parachute open!*

'You've got this, Maya! Let's do it!' François positioned us in front of the opening, lifting me up when my legs refused to cooperate. 'Three . . . Two . . . One . . .'

BISMILLAH.

Then we were out, careening towards the ground at 120 miles per hour.

'OH MY GOOOD!' I screamed as we fell, the wind and the pressure pulling my cheeks away from my face, making my eyes bulge out. A moment later, I felt a tug, then resistance and then the parachute had been activated. It worked! ALHAMDULILLAH, it worked! I wasn't going smash into the ground and shatter every one of my bones. It bloody hurt though – the G-force causing the straps to cut into my thighs.

Once the parachute had been activated, I dared to open my eyes to the sight of the magnificent Palm Island, spread out below, surrounded by turquoise sea. Subhanallah, it was spectacular. We were no longer speeding down towards the ground, but gliding. I soaked it all up in awe, like a sponge in water. It was utterly breathtaking.

It was over all too soon and as we reached the ground, I bent my knees and braced myself for the impact, but it wasn't as bad as I thought it would be. I hit the ground, fell backwards and slid on my bum across the grass until I eventually came to a stop.

My cousins were waiting for me in the lounge and I wobbled my way over to them, my legs shaking from the adrenaline, a massive grin plastered on my face. As soon as they saw me, they began to jump up and down, screaming. I did the same and we hugged each other and continued to shriek, the earlier confrontation forgotten as we united over our shared experience of narrowly missing death.

That evening we went out to celebrate at a fancy restaurant. It was our last night in Dubai and our morning flight meant that we wouldn't be getting any sleep, so we might as well enjoy our last moments.

The three of us went all out with our clothes and makeup. Pretty was in a slinky, black calf-length dress with sky-high stilettos. Pinky was more modest, in a teal-coloured jumpsuit and gold hijab. I wore a red satin maxi-dress and with the help of the twins, applied matching lipstick and fake lashes. It was difficult to walk though, with all the bruises on my thighs from the parachute straps digging into them. It was worth it. I probably wouldn't be able to do it again – the hours before the jump were too stressful – but I was glad I had done it.

At least eight men tried to get our numbers, from Emiratis to a couple of white Brits. There must have been something in the water, I told myself, when the eighth guy, a good-looking Emirati in a pristine long white thobe, placed three business cards on our table as he walked past. Pretty was documenting the entire thing on Snapchat, capturing our giggles and our commentary.

'I can't believe he left three cards,' Pinky laughed, grabbing the shisha pipe and inhaling it like she was breathing in fresh air. 'Talk about not putting all your eggs in one basket.'

'What happens if we all call him?' I mused, stealing the pipe back.

'Ménage arba'ah?' Pretty quipped, using the Arabic for 'four'.

'Gross,' we all said in unison.

I took my phone out to take some pictures and nearly dropped it into my plate of kunafeh when I saw that I had a text from Zakariya. There had been no meaningful communication between us for so long, so I stared at the phone in confusion, unsure how I should feel:

ZAKARIYA: Salaams Maya, how are you? How's it going in Dubai?

I continued to stare at the message, wondering if I should reply. Who did he think he was, texting me out of the blue after ghosting me for weeks? It was unacceptable. I began to type this out and then stopped when common sense prevailed. I deleted the rant and put my phone down. Seconds later, another text came through:

ZAKARIYA: What's happening? You were typing something and then stopped?

What the hell? Was he stalking me? Something in my face must have given away the irritation and confusion I was experiencing because Pinky picked up on it immediately. Pretty was too busy smoking and tracing her fingers over the embossed business card of 'Salah Al Din Al Hashimi – CFO – Al Hashimi Group' to pay attention to me.

'What's wrong? Has something happened?' Pinky asked, worried.

'Err . . .' I stalled, trying to fabricate a believable story quickly enough for her to buy it. The twins didn't know about the dynamics of my relationship with Zakariya and I intended to keep it that way. The last thing I wanted, or needed, was my aunt and uncle finding out that we sometimes hung out. They'd be on the phone to my parents before I could say 'astaghfirullah' – I seek forgiveness from Allah.

I decided to keep my answer as close to the truth as possible. 'It's just some guy. He's texted me out of the blue when I haven't heard from him in weeks.'

'What's wrong with that?'

'Well . . .' I took a sip of my mocktail while I figured out how to phrase it. 'We sort of shared a special moment a long time ago. I thought we did, anyway. But then I never heard from him again . . . until now.'

'What's he saying now then? Has he explained his disappearance?'

'No.'

'Is it a booty call?'

'Pinky!' I spluttered, spilling a bit of my expensive drink in shock. 'He's asking how Dubai's going!'

'How does he know you're here?' Pinky continued, ignoring my reaction to her previous question.

'He's on my socials,' I replied. 'What do I do? Shall I reply? Ask him why he ghosted me? Ignore him?'

'Definitely don't ask him!' Pretty interjected suddenly. I guess she was paying attention after all. 'You don't want to look desperate.'

'I think you should ask him,' Pinky disagreed. 'He needs to know he can't treat you like rubbish and then expect a booty call.'

'Asking her about her holiday over text is hardly a booty call,' Pretty rolled her eyes. 'You're so dramatic, Pinks.'

'Oh and you're not? What about the time that guy asked you for your number and you spent the whole evening looking at wedding lenghas?'

'Piss off, I didn't!'

'You did! I bet while you've been touching up that business card, you've been wondering how much money that Salah guy has and if he'll buy you an Elie Saab dress for your wedding.'

'I haven't!' Pretty protested, her flushed cheeks suggesting otherwise.

'Liar. You've bought half of Van Cleef in your head already!'

As the twins continued to quarrel, I took out my phone and typed an aloof message:

MAYA: How do you know I'm in Dubai anyway?

His response came immediately:

ZAKARIYA: I saw it on Pretty's Snap.

My stomach plummeted faster than when I fell from the plane. WHAT. THE. HELL. DID. HE. SEE. ON. PRETTY'S. SNAP?

MAYA: What did you see exactly?

226

ZAKARIYA: You guys went skydiving? It looked incredible. Was that on your list?

MAYA: It was indeed. And it was pretty amazing. Did you see anything else?

ZAKARIYA: Where?

MAYA: On Pretty's Snap?

ZAKARIYA: Bits and pieces. Are you having a good time?

I was, until I got his message. *What did he see?* Did he see the dancing video? If he did, I would never be able to face him again. A vision of myself throwing my hair and body around like an uncoordinated whirling dervish came to my mind, blinding me for a second:

MAYA: Yep, great thanks.

My answer was cold. I knew it was. But how was I supposed to react when he had been ignoring me for so long? He was lucky I was bothering to reply at all. I looked at the screen and watched as he started to type something and then stopped. I opened up Snapchat to see what the latest incriminating videos my stupid cousin had posted were and almost laughed when I saw a picture of the three business cards on the table with the caption, 'Being propositioned everywhere we go'. Was *that* why Zak's boxers were in a twist?

'Preets,' I interrupted the full-blown argument that was taking place between the sisters as they each went further and further back in time to provide examples of how the other had dramatised a situation.

'Tell Pinky to shut up!' she responded, her face scarlet. 'Or I'm going back to the apartment!'

'Pinks, drop it, will you?' I implored. 'This is our last night, don't ruin it, please!'

'Fine!' Pinky huffed, crossing her arms.

Maybe being one half of a pair of twins wasn't that great after all. When they had both calmed down, I tentatively posed the question that was burning my tongue to Pretty.

'You know you said not many people had seen the video you posted of me dancing?' I began, trying not to sound accusatory in case she threw a piece of hot coal at me.

Pretty gave me an 'Are you serious?' look.

'I'm not trying to start a fight!' I protested. 'But I need to know if anyone I know saw it. I don't want people chatting about us! You know how the gossip mill works!'

'I can't remember,' she shrugged, blatantly lying to my face. 'We did jump out of an aeroplane today to support you, you know. Sorry if my memory's a bit shaky right now.'

I looked at Pinky then, who muttered, 'See? Drama queen!' under her breath.

'OK,' I said slowly. 'Do you know if Zakariya saw it? Or anyone else who knows me?' I quickly added so as not to give the game away.

Pretty's expression turned from one of defiance to one of guilt. She looked away and took a long puff of shisha and I had the answer that I needed.

Chapter Twenty-Six

Sheila was definitely giving me the cold shoulder when I returned to work on Tuesday. Given that iciness was her standard setting, I hadn't thought it was possible for her temperature to drop further. She barely grunted at me when I said hello, she ignored me during the team meeting and she refused the baklawa I had brought back to share. Surely all this wasn't because I had taken three days off?

'Ignore her,' Lucy whispered as I stared at my screen, unable to focus with the weight of anxiety pressing down on me. 'She's annoyed because she flopped her meeting yesterday.'

'Flopped it how?' I asked as I tried to get through my emails.

'Well, you weren't there obviously and instead of asking one of us to set up the room like she should have, she thought she'd do it herself.'

'Literally everything went wrong,' Arjun sniggered, joining in. 'The tech didn't work, she forgot to put out the water bottles, her printouts were faded because the printer had run out of ink, she was late, like *everything*.'

'Shit.' Instead of rejoicing at karma paying Sheila back, I felt worse. No wonder she was screwing at me. She was going to make me pay for this.

Too scared to take a lunch break or even a tea break, I stayed glued to my seat for the entire day, only getting up when my bladder couldn't take it anymore. The only non-work-related thing I dared to do was open Noah's notebook, which made it look like I was still working. Turning over the page, I stared at number eighteen on the list, wondering how the hell a *notebook* knew what I needed. To be honest, it was something that I had considered in the past but never had the courage to do – or the inclination to spend money on.

But if the notebook said I had to do it, then I would. Besides, these days I was throwing around money like I was printing it all off myself at home, so what was another few hundred pounds if it meant I might finally have some peace in my life?

The rest of the afternoon passed quickly and by five, I had gone through all my emails, actioned what was urgent and put into motion what wasn't. The tension in my neck had spread all the way to my temples, destroying my skull as it travelled. I managed to beg some Ibuprofen off Arjun and ploughed on, despite the burning in my eyes and the throbbing in my head. Shortly before I packed up to go, a text came through from Zakariya:

ZAKARIYA: Are you coming to Arabic on Thursday?

That was random. I didn't have the energy to analyse it further, so stuffing my things into my bag, I sent a quick thumbs up and put my coat on:

MAYA: 👍

ZAKARIYA: What are you doing afterwards? Do you want to grab a meal?

Woah. Who knew that all I had to do to catch Zakariya's attention was fly to Dubai with my cousins and then get one of them to post evidence of us getting hit on by men?

'Shall I?' I asked Lucy quietly as we walked out of the office and towards the lift.

'Do it,' she replied distractedly as she typed away on her phone. 'It's not like you guys were together or anything when he ghosted you. It's not like going out with someone for over a year but they refuse to make things "official" and keep avoiding conversations about the future.'

'Are we still talking about me?' I asked as we stepped out into the warm evening towards the station. It was almost June and we finally had weather decent enough to ditch our jackets.

'No,' Lucy sighed, turning to look at me. 'Sorry. Just got a lot going on.'

'Do you want to talk about it?'

'Not really. Anyway. Yes, you should meet Zak and hear what he has to say, but call him out on his behaviour so he knows he can't get away with it.'

The next day, I went for my first-ever therapy session, as per number eighteen on the list. I had found a Muslim female therapist online, who had lots of good reviews despite being relatively new on the scene. She also had a cancellation and was available immediately, so I booked the session before I got cold feet.

Having a Muslim therapist was important to me. I wasn't surprised that it was hard to find one and that those I did find didn't have years and years of experience. Mental health is still such a massive taboo in my culture. In fact, sometimes it's worse than taboo; it's invisible. People think it doesn't exist or that it's a weakness of faith and spirit. I needed someone who understood my cultural context and why I behaved in a certain way.

After telling Lucy and Arjun about my appointment, I found out that Arjun had been having therapy for years. Then Lucy told me that she had also had some counselling when her parents got divorced and she had seen someone else after a friend had passed away. I was surprised by both admissions, but I suppose that was a reflection of my prejudices about what someone who went to therapy looked like.

The therapist was a woman called Fareena and she had a home office in Shepherd's Bush, so after bidding Lucy farewell at the station after work, I caught the bus there. I felt nervous about seeing her, more so because I was going to her home. It felt too personal somehow.

The house was on a quiet, tree-lined street with Georgian townhouses on either side. I walked up the stairs to the shiny black front door and hesitated a moment before I rang the bell, not knowing what to expect. Seconds later, the door opened and Fareena stood on the other side, smiling warmly at me. She was an older lady, probably older than Ma, and wore a plain white hijab over a white blouse and black trousers. She looked sensible and mature and made me feel more at ease when she offered me a cup of tea before leading me through a beautiful hallway with black and white chequered floors, wall panelling and high ceilings.

The office was at the rear of the house and it was light and spacious, decorated in neutral tones. As I expected, there were plants everywhere and a comfortable-looking sofa set. On the herringbone flooring was a silky Persian carpet, in the same brown and beige tones. I felt guilty stepping on it with my shoes on.

'Please, take a seat, Maya,' Fareena said, gesturing to the double sofa. I did as she asked and gratefully accepted the tea from her. I needed something to calm my nerves and it wasn't going to be an alcoholic beverage, so tea would have to do. I took a gulp and instantly scalded my mouth.

'Thanks,' I squeaked, as she sat down opposite me on the beige armchair. I looked around the room, at the plants, the art, the books and ornaments on the bookshelf. It all looked inviting but staged. It wasn't possible to be naturally this neutral, surely?

'How was your day?' she began, looking at me with kind eyes. The rest of her expression was impassive yet interested.

'Not that great,' I replied bluntly. I think she was making small talk, but I jumped straight into Sheila and work and how useless and incompetent I always felt, acutely aware that I was paying for this session and therefore had to make every minute count. With Fareena's gentle questions, I ended up talking about my education and how unsuccessful I felt – especially compared to Malik, who was far more accomplished than me.

'How is your relationship with your brother?' she asked, writing something in her notebook.

'It's normal, I think,' I began. What *was* our relationship like? I said it was 'normal', but I didn't have much to compare it to. Most of the cultural references in my life weren't from my culture. The brothers in the books I read and films I watched weren't Bengali Sylhetis in London. They weren't revered, they weren't put up on a pedestal, they weren't pampered to the point where they didn't know where the cereal bowls were kept.

'What does "normal" look like to you?' she probed.

'I don't know. We get along fine, but I suppose it's everything he represents that I find difficult to navigate.'

'What does he represent?'

'Erm . . . Unfairness. Double standards. The patriarchy. You know I only recently went on my first trip abroad with my female cousins, because all these years my parents haven't let me go. But they let my brother go all the time and he's younger than me. How does that make sense? And that's only the tip of the iceberg.'

Once those floodgates opened, they didn't stop. I started telling her everything. Like how when we were kids, Ma would make me mow the lawn, but when Malik wanted to do it, she told him not to because he might get hurt. It was fine for me to get hurt, it seemed. Or when she would make me stay up late helping her clean when I had coursework due in the next day, while Malik sat around watching TV. His schoolwork and homework always took precedence over mine. He was doing his GCSEs the year I was doing my A-levels and one of Baba's random relatives came over to stay from Bangladesh. I had to give up my bedroom two weeks before my exams and study in the dining room among all the noise and the bustle, while Malik got to hide away in his room and study properly.

And they wondered why he always got better grades than I did.

By the end of the hour, I was an emotional wreck and used a few of the tissues that were on the oak coffee table in front of me. Fareena was a great listener, although I didn't know why that came as a surprise to me. It was her job. She was literally being paid to listen to me go on and on about my childhood. But the difference between her and anyone else I had ever offloaded on – namely Dina or the twins – was that she didn't offer advice or judgement. She listened and asked questions and the questions made me realise things on my own.

I thought I would leave the session lighter, but I didn't. I felt heavier. I didn't know that my relationship with Malik was a cause of stress and anxiety. I thought I was going to waltz in there and lie down on the couch like they did in American movies and talk about Sheila, Zakariya and possibly Dina. I didn't know that there would be so many questions about my family and my childhood. And we had only just started.

Underneath '18. TRY THERAPY!' Noah had added in his now-familiar scrawl, 'Commit to at least six sessions. You're not going to achieve anything with only one!'

He was right. One session had unearthed so much that needed exploring, unpicking and possibly unlearning.

'Same time next week?' Fareena asked as we wrapped up.

'Definitely,' I sniffed, blowing my nose into another tissue. I hoped that once the hard parts were over, I would get to a stage where talking about all the things that weighed me down wouldn't require quite so many tissues.

The following day was Thursday, which meant Arabic class and I wondered if I'd bump into Zakariya. I had completely forgotten to reply to his invitation, what with therapy, Sheila and everything else on my mind. It was only when I was walking down Fieldgate Street, moments away from the building where the class took place, that I remembered. A part of me really hoped I would see him, but the more sensible part of me told me not to entertain the thought. What was the point? He was moving abroad in months. I didn't need a pen pal. To be fair, I didn't need a husband or partner either. Or even another friend.

It was while I was chanting this mantra in my head that I saw him. He was in the hallway outside both our classes, looking at his phone. He looked good, too good, with his work shirt unbuttoned at the collar and slightly messy hair. Something inside me stirred as I ducked into my classroom before he could spot me. As soon as I sat down, I replied to his last message, my mantra forgotten:

MAYA: Hey, sorry for the late reply, been really busy. Let's grab a bite tonight if you're free, I'm starving.

That was chill, right? I wasn't coming across as desperate or even interested. Just hungry and busy. At least, that was the impression I hoped I had given. Putting my phone away, I forced myself not to check if he had replied until after the class was over. This meant that every minute passed agonisingly slowly and I couldn't focus on a single thing the teacher was saying.

'Maya,' Ustadha Salma called out suddenly and I jerked upright in my seat.

'Na'am?' I replied in my almost-existent Arabic.

'Hal ata bil bus, am bil qitaar?' she asked, looking at me expectantly and completely catching me off guard. I stared stupidly at her.

'Ummmm,' I began. 'Uhhh. La?' Assuming it was a yes and no question, I responded with 'no', hoping to end the conversation.

'Which one, Maya?' she said slowly, in English now. 'Hal ata bil *bus*, am bil *qitaar*?' She asked the question again, as if hearing it a second time would somehow make me understand through a magical osmosis of sorts.

'Qitaar,' Nadira whispered to me as the entire class watched the Dunce at the Front. Why did I go and sit in the front row anyway?

'Er, qitaar?'

Giving me a hard look, Ustadha Salma moved on and I exhaled in relief. Hopefully I would be less distracted next week.

When the lesson was finally over, I checked my phone to find a message from Zakariya. With a mixture of dread and anticipation, I opened it:

ZAKARIYA: Tayyabs? Meet you outside after class.

Oh gosh, I hadn't looked at my face in hours. I wasn't ready to see him right now! Grabbing my bag, I rushed to the toilets and touched up my makeup as quickly as possible.

Spraying myself generously with my expensive perfume, I tried not to calculate how much each spritz was costing me. I fluffed up my hair, which had flattened throughout the day and walked out of the bathroom to find Zakariya waiting for me by the main door.

'Hey, Assalaamu Alaikum,' I said as I approached him, trying not to let my nerves show in my voice. He turned and smiled at me before returning the greeting. There was something different about his smile though. It seemed thinner and more guarded than it was the last time we went for dinner, which was months ago by then. What had changed in that time?

'So you've been really busy then?' he asked casually as we walked towards the restaurant, careful not to accidentally bump into each other. Nine weeks earlier, I had fallen asleep on him and now, if my arm touched his by mistake, he jumped away as if he'd been scalded.

'I have,' I confirmed, not sure what else to say, or how much about my life I should reveal. We arrived at the restaurant before I could add anything else to my dry response and while the waiter showed us to an available table, I tried to gather my thoughts. If I didn't snap out of whatever funk I was in, the next few hours were going to be excruciating.

Zakariya and I sat down opposite each other and flicked through the menu. I had been there enough times to know I wanted the lamb chops, daal and naan. Zakariya agreed with my choices and added a meat curry, samosas and chicken biryani to our order, together with mango lassi. If only we could just as easily order the awkwardness away.

'How was Dubai?' he asked when the waiter left. I remembered then that he had seen that God-awful video of me dancing like a lunatic in the desert and I wanted to curl up into child's pose and disappear. How could I have forgotten that crucial fact? How did I have the gall to face him after what he had seen? Well, it was too late to back out now. I had to own it or I'd look more ridiculous.

'It was fantastic,' I said with faux cheeriness. 'We did so many new things and had such a laugh. You should have come!'

'Uh, with you?'

I realised then what I had said. It was a standard response to someone who had missed out on a good time, I didn't literally mean that he should have come with us.

'No! Not with me!' I retracted. 'I meant that you should try skydiving, it's exhilarating.'

'The desert safari looked fun as well,' Zakariya said with a mischievous smile and my face instantly burned, much to my chagrin. The samosas and poppadum arrived, with a selection of chutneys and I took a bite of my flaky samosa to buy myself some time and figure out how to respond. I chewed the bite so long that it turned into soup in my mouth, while Zakariya – the little git – waited patiently for me to respond to his blatant dig at my Zumba routine gone wrong.

'It was the most fun I've had in forever,' I said at last, when I couldn't chew any longer and whatever I had swallowed was now threatening to rise back up my throat. 'We did this dance challenge thing, where we had to impersonate other . . . uh . . . creatures when we moved.'

'What? What do you mean?' Zakariya was about to take another bite of his samosa when I said this, but the surprise made him stop and stare at me instead. 'Other *creatures*, did you say?'

'Yeah,' I reiterated, avoiding his eyes. 'Pretty, for example, did a snake dance.'

'A what?'

'A snake dance. You know, when you slide along the sand and roll around and suddenly hiss at someone?'

Zakariya looked taken aback. 'No, I can't say I've seen something like that before. Pretty didn't post it on her Snapchat.'

AH HA! So, he *had* seen the video on her Snap. I knew it!

'Of course she didn't,' I said smoothly. 'She only posts the most curated moments of her life. It's not real.'

'It isn't?'

'Nope. As for Pinky, she decided to dance like a . . .' I wracked my brains. What could possibly look worse than my dance? 'Turkey.'

'Turkey? Like the Christmas bird?'

'Like the Christmas bird, not the country. It was so funny, she kept making gobbling noises and jerking her neck forward and backwards.'

Zakariya smiled then, shaking his head, almost as if he had resigned himself to all this madness. 'You girls are crazy. What was your dance? No, don't tell me . . .' He chewed his food while he thought and I took the opportunity to eat the rest of my samosa and a poppadum, which was divine dipped in mango chutney.

'I know,' he said, his eyes lighting up. 'Did you do an octopus dance? You waved your arms around a lot.'

Suppressing the urge to grimace, I was about to reply when he interrupted me.

'No, but then you were shaking your hair around as well. Was it a wet dog dance?'

Was he taking the mick?

'NO, it wasn't a wet dog dance!' I replied, tersely. 'It was a jinn dance, OK?'

'A jinn dance? Since when did jinns dance?'

'When do octopuses and turkeys dance? It was *performance art.*'

By the time the main courses arrived, we had finally abandoned the topic of dancing and had moved on to more normal subjects, like work, family and my list. It had taken a while, but I was seeing glimpses of the pre-Snowdon Zakariya again. Fun, smart, considerate, unassuming. I confessed that I was seeing a therapist and instead of bolting at the admission, he listened attentively. Although to be fair, I did keep stressing the fact that I was only doing it because of the list.

'I think we could all benefit from a professional perspective sometimes,' he said simply. 'Maybe if it wasn't so uncommon in our culture, there would be less trauma that keeps getting passed down through the generations.'

After polishing off our food, we went in search of mishti and tea for dessert. We walked through Whitechapel in comfortable silence and this time, whenever his arm brushed against mine, he didn't yank it away like I had a contagious disease. I had to suppress my natural urge to slide my arm into his and hold on to him as we walked. It wasn't something I had experienced much, that desire to be physically close to someone and not in a sexual way, but out of companionship.

'Can I ask you something?' I asked when we stopped at the tea shack and Zakariya insisted on buying me a karak chai and a massive piece of orange, crispy jalebi dripping with syrup.

'Anything,' he replied, smiling at me.

'Why did you disappear?' I asked quietly, looking down at the Styrofoam cup I held in my cold hands. 'We went to Snowdon, I thought we were friends and then you suddenly just ghosted me. What happened?'

Zakariya looked uncomfortable then, the smile fading from his lips. 'I didn't ghost you. I . . . I just—'

'You just what?' I interrupted his stammering. 'You just thought it was OK to treat me like that? Friends aren't supposed to do that.'

'I didn't disappear,' he said, getting agitated. 'I just didn't proactively seek you out. If I had seen you somewhere, I would have talked to you. Why wouldn't I? We're friends, right?'

'Friends like those girls you were flirting with in Snowdon?' I blurted without thinking.

'What?' His brows furrowed, Zakariya stared at me as though I had just announced that I had seen him fly off in a UFO.

'Snowdon? You went off with a group of girls and basically just ghosted me ever since.'

'What are you talking about?' he said, stopping so abruptly that I almost knocked into him. 'They were kids! They wanted to talk about the charity. Why do you care who I talk to?'

'I don't care!'

'So why are we arguing?'

'Because you ghosted me!'

'I didn't!' Frustrated, he waved his hand in the air to emphasise his point, forgetting that he was holding a cup of tea in his hand. The tea went flying and I yelped and jumped back, narrowly avoiding the hot liquid from staining my clothes.

'I'm so sorry!' he said, staring miserably at his own shirt, now soaked in tea.

'Are you OK? Here, let me help you!' I handed him my cup and paper bag and attempted to wipe his chest with some tissues I found in my bag. I did it instinctively, but after a moment or two I realised that I was standing much too close to him. So close that I could smell his musky scent. The gesture was supposed to be practical and helpful, but I heard him draw a sharp breath and, suddenly, it became intimate.

Without thinking, I let my hand linger on his chest for a brief second. Time froze and I could feel the warmth of his skin and the steady thumping of his heart beneath the cotton of his shirt. What would happen if I stayed like this forever? At that moment, I wished more than anything that I *could* stay like this forever, in the middle of Whitechapel, home to thousands of Bengalis. *Where any one of them could see us and report our inappropriate behaviour to our parents.*

Snatching my hand away, I bustled over to the overflowing bins a few metres away and carefully dropped the tissues on top, so as not to touch the rim or any of the rubbish.

'All good?' I asked, coming back over to him to relieve him of my cup and bag. Our fingers brushed and a spark flew through me, making my heart strain against my ribcage.

'All good,' he murmured, looking down at me, holding onto my bag for a second longer than necessary before he let it go.

'It's getting late,' I said, trying to inject reality into the charged atmosphere. The way he was looking at me was unnerving; it was as though he was seeing right through my confident, indifferent facade and straight into my soul, where he was reading an entire book about who I was and what I was feeling.

'It is,' he echoed, his voice low and husky. 'Shall we go? I have my car so I can drop you home.'

I knew I should reject the invitation. The atmosphere was too charged and I needed to remove myself from this intoxicating moment, but I couldn't bring myself to end the night so abruptly.

'Sure,' I said, trying to keep my voice steady and not betray the plethora of emotions that I was experiencing; everything from fear to elation. As we walked silently over to his car, I lied to myself repeatedly, telling myself that I was reading too much into the moment and nothing was happening between us.

Deep down, I was well aware of something brewing. It wasn't blossoming love or anything cheesy like that. It was worse, it was a storm.

Zakariya opened the door for me and once again, I was hit by a wave of desire to be held by him. I had spent my entire life being mindful of my behaviour as a Muslim. Intimacy was after marriage, end of. Was I about to ruin it by putting myself in a dangerous situation with a guy who had no interest in marrying me and was about to piss off to another country?

'Actually, I think I'm going to take the Tube,' I said quickly, when I was already halfway into the car. Before my hormones made me change my mind, I moved back, narrowly missing bumping into him with my ample bum cheeks.

'I need to . . . um . . . stop off and drop this . . . thing off to my friend on my way home,' I stammered as I turned to face him. Would he object? Would he be annoyed? Would he try and persuade me to accept the ride? If he did, I knew I would be too weak to resist. A part of me *wanted* him to protest.

'Oh. OK,' he said, the confusion written all over his face. 'Thanks for a lovely evening. Insha'allah see you soon?'

'Insha'allah,' I repeated. *God willing*. 'Goodnight.'

With that, I walked away from Zakariya and his alluring broodiness and headed towards the train station.

Chapter Twenty-Seven

'So, then what happened?' Dina demanded when she came over the next day with Sami and baby Sama. Aunty Noura had finally left to go back to Australia and we were both secretly relieved, although a little worried about how Dina would cope on her own.

We were up in my room enjoying tea and biscuits after dinner and prayers. Dina was breastfeeding Sama pretty much 24/7, dropping biscuit crumbs all over the baby blanket as she did so. Ma and Baba were entertaining Sami downstairs and he was thriving off all the attention. Ma loved children and was fussing over him like a grandmother hen, feeding him all sorts of sugary things that Dina would never have allowed had it been anyone else offering. During dinner, Ma kept making comments like, 'Who knows when I'll be a Nani or a Dadi?', scowling first at me and then at my brother.

'Nothing, I got on the train and I haven't heard from him since,' I admitted, as I dunked a cake rusk into my tea for a moment too long and watched the whole thing collapse into the bottom of my mug.

'Maybe you should text him,' Dina mused.

'Why? I don't have anything to say.'

'He's blatantly into you, Maya. Why don't you give him some sort of indication that you're into him too?'

'Firstly, I'm not *into* him,' I said weakly, aware of how lacklustre my response was. 'And secondly, he's leaving in a few months. There's no point.'

'So, tell him to stay!' Dina began flailing her free arm about, as if the more she waved it around, the more I would be inclined to listen to her.

'I can't do that!'

'Why not?'

'He's got a job out there! He's been planning to go for years. I'm not going to make him give up his dreams for something that might turn out to be nothing.'

'How will you know if it's something unless you give it a go?'

'How can I give it a go, Dina? What if he asks me to go to Dubai with him? I'm about to go back to uni! I've been offered a place *and* a scholarship. I can't jeopardise all that I'm trying to achieve because I fancy some guy!'

Dina grimaced and her silence confirmed that I was making sense. Maybe Zak did like me, but 'like' wasn't enough for us to completely put our plans on hold. And what did I know about 'fancying' someone anyway? I'd never been in a real relationship before. I hadn't even been in a fake one. I had no idea what I would be like as a fiancée, partner or whatever I would call myself while we were courting. I didn't know what it was like to have real feelings. For all I knew, this was a passing fancy. Albeit a mighty fine fancy. My insides tingled whenever I remembered him standing close to me, looking at me so intensely that it took all my self-control to walk away.

Dina and her babies left shortly after, as it was already past Sami's bedtime and he was beginning to get cranky. Ma reluctantly let them leave, filling containers with rice and curry because apparently Sami really enjoyed her fried fish and daal and Dina needed to eat well as she was breastfeeding.

After doing the rest of the clean-up, I politely declined Ma's offer to watch the latest Bollywood movie with her and Baba and went back into my room to peruse the list.

Climbing into bed and pulling the covers over me, I opened the weathered notebook. It was so fresh and pristine when I first found it on the Tube. Now, the black leather was wrinkled and worn, with creases in the spine and stains on the pages. If I ever met Noah again, there was no way I could return it to him in this condition, especially as I had scribbled my notes all over it. After completing each task, I wrote a few lines on how I felt about it. Nothing too deep, but nothing I wanted Noah to see.

Flicking through the pages, I got to number nineteen and swore under my breath. FFS, seriously? There, in the same ink as all the others, Noah had scrawled:

19. JOIN A DATING APP AND GO ON A DATE YOU MISER-ABLE SHIT ✓

Tinder= hookups, Bumble and Hinge seem more meaningful. RateYourDate next?

There was no way I was going to join a dating app. No bloody way. Especially not after my social-media debut, when Lucy had plastered my before and after all over her accounts. I never wanted to go through something like that again, where strangers judged me solely on my appearance. I'd spent too much time trying to persuade myself that there was more to me than my looks to now go and put myself on display for a bunch of shallow, immature men to reject me. Not when I had come so far in my journey and was finally starting to believe it.

'I'm not doing it, Luce,' I said to Lucy as we sat at our desks on Monday, messing around on our phones but with PowerPoint open so it looked like we were working. Sheila was away meeting clients up in the north somewhere, so we were taking the rare opportunity to mess around all day.

'Why not?' Lucy asked as she put together her latest Instagram post. Her social-media presence was gaining traction after she had managed to persuade a couple of micro-influencers to let her style them. My ugly little post was now so far down her feed that you had to scroll quite a bit to get there. It was a massive relief for me and I was working up the courage to ask her to delete it altogether. She had enough content now; she didn't need my crappy self sullying her aesthetics.

'I don't want idiotic men who don't know me judging me based on my looks,' I replied.

'But you look good now,' Lucy replied, completely missing the point.

'That's not the point.'

'What *is* the point? I get that you don't want to be objectified, but you're not doing it to find love. You're doing it to try something different and to complete the list. Are you really going to skip number nineteen to make a point to no one but yourself?'

'I don't like the idea of people reading a paragraph about me and then ticking a box like they're doing online grocery shopping. What if I show up and they send me back because I'm not what they were expecting?'

'Err, firstly, you're not a balsamic vinegar being substituted for a balsamic glaze. Secondly, how is it any different from that marriage CV thingy your parents made for you?'

'Did I tell you about that? I can't remember.'

'I remember and it sounds the same as online dating to me.' She had a point there. It was the same, but I didn't want a biodata in the first place. I only did it to get my parents off my back. But if I didn't do this, I couldn't tick it off. *And I HAD to.* I had jumped in a freezing-cold lake because I was determined to complete that blasted list. I had leapt out of a plane for God's sake! All I had to do was make a profile and go on one date and then I could delete it forever, tick it off the list and move on to number twenty. With any luck, it would be something pleasant like learning how to arrange flowers. I'd always wanted to do that.

'Fine, let's do it,' I sighed, handing my phone over to the expert. 'You sort it out for me. I'm going to make some tea. Choose anything from the favourites folder in my camera roll.'

When I got back from the kitchenette carrying two mugs, Lucy was nodding and whispering with Arjun, who was typing away furiously on my phone.

'There, all done,' he said with a flourish when he spotted me. 'You need to verify your face by taking a selfie now and you're good to go. Thank me later, jaanu.'

Grabbing my phone, I did as he asked and then checked out the profile he had created with trepidation:

MissMayaMarvel
27
London
5'4

Born-and-bred Londoner, lawyer-in-training, lover of fine food, books, films, the Marvel Cinematic Universe and adventure. I make the best curry on this side of the Indian Ocean. Enjoy thrills and keeping fit. Looking for someone who knows their Ulysses *from their* Iliad *and can match my passion and enthusiasm for all life has to offer* ☺

As far as profiles went, it wasn't that bad. It made me sound interesting. Intelligent. Adventurous. Fulfilled.

'*Can make the best curry on this side of the Indian Ocean?*' I raised an eyebrow.

'Creative licence,' Arjun replied casually. 'You're welcome.'

Turning back to my phone, I browsed through the pictures they had chosen and I was surprised to see that I didn't look completely out of my depth. There was a customary #goldenhour selfie, a picture from a wedding and a couple from Dubai. Looking at the profile felt like an out-of-body experience, like I was seeing myself for the first time. This profile didn't look like it belonged to a confused introvert who lacked confidence and always felt inferior.

'Thanks,' I whispered, my eyes beginning to sting. Was this how people saw me? For so long I had felt unworthy, second fiddle to my brother, the twins and my work colleagues. I walked about in a fog, not knowing who I was or where I was going. But now, I felt like I had some clarity. I may not have known exactly who I was, but I knew where I was going.

Arjun began explaining how the app worked and I tuned in and out of his tutorial. All I was going to do was go on ONE date and that was it, I didn't need to become an expert on swiping or reading between the lines.

'Whatever you do, DON'T give your number to any random person and don't meet anyone without telling us and letting us investigate him first, OK?' he said sternly. 'I really don't want to read about you in the papers the next day.'

'Stop freaking me out! I didn't want to do this in the first place,' I wailed.

'It's good you're freaked out. And also, don't send money to anyone or click any links. Or agree to go on a private jet.'

'All right!'

Someone clearly took their Netflix documentaries too seriously, but deep down, I knew he was right. If Arjun was offering to do due diligence for free, then I wasn't about to turn down an opportunity to preserve my life for a bit longer.

'Hey, Luce, how's it going with you and that guy you were seeing?' I asked her later that afternoon, as I carried on doing fake work. I'd had the same Excel spreadsheet open for the past two hours and hadn't made a single change on it.

'Same thing,' she all but growled at me. 'He won't commit and I'm done. I'm *so* done.'

'He doesn't deserve you, hun,' I said sympathetically. He really didn't. She was a catch in every sense of the word. She was kind, caring, fun, smart, beautiful. She could have anyone she wanted. She didn't need a wasteman who wouldn't commit to her. I said all this out loud and she suddenly stood up, her eyes ablaze.

'You're right!' she said. 'He doesn't deserve me. Look at me! Do I look like someone who waits around for a man to make up his mind if he wants to be with me?'

I stared at her as her voice grew louder, causing colleagues in different departments to look over at us.

'WELL? DO I?'

'Uh no, you don't. Sorry, I thought it was a rhetorical question.' I looked at her nervously and at all the curious faces watching us. Rachel in accounts in particular. She'd had it in for us ever since that time she asked if she could join us for lunch and we had slipped off without telling her. 'Err, Luce, do you want to keep it down a bit? People are looking.'

Lucy sat down in a huff, her face as pink as a marshmallow. 'You know what? I'm making a profile too. That's what I'm going to do. I'm not wasting a second further on some mummy's boy who's too scared to bring me home.'

Later that night, when I was in the privacy of my room, I checked RateYourDate and tried to figure out how to use it properly, wishing I had paid more attention to Arjun's lesson. Mind you, it wasn't exactly neurosurgery, quite the opposite, in fact. Some of the profiles made me wonder if the person writing them had a single brain cell. Said the woman whose friends curated and created her entire profile for her. I know, I'm a hypocrite.

Soon, I was having quite a lot of fun swiping this way and that. What made this app different was the fact that dates could rate each other after meeting up and the higher the star rating, the higher the profiles ranked.

Judging people on their dodgy profile pictures (heavily filtered ones being the worst) and their badly written bios was just what I needed after a long day at work. With some of the guys, it was obvious that they were there looking for a sneaky link, but it was more difficult to tell with others. The app wasn't a Muslim-centric one but there were still plenty of Muslim men on it. It didn't matter to me either way. I was after one platonic meeting and that was all. Number nineteen would be done and dusted.

It didn't take long to get bored of constantly swiping, so I decided to call it a night. I would check out my own notifications the following morning to see if anyone was interested in me, but it was late and I didn't want to get sucked into a conversation with anyone.

Just as I was about to log out and put my phone away, a profile caught my eye. The guy looked familiar, but I couldn't place him immediately. There was only one picture, so I moved down to the bio and gasped as realisation struck me in the centre of my chest like a lightning bolt:

NoahPT29
30
London
6'3

Hey everyone, Noah here. I'm a half-Lebanese, half-English personal trainer looking for someone who's smart, fun, easy-going and enjoys going out, working out and experiencing new things. If that's you . . . well, who knows where swiping right could lead us?

WHAT. THE. HELL?

My fingers trembling with excitement, I read his bio over and over again until I knew it off by heart. I analysed every millimetre of his picture, lapping it all up like a thirsty horse in a desert oasis. The beautiful, wavy, light brown hair, the twinkling green-grey eyes, skin the colour of molten gold, perfect straight white teeth, the bump in his nose. He was looking straight into the camera and it felt like he was looking straight at me.

Hurriedly, as though I was afraid that the profile would disappear, I took a screenshot and sent it over to Lucy, who called me immediately.

'OH, MY BLOODY GAWD, MAYA!' she shrieked so loudly that I had to move the phone away from my ear.

'It's him, Lucy! It's Noah! From the list!' I yelped. 'What shall I do?'

'Swipe right, you idiot! Do it now before he deletes his account or meets someone else! Do it now! He's so bloody hot.'

'OK, OK. I'll let you know what happens.'

Hanging up the phone, I took a moment to compose myself by closing my eyes and doing a bit of deep breathing. I couldn't believe I had found him and I didn't have to go to a triathlon to do it.

Whispering 'Bismillah', I swiped right and waited, praying that he would do the same.

Chapter Twenty-Eight

I didn't sleep a wink that night. It was impossible with the prospect of Noah matching with me hanging over me like fog, blurring my vision and clouding my senses. I must have checked my phone at least fifty times, if not more, waiting to see if he would accept my swipe, or whatever the correct terminology was. I went through a conveyor belt of checks – was my phone on silent? Were my notifications on? Was my phone even working? – more times than I cared to admit. I knew that he was most likely asleep and therefore hadn't seen my request. But after hours of evading sleep, I wasn't exactly thinking rationally.

At around five, I gave up on sleep entirely and pulled on my running clothes. I peeped into Malik's room to see if he wanted to join me and to my surprise, he was also wide awake, mindlessly scrolling through his phone and looked dully over to me when I opened his door.

'Hey, wanna go for a jog?' I whispered.

'Gimme two mins,' he murmured back, dumping his phone and getting up immediately. I guess I wasn't the only one suffering from insomnia that night.

Malik and I jogged steadily and silently together, side by side like equals, not like the first time we went running together when he kept lapping me and then gave up and went home without me.

As our feet pounded on the tarmac, I wondered if Noah would remember who I was. I doubted he'd spent half as much brain power on me as I had on him. That was because of the list, though. If I had left something intriguing behind – like a photo album, for example – then I'm sure I would have become equally as interesting to him. Well, maybe not, remembering the state of my camera roll pre-makeover. Fine. Case notes? Nope, boring. My phone messages weren't interesting before the list, either. They consisted mainly of texts from Dina of the 'I'm running late' variety, shopping lists from Ma or the odd message from Malik.

My life, I was ashamed to admit, was utterly boring before the list. Now, my phone was full of me making plans with my friends and cousins, cool pictures from all the experiences I was having and the occasional text from Zakariyah.

I nearly tripped over the uneven, chewing gum-studded pavement when I remembered Zakariya. Shit. I had forgotten all about him in my Noah-induced haze. Stopping abruptly, I bent forward and clutched onto my knees, trying to gather my breath and my thoughts. The most beautiful sunrise was illuminating the sky, casting the world in an orange glow, but I couldn't appreciate it because suddenly I felt overcome with guilt.

'You OK, Dimple?' Malik asked, stopping beside me. 'Have you pulled a muscle?'

'No,' I panted, turning to look at him. 'Question. If you were casually chatting to someone as a friend, but you knew they sort of liked you, but you'd never given them any indication that you sort of like them . . . Is it bad to join a dating app and then swipe right on someone else?'

'I don't really want to participate in this conversation,' Malik grimaced. 'Ask one of your girlfriends.'

My brother jogged away and I stood there, bent over with my hands on my knees, feeling floored. What was I doing, thinking about Noah, *swiping* Noah, when there was a man out there who I had been talking to, leaning my head on, having dinner with, attending the same Arabic class with . . . what was I, a two-timing floozy?

'You are not a two-timing floozy,' Lucy yawned down the phone when I called her in a panic. Her voice sounded gravelly and dry. I checked the time. Oops, it wasn't six in the morning yet.

'Sorry, did I wake you?' I said as I continued to jog home.

'You did, but I needed to get up soon anyway so it's OK. But listen, before I go to the loo, please don't do anything silly. You are not two-timing anyone. You and Zak aren't a couple, he hasn't said anything to you to imply that you should put all your eggs in his basket.'

'Yes, but—'

'But nothing. You owe him nothing. And now let me go before my bladder bursts.'

Hanging up the phone, I pondered Lucy's somewhat logical reasoning as I slowed down to a brisk walk and made my way back home. I knew she was right, but knowing something and feeling it can be on opposite ends of the spectrum.

By the time I left work in the evening, Lucy had all but banned me from checking my phone for the rest of the night. Sheila was back in the office but not even the danger of her finding me on RateYourDate was enough to make me stop looking at the blasted thing. Noah still hadn't responded to me and it had almost been twenty hours and three minutes. Not that I was counting, of course. Was he really so busy that he couldn't check the app that he pretty much *forced* me to join?

I had to snap out of it though, because on Saturday I would be participating in Race for Life and I needed to focus. I had met my fundraising target ages ago and the months of training were all about to pay off. I had managed to do a 5K run the other week, so it shouldn't be too difficult to do it all over again. I kept having visions of myself running like Rocky Balboa and had taken to listening to *Eye of the Tiger* during my training. I had to keep my head in the game.

Unsurprisingly, no one in my household thought to attend the race to cheer me on. I was relieved. The last thing I wanted was Ma going into paparazzi mode and taking a million pictures of me sweating like a goat and posting them on Facebook. She had only recently got into social media and instead of carefully capturing the best moments of her life, she was prone to posting anything and everything. She was also really into sharing dodgy conspiracy theories, which I tried to ignore. But then she would text me and tell me to re-share them because it was important that everyone knew that the government was putting hormones in the water to prevent fertility in women.

On Saturday morning I woke up early, did a Pilates workout to stretch my muscles and activate my core, had a banana and then forced Malik into dropping me off at the park, where Lucy was waiting for me.

'Can't you take the bus?' he grumbled when he came down the stairs, his hair sticking up in all directions. 'I'm not your personal taxi driver.'

'You know I need to save my energy,' I replied testily. 'I can't waste my strength now, not when I have 5K to run.'

'It's five bloody kilometres. It's hardly the London Marathon.' Malik had run the London Marathon a couple of years ago. The entire family – Chacha, Nani, the whole lot – had turned up to cheer him on. Gritting my teeth, I took my phone out to book a ride. I didn't need my stupid brother ruining the day for me.

'Whatever, I'll take a taxi,' I said, turning away from him.

'I'm up now. Get in the car.' He stomped off outside and I stared at his back, wondering why he was making such a big deal of it. He often moaned when I made him take me places, but never this much. I was tempted to ignore him and get an alternative ride anyway, but I forced myself not to. I needed positivity, not a fight.

The journey to the park was quick and silent but the atmosphere both in and outside the gate was anything but. There were women dressed in pink everywhere and friends and family holding pink balloons and banners walked alongside them. I couldn't spot Lucy and wasn't sure if this was the entrance she was waiting at.

'Hold on, Malik, can you stop there for a second?' I asked my brother and he complied silently, pulling over to the side and putting on the hazard lights. Taking my phone out, I called Lucy, who answered after a couple of rings.

'Maya, hi! Where are you?'

'At the park, which entrance are you at?'

'Seven Sisters Road. You?'

'I'm on the other side, I'll be there in a bit.'

'Can't you walk the rest of the way?' Malik said tersely and I ignored him, waiting for him to take me to the right entrance. I didn't know what his problem was, but at that point, I didn't care. I wanted to get on with the day and smash the race.

'Pull up here, please,' I told him when I spotted Lucy in her hot-pink vest and matching yoga pants, opening my window and waving at her. Why was it that when I wore similar bottoms they looked like leggings, but on Lucy they looked like yoga pants? Even with no makeup and her hair scraped back into a ponytail, she looked like a model for gym wear.

She was on her phone when the car came to a halt, so I called out her name through the open window to get her attention. When she looked up at me, she looked strange; bewildered, almost.

'Thanks for the lift,' I muttered as Malik all but shoved me out of the car and roared away.

'Hey, Luce, you OK?' I asked, giving her a hug. 'You look like you've seen a ghost.'

'I'm OK,' she said quickly, giving me a strained smile. 'You ready for the race?'

'As ready as I'll ever be.'

The Seven Sisters Road entrance to the park was grimy. There was pigeon poop everywhere, and the distinct stench of weed, wee and desperation. Still, nothing could quell the excitement brewing in me. I had been training for this moment for months and I was ready to put my stamina to the test. Fine, it wasn't twenty-six miles like Malik's stupid marathon, but it was worlds away from my fitness levels pre-list and I wasn't about to let him or anyone else bring me down. The fact that there was a greater purpose to this than proving that I could run without fainting made it all the more worthwhile.

We followed the crowds of people to the starting point. It was mostly women, all dressed in pink. There were children, old people and everyone in-between, all coming together to raise money for vital research. The atmosphere was warm and supportive and all along the route, friends and family had set up deckchairs and picnic blankets to cheer their loved ones on. I felt a slight pang that I had no one, but then, neither did Lucy.

The race began and to be honest, it wasn't really a race. There were people walking along the route that took us around the perimeter of the park like they were on a casual stroll. I wasn't one of those people. When the buzzer went, I shot off like a firework and ran like my future depended on it. With adrenaline coursing through me, I focused on the finish line and ignored all the noise around me. There were no other people, strolling or otherwise. There was no Lucy looking panicky, no Malik getting pissed off, no Noah ignoring my swipe, no Zakariya dropping me hints, no Sheila harassing me, no Ma and Baba overlooking me, no Pinky and Pretty undermining me, no aunties at weddings making me feel ugly and useless.

There was just me and my feet pounding against the tarmac, the blood thumping in my ears, the wind rushing through my hair. Nothing else mattered.

I finished the race in thirty-four minutes, which wasn't fast – there were plenty of people who finished before me – but I did have to wait fifteen minutes for Lucy to join me. While I waited, I did my stretches, took some pictures and talked to other participants. There were so many women there who had either survived cancer or had lost loved ones to the disease. Talking to them was humbling. In that moment, I decided to commit to fundraising for Cancer Research regularly and to participate in Race for Life annually.

Lucy finally managed to hobble across the finish line, gulping for air and clutching onto her side like an appendix had burst. It was pretty funny, seeing her with her face the shade of beetroot, strands of hair sticking to it, sweat dripping in rivulets down her neck.

'W-water,' she gasped, grabbing a bottle from a volunteer and downing it so fast that she spilt half of it over her pink vest. Collapsing onto the grass, she lay there spreadeagled and I sat cross-legged next to her while I waited for her to get her breath back.

'How come you're not suffering like I am?' she said when her skin eventually paled from tomato soup to more of a candyfloss pink. 'I think I have a stitch. It's worse than a stitch.

It's like surgery. Except the surgery went wrong, because I was being cheap and went to Prague to do it. And now I have an infection.'

I tried not to laugh as I surveyed the hot mess that was Lucy Robinson sprawled out on the ground talking nonsense. She was usually so perfect and composed and the reversal of roles tickled me.

'Luce, you know I've been running for months now, right? Training for this very moment? I think I could have managed 10K, you know. It would have been hard but I reckon I could have done it.'

'I know you said you were training but I thought you were exaggerating,' she moaned, rolling over to her front. 'How am I going to get home?'

'Don't worry, I'll ask my brother. He's being a moody git today but there's no way he'll say no to a pretty woman.'

At this, Lucy sat bolt upright. 'NO WAY. I'll book a ride.'

'Why? Because you look like a trainwreck? Who cares, it's just Malik. And you still look good, sweat patches and all.'

'It doesn't matter. Don't ask him, OK?'

'All right, calm down, I won't!'

True to her word, Lucy went home in a taxi, too exhausted to go out for a meal in Green Lanes like I had originally planned, so I plodded over to the bus stop. I was on such a high from the race that I didn't fancy seeing my brother's moody mug.

Checking my phone, I saw that Zakariya had replied to one of my Stories, congratulating me on completing the race.

'Thanks,' I typed out as I sat at the bus stop waiting for the number 29 to take me home. 'I'm not gonna lie, I smashed it.'

ZAKARIYA: I wouldn't expect anything else from you. How are you celebrating?

MAYA: Lucy got a stitch so she went home. I'm celebrating with takeout and a hot bath.

ZAKARIYA: Not all at the same time, I hope?

MAYA: Soggy doner kebab is the best, haven't you heard?

Ma and Baba were out when I got in and so was Malik, so I did exactly as I had planned. I soaked myself in a hot bath with Epsom flakes until my skin shrivelled like a raisin and the water grew murky and tepid. I followed this up with a greasy kebab from my local Turkish takeaway and ate it in front of the TV while a mindless movie played in the background.

For the first time that day, I checked RateYourDate. As usual, there was nothing from Noah. I no longer felt a crushing sense of disappointment when I saw that he hadn't responded to me, but I still felt a niggle of it. I kept telling myself that it was probably because he hadn't logged in. Maybe he wasn't checking the app intentionally, because he was already seeing someone?

Oof. The thought of Noah with someone when I was *this* close to meeting him again, when he was finally within my reach, was a tough pill to swallow. Like one of those huge Omega 3, 6 and 9 ones that always got lodged in my throat.

While there was nothing from the object of my desire, there were, however, hundreds of other men who had matched me.

I began scrolling through matches one by one. At first, I took the time to read the profiles properly, even when they were clean-shaven with weak jawlines. This took forever and I soon learnt to scan the profile and details quickly and only bother to read the bio if the rest was decent. It was almost like being in Yo Sushi; plates of maki flying by and I had three seconds to decide if I wanted to grab one or not:

Bashir. 28. 5'5. Indian. London. Blurry photo. Swipe left.

Alan. 38. 5'11. White English. Milton Keynes. Photo of a blond, stout man with skin that reminded me of mayonnaise. Swipe left.

Rayan. 32. 5'9. Pakistani. Southampton. OK-looking with a buzz cut.

Interesting. I clicked to read his bio, curious to know how he would introduce himself. *Lookin for ma wifey n tingz. Been locked up but a changed man. Living with mumsy is a must.*

I re-read the bio three times, trying to decipher what it meant. Was he trying to say that he was a criminal who had been locked up in *jail?* And after failing his DBS check, he *still* wanted a woman who would be happy to live with his mum? Was he serious?

Going on a dating app, I soon realised, was a bit like going on TikTok. You could get sucked into spending hours of your life mindlessly scrolling and in the end, you were no better off in life. Whenever I came across a profile that I thought was promising, the bio soon revealed that it was another waste-man looking for a quick hook-up or a stay-at-home 'wifey' to look after his elderly parents. And the ones in-between were the wrong age, wrong height or in the wrong geographical location. It was hopeless. Was this it? Was this what was available in the UK's Muslim dating scene right now? I felt as though I had shown up to the buffet too late and all the good stuff had already been taken.

As I continued mindlessly scrolling, a message pinged through. Probably from some forty-three-year-old who had his own 'business' (code for unemployed), still lived with his parents in an overcrowded flat and couldn't put a sentence together without three spelling mistakes.

Opening it half-heartedly, I didn't bother to check the profile of the person who sent it and read the message itself:

NOAH: Hey Maya, Love your profile – we seem to be interested in the same things! Are you free to grab a coffee/drink sometime this week? Noah x.

Chapter Twenty-Nine

'I knew he was going to match you!' Lucy squealed when I showed her Noah's message on Monday morning. My stomach had been churning non-stop since he got in touch and I had barely slept all night. I had waited for this moment for so long and now that it was almost here and I was on the cusp of finally seeing him again, I felt sick with anticipation. So much so that I hadn't replied to him because whenever I tried, my mind either went completely blank or filled itself with nonsense.

'How shall I respond?' I whispered, my eyes darting around the office until they landed on Sheila, who was walking across the open space with a mug in her hands and her earphones in her ears. Still, for all we knew, she was pretending to be on a call and was secretly listening in to our conversations.

'Let's chat later,' Lucy murmured nervously as Sheila got closer to our desks. I needed to talk to her about my working hours, but I had been putting it off for days because the thought of approaching her and asking for something was too frightening a task. It was scarier than the prospect of seeing Noah again, but until I did, I wouldn't be able to decide whether to do the degree full-time or part-time.

'Sheila, do you have a moment?' I said, getting up and following her across the room, trying to keep up with her long strides. She stopped abruptly and spun around to face me, her eyes narrowing.

'Make it quick,' she snapped and continued to stalk towards her office with me trailing behind like a toddler.

Sheila's office was a lot like her: cold and functional. Everything was steel or chrome, or whatever that silver-coloured metal was and what wasn't silver was a brilliant white. There were no plants, no pictures, nothing personal at all. Closing the door behind me, I waited for her to tell me to take a seat and when she didn't, I stood awkwardly, shifting my weight from one foot to another.

'Well? What is it?' she said, raising an eyebrow expectantly. It didn't lift much and I wondered if it was because she'd had Botox. That would explain her lack of expression most of the time.

'I wanted to talk to you about my working hours,' I said, trying my best not to stammer and to look her in the eye. 'I'm starting an LLM in September and I want to do it full-time so I can finish it quicker.'

'Right. So how are you planning to work here at the same time?'

'It's in the evenings,' I said quickly, my throat dry. 'If I do it full-time, it would be two evenings a week. The classes start at six, so it means that I would have to leave at five to get there on time. But I'd make sure to come in at nine on those days, so I won't be doing fewer hours than I'm contracted to do or anything.'

Sheila sighed and looked away while I waited for her to respond. For someone who was in a hurry and didn't have time to talk, she was taking a long time to reply.

'Well, Maya,' she sighed. 'You do know that this isn't a nine-to-five sort of job. What am I supposed to do if I need some photocopying or filing at five and you've gone off to uni?'

'Erm, ask Lucy or Arjun?'

Sheila glanced at me sharply and I wished I hadn't answered her rhetorical question.

'And if you do it part-time?'

'It's one evening a week. But I'd really prefer to do it full-time so I can finish it quicker.'

'What's the rush? I think I can manage to let you go once a week despite the inconvenience, but twice a week? That's too much and it's not fair on Lucy or Arjun to have to pick up the slack. You don't need a master's degree in Law to perform your paralegal duties. I'll email you later with the confirmation.'

With that, she began typing on her computer, signalling the end of the conversation and my cue to leave her space.

I turned around and left, my legs unsteady and my insides simmering with a quiet fury. Did she really say I couldn't do it full-time in case she needed me to photocopy? Angry tears burned at the back of my eyes and I blinked them away, determined not to let her see how much she had upset me. She didn't even say that she would think about it.

'What happened to women supporting women?' I asked Fareena in therapy later that day. 'What happened to sisterhood? Uplifting each other? I didn't ask for any time off! I'll still be working what I'm contracted to do. Why is she being like this? Why does she hate me so much?'

'It's not about you,' Fareena said calmly. 'I doubt she hates you. Sheila's projecting her own issues onto you. The question isn't why is she being like this, it's how are you going to navigate the hurdle?'

'What can I do? She's said it now. She's ruining my entire future.'

'Let's figure out all your options,' Fareena said. 'What can you do besides accept it?'

I thought for a moment. 'I could speak to HR, but then she'll make my life more difficult. I don't think I could bear that.'

'What else? What other options are there?'

I sat silent for a minute as I pondered the alternatives. 'I could resign,' I said after a moment. 'I could apply for a part-time role somewhere else and then resign. Or apply for a full-time job somewhere that's more flexible.'

'How would working part-time impact you?'

'Not much, to be honest,' I shrugged. 'I don't have rent or anything to worry about and I have loads of savings. In fact, it would probably be better for me as it would give me more time to study properly.'

'Is it an option to work part-time at your current place?'

'I'm not sure, I guess I could find out. But I can't bring myself to speak to Sheila again. Last time was torture.'

'You could always email her instead, so you will have a paper trail and everything documented properly. That way, she'll have to be careful in how she responds as well.'

Fareena and I moved on to talking about Noah's message until the hour was up. She made me think about why I hadn't replied to him yet, having spent days waiting for his response. She asked me what I was afraid of. He was someone I had already met before and had connected with. He had shown interest in me then and was still showing interest in me now. Why was I still afraid?

'I guess I'm scared that he won't like me if we spend longer than half an hour together,' I admitted at last, picking at the skin around my fingernails. 'I've thought about him so much over the past nine months or so and it could have all been for nothing.'

'Why would it be so bad if you met and didn't connect in the same way?' Fareena asked. 'Fear of rejection can stand in the way of so many wonderful opportunities, relationships and connections in life. You won't know which way it will go unless you do it. And if it doesn't go well, at least you'll know. And I'll be here to help you process your emotions afterwards. We'll do it together.'

With Fareena's words echoing in my ears, I decided to reply to Noah while waiting on the train platform:

MAYA: Hey Noah, sure, coffee sounds good. How's Thursday after work? I'm in north London but I work in west London, so anywhere in-between works for me.

The rest of the Tube journey was excruciating. Every time I got a patch of Wi-Fi, I checked my phone to see if there was a response. In the end, I took out his notebook and thumbed through the pages; all his little scribbles accompanying the items on the list and my doodles and notes beneath his. His messy scrawl next to my neat print. How could I give him back his notebook now that it was full of my own drama? Under '1. APPLY FOR A PHYSIO COURSE' I had written, *No thanks . . . I'm gonna do something relevant to ME. LLM? SQE? SQE too hard esp as haven't studied in a while. Research MAs, find the easiest one that isn't at a shit uni. Look for funding opps.*

It wasn't too incriminating, but it wasn't something I would want Noah to read. I turned to the next page and read what I had written under 'READ ULYSSES'. *What a load of effin' BS. Can't believe I wasted so much of my life on this overrated piece of shit. That bloody Noah is a pretentious git. Probably wants to use the fact that he's read this tome as a chat-up line.* Ouch. No. I definitely couldn't give it back to him, not unless I Tipp-Exed the whole lot.

Now that I had arranged a date, as per the list's requirements, I moved on to number twenty. Noah had written 'Donate £500 to charity'. Next to it was a giant tick and, *'Done. Donated to Save the Children. Hope they don't add me to their mailing list though.'* OK, that was easy enough. I wondered if I needed to do this. As Muslims, we are required to donate 2.5 per cent of our wealth every year to charity, which is called Zakat. I usually did it every Ramadan and the amount increased every year, since my savings tended to grow every year.

I decided that donating extra money could only be a good thing. Since I'd already given to Islamic Relief and Cancer Research when I did the trek and the run, I would donate to each of them again as soon as I had access to Wi-Fi.

I liked how Noah had charity on the list and not just poncy stuff to improve his own life and clout. Only good, kind people bothered to give to charity, so he must be both. I shut out the voice in my head reminding me that Zakariya didn't just donate to charity, he volunteered as well.

Number twenty-one, however, wasn't as simple:

21. GET A TATTOO ✓

Bloody hurt more than I thought.

That's all he had to say about it. There were no descriptions of where it was, what it looked like or which artist had done it for him. How was I supposed to get a tattoo? Ma would kill me, no doubt about it. I could get it somewhere she wasn't likely to see, but even if she couldn't see it, God could. As far as I knew, any sort of permanent alteration to our bodies technically wasn't allowed in Islam, unless it was for medical reasons. With a sigh, I closed the notebook and stood up as Turnpike Lane approached. I could either defy God and my mum in order to stick to the list, or I could alter it and make it more Muslim/Bengali/Ma friendly.

While I was walking home, enjoying the fact that sunset was getting later and later, my phone buzzed. Hurriedly pulling it out of my bag, I saw a message from Noah.

NOAH: Thursday is perfect and guess what – I also live in north! Whereabouts are you?

Smiling, I typed out a quick response:

MAYA: Turnpike Lane. Not the most glamorous location but I like the kebab shops.

NOAH: Oooh kebab, stop talking dirty to me! I'm not far from you, a little further north in Southgate. Anywhere in particular you want to meet?

MAYA: Will coffee in Crouch End work?

NOAH: Done. 6 p.m.?

MAYA: Assuming I get out of work at 5, yes. But my boss is a nightmare. Shall we make it 6.30 to be on the safe side?

NOAH: It's OK, I don't mind waiting for a good thing. I'll be there at 6 – see you in front of the clocktower x.

Staring at the little kiss at the end of the message, I couldn't stop my smile spreading into a huge grin. I was finally seeing Noah again! OK, he didn't seem to remember me from our Tube encounter, but that was fine. To be fair, I did look completely different. And he wasn't the one who had been perusing my notebook for almost a year either. If he had, the memory of our meeting wouldn't have faded so quickly.

Putting my phone back into my bag, I started down Turnpike Lane and towards my house with a silly smile still on my face. I would have to ask Lucy to help me come up with the perfect casual date outfit. As I continued down the main road lined with shops on either side, going through all the items in my wardrobe one by one, I spotted a familiar car drive past. It looked like Malik's Beemer, but as I lifted my arm to wave at my brother, I thought I saw a mane of either light brown or possibly blonde hair in the passenger seat. I hurriedly dropped my hand and watched the car disappear down the street.

Malik arrived home an hour or so after me and I grabbed hold of him when he came upstairs, before he could lock himself in the bathroom for an hour and yanked him into my room.

'Malik! I saw you on TPL with your girlfriend!' I whispered as he stumbled into my room, holding onto the door frame to stop himself from falling over.

'W-what?' he stammered, visibly paling before my eyes. 'What did you see?'

If Malik had turned white, I'm certain I turned green at the thought of him doing something he didn't want me to see.

'Ew, why would you get up to no good on your doorstep? If you don't want people you know to see you with a girl, you shouldn't be driving down the ends with her!'

'I was dropping her home,' he mumbled, edging away from me. 'It's not a big deal.'

'What's going on with her then? Have you sorted out your issues?'

'Dimple, do you mind?' he snapped, in a way that suggested that they hadn't sorted anything out. 'I just got home, I need a shower and I don't fancy being interrogated right now!'

With that, my brother stomped into his room and slammed the door behind him, leaving me baffled on the other side.

Chapter Thirty

The next day, I discovered that there were such things as semi-permanent tattoos, so I half-heartedly ordered a pretty-looking Arabic one online, which Lucy helped me apply at work on Wednesday ahead of my meeting with Noah. It looked sort of sexy along the side of my hand, positioned exactly where Noah was bound to notice it. Lucy was a genius like that.

I didn't feel excited about meeting Noah, despite what my strategically placed 'tattoo' may have suggested. There was too much going on in my mind for me to process and it was overwhelming. There was work, Noah, Zakariya and seeing my brother with his mysterious lady-friend and cagey behaviour, all weighing on my mind.

'Can I style you for your date?' Lucy asked as we walked back to our desks, letting out collective sighs of relief when we saw that Sheila wasn't in her office. I had yet to send her the email asking about going part-time. I had written it but was planning to send it when I wouldn't have to run into her immediately afterwards, like a minute before logging out to go home. The thought of sending her that email stressed me out a lot more than my upcoming date with Noah, although that was also up there on my 'most nerve-wracking moments this year' list. Not that I had a list like that. One list at a time was more than enough for me, thanks.

'Yes, please,' I said, although the thought of trying on hundreds of outfits exhausted me. 'I don't want to look like I've made too much of an effort though.'

'I know, hun, but you do need to get your hair done. It's been months and it's looking messy. And you could do with a manicure to go with your tattoo and we haven't got you a spring/summer wardrobe yet either and—'

'OK! I get the point. But there isn't enough time.'

'Let's go to Westfield after work. We'll make it quick. I'll see if I can get you a hair appointment and while you get your hair and nails done, I'll buy you some bits and pieces.'

A few hours later, I was sitting in a salon with foil in my hair and my hands spread out while one lady worked on my hair and another worked on my hands as if I were some sort of celebrity. It felt good but I couldn't help but wonder if Noah was doing anything remotely like this in preparation for his date with me. Probably not. Why were women the ones who were always under pressure to perform like a show horse, while men could wash their faces and brush their teeth and that would be considered making an effort? And why was I letting Lucy coerce me into continuing this toxic cycle?

Because the sad reality was, I needed it. How I looked directly correlated to how I felt. Maybe one day it wouldn't. Maybe one day I wouldn't care, but right then I did. And that didn't make me a bad person, or anti-feminist, did it? I made a mental note to hash it out with Fareena next week.

A couple of hours later, I met Lucy again – thankfully she hadn't gone wild with my credit card, but she did still have a fair number of high-street bags on her arms.

'Here, let me show you what I got,' she said, pulling me over to a bench.

'Aren't we going to eat anything? I'm starving.'

'Sorry, I'm meeting someone in a bit,' she replied vaguely, rummaging through the shopping bags so she could avoid making eye contact with me.

'Not that guy you ended things with?' I asked, my heart sinking. 'You told me to never let you see him again until he was ready to commit.'

'I know,' she said quietly. 'I sort of ran into him recently and he's been calling me since then. I'm going to let him say his piece.'

'OK,' I leant over to hug her. 'I hope it goes well. Remember that you deserve someone who's proud to commit to you and introduce you to his family and friends.'

'I know. Now let me quickly show you what I bought before I dash.'

Lucy began taking various shirts, dresses and jackets out of the bag and showed me what she wanted me to wear to work on Thursday: a silky sage green shirt dress with a belt and black boots.

'Err, you know I don't show my legs, right?' I reminded her.

'I know, so I bought you these wool tights to wear with them. You can't see your skin through them. You're going from work so you can't meet him in jeans and a shirt, Sheila will kill you.'

'She's already going to kill me. I sent her the email about wanting to change to part-time hours and now the thought of facing her tomorrow is making me sick.'

'You've got nothing to fear. Don't you get it? You have the upper hand because you don't need this job. You can leave whenever you want and focus on your studies.'

'It's a lot easier said than done.'

'I know, but you've got this. Anyway, here, I got this necklace and these earrings, wear them with that bracelet I gave you last time and keep your makeup fresh and neutral – go for a glossy lip. It will draw his eyes to your lips.'

'Why would I want him to do that?'

'Oh, Maya, you're so clueless sometimes.' With that, she got up, gave me a quick hug and began to hurry away.

'Good luck!' I called after her retreating back, but she didn't turn around. With a sigh, I gathered all the bags and began the long journey home.

Ma and Baba were out when I got in, visiting some relatives and Malik wasn't home either, so I rummaged through the various butter tubs and ice-cream containers to see what leftovers had been stored in them. I really needed to get better at cooking. Here I was, trying to become more confident and independent in every way, yet I was rubbish at one of the most important life skills.

As I waited for the leftover fish and green mango tenga to warm up – a yummy soup-like curry that was mostly tangy but also a little sweet – I checked Noah's RateMyDate profile for the hundredth time. He really was something to look at. He had that All-American look about him, but with a bit of British rough and readiness. There was a new picture on his profile and I opened it up eagerly. He was outside an old building, possibly a town hall or a listed building of some sort and wearing a charcoal-coloured suit that clung to every muscle and hard line of his body. I don't think I had ever seen a suit that looked that good. It was like something you would find on the runway, not north London. Men like that should be made to wear pillowcases over their heads to hide their beauty and shapeless sleeping bags on their bodies to hide their physique. Why had he uploaded this picture? Was it because he was trying to attract more women in case our date went badly? I resisted the urge to screenshot the picture and send it to Lucy for her opinion. She was busy sorting out her own life and I needed to be less reliant on her. After seeing the picture, I was glad that I let her talk me into a bit of beautification. At least I'd be putting my best foot forward as well.

A text pinged through and I immediately assumed it was Noah cancelling, before I remembered that he didn't have my number. Grabbing my phone, I opened it up to find a message from Zakariya:

ZAKARIYA: Hey Maya, how are you? Are you free after Arabic on Thursday?

Instantly, I felt awash with guilt. I wasn't free. In fact, I was bunking Arabic altogether to meet Noah. What sort of woman had I become, texting one man while meeting up with another? I replied, wondering what excuse to give:

MAYA: So sorry, I'm not going to be at Arabic, I've got an appointment after work. A really important one that I can't cancel I'm afraid. Sorry.

As I re-read what I had sent, I realised that I had been rambling; something that wasn't supposed to be possible over text, when you had the chance to edit before you sent. I should have just kept it simple; the more I went on, the more insincere I sounded. He wasn't stupid, he would know that something was up. He deserved more respect, more honesty than that.

Picking up my phone again, I continued to write:

MAYA: Actually. I'm meeting someone for the first time. Kinda like a date, I guess.

ZAKARIYA: Wow, OK. Well, good luck! 👍

I re-read his message at least five times. What did he mean by 'Wow'? Was he disappointed in me? Why did he write 'well' before 'good luck?' I replied with a simple, 'Thanks 👋'.

Sheila wasn't in the office the following morning and according to her calendar, she had external meetings all day. I had brought my makeup bag into the office, hoping to do a little touch-up before I left for my date. Now that my boss wasn't around, I had more time to make myself presentable, so at four o'clock, Lucy and I disappeared to the toilets to sort my face out. The other night, I had felt bad about depending on her so much. But this morning, I saw that she had turned our shopping trip into content for her social media and the guilt faded away. We were helping each other out.

'How did it go with your mystery man?' I asked her as she got to work on my face, trying not to move my facial muscles too much.

'I don't know,' her voice was quiet and I waited for her to elaborate. I didn't want to be too forceful and drive her away.

'What don't you know, hun?' I asked quietly after a few minutes of silence. 'You don't have to talk about it if you don't want to, but I'm here to listen if you do.'

Lucy didn't say anything so I closed my eyes and let her get on with my makeup, but when she got to my lips, she sighed.

'I really like him, Maya,' she began. 'He's a good guy and there's so few of them around. He's smart, he works hard, he's successful. He looks after his family and respects them. He's respectful towards me.'

'He sounds great.'

'He is, but there's a massive cultural difference and I think he thinks his family would disapprove, which is why he hasn't told them and doesn't want me to meet them. And until he does that, we can't move forward. He'll never live with me outside marriage, but it looks like he won't marry me unless his family is happy with our relationship.'

I thought about my own parents and culture and as much as I wanted to slate this guy who had my friend in pieces, I had seen all this play out countless times. Boys who weren't allowed to marry their girlfriends and then had arranged marriages to unsuspecting women who never knew that their husbands' hearts were elsewhere. Boys who defied their parents and ended up miserable later because the odds were against them. There were, however, some positive examples where the family accepted the non-Bengali spouse and these cases were slowly becoming more frequent. To me, the fact that Lucy didn't know what her man was thinking, or if he had told his family, meant that he wasn't serious.

'I don't know how traditional this guy's family is,' I began carefully, 'but if I were in the same situation, I would tell my parents if it was serious. There are more and more mixed-race marriages these days and if you want to be with someone enough, at the very least you'd tell your parents. You can't know how they'd react unless you give them the chance and respect to do so.'

'What do you think your parents would say, if it were you?'

'I don't know,' I replied honestly. 'It could go either way, but I think they would come around if they saw that the man was good.'

'And what if he isn't Muslim?'

'If he wanted to marry me, he'd have to become Muslim, that's non-negotiable, regardless of whether he was Black, white, or anything in-between.'

I had to stop myself from picking at my nails throughout the Tube journey back to north London, as anxiety overcame me.

I did the breathing techniques that Fareena had taught me to try and manage the sensation of everything inside me coiling up into a tight ball: breathing in for four seconds, holding that breath for another four and then exhaling for four seconds. I was meeting Noah, *my* Noah, from the list that had changed my life and I was terrified of what would happen. Yes, there was the fear of us not connecting again, which would tarnish my perception of the past nine months. But what would be worse would be him not turning out to be the person I thought he was. All this time I had been going through pages in this notebook belonging to him, tracing my fingers over his words, looking into his mind as he worked his way through the list, doing my own version of his ideas and plans. We were bound together by this book, by our shared experiences, but he had no idea about it all. How was I going to hold myself together? How was I going to stop myself from confessing it all?

I had to, though, because if he found out what had been going on, he would probably think I was a stalkerish psychopath. He would run and never look back.

I got off the train at Finsbury Park and hopped from one foot to another as I waited for the W7 bus to Crouch End. I had to pull myself together. I could *not* mess this up. There was no reason why I should mess it up, I told myself over and over again. Noah seemed to like me before my makeover and before the list; when I was simple, boring Maya with a simple and boring life. Look at me now. I was going back into education. I knew where I wanted my career to go. I had run a race for charity. I was strong, I was sort of independent. If I could handle jumping out of a plane, then a coffee with some guy I'd met briefly in the past would be an absolute doddle.

Topping up my lipstick on the bus and giving myself three sprays of my eye-wateringly expensive perfume, which I had now calculated to cost approximately 25p per spritz, assuming there were 1,000 sprays in the 100ml bottle, I did a bit more deep breathing, recited a prayer and then got off the bus right outside the clocktower where we were due to meet, my body trembling with nerves.

It was almost six and I was bang on time. When the bus drove away and cleared my line of vision, I saw him. He was standing beneath the tower in a leather jacket and jeans, scrolling through his phone. He looked like he belonged on the front of an estate agent's leaflet, encouraging young, trendy people to move to Crouch End.

Before I could back out, Noah looked up from his phone and the biggest smile spread across his face. And then he was walking towards me. I was rooted to the spot, my face contorted into an expression that was part startled, part nervous; my smile more of a grimace than the thing we do with our mouths when we're happy. Because I wasn't happy, I was bloody *terrified*.

'Maya? Hey! I'm Noah!' He spoke in exclamation marks and leant over for a hug. I stiffened, did something that resembled a return hug and inhaled his gorgeous scent. He smelt clean but with some sort of musky undertone.

'Hi,' I squeaked, my face already flushing. 'It's nice to meet you.'

'Likewise! Do you fancy grabbing some food instead of a coffee? I'm a lot hungrier than I thought I'd be and there's a nice Thai place up the hill if you fancy it? My treat?'

I knew the restaurant he was talking about and it happened to be halal as well, so I nodded my consent and followed his long strides towards Crouch End Hill, my brain working in overtime to try and process what was going on.

When we got to the restaurant, Noah helped me out of my brand-new, tan-coloured suede trench, the most expensive of the items Lucy had bought for me the day before. It was a bit embarrassing, with the material clinging to my shirt dress and him having to work a little harder to get it off. And when he did, I noticed that the bloody label was still on the jacket. He must have seen it, it was too conspicuous not to and once again I felt heat creep up my neck, giving me the appearance of a scarlet fever patient.

We finally sat down across from each other but I couldn't bring myself to stare at him the way I could feel him staring at me. Was this normal for an online date? It didn't feel normal. I had heard horror stories about guys refusing to pay for a single drink, or trying to get away with a free walk in the park to save money and here was Noah offering to pay for a meal? What was his endgame?

'So,' he began after we'd ordered our food, 'I really liked your RateMyDate profile. You sound like you're into the same sort of things as me.'

'I do?'

'Yeah! Well, that's the impression I got. What sort of things do you do in your free time?'

'I run, read, go out with my friends. I'm really into trying things I've never done before,' I replied slowly, trying not to give away the fact that the latter part of my statement was all thanks to him and his list.

'Me too,' Noah grinned, taking a bite out of the prawn crackers that had appeared at our table. 'What was the last thing you read?'

I thought for a moment, wondering if I should come out and say it. It almost felt wrong, but it was the truth, sort of. It was *one of* the last things I read anyway.

'*Ulysses*,' I croaked, trying to keep my expression and voice neutral.

'NO BLOODY WAY,' Noah stared at me, his beautiful eyes, almost the same colour as my dress, wide in shock. 'I've read that. What did you think of it? I can't believe it.'

I wracked my brain, trying to remember what Noah had said about it. Oh yes. *Epic.* 'It was pretty epic,' I lied casually as I tried to recall positive things people had said about that blasted book. 'It's the most complete literary compendium of human experience, don't you think?'

Noah continued to stare at me, like he couldn't believe his luck. 'I agree completely.'

Changing the subject away from the book, because I didn't know what else to say about it, I asked him what sort of new things he had tried recently.

'Well, I went skydiving,' he told me. 'It's something I'd always wanted to do and I finally did it last year.'

'Guess what?' I said, taking a bite of the duck spring rolls that had arrived with some Thai fishcakes. 'I went skydiving recently as well, in Dubai.'

I had to stop myself from laughing when his jaw dropped open in surprise.

'You really don't look like the sort of woman who reads *Ulysses* and jumps out of planes.'

'Don't I?' I giggled. 'Do I look more like the Bollywood and knitting type?'

'Ha, no. You look like the type who likes fine dining, complicated cocktails and social media.'

'You're lying,' I almost choked on my drink. 'I don't look like that at all.'

'You do,' he insisted. 'You must know that you're beautiful. I can't tell you how nice it is to sit and eat and talk without you feeling the need to take pictures or document it all.'

He thought I was beautiful? He liked that I wasn't obsessed with social media? The latter, at least, was the real me, even if skydiving and *Ulysses* wasn't. And that was good enough for me.

'What else have you tried recently?' he asked as we continued to eat.

'Loads of things,' I said, wondering what I should reveal next. 'I ran Race for Life last month.'

'Wow! A runner who's also into charity? I feel like I've struck gold here,' he gushed, his face illuminated with joy. I felt the food swirl around in my stomach and tried to push aside the guilt.

'It's an important cause,' I shrugged nonchalantly, as though I had come up with the idea all on my own. 'I did a sponsored charity walk up Snowdon not too long ago as well.'

'No way!' he gasped. 'I trekked it last year. I'm hoping to do Kilimanjaro one day.'

'Me too!' I lied enthusiastically. 'I've always wanted to go to Nepal.'

'Nepal?' he repeated, his forehead creased in befuddlement.

'Kilimanjaro?' I reminded him.

'That's in Tanzania. Maybe you mean the Himalayas?'

'Oh yes, sorry, my bad,' I coughed, my cheeks flushed. 'My geography isn't great.'

'At last, she has a flaw,' Noah smiled good-naturedly as he scanned his beautiful eyes over my face, as though he couldn't believe his good fortune in meeting someone like me, who shared all the same interests as him.

When it was time for desserts, I reluctantly pretended that I was full, having barely touched the main course in my eagerness to appear as health-conscious as Noah. He also patted his belly and claimed to be stuffed. We ordered healthy green teas instead and I suddenly remembered Zakariya's plate piled high with rice and curry and how he was always encouraging me to eat more.

But before I could dwell on Zakariya and the moments that we had shared, Noah reached over and traced his finger over my 'tattoo' and I nearly died from the electric shock his touch sent buzzing through my body.

'I can't believe you have a tattoo in Arabic,' he said, his voice a little louder than a whisper. 'Do you speak Arabic?'

'A little,' I shrugged, trying to keep it cool, though inside I was anything but. Inside, I was a raging inferno, a hot mess of feelings and sensations I had never experienced before. Not with Zak, not with Kaito from uni, not the Duke from *Bridgerton*. What was happening right then was on another level. 'I've been taking lessons.'

'So have I,' he replied, his eyes moving from my wrist to my lips. 'I'm not surprised by how alike we are anymore. This is obviously destiny. Let me see what it says.'

Once again, his finger brushed against my skin and I felt instant goosebumps form along my forearms as he took my hand and brought it closer to his face as he tried to decipher the complicated calligraphy which was woven into a pattern until it was almost illegible.

'That's a "ha" and I think that's a "meem" and . . . is that a "ra"?'

'Hmmm?' I knew he was saying something but I could barely focus on anything but the sensation of my hand in his, on his warm breath tickling my skin. If this was what a mere touch was doing to my senses . . . for a brief second, I allowed my mind to fantasise further.

'Hmar? Your tattoo says Hmar!' Noah began to laugh, shaking me out of my drunken-esque stupor.

'Huh? What? What does that mean?' I felt groggy as I tried to surface from the pool of desire I was floating in. As my eyes began to focus and my mind sharpened, I realised that Noah had turned red from the exertion of trying to contain his laughter.

'Noah! What does it mean?' I repeated, my voice rising as the heat within me began to fizzle out.

'It . . . it means d-donkey,' Noah spluttered as he gave up trying to conceal his laughter and let it all out.

Mortified, I snatched my hand away and covered my face. I couldn't believe it! How could I not know that I had stuck a semi-permanent tattoo that said DONKEY on my hand? What sort of Arabic had I been learning for the past few months if I was too ignorant to notice it?

It took a while for Noah's hysterics to cease and when they did, he apologised profusely, his grey-green eyes still glistening with amusement.

'It's OK,' I sighed, my shoulders slumped in shame. 'I'm the fool. I should have done my due diligence, but it was difficult to make out the letters. I'm an idiot.'

'You're not,' he smiled, taking my hand again. 'You're funny, smart, exciting and possibly a bit crazy. But you're not an idiot.'

My heart began to speed up again and this time when I looked into those pools of green, the amusement was replaced with a sort of wonder.

Chapter Thirty-One

The following morning I woke up to a text and, in my sleepy state, I opened it, hoping it was from Noah:

ZAKARIYA: Hope your 'kinda date' went well.

Confused, I yawned and then rubbed my eyes before reading it again. It was from Zakariya, not Noah.

My eyes flew open, all traces of sleep gone.

I had had such a good time with Noah that I hadn't spared a thought for Zak at all. His weird text had disappeared from my mind altogether. Maybe I shouldn't have told him that I was going on a date? Maybe I should have lied to him? Did I owe him the truth? I had no idea, but I still felt guilty.

It was OK, thanks for checking in, I typed out, trying my best to sound nonchalant yet friendly. Were all male–female friendships this exhausting? I posed the question to both Dina and Lucy via voice-notes as I got ready for work. Dina replied with a simple 'shrug' emoji and Lucy's voice-note came back as I was walking downstairs, about to leave for work.

'Babes, male–female friendships are rarely simple, especially if one party has ever expressed romantic interest in the other,' her voice rang out from my phone as I entered the kitchen. 'In fact, all men are just a waste of time.'

I had cut it too close to have breakfast so was planning to grab a banana and make a dash for it, but the sight of my brother standing there scowling, still in his flannel PJs, made me stop for a moment.

'Everything OK?' I asked warily, stuffing my phone into my pocket.

Malik grunted and turned to look at me. He had dark circles under his eyes and his beard had gone from a perfectly manicured lawn to an overgrown forest. He looked rough.

'Yeah, fine,' he muttered as he opened cupboard after cupboard.

'What are you looking for?'

'Coffee, where the hell is it?'

'Err, right in front of you. Where it's been for the last decade or so.' I pushed the coffee and sugar canisters that were kept on the counter towards him.

'You always have to add something extra, don't you? Why couldn't you pass it to me without adding a snarky remark?'

My hand froze by the fruit bowl. Making snarky remarks was our thing. It was what brothers and sisters did. It wasn't just a global tradition, it was a rite of passage. Why was he crying about it now?

'Because it's pretty ridiculous that a grown-arse twenty-five-year-old who has lived in the same house his whole life is so pampered that he doesn't know where the coffee's kept!' I replied, grabbing my banana and turning to leave the kitchen. Honestly, I didn't know why I bothered with him half the time.

'More ridiculous than a twenty-seven-year-old spinster who doesn't pay for a single thing at home deciding on a whim to go back into education so she can carry on burdening everyone?'

The words came at me like bullets from a machine gun, lodging themselves into my flesh and I stopped mid-stride, too stricken to move. Was that what he really thought of me? Was that what *everyone* thought? I opened my mouth to respond, but I didn't know what to say. So I closed it and without a word, I continued my way out of the house. It was only when I got to the station that I realised the banana in my hand had been squashed to a pulp.

'Your brother said that?' Lucy asked in disbelief when I relayed the morning's encounter to her.

'Welcome to my world,' I responded flatly. 'Where my brother reigns supreme and I am but a lowly, unworthy scullery maid.'

'I'm sure he didn't mean it, babe,' Lucy looked at me sympathetically, the pity on her face making me feel worse. 'Maybe he's stressed about something else and took it out on you?'

'Maybe,' I shrugged. 'But the truth usually comes out when people are stressed. He's right. I *am* a burden.'

'You're not! Are you telling me that your parents would rather you moved out?'

I couldn't help but snort at that. Moving out of my parents' perfectly adequate London house, when I worked in London, would mean only one thing to my extended family and community: I was up to no good.

'Fair point,' I conceded. 'Anyway, let me tell you about my date with Noah before Sheila gets back from her meeting.'

As Lucy, Arjun and I sipped on our masala tea, I gave them a rundown of the date.

'It couldn't have gone better,' I concluded. 'We were on the same page about everything. It was like we were made for each other and I could tell he was thinking the same thing.'

Arjun and Lucy exchanged glances.

'What is it?' I asked, looking at one and then the other as they sat there, both the epitome of a perfect poker face.

Lucy remained stoically silent, so Arjun piped up. 'Well,' he began in his Essex drawl, 'maybe it *felt* like you were made for each other because you're doing all the things on his list, so now he thinks that you're kindred spirits . . . but you're not.'

Ouch.

'I see what you're saying,' I began slowly, heat flooding my cheeks. 'But the fact is, I *am* doing those things. It's me doing them, so what if his list inspired me? It's not like I'm lying. This is the new me.'

'Did you tell him that you hated *Ulysses* so much that you fantasised tearing out the pages one by one, but the only reason you didn't is because you like the prestige of it sitting on your bookshelf for potential suitors to spot?'

'I didn't hate it!' I protested weakly. 'Look, guys, Noah and I are obviously hitting it off and yes, he met the new me, but if you remember, he met the *old* me on the Tube and he liked that version as well!'

'Did you tell him about your Tube encounter and having his notebook?' Lucy finally asked, when I was beginning to wonder if her larynx had had a seizure.

'No,' I admitted. 'How can I? He'll think I'm crazy!'

The two of them looked down at their desks in a way that made me feel like they definitely thought I was crazy. Well, the pair of them could get lost. They were supposed to be happy for me, but instead they were ruining it all. First my brother and now my friends.

Later that afternoon, Sheila finally responded to my email:

To: Maya Rahman
From: Sheila Steadman
Subject: Re: Hours

Dear Maya,

Thank you for your email. Unfortunately, it will not be possible to offer you part-time hours, as your role is one which requires full-time hours. Please find your contract attached.

Do let me know how you would like to proceed.

Regards,

Sheila

This day had delivered one emotional blow after another. Tears threatening to flow, I grabbed my jacket and bag and left the office, despite it being only 4.45. Bursting out into the warm evening outside, I began walking in the opposite direction to the station. And then I began to run like I was on one of my morning jogs, not wearing loafers and chinos and carrying a cumbersome tote. I ran past the shops and office buildings, my feet pounding on the hard concrete beneath me. I ran until I was on a wide, leafy residential road with huge, terraced houses glued to each other like Lego pieces.

Why did Malik turn my banter into something darker? Why did Sheila use her power to try and quash my dreams instead of uplifting them? Why did my friends think that Noah didn't like me for *me*?

Maybe, a voice inside me whispered, *no one liked me for me*. I simply wasn't good enough and it was only through the process of the list that I had become palatable. There was a reason why I had never had a relationship before, halal or otherwise. Even Zakariya, who seemed to like me, only really knew the *new* me – the one who took Arabic classes and trekked mountains like him. He wouldn't have given the old me the time of day.

Heart thumping, knees aching, feet blistered, I came to an abrupt stop. As I gasped for breath, tears streaming down my face, I felt a hand on my arm. I spun round, half expecting to be attacked – because what woman doesn't fear for her life when she's out on her own? – but then I saw that it was Fareena, my therapist. My eyes darting wildly around the road, I realised I was a street or two away from her home office.

'Maya? Are you OK?' she asked me, her face lined with concern. When I couldn't answer through all the gasps, she placed both hands on my arms and instructed me to breathe slowly, in through my nose, hold it and then out through my mouth. When I finally managed to nod, she gently took my arm and led me to a nearby coffee shop. Ushering me inside to an empty table, she disappeared to the counter and then returned with two herbal teas. Through the haze, the sensible part of me wondered if she was going to bill me for this. Surely, she was going against standard therapist–patient protocols by acknowledging me in public?

'Do you want to talk about what happened?' she asked after a few minutes of the two of us sitting in silence drinking our tea. I shrugged unhelpfully and stared out of the window, too emotionally and physically wrecked to attempt to pretend to be OK.

'I don't know,' I said when the silence stopped being comforting and started becoming embarrassing. 'I'm so sorry you saw me like that. How much do I owe you for the tea?' I started rummaging through my bag for my wallet and Fareena stopped me.

'Don't apologise for your feelings,' she said, more firmly than I had heard her speak before. 'Whatever is going on, how you feel is completely valid. I'm here if you want to talk but I won't push you if you don't.'

'I really don't know,' I said again, feeling stupid. 'I don't know why I'm crying like this. It's ridiculous. I'm lucky, I know I'm lucky, to have a good life, good health, good friends. My problems are insignificant in the grand scheme of things.'

'But we're not living in the grand scheme of things, we're also living our own lives, in the micro scheme of things. And in this micro scheme, it's OK to feel upset, or angry, or let down, or whatever you're feeling. You don't have to compare yourself to anyone better or worse off. This is your life, your space and your problems and feelings,' she told me.

So I began to talk and Fareena listened, asking me questions every so often, but mostly letting me talk.

'Have you ever told your parents or your brother about how you feel like you've been ignored and sidelined most of your life?' she asked me after I told her about Malik's comment and how, in the past, whenever I went to my parents with any issues I had with him, they always belittled me and essentially gaslit me.

'No, never. It's easier to keep the peace, you know?'

'I do know,' she said after a moment. And then, looking me straight in the eye, she added, 'I get why you want to keep the peace around you, but what about the peace *inside* you?'

I was exhausted when I made my way to the nearest Tube station. Although all I wanted to do was climb into my bed, I wasn't ready to go home yet, so instead of getting off at Turnpike Lane, I continued all the way to Oakwood and to Dina's house without calling or texting to let her know I was coming.

Dina opened the door, baby Sama attached to her in a sling. If she was surprised to see me, she didn't show it. Instead, she welcomed me into the house as though she had been expecting me and little Sami came running over and hugged my legs. That nearly set me off again, but I controlled myself. I had cried enough for one day.

Later, after Sami was in bed, Mohammed gracefully excused himself under the guise of wanting to get some reading done and left Dina and me to catch up. Dina made us both fancy hot chocolate with her Velvetiser while I held the baby and told her what had been going on.

'That was really harsh of Malik,' she sympathised, bringing her fancy porcelain mug to her mouth. The baby began to cry and root for milk and with an exhausted sigh, Dina took her from me to feed her.

'I don't know how you do it all,' I told her as she latched the baby onto her breast and closed her eyes. 'How are you coping? What can I do to help you?'

'I'm OK, hun,' Dina replied quietly. 'Just tired. I didn't breastfeed Sami so I really wanted to give it a proper go with Sama, but it's bloody hard. She's glued to me 24/7, no one else can feed her but me. She won't take a bottle so I can't express. I'm desperate to sleep.'

'And here I am keeping you up.' I hung my head in shame.

'No, I'm glad you're here. It's a nice distraction from all this.' She gestured to the living room, which was littered with toys. I had never seen Dina's house so messy. Cluttered, yes, but never like this. There were Mega Blocks scattered all over the floor, toy cars, trains, dinosaurs, balls, those fruit and vegetables that were joined with Velcro . . . everything was everywhere.

Downing my hot chocolate in one go, I got down on my hands and knees and began tidying away the toys into the correct boxes. Dina protested weakly but I ignored her and got on with it in silence. My throat was sore from all the crying and talking with Fareena and it felt good to quietly get on with something easy and methodical.

'By the way,' Dina began after all the toys had been tidied up and I was putting away the arts and crafts supplies, 'I've been meaning to tell you; I saw Malik with a woman a few weeks ago and they were definitely more than just friends. Maybe that's why he's been acting off?'

'What were they doing? Or is it better I don't know?'

'Nah, it wasn't anything crazy. They were in Morrisons in Palmer's Green shopping for groceries, holding hands. It was cute but I didn't go up to them in case he got embarrassed.'

'What did she look like?'

'Pretty. Really pretty, in that traditional English girl-next-door kind of way. Long blonde hair, blue eyes, banging figure. I wish I had taken a picture to show you. You could have searched her picture on Google and figured out who she was.'

'She must live around there then,' I mused, half to myself, putting my detective hat on. 'Why else would anyone be in Palmer's unless they lived there?'

'True,' Dina said. 'Do you know anyone who lives there?'

For the fifth time that day, I felt my blood turn cold. I *did* know someone who lived in Palmer's Green. My hands beginning to tremble, I took out my phone, opened up Instagram and scrolled through my followers until I had the page I was looking for, all the while praying I was wrong. Because if I was right, it meant that two of the people closest to me had been lying to my face for months. I handed my phone to Dina and she squealed in delight.

'Yes! That's her. Oh, wait. Is that Lucy as in . . .'

'Yes. My work colleague and friend.'

'Damn. And she never told you?'

'Nope.'

Dina and I both stared at Lucy's page, at the carefully curated snapshots of the version of her life that she shared with the world. There wasn't a single hint of her dating someone, let alone my brother.

I didn't bother going home that night. I sent my mum a text telling her I was staying over at Dina's house and spent the night tossing and turning next to Sami's warm little body. His arms and legs were all over the place and all night he alternated between flinging his body across mine, thumping me in the face and kicking me in the ribs. He could have been as still as a statue, but I still wouldn't have slept. I couldn't. There was too much going on. My head was so messed up that I hadn't even been able to bring myself to text Noah back. He had messaged at some point, asking me if I was free to meet up over the weekend. I was free, but after Arjun and Lucy's comments about him only liking me because he thought we were similar, I was left with a bitter taste about the whole thing.

I tried to remember what Malik had told me about Lucy but the details were blurry. It was something about her not being suitable enough to have a future with. How he thought she was into her career more than having a family. Of all the women in London, why did he pick her? My colleague? My friend?

What felt worse than his lies, though, were hers. It all made sense now, why she was so happy to help me with my stupid list. I wasn't simply Maya, her work colleague. I was Maya, her potential future sister-in-law.

Then there was Sheila. What was my future going to look like if I packed in my job?

Looking around Sami's bedroom at three in the morning, at the sage green walls with a mural of a whale painted over the fireplace and all the toys neatly organised in wicker baskets, I wondered if I would ever get all this for myself: a pretty house in the suburbs, an adorable baby and toddler, bougie hot chocolate in a fancy mug. The strange thing was, I didn't know how badly I wanted it all, until now.

Chapter Thirty-Two

The next morning I woke up with a banging headache. Sami was no longer next to me and I could hear him pottering around somewhere in the house. As much as I wanted to, I couldn't hide in Dina's house forever – she had a newborn baby to deal with and I didn't want to burden her like I had apparently been burdening everyone else – but the thought of facing Malik made me ill. It was unlikely that he would be at home on a Saturday, so I dragged myself home later that morning, praying that he wouldn't be there.

The house was quiet and still when I entered, everything pristine without a speck of dust in sight thanks to Ma's obsession with cleanliness. No one was home, so I shuffled about in the kitchen for a bit, making myself some tea and toast before heading up to my room. Ma had left a basket of my clean clothes fresh off the clothes horse and once again, I felt the sting of Malik's accusation.

Once I had put my laundry away, I half-heartedly pulled out Noah's notebook and flicked through the pages until I got to the next item on the list. I wasn't in the mood for Noah's antics, but I needed a distraction from the mess that was my life:

22. PAY OFF CC ✓

DONE!!! £6,790 all gone – finally debt-free and it bloody feels amazing! DO NOT EVER PUT YOURSELF IN THIS SORT OF SITUATION AGAIN!!!!

I felt bad as I read number twenty-two. Now that we had met again in real life and he was no longer a fantasy, but a real-life person I was possibly about to go on a second date with, it felt like an invasion of his privacy. What if he didn't want me to know that he used to have credit-card debt?

Thanks to the fact that I had been 'burdening' my parents all these years and that I didn't have much of a life or style until recently, I had zero debt and hefty savings. Under Noah's note, I wrote, *Alhamdulillah, this isn't something I need to do. Maybe look into investing money instead?*

Moving onto twenty-three, Noah had written:

23. GET OVER FEAR OF KARAOKE! ✓

Bloomsbury Lanes private room – was jokes! Still can't sing but all good.

The thought of doing karaoke made my stomach turn. Some people liked getting up there and having everyone watch them fooling about, but I didn't. I couldn't think of anything worse than being the centre of attention. I would never be able to relax or let myself go. How was I supposed to do this?

Something Fareena had said once came to me, about how sometimes we're the ones who cause our own difficulties and that if we got out of our own way, then incredible things could happen. I didn't think she meant going to karaoke, but the sentiment still rang true.

Before I could persuade myself otherwise, I opened up Noah's last message asking if I wanted to meet up at the weekend and texted him back. I was in desperate need of a distraction and some fun, something to take the edge off the pain that was currently residing within me:

MAYA: You up for some karaoke?

NOAH: Count me in! Tonight?

MAYA: If you're free?

NOAH: I have a client at 5, so can meet around 8?

MAYA: Perfect, I'll see what's available.

The place Noah went for karaoke was fully booked, so I booked the smallest private booth at a place in Holborn and arranged to meet him there.

As I got ready for our date, I was acutely aware that I still didn't know if Noah was Muslim or not. If he wasn't, whatever we were doing wasn't going to lead anywhere, so why was I still doing it?

Noah was already there waiting for me when I walked up to the doors leading down to the basement that housed the various private karaoke booths. I felt nervous as I approached him. He was looking down at his phone and I got a few seconds of observing him unnoticed and he didn't disappoint in a white T-shirt that showed off his beautiful colouring and faded, ripped jeans. We were sort of matching and for the first time in my life, I felt the overwhelming need to get a picture of us together so I could forever remember the time I matched outfits with the hottest man in London.

'Hey,' I called out as I approached him. He smiled when he saw me; a wide, easy, unassuming smile, causing my belly to do a little somersault and pushing away the darker thoughts that had been plaguing me since the day before.

'Hello,' he replied, his voice warm and smooth, like custard when it's made right. He reached over to hug me and I let him, feeling another stab of guilt. *Was this going to go any-where? If not, why was I letting this random man touch me?* I persuaded myself that I wouldn't cross any more lines, that this would be the extent of any physical moments between us. It's not as if I was behaving like my brother – going on holidays and shopping in Morrisons with a woman I had no intention of marrying. It was karaoke. There was a vague hug. That was it.

'Fancy a selfie?' I asked him before we made our way inside the venue. 'We're sort of matching.'

Noah laughed at that and pulled me closer to him as I angled the phone and took a picture of us both. His body was warm, his muscles defined but not in an over-the-top, body-building kind of way and it felt good to be nestled against him.

We followed the hostess down to our private booth, a small, dark room with a leather bench along one wall, a TV screen and a couple of microphones. The hostess gave us a rundown of how to use the system and order food and drinks and then she was gone and it was Noah and me, in the dark.

Gulp.

'What do you want to drink?' Noah asked, his voice slicing through the silence, punctuated only by my heartbeat.

'Red Bull, please,' I said quickly. 'Err, I don't drink,' I added hastily. 'I'm Muslim.'

'I thought so,' he said easily. 'I am too, so I'll get us two Red Bulls. Anything else? I'm thinking of nachos and fries.'

'Sounds good,' I said calmly, maintaining a composure I certainly wasn't feeling inside. Inside, I was laughing hysterically. HE WAS MUSLIM! What a relief!

The conflict I had been experiencing only moments before ended as though a white flag had been waved. This was no longer a pointless date; it could actually lead somewhere!

I settled into the bench as we chose the list of songs. I said 'we' but it was more Noah who did the choosing; I sat back and let him take the lead. His enthusiasm was a welcome change from Zakariya's cool indifference and he worked through the lists adding mostly R&B and hip-hop tracks.

'You know, I've never done karaoke before,' I told him as I watched him staring intently at the little computer, scrolling through the songs.

'I've only done it once before,' he replied and a stab of guilt pierced through me. I knew this already.

'How was it?' I croaked, taking a gulp from my drink.

'Better than I thought it would be. I had a sort of irrational fear of it, but I got over it after that night. We had a lot of fun.'

'Yeah, I'm a bit nervous,' I admitted. 'I don't have the worst voice but it's the thought of being up there with people watching me that stresses me out.'

'Well, the only person here is me,' he said, turning to smile reassuringly at me. 'And we'll sing together anyway. Here we go, I'm going to start the music. You ready, Ariana?'

'Ariana?' I squeaked. 'Talk about setting the bar high.'

Noah shrugged. 'You kinda look like her.'

I most certainly did not. Was he playing me?

The music started and I giggled when I recognised the opening notes to 'Gangsta's Paradise', relieved that I wouldn't have to *actually* sing.

'You ready for this?' Noah asked, moving his body to the music.

'As ready as I'll ever be,' I replied, standing up to join him, getting ready for the rap to start. '*As I walk through the valley of the shadow of death . . .*'

The next two hours sped by in a blur of music and food. Sometimes Noah sang and danced alone as I caught my breath, sometimes he watched me bop along like a fool to noughties pop, sometimes we sang duets, other times we didn't bother singing, we just sat back and talked over the music. At the beginning, I was painfully self-conscious, thankful that the room was dark. By the end, I was sweating from all the jumping around, my throat ached from the shouting and singing (more often the former than the latter) and my belly hurt from all the laughter. My inhibitions became smaller and smaller as the night progressed and by the time it hit 10 p.m. and our two hours ran out, I no longer cared what I looked like with my wild hair and red face. We were having so much fun that it didn't matter.

Emerging out into the cool night was a welcome relief from the heat and humidity of the booth. Noah tried to slip his hand into mine but I pulled it away, embarrassed.

'Sorry, my palms are sweaty,' I explained, rubbing them onto my jeans.

'Are your knees weak and arms heavy, as well?' he replied, a twinkle in his eye.

Laughing, I continued the lyrics and once again, the atmosphere was light and fun and we continued to sing the rest of the song together. When Noah grabbed my hand again, I didn't stop him. Now that he was marriage material, surely a bit of hand-holding was OK?

'Shall we get some proper food?' he asked as we walked through the backstreets of Holborn towards Covent Garden, which was buzzing despite the hour. 'I'm starving after all that dancing.'

'Sure,' I replied genially and allowed him to lead me to a restaurant in the centre of the plaza, still relishing the feeling of his hand in mine.

'This place is halal,' he said as we stood outside the restaurant and perused the menu. I didn't care what or where we ate. I was happy to do anything that prolonged the night.

'You know, I can't shake this weird feeling I have,' Noah said as we sat down and ordered our food: chicken bao buns for me and a steak sub for him.

'What is it?'

'I don't know, I keep feeling like we've met before. Odd, right?'

'Uh yeah, very odd,' I agreed, shifting uncomfortably in my seat. 'I've been feeling like that too, but, uh, I don't know how we could have possibly met before.' I was rambling, I knew I was and I wish I had admitted the truth to him there and then. I didn't though. Something stopped me and when I had finished rationalising everything, I opened my mouth to suggest that we had perhaps met on the Tube – but he started speaking at the same time and the moment passed.

Chapter Thirty-Three

Over the next few weeks, Noah and I spent every free moment together, either in person or on the phone. We texted each other throughout the day and the messages went from friendly to flirty, making me wonder if we were officially a couple. I wanted to ask Lucy what she thought, but I couldn't because I was avoiding her like Coronavirus. I had no desire to confide in someone who didn't bother telling me that they were dating my *brother*.

'Maya, you're not going out today, are you?' Ma asked as she burst into my room at eight on a Sunday morning. I didn't get home until way past twelve after my cinema date with Noah and had barely slept the night before either. My head felt heavy, so I moaned and pulled my duvet over my head in protest.

'Wake up,' was Ma's unsympathetic response as she stalked over to the window and yanked the curtains open. With the duvet still over my head, I didn't see her do it, but I could hear her and I knew what was coming next.

Sure enough, a second later, the covers were pulled off my body.

'Your Nani's coming for lunch with your Aunt Lottie,' Ma informed me. Despite my eyes being squeezed closed, a last-ditch attempt to stay in bed, I could envision her glowering at me from the foot of the bed, her hands on her hips, her lips pursed. 'You've been out too much recently. Whatever plans you have today, cancel them and get up and clean the house and then help me in the kitchen.'

'Ma, I'm tired,' I groaned, refusing to open my eyes.

'I don't care. Khe tumareh khoiseh khali bareh bareh fakhai tai?' Ma snapped, berating me for going out so much. 'Now get up.'

Fearing a slipper slap next, I dragged myself out of bed and into the bathroom, where I wasted another half an hour on the toilet, scrolling through TikTok and responding to all my messages. While doing so, I remembered that I hadn't responded to Zakariya's last text. With everything going on with Noah, Lucy and work, I had completely forgotten. What could I say that was uncomplicated and polite, yet friendly and warm, without giving the wrong impression?

MAYA: Hey Zak, how are you? Sorry things have been really busy. Will be at Arabic next Thursday; shall we catch up then?

His response came immediately, while I was still on the loo: a lacklustre thumbs-up emoji. I felt oddly deflated. Was he being passive-aggressive? Was I the toxic one? I wouldn't know. My life was like a nuclear-power plant. I was so used to toxicity that I no longer knew how to recognise the signs.

The rest of the morning was spent cleaning the house to Ma's impossibly high standards and then helping her in the kitchen. Whenever Nani came over, Ma cooked at least eight curries, mostly fish and vegetables, the things my grandmother enjoyed. There was always meat and chicken though, as Malik wouldn't touch fish and would only tolerate vegetables. The annoying voice in my head added *and you're the burden, huh?* It had been a few weeks since he made that remark and I was becoming a bitter old hag because of it, the feeling intensifying whenever I walked past his closed bedroom door, the sound of his gentle snoring insulting my ears.

As I vacuumed the first floor, I made sure to knock the contraption against Malik's door several times. The resentment was steadily bubbling away inside me, ready to erupt like a volcano that had been lying dormant for decades.

'You're ruining the fish,' Ma gasped when I went down to help her in the kitchen. She had optimistically given me the job of de-scaling three different types of fish. 'Give it here, I'll do it. You de-skin the chicken instead and don't ruin it, I'm making tandoori chicken.'

'Why don't you ever get Malik to help?' I grumbled as I tried, in vain, to get the wet, slippery skin off the chicken pieces without taking the flesh off with it. 'He could have done the cleaning while I helped with the cooking and then everything would have got done faster.'

'Why are you always starting on your brother? He works really hard; he needs a bit of rest at the weekend.'

'And I don't work hard?' I dropped the piece of raw, skinless chicken that I was holding and stared at my mother with incredulity.

'Of course you do,' Ma said quickly, sensing a storm brewing. 'But you're so much more capable than he is. He's useless; if I asked him to hoover, he'd break it. You know what he's like.'

I was finally allowed out of the kitchen at noon, stinking of onions and garlic. I went to the bathroom to take a shower and get ready, but Malik had finally decided to wake up and was occupying the one bathroom we had in the house. Seething, I ironed mine and Ma's clothes while I waited for the bathroom to be free, all the while plotting ways I could get my own back on my stupid, lazy, entitled, *lying* brother.

'About bloody time,' I snapped when Malik emerged from the bathroom, wafts of steam and the scent of luxurious manly products following him out of the room. 'There are other people in this house, you know, who might need to use the bathroom.'

'What's your problem?' he glared at me, pushing past me and into his room.

'You!' I said to his retreating back, stomping into the bathroom and slamming the door behind me.

I had exactly three minutes in the shower, thanks to Malik hogging the bathroom and leaving me with barely any time to get ready. I also had to clean it again thanks to his hair being everywhere. He was shedding like the snake that he was. I forced myself to do deep breathing to calm myself down, but the flame in my belly was growing with every second. It was no longer a mere candle; it was well on its way to becoming a blazing forest fire and I didn't know how to make it stop.

I didn't have time to bother with my hair, so I threw on the cotton shalwar kameez I had ironed, secured my damp tresses with a clip and slapped on just enough makeup to look like I wasn't ill. Ma came up to shower and change, instructing me to keep an eye on the oven and stove. Which meant I was going to smell all over again. With a sigh, I went downstairs.

Baba and Malik were in the living room watching cricket and I scowled at them both for lazing around like kings while my mum and I rushed around like maids. I was about to open my mouth to make a cutting remark when the doorbell rang.

'Nani!' I cried out when I found my little grandmother on the other side of the door clutching her trusty handbag in one hand and a Tesco bag full of goodies in another. The anger that had been simmering all morning dampened the moment I saw her beautiful plump face and the eyes that lit up whenever she saw me.

'Yallah, amar Maya ni?' she asked, like she always did, like she didn't know it was me. In Arabic, Maya means princess, in Persian, it means gracious, but in Bengali, it means love.

That's why my grandmother named me Maya, apparently, because she always wanted me to feel loved. And by her, I did.

'Ji oi Nani,' I replied like I always did, confirming that it was, indeed, me, Maya, who was standing before her. I gave her a hug and ushered her into the house, greeting my uncle, Aunt Lottie and little cousin Ahmed as I did.

'Here, this is for you,' Nani whispered to me in Sylheti, handing the entire Tesco bag over to me. 'Don't share it with anyone.'

Laughing, I took the bag from her and put it in the kitchen, before helping her with her shoes and leading her to the living room to sit down with my dad and brother.

Now that our lunch guests were here, I had to rush around setting the table while Ma and Aunt Lottie began heating up all the food so that it would be piping hot when everyone sat down to eat. If it wasn't, you could be sure that if Nani didn't comment on the tepid temperature, Baba certainly would.

We finally sat down to eat, with Nani telling us about the latest dramas in our extended family and everyone gushing over Malik's latest achievement – trading in his BMW 5 Series for a bigger, more family-friendly X5, which he claimed was for Ma's comfort.

'What a thoughtful soul you are,' Nani said, mixing up a handful of rice with meat curry and feeding him with her hand; the epitome of demonstrating love in my family. If my eyes had rolled any harder, they would have fallen out of their sockets and spun across the room.

At some point, Aunt Lottie made a comment about me still being single – how I had to get a move on if I wanted to have kids – and Malik snickered as he shovelled food down his throat like he had never seen a curry before.

'Haven't you heard? Maya's going back to university so she'll be single for longer,' he said, chewing noisily. I hadn't mentioned this to my uncle or aunt, or Nani even, which caused the questioning to begin. Everyone started talking about what they thought I should or shouldn't do with my life. It was like I wasn't there, as they discussed whether studying further would increase or reduce my chances of finding a husband. Like I wanted to find a bloody husband!

Nani's presence usually calmed me, but having them all dissect my life was grating on my nerves. Malik the snitch sat there throughout with a holier-than-thou expression on his face. He was enjoying making me squirm, I could see that he was.

'How are you going to fund it all?' my uncle asked and before I could say that I had won a scholarship, Malik piped up.

'Well, she doesn't pay anything at home so she has plenty of spare cash.'

'And why should she?' Nani interrupted indignantly. 'She's a girl. Girls don't have to contribute financially.'

'So it should all be on me to pay for the kitchen and loft extensions?' Malik answered back, giving me daggers as though I was the one who had replied, not Nani.

I stared back at him, utterly flabbergasted. Was this why he was acting like this and harping on about me not contributing financially at home? Why had he never mentioned this to me before? Why had he waited for us to have lunch with my grandmother, uncle and aunt before revealing his dissatisfaction?

'Yes, it should,' Nani said calmly. 'Firstly, your inheritance will be twice the amount of Maya's, according to Islamic law. Secondly, Maya will get married and move out and you'll be here with your wife enjoying the extra space. That's how things work.'

'And for your information, while I may not contribute financially to running this house, I do other things,' I said, trying to keep the hurt and anger out of my voice. 'I'm the one who was up at the crack of dawn dusting skirting boards and de-skinning chicken, while you slept in!'

'Oh, big deal, you did a bit of housework,' Malik spat back and before I knew it, we were in a full-blown argument, all of us. I was shouting at my brother, he was shouting back, Ma was trying to make him stop, Baba was saying something to my uncle, my eight-year-old cousin Ahmed was crying and Nani was begging us all to be quiet.

'You're always so bloody miserable!' Malik shouted at me, both of us standing up and facing each other. 'You drain the life out of everything!'

'Oh and you're a bundle of joy yourself, aren't you?' I screamed back. 'Crying like a baby because your life is soooo sad while you mess around with MY FRIEND and refuse to commit to her!'

Malik shut up then. In fact, everyone fell silent.

'What are you talking about?' Ma demanded, looking from me to Malik in bewilderment.

'Ask your beloved son about who he took on holiday to Thailand! That's why he hates spending money at home. He's trying to keep up with his girlfriend, Lucy. She's white-English by the way and has very expensive taste—'

'Who's English? Who's "Loose"?' Nani interrupted, looking at us in confusion.

'Malik? What's going on? Is this true?' Ma gasped, the blood draining from her face.

'What's the meaning of all this?' Baba chimed in, as if he felt as though he had to say *something*.

'You stupid cow,' Malik snarled. 'You're jealous because no one's ever been interested in you!'

'That's what you think! FYI, there are two guys interested in me right now and both are willing to fight for what they want. They're not stringing me along and hiding me from the world like you're doing with Lucy!'

'What?' Ma turned to stare at me. 'What's going on? You have *two* boyfriends? Since when? La hawla wa la quwwata illah billah! A'oozo billiahi minash shaytaan irrajeem!' Ma started wailing Arabic prayers, asking God to get rid of Satan. *Fudge.* I hadn't meant to let that slip. In fact, I hadn't meant to let *anything* slip, but Malik kept pushing me until I was past my limit and well past the point of no return.

'Hope you're happy! This is all your fault!' I screamed at my brother before running out of the dining room. I heard Malik do the same. A second later, I slammed the door to my bedroom, Malik had stormed out of the house and everyone else remained downstairs, lunch long forgotten.

No one came up to bother me for hours and I sat there on my bed, sobbing like a teenager. Malik was right, I *was* a miserable old leech. I tried praying, but my mind was too distracted and I went through the motions shakily, without really focusing or connecting with God.

After my prayers, I flopped down onto my bed and took out Noah's journal. The book had become a lot of things for me over the past nine and a half months. It felt like the one, steady constant that gave me a sense of purpose. I always knew what I was going to do next, no matter how small or big the task was. The act of holding it in my hands helped soothe me; I ran my fingers over the soft leather, tracing over Noah's embossed initials.

My bedroom door opened and I dropped the book like a hot handesh, guilty at being caught. But it was only Nani, who shuffled into my room carrying a tray with tea, biscuits and mishti on it. I leapt out of bed and relieved her of it, feeling bad that she had carried it all the way upstairs.

'Nani, afneh ita kita khorrah? What are you doing? I could have carried this!' I scolded her gently, as I placed the tray on my vanity and offered her a seat on my bed. She sat down and I handed her one of the teacups.

'How, when you're hiding away in here?' she replied, giving me a sharp look. 'Tell me what's been going on, my Maya-shuna. Why are you and your brother fighting? You two only have each other, it's not nice seeing you fight like that.'

'He's been really awful with me recently,' I replied in my broken Bengali mixed with a heavy dose of English. 'He keeps making digs and comments about me being a burden. I feel like moving out.'

'Toubah ostoghrifullah!' Nani scolded me, imploring God for forgiveness in her heavily accented Arabic. 'How can an unmarried girl like you move out of her parents' home? Mansheh kita khoibah?'

'What will people say?' was my Nani's favourite phrase and could be applied to nearly any situation. Going back to uni. *What will people say?* Going to a life-drawing class. *What will people say?* Going on holiday with friends. *What will people say?*

'Tell that to Malik. He's the one who called me a burden.'

'You're not a burden, my shuna,' Nani said soothingly, stroking my hair as I leant my head on her shoulder. 'You're the opposite. You're the life and foundation of this family. Without you there would be no warmth, no soul.'

'Really?'

'Really. I'm sure your brother's reaction has nothing to do with you. He's probably worried about this shada girlfriend of his and what everyone's reaction will be.'

'I shouldn't have said anything,' I said, hanging my head in shame. 'He'll never forgive me.'

'You were only reacting because of the things he was saying to you. You've probably done him a favour, forcing it all out in the open. Maybe now he can move forward with his life. And you need to do the same. Move forward with life, however you see fit. If it's not with a husband, then progress in other ways, like studying. It's OK, my shuna. But first, what is this about two boys?'

'It's nothing important, Nani,' I admitted. 'I just said that to make Malik shut up.'

After Nani and co. had left, I picked up the notebook from where it had fallen on the floor. I hesitated every time I opened it now. Noah and I were sort of dating, if you could call it that when there was no kissing or hanky-panky going on. It was more like courting. The point was, he wasn't a stranger anymore and reading his list was like looking into his mind. It was private.

But I was so close to the end. How could I stop now? I pushed aside any feelings of guilt and opened it up to the next page:

24. PUT DOWN AN OFFER ON A HOUSE

Can't find anything decent within budget – keep looking, don't give up!

I re-read it, feeling proud of my man and everything he was doing to make his life better. What was it that Nani had said to me? Something about continuing to grow and progress in life, with or without a husband. Maybe it was time for me to put down some roots on my own. In fact, Baba had been telling me to look into property for a while, but I hadn't taken it seriously. I could easily afford a deposit on a flat, but if I was going to reduce my hours to part-time, or leave my job, I wouldn't be able to get a mortgage. I decided there and then to find a mortgage advisor and get the ball rolling while I still had the chance.

Zakariya seemed like the person who would know about this stuff, so despite the cold vibes I got from his earlier message, I texted him and asked him if he knew any mortgage advisors. Immediately, I felt a sense of relief and the lunch-time drama stung a little less. I knew what I was going to do next with my life and that's what mattered.

Chapter Thirty-Four

Malik had been ignoring me since the disastrous lunch and I did the same in return. Avoiding him meant I was holed up in my bedroom most of the time, more so because I had bunked work for three consecutive days, feigning the flu. By now, Malik had surely told Lucy that I knew about them and I couldn't bear to face her. I wasn't eating my mum's food and was surviving on cereal to avoid going downstairs when anyone was home. I had reached an all-time low.

My brother wasn't the only one who had aired me. Zakariya didn't respond to my message about the mortgage advisor and the rebuff stung. Whatever. I didn't need him. I asked Dina instead, who shared the details of the one she used, and I made an appointment for later that week and carried on scouring Rightmove, putting all the potential properties in my favourites folder.

There was a saying that when one door closed, another opened. Life felt like the other way round for me. When one door opened, four windows and doors closed. I had finally found Noah – the object of my fantasies for many months – and simultaneously lost Lucy, my brother, Zakariya and possibly my job. Things were strained with my parents and instead of helping me, therapy was uncovering feelings and issues that I hadn't realised I had.

Maybe the list could help. Taking a break from scrolling through property listings, I retrieved the notebook from my desk drawer and opened it up to number twenty-five:

25. COOK A BANGING THREE-COURSE MEAL ✓

Done. Starters: caramelised fig and goat's cheese tart. Mains: rib-eye steak with honey-glazed carrots, creamy mustard mash and garlicky greens. Dessert: white chocolate and raspberry cheesecake. The girls are gonna go crazy for this one.

I felt a little twinge of jealousy over the girls going 'crazy' over his menu. What else were they going crazy over? How many women had he wooed with his cooking? The list was nearly over and so far, he had done everything on it. I hadn't yet reached the point where he lost his journal. It took all my willpower not to forge ahead and find out what happened next in his life, but I had come this far without screwing it up, so I didn't want to do it now.

My bedroom door suddenly burst open and Ma stomped in, the concept of privacy completely alien to her. She made a face upon surveying the state of both me and my room.

'Maya, you need to come out of your room,' she implored, her hands on her hips, as she took in my unwashed hair with matching unwashed face, the crumpled sheets, the empty cereal bowls which had dry bits of Frosties encrusted in the sticky remnants of milk.

'Nah, I'm good,' I said sullenly, putting my AirPods into my ears like a teenager. Despite everything that had transpired during the family lunch from hell, Ma hadn't asked me *anything*. Maybe she had got the lowdown from my nani or maybe she didn't want to get into an argument with me.

'Good? You haven't been to work in two days!' Ma said.

'I'll go in tomorrow,' I replied, still not looking her in the eye.

'Make sure you do. You don't want to lose your job over this.'

'Of course not. Wouldn't want to be more of a burden.' I finally looked at my mum then and was surprised to see the sadness in her eyes.

'You're not a burden, Maya,' she said quietly, averting her gaze. Walking over to my desk, she began gathering up my dirty crockery. 'You're my daughter. Until you get married, your place is with me. And when that day comes, this house will become dark and empty.'

Her voice cracked then and I was a little taken aback by the pain in her voice. In her face I could see so many emotions flash past: sadness, confusion, regret. What did she regret? Did she realise that both she and Baba always treated Malik better than me?

I thought back to something Fareena had said, about how avoiding confrontations prevented change and growth. This year, the list, was supposed to be about me growing as a person and while I had in so many ways, I was also stuck because of years and years of hiding my feelings to avoid upsetting people.

It was finally time to tell Ma how I felt.

'I guess I feel like I take second place to Malik,' I said quietly, picking at the skin around my nails.

'You don't!' Ma protested weakly. 'We love you the same, but we treat you differently because you're different people. You wouldn't respond to us in the same way.'

There was another long pause while I tried to articulate what I wanted to say next. I could feel tears brewing and I was angry with myself. I didn't want to cry. I wanted to have a rational conversation without it turning into a fight. I wanted to be heard.

At this point, the old me would have let it go, but after everything I had been through and how far I had come, I decided not to back down for the first time in my life.

'Ma, you and Baba practically revere him,' I said, trying to keep my voice from wobbling. 'It's been like this since we were kids. Whenever he would do something, like break your favourite dish or kill your plants with his football, you would blame me.'

Ma looked uncomfortable then and as always, I felt a pang of guilt.

'That was a long time ago, Maya,' she said. 'Parents aren't perfect. We make mistakes too.'

'But it's not a long time ago, Ma. You're still like that. You never question him, you never ask anything of him, you never rely on him. You're always gushing over him, bending over backwards to make him happy, make him feel loved, going on and on about his achievements. It's tough living in his shadow.'

I looked up at my mum, hating myself for telling her how I felt, but at the same time, getting it off my chest was a relief.

And then she did something unexpected. She didn't continue to try and defend herself. She didn't deflect or gaslight. She put down all the bowls, spoons and mugs she was carrying, sat down next to me on the bed and put her arms around me.

'You're right,' she whispered. 'I'm sorry.' Pulling away, Ma looked me in the face with tears brimming in her eyes, mirroring my own.

'I was pregnant once before you,' she said, her voice thick with sadness. 'It was a boy and I lost him when he was nearly full term. When you were born, some members of your dad's family gave me a really hard time for not producing another boy. They made me feel like I was inferior somehow. I didn't care, at least I thought I didn't, but looking back it did affect me. When Malik was born, everyone was so happy that I'd had a boy and they spoilt him rotten. They were different with me after that, better, like I had finally given them what they wanted and if I'm honest, I relished the attention. It set the tone and I don't know why I haven't stopped. I'm sorry.'

Tears were streaming down Ma's face and I hugged her closer to me, my own face as wet as hers. We cried together, for our losses and our mistakes.

'It's OK, Ma,' I whispered after the tears ran out, yet we remained holding onto each other. 'It's OK.'

After Ma left my room, I opened my windows, changed my bed covers, took a long, hot shower and spent the rest of the day with her.

I told her that I wanted to learn how to make a 'banging' three-course meal so we went shopping for the ingredients together and then made lamb kebabs and a tomato and onion salad with poppadoms for starters, butter chicken, homemade naan and chana daal for mains and a mango and lime cheese-cake for dessert. It was spectacular and instead of waiting to have it for dinner with Baba and Malik the Muppet, Ma and I enjoyed a late lunch together and spent the rest of the afternoon watching Pakistani dramas. In the middle of a particularly exciting episode of *Mere Humsafar*, Ma turned to me and casually asked if what I had said about having two boys on the scene was true. My hand froze by my mouth and I put the piece of popcorn I was about to eat back into the bowl.

'Be honest, Maya,' she said, pausing the TV and looking at me intently. 'What's going on?'

'Honestly, not much,' I admitted, embarrassed. 'There's a guy I sort of like called Noah, but it's early days and we're just friends.'

'What do you mean by that exactly?' Ma probed, looking worried. 'I've always trusted you to do the right thing, Maya, and you've never let me down. Can I trust that you're not crossing any boundaries?'

'Of course!' I replied indignantly, my cheeks flushing. Was this the Bengali Muslim equivalent of the birds and the bees talk? 'We just talk and do activities here and there. Nothing haram, I promise!'

'OK,' Ma said after a while. 'But you will tell me if anything progresses?'

'I will, Ma, don't worry.'

'And what's this about your brother and that shada girl? Do I need to be worried about that?'

I shrugged and reached for a handful of popcorn. 'You need to talk to Malik about that. He barely tells me anything. I found out by chance.'

After a moment, Ma continued to play the episode and I exhaled in relief, thankful that the awkward conversation was over.

What I had told my mum was true though. I wasn't doing anything *overtly* haram. Not the sort of thing she was worried about anyway. Noah texted me consistently throughout the day, as he did most days. He had followed me on Insta and Snap and we had been exchanging reels and memes for the better part of the day. I sent him pictures of what we were cooking and he responded with a picture of his own meal. It looked very much like the three-course meal he had learnt to make recently – I doubted he happened to cook it that day. I obviously couldn't call him out on sending me an old picture, so I showered him with praise instead, feeling both tickled and guilty as I did so.

We hadn't put a label on what we were to each other, but with all the 'x's' that punctuated our messages and the increasingly endearing sentiments, it was clear that we were more than friends. Every time my phone buzzed, I felt a jolt of excitement shoot through me and eagerly checked for Noah's message. If it wasn't him, I'd feel a little deflated. I replied immediately to his texts, contrary to everything I had learnt about reeling a man in from popular culture and he did the same. We were fast becoming firm fixtures in each other's phones, although it hadn't quite translated to offline life yet.

'Why are you grinning?' Ma suddenly looked away from the dramatic scene of a woman running away from her evil husband on the telly, as I read Noah's latest text:

NOAH: I miss you. Desperately need to see you. Free tonight?

'I'm not,' I lied, wiping the grin off my face so quickly it was like someone had poured cold water over my head. When Ma went back to watching the rest of the show, I snuck my phone out and replied:

MAYA: Miss you too. And I'll make myself free for you x.

At around five in the afternoon, Ma went upstairs to rest so after I cleaned up all the mess we had made that day, I took out Noah's list. There weren't many items left to complete and the thought of going through life without this bit of guidance and direction made me anxious. I made a mental note to raise this during my next session with Fareena:

26. VISIT UNCLE F IN LIVERPOOL, MAKE AMENDS.

That was it. No notes. This must have been where Noah had got to when we met that day on the Tube, or maybe he hadn't had a chance to update it, or it was still in progress. Although I wondered who Uncle F was and why they needed to make amends, I was relieved that there were no further details and that I had reached the end of his notes. I already felt bad that

I knew so much about his personal life, things he would never have shared with me at this stage in our relationship.

It was pretty obvious how I would have to tailor this to suit my life. I would have to make amends with Malik and Lucy. How and when, I wasn't sure, but I knew it had to be done.

Chapter Thirty-Five

That night, I met up with Noah, feeling nervous and shy as if we were meeting for the first time. The all-day-and-all-night texting had brought us closer, but now that I was going to see him in the flesh, I suddenly felt embarrassed about the flirting and little innuendos that our messages had evolved into.

Noah suggested that we go for a walk and although 'walking' wasn't my idea of a perfect date (isn't walking what you did to *get* to the actual date?), I feigned enthusiasm and agreed to meet him at Alexandra Palace. The weather was nice at least and sunset wasn't until nine, so maybe he wanted to make the most of the sunshine.

'Maya, over here,' Noah called out as I approached him standing outside the palace, which stood at the top of a hill overlooking London as night began to fall. The evening was clearer than usual. Without London smog blurring the view, the twinkling lights of the city competed with the stars above us.

'Hey, Noah,' I replied, my hands suddenly feeling clammy. How was I supposed to act after he texted me that he 'desperately' wanted to see me? I didn't look my best following my three-day stint in bed and accompanying diet of sugary cereal, but he didn't seem to notice. He smiled broadly at me, not only with his sexy mouth but with those beautiful green-grey eyes travelling down my body as though I were in a ballgown, not a floral maxi-skirt and a plain white T-shirt.

'Come here,' he whispered, taking my hands and pulling me closer to him. For a second, I froze. What was he going to do? I couldn't let him *kiss* me, not unless we were engaged to be married, at least. We weren't even *close* to getting engaged. I didn't know *what* we were, besides texting buddies. I couldn't let some random man kiss me without the promise of a future! Kissing, or any physical contact, isn't permitted Islamically during the engagement period either by the way and the thought of starting a future with someone in a way that wasn't blessed didn't feel right to me.

Noah seemed to sense my panic and released my hands. I let out a sigh of relief and he placed an arm around my shoulder instead, drawing me closer and resting his head on top of mine. The bare skin of his arm brushed against mine, causing all the little hairs on my body to rise in delicious anticipation. He smelt like detergent and aftershave mixed together, a combination I never knew could be so alluring.

We stood there for a while, me nestled into him, staring out at London spread before us, talking about the things we wanted to do for the rest of the summer and beyond, until he suggested that we walk around Alexandra Park. I reluctantly moved away, instantly feeling his absence. But then he took my hand in his and we walked around the grounds of the park together like a real couple. Walking, I realised, was a pretty good date activity after all.

'What else have you been up to?' he asked as we strolled hand in hand. 'Apart from cooking amazing food?'

'I've been spending a lot of time with my mum lately,' I said, wondering how much detail I should go into. We hadn't had any deep conversations yet and I wasn't sure if our relationship had reached that level.

Noah didn't probe further and instead began filling me in on his week, which was full of exercise and sounded exhausting.

'I've been swimming outdoors in Hampstead a lot,' he said. 'You should try it. It's amazing.'

'Actually, I have,' I revealed. 'I did it back in April.'

'April?' Noah stopped in his tracks. 'It must have been cold!'

'It was,' I shrugged casually, as though it had been easy. 'But that made it even better, you know?'

'You're something else,' Noah breathed almost reverently, stopping to gaze into my eyes. 'You're perfect, in every way. I can't believe I found you on an app. I've never had this much in common with anyone before. It's unreal.'

'Thanks,' I said weakly, breaking eye contact. 'You're amazing too. I, err, also can't believe how similar we are.'

We continued to stroll and it was while we were heading back to the car and Noah was telling me yet another story about one of his clients that I spotted Zakariya climbing out of his Mercedes. Gripped with panic, I immediately dropped Noah's hand, although he was so engrossed in what he was saying that I didn't think he noticed. *What the hell was Zak doing here?*

A moment later, he saw me too and our eyes locked. An expression of shock flew across his face as he observed Noah, who continued walking towards his car, utterly oblivious to what was going on around him. Zak looked good, *really* good, in a form-fitting black T-shirt and jeans. I had never seen him in a T-shirt before and his bare arms were toned but not as muscular as Noah's. My heart pounded as I wondered what I should do, how I should react. Was I supposed to go over and speak to him? What was the protocol in this situation? How would I possibly be able to introduce them to each other?

Before I could figure it out, Zakariya made the decision for me. He waved his hand in a brief hello – turning away from me in a gesture that implied he didn't want to stop and talk – and went over to open the passenger door instead. A second later, as Noah and I walked past his car, a stunning girl in a hijab climbed out, smiling up at him. Zakariya's back was to me so I couldn't see his expression, but I could imagine the sort of look he was giving her. And inside me, my heart constricted painfully. His not stopping to say hello wasn't because *I* was with a man, it was because *he* was with a woman.

Plastering a fake smile on my face, I turned back to Noah and tried to tune into his chatter. My legs trembling, I followed him to his own car, a flashy two-seater, and somewhere in the dregs of my mind, I wondered how he could afford a car like this when he'd only recently paid off his credit-card debt. Sliding into the car, Noah continued to waffle, I continued to smile and inside, my heart continued to wilt.

I had to go into work on Thursday. I couldn't bunk for the fourth day in a row without a doctor's note confirming that I did have the 'virus' I claimed to have. The thought of seeing Lucy made me anxious and the thought of running into Zak in Arabic felt just as torturous, but it was time to face reality. And not because some list told me to make amends. If I could open up to my mum, then surely, I could have an honest conversation with Lucy?

On the way into the office, I checked Noah's notebook to see what number twenty-seven was, hoping it wasn't anything too intense:

27. GO ON A SOLO TRIP. EUROPE? ASIA? THERE'S SO MUCH TO SEE AND DO!!!

There were no notes, so I had no idea where he went in the end or if he had gone at all. Travelling solo didn't appeal to me in the slightest. I couldn't think of anything lonelier than being in another country and having no one to experience it with, no one to share meals with, no one to take pictures with.

I wasn't the type to strike up conversations with strangers. I was tempted to give the whole thing a miss, but the stubborn part of me wouldn't be able to. I had come this far. The end was *so* close. Everything I had done up to this point had either taught me something about life or taught me something about myself. A solo trip would do the same.

I wished Noah had more faith-related tasks on his bucket list. Maybe then, instead of drawing naked guys and getting temporary tattoos, I would have done more meaningful things, like go for umrah, the smaller Muslim pilgrimage, and started praying more regularly. It was time to start forging my own plans for how I wanted to improve my life, instead of solely relying on Noah's list.

'Hey, jaan, how are you feeling?' Arjun cooed when I walked into the office. I nearly dropped my bag in shock to see him there before me.

'Am I still delirious? How are you here before me? I must still be sick!' I gasped, collapsing into my chair.

'All right, no need to be so dramatic,' he grumbled as I laughed and turned my computer on.

'Hey, everyone.' I looked around to see Lucy walking up to our trio of desks, trepidation oozing from her. I could see it in the stiffness of her back, the way her eyes darted around the room, landing anywhere but my face, the whiteness of her knuckles clasped tight, the tremble of her lips.

Eventually she made eye contact as she sat down. 'How are you feeling, Maya?'

'Fine, thanks, how are you?' I managed to say, averting my gaze because looking at her was too painful. I loved Lucy so much and she had been a good friend to me over the past few months, but now I wondered if it was all a pretence to get closer to my brother through me. Ever since I found out the truth, I had wracked my brains to see if I could remember any conversations we had had about Malik, but I couldn't. I had been so busy with the list that everything else was a blur.

'I'm OK,' Lucy responded, her voice quiet. Arjun looked at me and then Lucy and back at me, the tension between us heavy, like smog settling around us.

'Oh, you're back, are you?' Sheila was the next to swan into the office, dressed head to toe in white, right down to the white stilettos. Lucy and I would have had a giggle about that before, but I didn't know what the correct etiquette was between us now.

'I am indeed,' I said to Sheila, my tone matching hers. She looked startled by my response and said nothing else as she continued to her office. If it had been possible to slam the door behind her, I'm sure she would have. But the glass offices had no doorframes, so it was physically impossible. *Ha*.

'Can we talk at lunch?' Lucy asked a few minutes later, her voice low. 'Please?'

I shrugged. 'If you want.'

The bravado I was feeling when I first got to the office faded with every second that brought us closer to lunch. Watched pots weren't supposed to boil, but the morning sped past at an alarming speed and soon it was lunchtime. Lucy and I both grabbed our phones and headed to the lift, without looking at each other or Arjun. Once we exited the building and were onto the busy street below, I turned to face her. I was done with playing games, beating around the bush, brushing things under the rug and every other avoidance idiom.

'Why did you hide the fact that you were dating my brother from me?' I asked plainly, trying to keep the emotion out of my voice. Lucy winced. She clearly wasn't prepared for how direct I was going to be.

'I-I'm sorry, Maya,' she stammered. 'I really am. There were so many times I wanted to tell you . . .'

'And what? The timing was never right?' I looked away. 'Be honest with me, Lucy. Were you trying to get to my brother through me? Is that the whole reason you've been so nice and helpful towards me?'

'No! Not at all!' Lucy shook her head vehemently, a stricken expression on her face. 'I wanted to tell you, but he asked me not to. He didn't want to complicate things more and I had to respect his wishes, Maya.'

'And what about me? Where was the respect for me?' I tried hard to keep the bitterness and pain out of my voice as I stared at her face, analysing every twitch, trying to deduce whether I was being played.

'Maya, I swear I never wanted to hide it from you, but he's your brother, he got priority over what he wanted you to know. He was adamant that his family shouldn't know about us. And if I'm honest, I was also scared of telling you. I didn't want my issues with Malik to get in the way of our relationship.'

I searched Lucy's clear blue eyes that were filling up with tears and I knew she was telling the truth. She began to cry and I pulled her into a hug.

'Shall we eat s-something?' Lucy sniffled after a few minutes of ruining my flimsy, pale blue cotton shirt with her tears and snot.

'Come on, let's get a quick Pret.'

We grabbed a sandwich and coffee and she filled me in on how she met Malik at some exhibition, how she recognised him as my brother from an old Instagram post of mine, how he slid into her DMs after. How guilty she felt when she saw him dropping me off at Finsbury Park. I didn't want to know too many details, but it was clear that she was really into him. But the fact that he was still hiding her from everyone made me wonder if he was ready to take things further. I didn't say this to her though. As angry as I was towards Malik, it wasn't my place. I kept my mouth shut and decided that the next time I saw him, I would have it out with him. I was on a roll, after all.

The text from Zakariya came through as I was packing my bag and getting ready to leave the office:

ZAKARIYA: Salaams Maya, are you going to be at Arabic tonight? Can we talk?

I opened my mouth to ask Lucy what to do and then found myself closing it. Now that I knew about her and Malik, I felt weird telling her all my private business. We were friends and I had forgiven her, but it would take me a while to get used to the change in dynamics. I wasn't ready to articulate what I was feeling either. How confused I felt when I got home last night. How I hated seeing Zak with another woman, even though I was with another man. How irrational the whole thing was.

Sure, I replied, swallowing away all the conflicting emotions. *See you then.*

My insides were wrought with nerves after Arabic, as I walked out of the building and into the cool night. My cotton shirt gave me enough comfort during the day when it was warm, but now that the sun had gone down and the sky was dark and brooding, it didn't feel like it was enough. I felt Zakariya approach before I heard his voice, causing a chill to run down the length of my body. I couldn't be sure if it was the temperature or seeing him that was making the hairs on my body stand on edge.

'Assalaamu Alaikum,' he said in his low voice. It was different to Noah's; deeper, slower. Noah's voice was always laced with excitement, but I had yet to hear Zakariya show enthusiasm for anything.

'Wa Alaikum Salaam,' I replied, turning to face him. 'How are you?' He looked tired and somehow older than when we first met. I wondered if I did too. I felt like I had aged a decade in the past ten months.

'I'm OK, Alhamdulillah. Shall we go and get some food?'

'Sure. Can we go to that ghetto Bengali place again? I couldn't eat properly last time because of the stupid Whole 30 thing.'

Zakariya nodded and we walked side by side in silence – and not the comfortable type. There seemed to be some sort of frisson in the air and whenever my arm, covered by the thinnest fabric, brushed against his, he snatched it away as if it was contagious. I wondered when he was going to mention our awkward run-in and decided not to bring it up myself. While a part of me was dying to know what the deal was with that girl and if it was serious and if she was the real reason why he disappeared on me, the other part of me wasn't ready to have the conversation. I would have to explain who Noah was to me and it all felt too complicated to go into.

'So . . . how's your week been?' I asked when we entered the restaurant, the strong scent of curry engulfing us. My stomach growled immediately in response, loud enough for him to hear, and I tensed it, begging God to make it stop.

If Zakariya had noticed the rumbles emanating from my belly, he was too much of a gentleman to point it out. He pulled out a chair for me and, as I sat down, my belly groaned again, louder this time.

'Hungry?' he asked, a small smile playing on his lips. So much for being a gentleman, but I didn't care because as he smiled, his entire face lit up and transformed. I wished he would do it more.

'What gave you that impression?' I rolled my eyes playfully. 'I haven't eaten properly in days. I'm marvin'.'

We collected our plates and began helping ourselves to the buffet curries. Unlike the last time, I piled my plate high with everything I fancied, not caring what Zakariya might think of me. If he thought I was a greedy pig, he didn't say so. Not that he would call me a pig. It wasn't a particularly Muslim-friendly insult.

'This is so good,' I mumbled, my mouth full of rice and mutton curry.

'Why haven't you been eating?' he asked, not looking at me as he tackled his own plate, also piled high.

'Oh, no reason,' I replied breezily. 'I've just been busy.'

My breeziness was clearly less of a breeze and more of a sticky, humid air, clinging to everything around it, because Zakariya looked right through the facade.

'You don't have to talk about it if you don't want to,' he said gently. 'But if you do, I'm a pretty good listener.'

So I told him. I told him about Malik and Lucy, about Sheila, about my parents, about growing up in the shadows, overlooked, my growth stunted and hidden under Malik's shine. I told him how I felt like a useless, unaccomplished burden and how I had originally started therapy because it was on the list, but now it was changing me and my perspective and I didn't know if that was a good thing. Now I had a voice; I had started speaking up for myself and people didn't know how to react to it.

'Do I sound completely ridiculous?' I asked, brushing away a stray tear that had the nerve to show itself at the most inopportune moment.

'You could never sound ridiculous to me,' Zakariya said, so solemnly that I couldn't help but laugh at his tone. 'But if I may: choose who you keep around you carefully. It's amazing how many people no longer find you useful when you're harder to control.'

I stared at Zakariya in awe, my spoon frozen in front of my mouth, which was slightly open. 'That's so deep,' I managed to say and he smiled his half-smile again, which was becoming cuter by the second.

'I have my moments,' he shrugged modestly and I had to stop myself from reaching across the table and squeezing his arm. He was seeing someone and so was I. It wasn't right.

'How are things with you?' I asked as we tucked into our second serving of dinner.

'Well,' he began, his tone sombre, 'I wanted to meet you tonight to explain about yesterday, in Ally Pally.'

'Oh, there's nothing to explain,' I replied casually, when inside, I felt anything but. 'You were on a date and so was I. There's nothing to say.'

'OK then,' he replied, looking at me warily. 'Was that the guy you mentioned you were going on a "kinda date" with?'

'Yes,' I replied uncomfortably.

'Looks like things aren't on the "kinda" vibe anymore. You looked pretty into him.' He looked pained as he said this and my hackles rose. He was with a girl himself! And how could he discern how 'into' Noah I was after seeing us together for a split second?

'I am,' I retorted. 'And you seemed pretty into your lady friend. Which is weird as you told me that you're moving to Dubai. Unless you've changed your mind?'

'I'm still going,' he replied, a defensive edge creeping into his voice.

'How's that going to work?' I said, my tone sharper than I had intended it to be.

Zakariya took a moment to respond and I watched his face. He looked uncomfortable. 'I'm not going forever. If it's meant to be, it will survive the distance.'

There was a pause as I digested this information. I suddenly felt sick and pushed my plate aside, the annoyance I had felt towards him dissipating.

'When are you leaving?' Though I tried to keep my tone light, I felt anything but. I felt heavy, like an anchor, stuck.

'September.' His voice was quiet for someone who was about to embark on an exciting new chapter, possibly with a love interest.

'That's soon. There's what, two months to go? How do you feel?'

'Nervous. A little sad.' He looked at me then and though his stony expression was difficult to read, like it always was, there was something about the droop of his eyes and mouth that felt as though he really *was* sad.

'Why are you sad? Family? Your lady friend?'

'Partly. I'll miss them for sure. But can you stop calling her my lady friend? This isn't the nineteenth century.'

'They'll come out to visit you,' I tried to reassure him, ignoring the latter part of his response. 'You know what it's like. Anyone who flies with Emirates will stop in Dubai in transit on the way to Bangladesh or wherever. You'll see people all the time.'

Zakariya put down his spoon then and looked me straight in the eye.

'What if I don't get to see the people I want to see?' he asked, his deep voice so low it was barely more than a growl.

Swallowing nervously, I replied, trying to keep my voice steady. 'Who do you want to see?' Was he implying what I thought he was, or was I completely misreading the situation?

Breaking off eye contact, as though looking at me was too difficult a task, Zakariya said nothing. The silence, however, spoke louder to me than anything he could have said. Not knowing how to respond, I also stayed quiet until he started talking about something else, and we both pretended that nothing had changed between us.

But everything had changed.

Chapter Thirty-Six

On Saturday night, my cousins called to ask if they could come over, so I took the opportunity to show off my new culinary skills with the three-course menu I'd learnt from Ma. Bengalis usually had at least five to six items or more on the dining table whenever guests came over – it was a travesty to offer anything less – but I didn't care. It was the only thing I knew. The methodical act of chopping and dicing also helped to keep my mind off Zakariya and everything that had been left unsaid between us.

'There's no way you made this,' Pinky said, awestruck as she savoured another morsel of the perfect butter chicken curry I had cooked all by myself. It was just the right balance of tanginess, creaminess and spice.

'I did! And completely on my own as well,' I said proudly.

'She did,' Ma affirmed, reaching across the table to give my arm a squeeze. 'I'm so proud of her.'

Since my heart-to-heart with Ma, she had been extra attentive towards me, but every time she showered me with praise, I felt embarrassed and uncomfortable. It would take me a while to get used to it.

'Kub moza oiseh,' Baba agreed. 'Ten out of ten.'

'Bloody perfect,' Pretty added and then covered her mouth. 'Oops, sorry. I mean, erm, ruddy perfect.'

'All right, Pretty, I think our delicate ears can handle the b-word,' Ma said, giving her a look.

'Which b-word?' Pretty asked cheekily and promptly received a smack from Ma. Pinky started laughing and even Baba looked like he was having a good time hanging out with us.

'There's still hope for our Maya becoming an excellent cook, like her mother,' Baba said, taking another helping of the curry, earning him a nudge from Ma.

'Eh-reh, you know your blood-sugar levels have been unstable lately,' she told him in Bengali. 'You need to go easy on the food, especially white rice and bread.'

Ignoring her completely, Baba took another two naans and tucked them protectively beside his plate, as if he was afraid Ma was going to clear up before he had the chance to eat his fill.

I looked around the table – at Ma who was trying hard, Baba who was letting go for a change and at my crazy beautiful twin cousins, who I had spent most of my life being compared to. I realised that I didn't care anymore. So what if they had fairer skin than me? Silkier hair? Smaller waists? It didn't make my life better or worse. Them having less wouldn't have made my circumstances any different.

It was time to let the resentment go. It wouldn't disappear overnight, I knew, but it was getting there. *I* was getting there.

'What's the latest with you guys?' I asked my cousins after the three of us cleared up after dinner and headed up to my room with our tea and dessert for some privacy. Pretty exchanged a look with Pinky, who indiscreetly nudged her. 'Tell her before I do.'

'What happened?' I asked. 'Tell me!'

'I've met someone!' Pretty squeaked, taking a sip of her mug of piping hot tea. 'Ouch! That burnt my mouth.'

'OMIGOD!' I squealed, partly shocked but mostly excited. 'Forget the tea! Back to the point, please. Tell me everything!'

'So my mum and dad made me meet this guy a few weeks ago,' she began, then explained how she liked the look of his biodata, how they met up for an informal coffee – her with her twin, him with his friend – and how the conversation flowed with no awkward silences, how they were on the same page about everything from their life ambitions to how many children they wanted.

'What does he look like? What does he do? How old is he? Where does he live? What's his name?' I interrupted when she got sidetracked by the crap coffee and stale cake in the cafe, missing out all the essential details.

'His name's Yahya and he's really cute,' she gushed. 'Let me show you, his picture. Like one minute he's in his hoodie and Jordans and he looks good and the next minute he's in a suit and my mind is like, blown.' She gesticulated with her hands, emphasising the 'blown'. 'Here, look.'

I took Pretty's phone and looked at the pictures carefully.

'He is cute,' I agreed. 'What does he do?'

'He's a data analyst. Twenty-nine. He lives with his family in Wembley. The only issue is that he's the eldest son.'

Ah. That *was* an issue. Eldest sons traditionally bore most of the familial load and many girls didn't want that sort of pressure when they got married. It wasn't always the case; I knew of eldest sons who didn't live with their parents after marriage or contribute financially. But they were the minority.

'How do you feel about that?'

'Surprisingly OK,' she shrugged. 'It's not ideal, but I've met his parents and siblings and everyone's lovely. They're not super traditional or anything. He said that as long as his parents are well and capable, there's no reason to live with them at all.'

'Preets, I'm really happy for you,' I said, feeling myself choke up as the realisation that my cousin and one of my closest friends was getting married dawned on me. 'But please don't become one of those annoying married women who can't do anything without their husband being there,' I added.

'I will kill you if you do,' Pinky warned. 'Just try answering my calls on speakerphone in front of him and see what I say to bejjot you.'

'I'm not that dumb, all right,' Pretty laughed. 'Will you girls be my bridesmaids?'

'Since when do Bengali brides have bridesmaids?' Pinky asked.

'What does a Bengali bridesmaid do?'

'I kinda resent being called a "maid",' Pinky added and we both started to laugh as Pretty picked up a pillow and began trying to beat us with it.

'Don't even think about hitting me with my own pillow!' I giggled, darting around her and grabbing one to thump her back with. Pinky also took hold of a cushion and within seconds we were cackling and screaming hysterically as we chased each other around the upstairs of our house, pillows and cushions in our hands.

'Stop! I'm going to wet myself!' Pretty gasped, collapsing onto Ma and Baba's bed.

'What's wrong with your pelvic floor? If it's like this now, what's it going to be like after you've had kids?' Pinky laughed, falling onto the bed next to her twin.

'Hang on, I haven't gotten engaged yet and you've already turned me into a mother?'

'It wasn't me who said it, it was your pelvic floor.' For some reason, we all found this line utterly hilarious and we laughed and laughed until tears streamed down our faces, our sides ached and black mascara streaked our cheeks.

'What on earth's going on in here?' Ma surveyed us from the doorway to her room, a horrified expression on her face.

'Pretty wet herself on your bed, Chachi,' Pinky said with a straight face and I started laughing again.

'I love you guys,' I said, my mood suddenly switching to the opposite end of the spectrum. 'I really do. Preets, I'm so happy for you. I can't wait to meet Yahya.'

We spent hours discussing what Pretty's wedding should look like (understated, elegant, with traditional touches like a paan stall, masala tea and Bengali music as well as Bollywood music). We spoke about Yahya and all the things she liked about him (smart, great timekeeping, kind) and what she was worried about (navigating in-law dynamics, the wedding night).

'Our whole lives we're taught not to go near the opposite sex,' Pretty complained as we sat on my bed with a box of chocolates that was growing lighter by the minute. 'The fear of God, tales of destroyed reputations and the warnings about the gossip mill are drilled into us so deep that until recently, I could barely make eye contact with a guy I fancied.'

'You're so extra. I have no problem making eye contact, as long as that's the only contact going on,' Pinky butted in.

'My point is,' Pretty continued, 'it's all well and good until we have to get married and then we're expected to jump into bed with him! How are we supposed to go from zero to one hundred in *one* moment?'

'That's why it's better to get the nikah done earlier than the actual wedding and walima,' I said. 'That way you're married Islamically and you can take your time getting to know each other the halal way, building up to your actual wedding night.'

'That's a good idea,' Pretty said. 'That's it. I'm going to tell my parents that I want the nikah at least three months before the wedding.'

It was nearly two in the morning when the twins left, yawning as they climbed into an Uber. It wasn't until I was in bed that I took my phone out for the first time that evening.

I had messages from Lucy and Dina and also one from Noah, asking if I was free to meet up on Sunday.

As I texted Noah back, a knot of guilt formed in my belly. Meeting him again after the connection I felt with Zakariya the night before felt wrong on so many levels. But Zakariya was leaving and more importantly, I reminded myself, he had met someone else. My heart constricted at the mere thought:

MAYA: Hey Noah, sorry for the late text, had a really busy night. Sure, I'm free to meet for a bit if we keep it local and it's not too early or too late xx.

I fell asleep immediately after sending the text and despite everything plaguing my mind, I slept so deeply that I didn't wake up until nearly noon the following day, completely missing the dawn prayers. As always, I checked my phone before I fully opened both eyes. Nestled among all the notifications about the picture of the meal I had posted the night before was a reply from Noah:

NOAH: How does coffee, cake and a walk in Southgate sound? 3pm?

When I went downstairs, I found Malik in the living room in his PJs, a half-eaten bowl of Frosties on his lap. I guess I wasn't the only one who had woken up late. I scowled at him – a waste of time and facial muscle movements since he didn't bother looking at me – and made my way to the kitchen to pour my own bowl of cereal. Reaching for the box on top of the fridge, it felt oddly light so I checked inside to find it empty bar one, lone flake. Trying to contain my annoyance, I had no choice but to go for the Shreddies instead. But when I went to get milk from the fridge, there was only a splash left in the bottle.

Now I was livid. I felt the rage bubble up inside me, threatening to boil over. I began to slam cupboard doors as I looked for bread to toast instead. I was *so angry* at my brother for spending his entire life as a pampered king and then having the nerve to call *me* a burden! I was furious with him for sneaking around with *my friend* and lying to my face about it. I was fuming at the way he was wasting her time and refusing to commit. Banging a plate onto the counter, I buttered my toast like I was flaying a prisoner, Ramsay Bolton-style, working myself up into a real rage. I never usually reacted like this. Pre-notebook, I had been the most passive, unconfrontational person. But something had shifted inside me and I could no longer bear the burden of his—

'BULLSHIT!' I shouted in the kitchen at the top of my lungs. Leaving my decimated toast on the countertop, I stormed into the living room, the almost-empty milk carton in one hand and the barren Frosties box in the other.

'Is it SO hard to throw empty containers in the recycling bin, KING MALIK?' I all but screamed his name at him and he stared at me, flabbergasted, like I had morphed into a dragon right before his eyes.

'Calm down,' he eventually drawled, taking a spoon of his cereal. 'It's not that deep.'

'Oh, of course it's not deep for the person who tramples over everyone like we're insignificant bugs!' I replied, feeling the veins in my neck bulging from built-up tension and fury. 'Yet I'M the burden, right? Me, who scrubs every inch of this house until my hands are sore!'

'Yeah, so what? I do other stuff, so stop bloody screaming at me! What are you, on your period or something?'

'YOU BEHAYA! BESHOROM! BIADDOB!' I shouted in Bengali, completely losing it. 'You're so shameless! Mannerless!' With that, I threw the milk carton at him, hitting him square in the head.

'Oi! Have you gone crazy?' my brother shouted back at me, rubbing his head like the weasel that he was, as if an empty milk carton was really going to inflict proper pain. 'What the hell is wrong with you? Calm the hell down!'

'*You're* what's wrong with me!' This time I threw the cereal box at him, Frosties crumbs flying everywhere, but I was too angry to control myself, even though somewhere deep beneath the lava I knew that it would be me who would have to clean it all up. As usual. AS USUAL! These thoughts stoked the fire that was now burning rampant.

'Your selfishness! Your entitlement! The way you get every little thing you want!'

'Are you bloody kidding me?' Now he was shouting at me. 'How do I get everything I want? I'm the one in the shitty box room, not *you*, when I'm the one who pays for stuff. Yeah, you clean and help Ma, big deal! I'm the flipping family Uber driver! You swan into my room whenever you want, waking me up and making me drive you to places at dawn. And I'm the one who's selfish? Book a bloody taxi, you lazy, cheap git!'

We were both screaming at each other so loud that my face was sweating and my throat hurt – my voice was on the brink of disappearing. Malik was no better off than me – at one point his eyes looked like they were going to fall out of his head.

And then I burst into tears, hating myself more as the tears streamed down my scarlet cheeks. 'Do you know what it's like, being the daughter no one wanted and the sister of the son that everyone reveres?'

'It's all in your psycho head,' he shouted at me, unmoved by the huge droplets of water that were spilling down my face. 'You've got issues, Affa. And it's nothing to do with me!'

'It's not in my head!' I sobbed. 'Even Ma agreed that it was true and she apologised for it! Why can't you see it? Do you have any idea what it's like for everyone to comment on my "dirty" complexion, feeling sorry for me that it's not as "clean" as my brother's? Do you know how many times I've heard people say what a shame it is for the looks to go to the boy when he doesn't need them?'

Malik stopped pacing the room and turned towards me. 'Are you serious?' he said quietly, as though hearing this had made the fight leave his body. 'Who the hell said that? Are they stupid?'

'It was the same at school! The only time someone wanted to be my mate was when they wanted to get closer to you. And then I finally made a friend at work and what do you do? You go and steal her from me!'

Malik looked uncomfortable and without him shouting back at me, fuelling my fire, I suddenly felt exhausted. Collapsing onto the sofa, I held my throbbing head in my hands, my throat so sore and dry that I couldn't swallow.

And then my brother did the most unexpected thing. He sat down next to me, put his arm around me and said sorry.

'You're not a burden, Affa,' he said quietly. 'I'm sorry for saying that. And your skin isn't moila, it's beautiful, OK? And I'm sorry for hiding the Lucy thing from you . . . it was all messy and confusing and I thought that adding you to the mix would make it all worse.'

'What's happening between you two, anyway? Ma asked me and I told her to speak to you.'

'I had a chat with Ma,' Malik admitted. 'I told her the truth. That I'm not ready to settle down and as much as I like Lucy, I don't want to get married right now.'

'Wow. So what now? You guys are over?'

'We are. But it was actually her who ended it with me.'

'I'm sorry too,' I whispered, my head still in my hands. 'For always expecting you to drive me around at ridiculous hours and for being a moody cow most of the time. But Malik, I need you to have my back more. Not everything needs to be an opportunity to get at me. Sometimes I need my brother's support, you know? And I'll be the same to you.'

Malik looked away as he admitted this, and although I felt a little sorry for him, I was proud of my friend who knew her own worth. I didn't say this, though. There was no need to run chilli powder in the wound.

Malik didn't say anything after that and neither did I. I suppose we had said everything we needed to and for the first time, we understood each other.

Chapter Thirty-Seven

I was emotionally drained after Malik and I had it out. My eyes were swollen, my mouth felt and tasted like sandpaper and I had zero desire to meet Noah. When I took my phone out to cancel, I saw that we were supposed to meet in less than an hour. How could I flake on him so close to our date?

I had forty minutes at most to make myself presentable, so after applying cucumber slices on my eyes for a few minutes to help reduce the puffiness, I washed my face and threw on an oversized shirt and jeans because they didn't need ironing. I tried my best to hide my dark circles with concealer and used blusher to give my sallow complexion some life, but it made little difference. I didn't have the energy or time for anything more elaborate, so sticking on sunglasses, I slunk out of the house and made my way to Noah.

Unsurprisingly, I was late getting to Southgate, given how little time I had between bawling on the sofa to leaving the house. If Noah was annoyed, he didn't show it.

'Hey, Maya! How are you?' he smiled, leaning in and giving me a long, tight hug. Still not used to the physical contact, I felt a pang of discomfort but I didn't pull away. I felt too embarrassed and I wondered how many women out there went along with men's wishes to avoid having an uncomfortable conversation.

What I did notice from the hug was that this time, I didn't feel as though my knees were going to give way. Yes, he still smelt nice; yes, it felt good to have his strong arms around me; yes, his broad back was pleasant to touch. But I wasn't electrocuted like last time. Was I too tired for chemistry or had the Noah-effect worn off?

'I'm OK,' I said simply. 'Sorry I'm late.'

'Five minutes doesn't count as late, not really,' he said kindly. 'There's a cool little cafe down the road. Do you want to sit inside or get a takeaway and go for a walk?'

I pondered the question for a moment. Inside meant taking off my sunglasses and letting him see my red, puffy eyes. But I had no energy to walk around aimlessly.

'Can we sit down inside?' I croaked. 'Maybe we can walk around after?'

'Sure.' Noah began energetically striding away in the direction of the cafe and I sighed, trailing behind. Hanging out with a personal trainer was tiring. They always wanted to be active. And all those endorphins from the exercise seemed to keep him in a constant state of cheeriness.

'How's your week been?' I asked once I had sat down with a hot mug of chamomile tea and a gigantic wedge of carrot cake, still wearing my sunglasses. Noah had ordered a black coffee and the world's smallest cannoli. He insisted on paying for it all despite my feeble protests.

'Really good!' he enthused. 'Wow, that cake is huge. How will you manage all that?'

I narrowed my eyes, not that he could see them through the dark lenses. 'Um, I haven't eaten all day and I had a crap week, so I think I'll manage.'

Noah didn't ask me why my week was crap, nor did he pick up on his faux pas. Instead, he continued talking about his own week, his clients, how he was house hunting. I was house hunting too, but I didn't get a chance to tell him because the pauses between his sentences were too short.

As I listened to him go on and on, I wondered if he had been like this the last time we met. I didn't think so. I was certain that he wasn't as obtuse the first time we went out either, nor the time on the Tube. Maybe *he* wasn't the issue, maybe it was me; I wasn't in the best headspace after my horrendous week and I was always irritable and moody a week before my period was due. I was being rubbish company and really should have cancelled the meeting. He was having to work extra hard to keep the conversation going.

'Hey, why are you still wearing sunglasses?' Noah asked suddenly, mid-way through recounting a story about one of his clients – a really big, built man who kept farting every time he squatted. It was a funny story, but it was putting me off my cake.

'Oh, I've got a really bad eye infection,' I lied smoothly. 'And I've got a fever too. I don't feel well.'

'Oh, God, why did you come out then? We need to get you home!'

'I didn't want to flake on you.' This, at least, was true.

'Let me call you an Uber,' Noah said.

'No, no, I can do it myself,' I replied, taking my phone out and regretting the lie that was now costing me twenty pounds.

'No way, I insist,' Noah protested, opening up his phone and I instantly felt bad for the mean thoughts I was having about him. He was a genuinely nice guy. And so what if he was always happy and excited? It was better than always being cold and unreadable like Zakariya. Noah at least made it clear that he liked me. He didn't wait weeks and weeks before initiating contact with me and then leave me with a silence to decipher.

The Uber came quickly and I was almost sorry to say good-bye to Noah so hastily. Almost, because I was also relieved. I needed a break from it all; not just his chatter, but from my family, work – basically from my life.

I remembered then that I had yet to book my solo trip, as per Noah's list. The activity couldn't have come at a better time. By the time I had reached home, my solo long weekend to Istanbul was all booked and paid for and I smiled for the first time that day. Now I just had to persuade Sheila to give me time off.

A couple of weeks later, I was on a plane completely alone for the first time in my life, in a bid to cross number twenty-seven off my list. Not that Ma and Baba knew I was on my own. They were so unimpressed when I told them that I wanted to go away again (twice in one year was incomprehensible to them) that I couldn't work up the courage to tell them I wanted to go alone as well. In the end, I lied and told them that I was going with Dina and the kids. They loved and trusted her too much to say no to me after that.

I also lied to Sheila, claiming a 'family emergency' was the reason why I needed to take two days off, creating an elaborate story about a fictional family member falling seriously ill. I asked Allah to forgive me for my lies and pleaded with him not to make the sick family member thing come true.

Both Zakariya and Noah had texted me consistently throughout that time, although the content of their messages couldn't have been any more different. Zak would send me funny phrases he'd learnt in Arabic, links to interesting political articles or ask me my advice on things like where to live when he moved to Dubai, sharing listings of fancy apartments near the sea, with pools and gyms, that cost the same to rent as a crappy basement flat in Hackney. And not the bougie part.

Noah, on the other hand, sent me motivational quotes, gym TikToks of himself – which admittedly made me a little hot around the collar (I am a red-blooded female after all) – and the occasional 'thinking of you' type message, with a little 'x' at the end.

Noah's texts were endearing, playful and he was clearly interested in me and trying to get a rise out of me. Zak's were intellectual, Islamic and a tad abrupt at times. I knew that I was an idiot for enjoying the fact that I was hearing from him more than usual, as platonic as it was. Though each time I received a message, I felt a pang of regret at the timing of us.

'Can't you forget about uni and follow him to Dubai?' Dina had said when I told her how I was feeling. It was the night before I flew out to Istanbul and we were talking while I was packing my suitcase. Sami and the baby were downstairs with Ma.

'Are you seriously telling me to give up my dreams and my career for a man? And one who isn't interested in me and is seeing someone else?'

'Err, not when you put it like that,' she responded weakly.

'What's wrong with Noah?' I demanded, as I struggled to choose between a red floral maxi-dress and a blue floral jumpsuit.

'Nothing's wrong with him, per se,' Dina said carefully. 'I just wonder if he's Islamically and culturally compatible with you, that's all. Plus, I really don't see your parents being happy about you wanting to marry a half-English personal trainer with no degree.'

'He's Muslim,' I said a tad defensively. 'He doesn't drink. That says a lot these days, you know. And you know he's trying to become a physiotherapist!'

'I know, but what are his life goals? Is he trying to become a better Muslim, a better person? Is he the man who's going to help you grow in this life and the next life?'

'He's already helped me grow massively!'

'How? You've known him for what? A month?'

'I feel like I've known him for nearly a year because of the list,' I admitted. 'The list has helped me grow so much.'

'It has,' Dina conceded. 'In some aspects. You're more assertive, more confident, you understand yourself more. But how else has it helped you grow? Are you closer to God? Are you a better human? Only you can answer that.'

As I sat on the plane, replaying Dina's conversation in my head, I told myself that while the list didn't help me get closer to God, it wasn't *supposed* to. That was a journey I was going to have to embark on myself, it had nothing to do with Noah or Zakariya or anyone else.

Landing at Sabiha Gokcen Airport in Istanbul, I managed to get a taxi that would take me all the way to my hotel, which was near the Galata Tower. The first thing I noticed was how hot it was, much hotter than I thought it would be. I broke out in a sweat before I made it inside the cool, air-conditioned cab despite the thin cotton of my shirt. But it didn't matter because I HAD MADE IT and as the car drove from the Asian side of Istanbul across the bridge to the European side, I couldn't stop staring out of the window and drinking up the sight of all the lights and majestic mosques.

Checking into the modern little hotel right next to the famous tower was easy enough and as I showered and got into bed, I struggled to fall asleep from the excitement and nerves of being in an unknown city completely on my own.

A text pinged through from Zakariya, straight to the point as usual:

ZAKARIYA: Salaams, have you arrived?

MAYA: I have! Thanks for checking in. You OK?

351

ZAKARIYA: Yeah, can't sleep for some reason.

MAYA: Me neither! I'm too excited to sleep!

ZAKARIYA: What's your plan for tomorrow?

MAYA: How do you know I have a plan?

ZAKARIYA: I know you love a good list, Maya Rahman.

MAYA: Haha, you're right, I do ☺ Basic touristy stuff tomorrow – Blue Mosque, Hagia Sofia, Grand Bazaar. And then there's other stuff I wanna do like go to Topkapi palace of course and a nice fancy dinner at Nus'ret hopefully.

ZAKARIYA: You're going to go to Nus'ret on your own? ☹

MAYA: Yeah . . . why not?

ZAKARIYA: Be careful, please. These Turkish guys are womanisers.

MAYA: LOL! You sound jealous! Don't go generalising people like that, alright? 🙈

I waited for Zakariya's response, but it didn't come. Either he had fallen asleep or I had pushed him too far. It didn't matter. I was in Istanbul, one of the most magical cities in the world, and I was going to enjoy every moment of it.

The next morning I woke up early enough to enjoy a traditional Turkish breakfast for one. The table was laden with cold meats, cheeses, bread, olives, jam, honey, cooked sujuk and scrambled eggs, all washed down with a glass mug of piping hot, sweet Turkish tea. At first, I felt self-conscious as I ate, so I read a self-help book at the same time in order to look less lonely. I took pictures of my food and as I became more comfortable and less bothered about what people were thinking of me, I posted a selfie of myself basking in the sunlight in my sunhat and pale blue and white maxi-dress onto my Insta Stories.

Zakariya was sort-of right about some of the men in Istanbul. I didn't know if they were all Turkish, or if they were tourists or immigrants, but not only were a large proportion of them incredibly good-looking, but they were also extremely forward. Everywhere I went barring the mosques, men approached me to make conversation and I'm not going to lie, it did wonders for my confidence.

The mosques in Istanbul were stunning. I carried a pashmina with me in my straw holiday tote so I could wrap it around my head before entering. I also made sure to keep myself in a state of ablution so I could pray in them and not only visit them like a tourist. Hearing the call to prayer outside was beautiful and it did something to my soul. I spent hours in the various mosques and in the end decided that my favourite was the Süleymaniye Camii, which was situated at the top of a hill. It was ancient and imposing, much older than the Blue Mosque and so the architecture was more simple and less ornate, but it was quiet and calm and it soothed my nerves.

Surprisingly, I prayed more in Istanbul than I had done since Ramadan. I prayed for God to direct me to a future that was good for me. I prayed for Him to give me the courage to go after my dreams, to become a better person, to help me with my anxiety, to give me the patience and wisdom to navigate difficult situations. I also prayed for everyone I knew. My parents, my nani, my brother, my friends. I wasn't on Umrah but the amount of time I spent in contemplation made me feel as though I was on as much of a spiritual journey as I was on a personal-growth journey. Dina was right, my connection with God was something I was lacking; something I needed to work on.

Noah texted me throughout my trip. Now that my period had come and gone, I felt differently towards his energy; I enjoyed it. Every few hours he would send me a link to a cool restaurant to visit, or gallery to check out, or sight to see and with the tips came heart emojis and kisses.

The Grand Bazaar was a lot of fun and I spent hours wandering through the maze-like halls sampling sweets, trying on jewellery and smelling perfume and soaps. I was certain I got scammed, although it wasn't as bad as it would have been were my skin tone ten shades lighter. I was Bengali after all. My haggling skills were on another level, honed as a child when I would watch my mum and grandmother barter everything down to half the original asking price in Whitechapel market. I bought a beautiful handwoven carpet for our living room, as well as some pretty hand-painted colourful dishes. I also bought silver jewellery studded with mother of pearl and turquoise for myself, Ma, Nani, Lucy, Dina and the twins and then boxes of baklava for everyone else.

Contrary to Zak's reservations, I *did* go to Nus'ret on my own, something I never dreamed I would have had the courage to do. I dressed up to the nines that night, in a slinky black satin dress, heels and red lipstick. I took my book with me as my date and I documented the whole thing on social media. My DMs blew up when I posted a picture of me and the Salt Bae himself, his arm casually draped around me and while Noah commented on it, Zak didn't. I wondered if he was too busy to check Instagram, or if he didn't like that I had gone out like that on my own. So I did what anyone would do: I checked who had viewed my Stories and after scanning the names one by one, I came across Zakariya's. He *had* seen my picture after all. Why was he being so cold?

'What does this all mean?' I asked an innocent man that night, as I sat in a coffee shop on Istiklal Street with a huge piece of kunafeh and ice cream. Ali, who was attractive in a boyish sort of way, had approached me and asked me if he could join me. After three days of eating alone, I nodded enthusiastically and gestured to the empty seat in front of me. After some small talk, which I had become really good at during this solo trip, I proceeded to offload my man problems on him.

'He's totally hot and cold. One minute he's driving me home and climbing a mountain with me and the next he's distant and aloof. I don't know what to make of it!'

'And you said that he once made his intentions known and you rejected him?' Ali asked in heavily accented, broken English, his forehead knitted together in concentration as he tried to keep up with the story.

'Well, yes,' I admitted reluctantly. 'But that was ages ago. I've made it pretty clear to him since then that I'm interested, but he's not reciprocating it.'

'And what of the other man? What was his name, Nuh?'

'Yes, but he pronounces it the anglicised way, Noah.'

'Strange. Why does he do that?'

'He's half-Lebanese, half-English,' I explained to Ali, wondering why I was explaining Noah's choice of pronunciation to a stranger. But I guess I had opened myself up to scrutiny when I involved a stranger in my business.

'You cannot trust Lebanese men,' Ali said seriously, his face expressionless.

'Why not? And he's only half-Lebanese!'

'You cannot trust English men either.'

'It's not like Bengali men are much better. It's not a race or ethnicity issue, Ali. Most men, I find, are lacking. It's about finding the one that lacks the least. Noah, at least, has made it obvious that he likes me.'

'If that is enough for you to be happy, then good luck, sister Maya.'

Chapter Thirty-Eight

The journey home from Istanbul was bittersweet. I ended up having a much better time than I had anticipated and I'd unexpectedly found a friend in Ali. We spent my last day there together and he took me to Galata Port, where we spent all day walking around, shopping, trying different foods from random little carts and drinking tea. We ended the evening at a shisha cafe near Taksim that played the best Turkish music and had a lively atmosphere. It was full of attractive people our age playing cards, smoking shisha and chilling out.

While we puffed away, Ali shared that he was in love with a girl called Zeynep but her parents wouldn't let her marry him because their family backgrounds were too different, in terms of politics, wealth and education. We spoke for hours about his dilemma, about my two love interests and everything in-between.

'If your heart is telling you to go to Zakariya, then you must,' Ali said solemnly, inhaling deeply and letting out the longest, strongest plume of smoke. 'You must not let him move to Dubai without knowing how you feel.'

'How can I?' I replied miserably. 'Firstly, he's started seeing someone. Secondly, I can't ruin his dreams, his ambitions. Everything with Zakariya is too difficult. Noah is so much easier.'

'Since when was the easier path the better path? I thought all you English people say that good things are worth fighting for?'

'You've been watching too many Hollywood movies, Ali,' I laughed. 'Real life is hard enough. Love should be easy.'

'So you love this Zakariya? Or this Nuh? I mean, Noah?'

'No! I don't love either of them. I feel drawn to them both. They're both so different from each other. Noah is light, Zak is dark. The thing is, I've spent months hoping to run into Noah and now that I've finally found him, I feel like I need to see where it will go. At the same time, I don't want to lose Zakariya, as a friend or as potentially something more.'

'It seems to me, Maya, that you are trying to have it all,' Ali said seriously, gesturing for the waiter to top up our tea. 'I know they tell women these days they can have it all, but you cannot. No one can have everything. You need to make a choice. Pray to God for a sign to show you who is the right one.'

I took Ali's words with me all the way back to London Stansted. Muslims believe that prayers are more likely to be answered while travelling, so I spent a significant portion of the flight back asking Allah to show me who I should be with – if either of them.

When there was an hour or so left of the flight, I took out Noah's notebook to cross out number twenty-seven on the list and check out number twenty-eight. Under twenty-seven, I wrote: *Had the best four days in Istanbul; fed my mind, body and soul and made a new BFF. ALHAMDULILLAH!!!*

I suddenly felt nervous about number twenty-eight. The end was so close and I felt as though I needed to come to a decision about Zak or Noah before I reached the end of the list. I was also feeling increasingly guilty about the fact that Noah didn't know that his list was not only in my possession, but that all the things he liked about me – the tattoo, the hike, the skydiving, the literature, the swimming, the movies – were only because he unknowingly made me do it.

With a silent *Bismillah*, I turned the page:

28. DATE A GIRL WHO ISN'T YOUR TYPE

Talk to one on the Tube? Or swipe one from a dating app?

I read and reread it, over and over again, feeling as though I was being slapped every time my eyes desperately scanned over the letters.

That day on the Tube, the day that changed my life for the better, the day I clung to as proof that Noah liked me for *me* – not just post-list me – was all a load of BS. He only spoke to me because it was something to check off a list. It wasn't because he *actually* liked me or fancied me. Why would he? Why would someone as good-looking as Noah have bothered to approach someone like me? *I was never his type.*

It was all a lie and I was the biggest idiot for falling for it, for wasting months of my life chasing a man, chasing a dream, chasing a new life.

I cried then. Silent tears fell down my face, splashing onto the page and turning the ink of Noah's pen into a blurry, illegible mess. Who was I fooling, thinking that a haircut, some makeup and some confidence were enough to turn me into someone that people noticed and liked?

Well, I had already done number twenty-eight, hadn't I? I was currently 'dating' a man who wasn't my type, for all the good it did me. Taking out my pen, I crossed it out, again and again, so hard that the pen tore through the damp page and on the page after. And then I closed the book and stuffed it back into my handbag. I couldn't bear to look at it again.

Walking through the arrivals section of the airport, I looked around half-heartedly, knowing perfectly well that there would be no one to meet me. For once, I was grateful for it. My eyes were red, my nose was sore and my tears had left streaks down my face that I didn't care enough about to wipe off. Let everyone stare at me. I didn't give a toss anymore.

Until I heard someone call my name.

'Maya!' The voice was familiar but it took me a second to place it. *SHIT, SHIT, SHIT.* What was he *doing* here? He called out again and with dread, I slowly turned around, following the sound of his voice. Sure enough, there he was, holding a massive bouquet of flowers, matching the size and vibrancy of his smile.

'Noah?'

'Welcome home, babe!' He rushed over to me, placed the flowers on my trolley and then picked me up in a giant bear hug, lifting me right off the ground. Being lifted by someone had always been a fear of mine – not that I ever expected it to happen. I was always scared that the person who tried to lift me would break their back, or gasp at my weight and drop me on my face.

Noah did none of those things. He carried me as though I were as light as a wisp of silk from the finest saree shops in Dhaka. He held me for ages, right there in the airport arrivals section, where anyone could see me and report my shameless behaviour to my parents, or worse, my grandmother. It was supposed to be a romantic gesture straight out of a movie, but it didn't feel romantic. I was absolutely mortified.

'What are you doing here?' I asked when he finally put me down after kissing the top of my head and giving me another hug when my feet were planted firmly on the ground. The pain of finding out the truth about why he approached me on the train was still raw and I tried to keep the steel out of my voice.

'I had to see you, I've missed you so much,' Noah said, his eyes crinkling in the corners as he continued to smile at me. 'I didn't want you to have to take a taxi home either.'

'Oh,' I said stupidly, as I attempted to subtly wipe the now-dry tear streaks off my face. The correct response would have been 'I've missed you too' but I was still dumbstruck that he was there.

'Aren't you happy to see me?' he asked simply, looking at me quizzically.

'Of course I am,' I protested weakly. Maybe I wasn't giving him quite the ecstatic greeting he had expected, but I couldn't help it. I had just found out that he only spoke to me on the train because of his list. The idea I had of being worth talking to by someone as handsome and driven as Noah had been shattered. And now he had materialised in front of me like an apparition and I was expected to gush over him?

The journey to north London was quiet. Noah assumed it was because I was tired and I let him think as much while he maintained a steady monologue for most of the way. All the while the disquiet, the strain, the lump inside me grew until I couldn't take it anymore.

'We need to talk,' I blurted as he came off the North Circular Road at the Wood Green exit. 'Can we stop somewhere?'

'What, right now? Shall we go and grab some food or something?'

'I don't think it can wait,' I insisted and Noah obliged, turning into a side road and parking up outside a pretty detached house.

'What's wrong?' Noah turned to look at me and I suddenly felt an overwhelming sense of déjà vu, of the first time we met on the train. Something in his expression felt the same; the curiosity mixed with nerves. I remembered thinking how drop-dead gorgeous he was then and since getting to know him, instead of becoming less attractive, he had become more. I remembered feeling awestruck at the fact that a man this good-looking was talking to me. Looking back, it was pathetic, the way I let a stranger on a train change my entire life, for no reason other than the fact that he was hot and *I was not*.

But as I sat there with my heart hammering loudly in my chest, trying to find the right words for my confession, I realised that what Noah had inadvertently done to me was nowhere near as bad as what I had done to him. I had knowingly led him to believe I was a fun-loving, adventure-seeking, *Ulysses*-reading, sexy-haired vixen who happened to be interested in all the same things he was.

I was nothing but a fraud.

'I need to tell you something,' I said quietly, forcing myself to look him straight in the eye, into those swirls of colour: green, grey, blue, hazel, mixed together like an oil painting.

'What happened?' His voice was quiet, nervous. He was usually such a bundle of excitement and it was unsettling, seeing him look so worried.

'Nothing's happened, but I haven't been completely honest with you,' I began, a tremor in my voice. 'Do you remember how you once said that you felt like we had met before?' I asked, watching his expression carefully as I spoke.

'Sort of,' he shrugged. 'You probably have one of those faces.'

'That's not why I felt familiar to you,' I ploughed on, desperately trying to swallow the nerves that kept rising up my throat. 'It's because we *had* met before. Before RateYourDate, I mean.'

'Really?' Noah's eyes lit up, like he was watching an exciting movie, not like I was about to tell him that I had invaded his privacy, big time. 'When?'

'On the Tube,' I confessed. 'I was on my way to work and I was doing my makeup. You made a comment about it and the next thing I knew, we were talking about Marvel movies and other random things.'

Noah pondered, his eyes searching my face and I could see recognition dawn on him as his mouth stretched into a huge smile.

'I remember you!' he exclaimed, taking hold of my hands. 'You drew a line across your face! And then I had to get off the train before we could exchange contact details. I proper kicked myself all day for that.'

'Did you?' I asked, my voice small as my palms began to sweat. I pulled my hands out of his.

'I did! I told my client all about you,' he grinned. 'And now look, you're right here in front of me. We were meant to be together.' He grabbed my hand again and brought it to his lips. Ordinarily, something like this would have sent a jolt through me, but I self-consciously snatched my clammy hand away and then sat on both my hands to stop them from trembling. The memory of the last time we laughed and sang about my sweaty palms hit me and I felt an intense wave of sadness wash over me.

'That's not all,' I croaked, wishing I had a glass of water. Maybe it was a mistake, doing all this in the car. It would have been safer in a restaurant, with witnesses around.

'Oh. What else?'

'That day, you left something behind.' I reached into my bag and pulled out the battered notebook, the edges worn and the leather scratched.

'What's this?' he asked, staring blankly.

'Hang on, is that my . . . notebook?' He took the book from me and opened it to the first page. 'I was wondering what I did with this! I'm so glad to have it back. But wait . . . I didn't write this.'

He looked at number one on the list. *Enrol in a physio course.* Under his notes was my own neat lettering in bright-pink Sharpie. '"Now is the time to get your ass back to uni and finally do that master's, girl",' he read slowly, his voice completely befuddled. '"But get a scholarship because you shouldn't be getting into debt at your age." What is this? Did you write this?'

'Yeah,' I broke eye contact then. 'You see, when I first found your notebook, I didn't want to open it and breach your privacy, but then I thought that it might help me find you again.'

'OK . . .'

'But when I saw that it was a list of things you wanted to accomplish before you turned thirty, it sort of inspired me.'

'To do what? Make your own list?'

'Uh, not exactly. I decided to do the stuff on your list.'

Now he looked surprised. 'What? You enrolled on a physio course?' he asked, incredulous.

'No, I changed the ones that were completely irrelevant into something that made sense to my life. But the rest I did.'

Noah turned the page to number two and I felt my ears burn as he read out loud, '"Read *Ulysses*. What a load of effin' BS. Can't believe I wasted so much of my life on this overrated piece of shit. That bloody Noah is a pretentious git. Probably wants to use the fact that he's read this tome as a chat-up line."'

'Ouch, that's harsh,' he said, his voice strained. 'I thought you said you liked it? I could have sworn you did . . . it was one of the things that got my attention when we met. I mean, when we met the second time.'

Noah looked confused as he continued to flick through the book, this time sparing me from having to hear my snarky thoughts out loud.

'So basically,' he began, his voice now cooler than I had ever heard it before, 'all the stuff I thought you were into, you only did because it was on my list?'

'Basically.'

'You're not really into sports and hiking and adventures and tattoos? I don't understand. Who are you?'

'I'm still me,' I said, trying to keep the wobble out of my voice. 'But before your list, I was more of an introvert. I spent my weekends at home watching TV or meeting my friend for dinner. Your list made me get out and experience life. And my tattoo was only temporary, by the way.' I held up my hand to show him and he blanched.

'This is a lot to process, Maya,' he said after a long pause. 'I feel like I don't know you.'

Noah turned the engine on and I said nothing to defend myself.

The rest of the trip continued in deadly silence with Noah staring stonily at the road ahead and me looking out the window, willing myself not to cry. What did I think was going to happen? This wasn't a movie. He wasn't going to hug me and tell me that he liked me anyway and it didn't matter that I only did those things on the list because of him . . . Because at the end of the day, I *did* do them. It was my grit and determination that made me swim in the ice-cold pond. It was my hard work that won me a scholarship. It was my courage that allowed me to jump out of that plane. It was *my* perseverance that got me to the end of *Ulysses*. Yes, the list inspired me but it was my mind, my body – ME – that got me through it all.

We arrived in Turnpike Lane and as we pulled into my road, I turned to look at him one last time.

'You know, you're so hung up about feeling tricked, but what about me?' I began softly, my voice barely louder than a whisper.

'What do you mean?' Noah didn't look at me but continued staring straight ahead.

'The day you spoke to me on the Tube was only to tick off number twenty-eight: "Date a girl who isn't your type." All this time I thought you liked me for me and that's why you had approached me. I thought you liked who I was before the list. But clearly you didn't. I was never your type. I was just a challenge for you, like reading a difficult novel or climbing a mountain.'

I opened the car door and went over to the boot myself to lug my big, twenty-three-kilogram suitcase out. Noah didn't come out and help me. He stayed in the driver's seat, the engine still purring, and as I dragged my case along the uneven, cracked pavement, I heard his car roar away. I didn't look back.

Chapter Thirty-Nine

A couple of weeks went by and before long, we were in hot, humid August, which was made infinitely more bearable because Malik and I had air-conditioning installed downstairs. It was Malik's idea but I persuaded him to let me go halves with him. He had made a fair point about me not contributing financially and I had heard him.

My parents moaned and groaned the entire week the builders were there, drilling through the bricks and fitting the pipes and vents. They thought it was an unnecessarily extravagant expense. Now that we had got our house back, they were loving it. We ended up spending less time isolated in our rooms and more time together sprawled out in the living room, enjoying the coolness. Even Nani had been coming over more often to escape the heat in her house.

'Oh, did you hear about that boy?' Ma said one night as we loafed around in front of the TV with the AC on full blast. Baba was watching Bangla TV as usual, the newsreader talking in formal Bangla so fast that I barely understood a word she said. It could have been Urdu, or Farsi, for all I knew. I gave up trying and closed my eyes instead, resting my head on Nani's shoulder.

'What boy?' Baba asked distractedly.

'You know, the one who gave the alaf for Maya? What was his name, Zaki?'

'Ohh, Jakariya,' Baba continued, chewing the triangle of paan that Nani had made for him. 'What about him?'

My ears pricked up at the mention of Zak's name and I tried my best not to move or give any indication that I was listening to the conversation.

'Lovely boy,' Nani piped up, despite never having met him. 'Such a shame that it didn't work out.'

'Ask your beloved granddaughter why,' Ma grumbled. I imagined her side-eyeing me as she said this, but I didn't open my eyes to check. 'Anyway, did you know that he's moving to Dubai?'

'Oh, yes, I heard about that,' Baba replied. 'He got a fantastic offer from a big investment bank. Such a shame. Imagine, Maya could have gone with him and made so much tax-free money. What a loss.'

My eyes flew open and as I was about to sit upright and say my piece, Malik spoke up.

'Maya's about to do her master's, Baba. She can't run off to another country now.'

Baba harrumphed audibly. 'There's a time and a place for everything. The time to study is over. Now is the time to get married. If she married this Jakariya, she wouldn't need a better job, he earns enough.'

'It's never too late to study,' Malik replied. 'And I thought we believed that everything is in Allah's hands? If Maya and Zakariya are meant to be, it'll happen.'

My brother and my dad continued to debate and I settled back down in my comfortable position beside my grandmother, inhaling her familiar scent of Arabic-style oil perfume mixed with lavender detergent and Astral face cream. Malik finally had my back. He had heard me too.

That night, I tossed and turned in my stuffy bedroom, my skin sticky with sweat and contemplated sleeping downstairs like my parents had been doing. The windows were wide open – no doubt all sorts of spiders and mosquitoes were taking up residence in my room – and thoughts of Zakariya and Noah kept turning over and over in my mind.

I hadn't heard from Noah since that awful drive back from the airport when he all but threw me out of the car. The strange thing was, I wasn't broken. I missed him and I missed all the possibilities for the future that our relationship had held, but I knew what the stakes were when I told him the truth about the list and I was ready to pay the price for it. If I was being completely honest, I wasn't that into him, which made me feel rather pathetic. I think I was more into his incredibly good looks than anything else. The truth was, we didn't connect on an intellectual, spiritual or emotional level. If I had been getting it on with him and enjoying his spectacular body, it would have been worth it . . . but I wasn't even doing that, so what was the point?

'Why did I continue with it when I knew that he wasn't the right one?' I had asked Fareena once it became clear that I wouldn't be hearing from him again. He disappeared from all my social media without a trace and yes, I experienced a pang of . . . something. Disappointment. Embarrassment. Loneliness. But it certainly wasn't heartbreak.

'But you didn't, did you?' she said gently. 'When you told him the truth, you overcame your need to feel wanted and the desire for companionship. You realised that you couldn't find the new when you were still holding onto the old, so you let go.'

'The new? There is no "new".'

'Maybe not right now, but it's there. All this time you've been shackled by Noah's list. And yes, a lot of good came out of it, you experienced new things, you developed self-esteem, but you were using it as a crutch. Now the list has gone, Noah has gone, it's time to find your own new things. It's time for your own truth.'

It was a nice sentiment, but I didn't have *time* to find my own truth. It was Pretty's nikah in a couple of weeks and there was still so much to do. As joint chief bridesmaids (don't ask), Pinky and I found ourselves lumbered with a mammoth list of things to organise, from planning an epic bridal shower to organising the mehndi night to putting together all the favours. It was beyond time-consuming, but at least it kept my mind off other things. And this wasn't the big shebang; it was the Islamic ceremony to make them legit in the eyes of God so they could hang out the halal way. The big, fat Bengali wedding was going to take place the following spring.

Now that Arabic classes were over for the summer holidays and Zakariya was getting ready to leave for Dubai in less than a month, we hadn't had the opportunity to see each other. Every night I'd pick up my phone to text him to see if we wanted to meet before he left and every time I'd chicken out and put it back down, my heart contracting as I did. With his imminent departure and some other girl on the scene, what was the point?

On the day of Pretty's mehndi, Pinky and I spent the morning at the venue in east London making sure the events team set up the decor properly. Pretty wanted a traditional Bangladeshi-style henna party, which meant lots of flowers and brightly coloured sarees draped to look like decorations. The dress code for the event was yellow and as per our Bridezilla's instructions, Pinky and I had to wear matching sarees, along with their first cousins from their mum's side.

As the nikah was going to be a simple, holy affair at the mosque, Pretty wanted the mehndi to be the complete opposite: a DJ, dancing, shisha, the lot of it. Pinky and I therefore spent all of our free time trying to make her vision come alive and as I stood back and surveyed the scene, I decided that we had succeeded.

The hall was packed with friends and relatives; aunties dressed in colourful jamdani and kathan sarees were huddled around the tables, enjoying biryani, tea and their favourite past-time: gossiping. If they weren't boasting about their offspring, they were keeping their beady eyes peeled for an unsuspecting future daughter-son-in-law. A handful of uncles in either traditional cotton shalwar kameez or casual shirts and trousers sat in the opposite corner of the hall, chewing paan stuffed with betelnuts and talking politics, religion and basically all the topics white people considered bad form at weddings.

Meanwhile, kids were sweating on the bouncy castle, teenage girls self-consciously shimmied on the periphery of the dancefloor to the latest Bhangra beats, teenage boys watched them from afar and the rest of us did a bit of all the above. I found it hilariously ironic that we were never allowed to go clubbing, but it was fine to turn the ancient tradition of applying henna to a bride into a nightclub.

'Pretty looks stunning, doesn't she?' I breathed in awe to my mum, as I watched my cousin sitting on the stage, her arms spread out as the mehndi artists decorated her pale, buttery skin with intricate henna designs. She wore a classic Bangladeshi green and gold saree and had red flowers trailing all the way down her curled hair. Instead of sitting on a regal sofa like most brides, she sat on the floor like they used to do back in the day, on a luxurious silk carpet surrounded by patterned Aarong cushions. She looked like something out of a colonial-style Bangladeshi poster, right down to her dark, kohl-rimmed eyes.

Ma had dressed me in the yellow and gold chiffon the bridal party were all wearing and helped me fasten little flowers in my hair, which we had styled into a chic updo. Like Pinky, I wore a deep red lipstick and a golden tikli sat majestically down my middle parting. Fake lashes and bangles completed the look and I had to admit that I looked pretty amazing. Until I moved. My movements were restricted by how tightly Ma had wrapped the nine yards of cloth around me, secured by safety pins everywhere so I had to shuffle rather than walk, trying my best not to trip over the pleats. When I was stationary, I looked elegant, but as soon as I began to walk, I turned from swan to duckling, yellow feathers and all.

'She does look beautiful,' Ma agreed. 'Now come, I want you to meet your Lilly khala, she's looking for a bride for her nephew, you know.'

'Ma!' I moaned as she pulled me across the room. 'I'm not ready to do this whole biodata thing all over again.'

'Well, get ready,' my mother said curtly. 'That was the agreement.'

My mum all but dragged me over to the potential mother-in-law and plastered a fake smile all over her face.

'Assalaamu alaikum Lilly Affa, bala asoinni?' Ma greeted the aunty. 'This is my daughter, Maya. Maya, this is your Lilly khala.'

'Asaalaamu Alaikum khala,' I squeaked, as Ma pushed me forward to allow me to be inspected by this woman who had an eligible nephew. The aunty began interrogating me about what I did and when I mentioned that I was going back to uni to do my LLM, Ma elbowed me so sharply she almost poked a hole in me. The last thing she wanted was people knowing I had commitments for the next year.

Surprisingly, Lilly khala didn't seem put out that I had aspirations that went beyond getting married and popping out babies. She gestured for me to sit down next to her and asked me about the course, where I hoped it would take me, what I liked doing for fun. The conversation was easy.

'See? That wasn't so bad, was it?' Ma stage-whispered when we walked away ten minutes later. 'You did so well! I bet she's going to call to arrange a dekha dekhi soon!'

'Don't arrange anything until I've seen his biodata, please,' I warned Ma as her pupils practically morphed into hearts right before me. Ma spotted another distant relative's cousin's wife's aunt or something and disappeared to talk to her, so I took the opportunity to duck outside for a breather.

The night was sticky and humid and the faint sounds of Coke Studio Bangla could be heard through the closed doors of the venue. The heat, together with the music and scent of biryani, made me feel as though I was in Bangladesh. Not that I knew what being at a Bangladeshi wedding *in* Bangladesh was like; I hadn't been since I was seven years old. But this was exactly how I imagined it: the smells, the sounds, the air, the heat. Leaning back against the cool of the steel fire exit door, I closed my eyes. In two days, Pretty was going to get married. Pinky was going to lose her identical twin sister. I was going to lose a friend. But I was hoping rather than an immense loss, we were going to gain a new brother.

'Maya?'

His voice brushed against my ears, causing the flesh on my bare arms to instantly prickle in anticipation, interrupting my thoughts in the most delicious way. Taking a deep breath, I tried to compose myself as I opened my eyes.

'Hey, Zak, salaams,' I said quietly, a tremor in my voice as I stepped away from the wall and turned to face him. He was wearing a jet-black kurta with black embroidery along the neck and baggy black shalwar trousers. He looked dashing, like the hero of a Bollywood movie, and I felt my stomach twist and turn like a blender as he stared down at me. Why had

I never noticed before how kind his eyes were? His expression may have been in a permanent state of sullen indifference, but his eyes were different. They were so expressive. Forget being windows to his soul, they were like trapdoors that you could fall through if you weren't careful.

'How are you?' I managed to croak.

'Tired,' he shrugged. 'I've been packing all week. Can't believe I'm flying out in a couple of weeks. You look nice, by the way.'

'Thank you,' I replied dully, looking down at the ground. 'I can't believe you're leaving so soon either. How do you feel?'

'Excited. Nervous. What about you? Are you ready to start your course in a few weeks?'

'As ready as I'll ever be,' I shrugged. 'My workplace is making things hard for me, so I'm handing in my resignation on Monday.'

'What? That's big.' Zak looked taken aback by my admission and ran a hand through his hair.

'It is,' I sighed. 'But I want to do my LLM full-time. I don't want it to drag over two years. My manager's refusing to be flexible so . . .' I let my sentence trail off.

'So . . .' he repeated thoughtfully. 'Why are you in such a hurry to finish the course? What's the rush?'

'There's no rush,' I lied. 'I want to be able to move on with my life, that's all. I don't want to long it out unnecessarily.' *I want to hurry up so next time someone like you comes along, I'm ready.*

'"Long it out", huh? I like it when you go all street on me, Maya Rahman.'

I glanced at Zakariya in surprise. Was Mr Too Cool for School *flirting* with me?

'It's funny hearing you talk like that,' I smiled, nudging him playfully.

'Hey, I'm a Camden boy,' he said, smiling easily back. 'I'm just as much of a north Londoner as you are.'

'Not for much longer. You'll be wining and dining with sheikhs in Dubai soon.'

Zak grimaced. 'I wish I wasn't going out there alone.' He inched closer to me, a move so subtle that I didn't think he had noticed it himself. But I did. I shuffled nervously away from him until my back was once again pressed against the wall.

'What about that girl?' I managed to say, avoiding looking into his eyes. 'Why don't you get your nikah done so she can go with you?'

'What girl?' Zakariya looked confused, as though he had no idea who I was talking about. His reaction irritated me and my voice rose a level.

'The Ally Pally girl?' I said, watching his reaction carefully. 'The one I saw you with? Why are you acting like you don't know who I'm talking about?'

'Oh, her,' he chuckled softly, refusing to rise to the bait. The sound of his laughter tugged on my heartstrings and instantly calmed my frazzled nerves. 'The thing is . . . she's actually my cousin.'

'What?' I stood upright in horror. 'You're marrying your *cousin?*'

'No! She lives in Scotland. I was showing her around!'

'I could have sworn you said—'

'What was I supposed to say, when you told me the guy you were with was your date?' Zakariya interrupted me, agitated. 'I didn't want to look like a fool who was holding on for no reason.'

There was a silence as I digested this and searched his face for clues about how he might have been feeling. He looked back at me and there was no mistaking what was in his expression, his voice, his eyes.

'What were you holding on to?' I whispered, the electricity crackling between us.

'You,' he said simply. 'I was holding on to the thought that maybe one day, you would like me too. I wish *you* were coming with me. I know I have no right to ask it from you, but I can wish it, can't I?'

My breath caught in my throat as I struggled to come up with a witty reply, some sort of joke to diffuse the charge in the air. My mind didn't comply and I stood there, silently and stupidly, my legs like panna cotta. I dared to look up at him again and this time, his eyes were sad. Every part of me ached to wrap my arms around him and make that sadness go away and just as I geared myself up to give in to the overwhelming urge to be close to him, my phone buzzed, interrupting the moment and releasing the tension. I both resented the intrusion and was grateful for it. What was I thinking, planning to hug a man *outside my cousin's mehndi party, where all my family had gathered?* I was going crazy, there was no other explanation.

'Excuse me,' I managed to say as I checked it.

NOAH: Maya, can we talk? I really miss you and I've realised that I don't care if you copied my list. It doesn't mean that I didn't know the real you. I'm really sorry for how I reacted . . . I guess I needed some time to process it all. Please forgive me x.

I read and reread the message, my hands trembling. Why was Noah messaging me *now*, at this precise moment, after ghosting me for weeks? Was it a divine sign that Noah was the one I was supposed to be with, not Zakariya? I had been praying for clarity, direction. Was this the answer to my prayers?

'Everything OK?' Zak asked, shuffling from one foot to the other, discomfort oozing from him. His voice snapped me out of my stupor and I looked up at him standing there in his black shalwar kameez and all our little moments together began to flood my mind. The way he always looked out for me, was always ready to help me. He was dependable. And sexy AF. I thought back to how I had rejected him more than once, but yet there he stood, baring his soul once again, despite claiming that he never would.

'Everything's fine,' I replied, as clarity dawned on me like a new day, pushing away the clouds and filling my life with light. The sign *wasn't* Noah's text. The sign was Zak, here in front of me, liking me for exactly who I was, not who he thought I was, jinn dance and all.

I put my phone back into my clutch bag as the tension that had been gripping my shoulders began to ease. I would respond to Noah later. I needed to do it properly, not in the middle of my conversation with Zakariya.

'In fact,' I continued, smiling up at him, everything's *better* than fine. Shall we go inside and sit down with a cup of masala tea?'

'Uh. OK?'

'We've got a lot to talk about.' Grabbing his hand, I gently led him towards the door. He looked at my hand like it belonged to an alien, as though he couldn't quite believe what was happening, and I dropped it the moment I opened the door to the hall. It wouldn't do to give the aunties fodder for their gossip session.

'We do?' he asked, looking confused as he followed me through the corridor that led to the hall, which felt like utter chaos after the calm outside. It was noisy, people pushed past us as they looked for the toilets, children ran by chasing balloons, but despite the mayhem, I had never felt so at peace.

'We need to figure out how we're going to do this,' I said boldly, tiptoeing to bring my lips closer to his ear, so he could hear me above the music and chatter. 'You're leaving in two weeks, I'm not. My course is only a year. I'm sure we can figure something out.'

'What? Are you messing with me?' Zak stopped to stare at me, his mouth falling open in shock.

'I'm not messing with you, fam,' I said in my most London, *Top Boy* accent, looking up at him as he continued to gawk at me as though waiting for the punchline. 'You wanna do this or not?'

'I do,' he said, and a smile so bright it could illuminate the room spread across his face.

We stood there in the doorway to the hall and smiled at each other. Big, cheesy, silly smiles. All around us, people danced, kids jumped away on the bouncy castle, elders sat around the tables chewing paan and drinking tea, but at that moment, it felt like we were the only two people in the room.

Later that night, when I was back at home and in bed, my feet sore and my mind still blown from all that had happened at the mehndi, I replied to Noah:

MAYA: Hey Noah, thanks for reaching out to me, I appreciate it. I honestly didn't mean to trick you into thinking I was something I wasn't. I suppose I've had a hard time lately figuring out who I am and I'm sorry for getting you caught up in it.

Thank you for everything you have shown me and taught me through your list – I will always be grateful to you for giving me the gift of adventure and exploration, both within me and in the world around me. I've enjoyed getting to know you, but you were right when you said we are too different.

Take care, Noah. I wish you all the best, always x.

Epilogue

One year later.

Maya's 30 Before 30

1. Pass SQE
2. Get a training contract
3. Put an offer down on a house
4. Go for Umrah
5. Go to Bangladesh with Ma and Baba
6. Learn to speak Arabic fluently
7. Run the London Marathon
8. Be able to do five chin-ups
9. Watch the *Godfather* trilogy
10. Visit every county in England
11. Climb Ben Nevis
12. Make up all missed fasts
13. Meditate daily
14. Go on a girls' trip with Dina
15. Watch a ballet
16. Grow something edible in the garden
17. Learn how to arrange flowers
18. Go skiing
19. Do thirty random acts of kindness
20. Pray five times a day consistently
21. Go for a bike ride around London
22. Learn how to swim 5 km

23. Invest in gold
24. Learn how to make samosas from scratch, including the pastry
25. Take a public-speaking course
26. Learn self-defence
27. Make a biodata for Malik
28. Read the whole Qur'an in English and Arabic
29. Host an epic thirtieth birthday party
30. Get married to Zakariya

Acknowledgements

As always, a huge thank you to Ammu, Abbu, my family and my friends for their unwavering support; for listening to me talk about characters, plot and dialogue, giving me ideas, showing me up at my events, bigging me up to strangers, buying my books, for understanding when I'm too busy to hang out and giving me space when I need it. You know who you are! (Faaria, I know you wanted me to list everyone's names but sorry, there are just too many and I'm petrified of forgetting someone!)

To my husband and children for continuing to put up with me and my absences as I navigate 'writer life' – I wouldn't be able to do this without your patience and support – thank you.

A special shout-out to my siblings – all six of them – who taught me how to write about sibling relationships. We pretty much have every personality trait possible between us. Thank you for always making sure I keep things real . . . ish.

To my wonderful agent, Abi Fellows from DHH Literary Agency, for listening to my crazy ideas and helping me shape them into stories, always having my back, writing those awkward emails and listening to my rambling voice notes! I'm so blessed to have you!

To the OG editor Sarah Bauer, who heard my thirty-second elevator pitch and loved it enough to give me a two-book deal – thank you for believing in me.

To Salma Begum, without whom the gates would have continued to be locked. I owe you everything.

To the fantastic Melissa Cox and Misha Manani in editorial – for jumping on board midway, taking my book baby under their wings and making sure that it became the absolute best it could be – I'm very grateful!

To Jenny Richards for bringing my vision to reality with this gorgeous cover – I'm in love with it. Thank you!

To Sophie Raoufi, Clare Kelly, Elinor Fewster, Alex May, Eloise Angeline, Kim Evans, Kate Griffiths, Vincent Kelleher and everyone in the Bonnier team who has contributed towards the production, publicity, marketing and sales of this book. So much goes on behind the scenes, and I'm really thankful for your efforts in bringing *The Thirty Before Thirty List* to life, and to bookshops!

To everyone else who has ever talked shop with me followed or engaged with me online, shared their stories and platforms with me, inspired me, let me sit in their cafes to write, interviewed me for podcasts, TV shows, articles, zines and Insta lives – thank you. This book is a collective effort of that love and support, and I owe you all so much!

And lastly, a massive thank you to everyone who read, bought, supported, reviewed, shared and talked about *Finding Mr Perfectly Fine*. I don't think I would have written another book if that one had flopped. Thank you for making me believe in myself, my stories, my experiences, my writing and my truth. Alhamdulillah.

If you enjoyed *The Thirty Before Thirty List*,
you will love Tasneem's debut romcom,
Finding Mr Perfectly Fine.

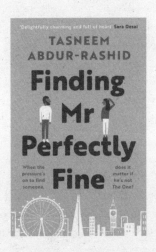

**When the pressure's on to find someone,
does it matter if he's not The One?**

'I loved it. Utterly charming'
Jenny Colgan

'Full of heart and brimming with emotion . . . a delightfully
charming story about finding yourself before you can
find love. I couldn't put it down'
Sara Desai

'If there's one book you need to read this summer it's
Finding Mr Perfectly Fine'
Yousra Imran